01/21

OLIVE BRIGHT, PIGEONEER

OLIVE BRIGHT, PIGEONEER

Stephanie Graves

KENSINGTON
PUBLISHING CORP.

www.kensingtonbooks.com

This book is a work of fiction. Names, characters, businesses, organizations, places, events, and incidents either are the product of the author's imagination or are used fictitiously. Any resemblance to actual persons, living or dead, events, or locales is entirely coincidental.

To the extent that the image or images on the cover of this book depict a person or persons, such person or persons are merely models, and are not intended to portray any character or characters featured in the book.

KENSINGTON BOOKS are published by

Kensington Publishing Corp.
119 West 40th Street
New York, NY 10018

Copyright © 2021 by Stephanie Graves

All rights reserved. No part of this book may be reproduced in any form or by any means without the prior written consent of the Publisher, excepting brief quotes used in reviews.

All Kensington titles, imprints, and distributed lines are available at special quantity discounts for bulk purchases for sales promotion, premiums, fund-raising, educational, or institutional use.

Special book excerpts or customized printings can also be created to fit specific needs. For details, write or phone the office of the Kensington Special Sales Manager: Kensington Publishing Corp., 119 West 40th Street, New York, NY 10018. Attn. Special Sales Department. Phone: 1-800-221-2647.

Library of Congress Card Catalogue Number: 2020944009

The K logo is a trademark of Kensington Publishing Corp.

ISBN-13: 978-1-4967-3151-7
ISBN-10: 1-4967-3151-4
First Kensington Hardcover Edition: January 2021

ISBN-13: 978-1-4967-3157-9 (ebook)
ISBN-10: 1-4967-3157-3 (ebook)

10 9 8 7 6 5 4 3 2 1

Printed in the United States of America

For those whose stories have not yet been told.

Acknowledgments

A debt of gratitude to the men and women who pulled out all the stops, in the face of incredible odds, in their pursuit of VE Day.

Heartfelt appreciation for the survivors of World War II and their children, who dutifully recorded experiences and memories for the archives of BBC's *WW2 People's War*. It's truly a treasure trove of information.

Thanks to Emma Martin for inspiring Miss Husselbee's "nothing better to do" line.

For my editor, John Scognamiglio. Olive couldn't be in better hands.

For my agent, Rebecca Strauss. I'm fortunate to have you by my side on this journey.

For Janice Rossi Schaus, whose cover design is everything I could have hoped for.

For Rosemary Silva, copyeditor extraordinaire. Thank you for fixing all my little mistakes.

For Holly Faur, critique partner, cheerleader, Netflix and PBS partier, and general sounding board. Everyone should be so lucky to have such a friend. And for the Family Faur, for making me feel much more mysterious than I really am.

For Blake Leyers, Carin Thumm, and Deanna Raybourn. Sweet butter crumpets, you girls are the bomb!

For my boys, Zach and Alex. Twenty years passed in a flash. GG.

And most of all, for Jason. My inspiration, my love.

"If it became necessary immediately to discard every line and method of communications used on the front, except one, and it were left to me to select that one method, I should unhesitatingly choose the pigeons."

—Major General Fowler, Chief of Signals and Communications, British Army

Saturday, 9 September 1939
Peregrine Hall, Pipley
Hertfordshire

I admit, my introduction to Mass Observation did little to convince me of the project's worth or significance. The efforts expended in gauging popular opinion and collecting general observations on the coronation of King George VI likely yielded nothing of much use to anyone. However, the situation has changed. Britain has engaged in a second war with Germany, and as such, I have decided to answer that organization's appeal to take up our pens and record our experiences of these long, bitter days ahead. Let there be no misapprehension; my intention is not to record the tedious daily minutiae that will fill the pages of other diarists, but to capture the triumphs and hardships that will create the landscape of this war on the home front. Days will be dark, and each of us will be tested, our true natures laid bare. I won't promise to stay silent when coming face-to-face with treachery, but in these pages, I will endeavour to allow all to remain anonymous. Nevertheless, truth will out, and we will persevere. Rule, Britannia!

V.A.E. Husselbee

Chapter 1

Thursday, 1st May 1941
Pipley, Hertfordshire

Olive Bright coasted to a stop beside a familiar figure, turned out respectably in the Wedgwood-blue uniform of the British Royal Air Force, her gaze arrowing to the telltale white flash on his cap, which signified he hadn't yet completed his training. He was waiting just shy of the St Margarets station platform, away from the bustle of activity, but close enough to hear the boarding call. Waiting to tell her goodbye.

Swallowing down emotion and schooling her features, she slid off her bicycle, propped it against the brick wall of the station, and unlatched the wicker carrier basket strapped to its handlebars. When she turned back, her face was suffused with mischief.

"Olive . . ." George was always saying her name that way: a gloss of warning over exasperated finality.

"For luck," she insisted.

George's blue eyes met the glassy dark one peering at him from a narrow opening in the wicker. Olive considered his dubiousness rather disheartening, but she wasn't about to let it bother her today. He and his stolid lack of imagination were so dear to her; it was entirely appropriate that he shouldn't make this easy. "You know I can't take her," he said, his Adam's apple roving uncertainly.

Even as she smiled at him, she could feel the nervous tension undoing her efforts, threatening to thwart the stiff upper lip that was to have been her last resort. Needing a moment, she rolled her eyes away from him, blinked up into the apricot clouds that crowned a pale lavender sky. It could have been any other spring morning. Except that it wasn't.

She swallowed past the lump in her throat, her gaze swinging down again to clap solidly on the tall, dark-haired, square-jawed fellow in front of her. He was a perfect melding of his father's rough masculinity and his mother's classical features, but he was like neither of them. It would be a long while before he came home again—she refused to even consider the possibility that he might not.

Olive had managed mostly to ignore the sharp nip in the air on her ride to the village, but the chill that swept over her now seeped through her jumper and goosefleshed skin, straight to her bones. She tipped her head down quickly and scuffed her feet over the gravelled road. She'd been fiercely proud when George had joined up, prouder still when he'd graduated from the Elementary Flying Training School. Now he was being shipped off for training in service flying—all the things he'd need to know for piloting an aeroplane in war. It was the last step before he'd earn his sergeant stripes and Royal Air Force wings.

Olive beamed at him, clenching her jaw to hold the smile in place as her eyes ranged over his face, urgently memorising the deep dimple in his left cheek, the snapping blue of his eyes, and the two tiny pale white scars on his temple, which served as markers of a long-ago cautionary tale. The dutiful Watson to her high-handed Sherlock, George had chivalrously let her run herd on him for the better part of their still young lives. After today, she'd no longer have a part in his adventures; he was leaving her behind. And that was intolerable.

Her older brother Lewis had been gone for over a year now, serving as a British liaison officer in Greece. They hadn't had a letter from him in three months, and Olive couldn't look at the little framed photograph of him, dashing in cricket whites, posing on the village green, without succumbing to a crushing feeling of helplessness.

Forcibly tamping down the negative emotions, she lifted her chin, even at the risk of exposing the quiver in her lower lip. There'd be time for a good wallow later. Right now, George needed one last knuckling under before he stepped beyond her reach.

"*Why* can't you take her?" she demanded.

"This is the real thing, Olive. The War Office, official business. Packing a stowaway"—he eyed the basket with exasperation—"is surely grounds for an unpleasant sort of punishment."

Olive's lips twisted with nostalgia. George could always be depended upon to muster a cautious, sensible objection to every impulsive suggestion. Who would temper her wilder impulses while he was gone?

She propped the basket under her arm and released the catch. A rounded grey head poked itself curiously into the conversation, as if to say, "Who would dare object?"

George's shoulders slumped farther, and Olive grinned encouragingly.

"It's not as if the RAF is anti-pigeon," she reminded him. "Quite the opposite. These birds have been carrying messages since the beginning of the war, selflessly doing their bit. Before that it was the Great War, and before that—"

"Save it," he said dryly.

"Poppins is a racer. She's trained for this sort of thing," Olive pressed. "Release her wherever the fancy strikes—the farther away the better—and she'll fly right home." She flashed a broad smile. "With no one the wiser."

He let his gaze roll away, a hint that he was caving. "But Poppins is a civilian," he said, his tone no longer quite as adamant.

"For now," Olive countered, her brows lifting defiantly. "She is at His Majesty's service." She attempted an awkward curtsy. "You know Dad notified the Pigeon Service committee that our lofts are available for the war effort," she reminded him. "We simply haven't received our certification. I'm sure it's an administrative oversight," she said crisply.

It was more likely that her father's imperious manner had raised the committee's hackles. While he'd jumped at the opportunity to enrol the Bright loft with the Service, envisioning their birds winging top-secret, mission-critical messages across the Channel for Britain, he'd been considerably less enthusiastic about relinquishing control of his loft. He had, in fact, informed the committee of fanciers put in charge of vetting local lofts that if they wanted his racers, then they were going to get him, as well. If he imagined that might sweeten the deal, he was mistaken: it seemed they wanted neither.

Olive was convinced that if the Bright loft had a file at the National Pigeon Service, it was surely marked LAST RESORT, but she was determined to calm any ruffled feathers, so to speak. The war effort needed excellent pigeons, and if the racing sheets were any indication, the birds she'd trained were some of the best.

George hoisted his duffel higher on his shoulder and eyed Poppins distrustfully. "And what, may I ask, did Mr Bright have to say about you absconding with the loft's champion pigeon and entrusting her to my care?"

Olive's spine straightened, her chin levelled, and her eyes calmly met his. "He didn't say a word."

"You didn't tell him, did you?"

When she didn't respond, the barest smile tugged at the corners of his lips. He knew her very well indeed.

And yet, Olive couldn't help but acknowledge that he was a far cry from the boy who'd tripped along beside her for so many years. His hair, beneath the cap, was slicked back; his jaw shaven smooth; and his eyes were heavy with responsibility. She didn't want to think about her own eyes and hair; she probably looked a fright, but George didn't bat an eye.

He had never borne up well against tears, and if she'd chosen to manipulate him with their sudden appearance, he wouldn't have stood a chance. But they both knew she wouldn't stoop to such a deceit. Her heart was being ravaged, and tears were coming whether he liked it or not. In what was surely a last-ditch effort to stave them off, he extended his hand for the basket. Sighing with relief, she offered it, then quickly turned her face to the wind, in the hope that it would dry her eyes and cool the achy flush in her face.

"No promises," he said as she turned back. "It's entirely possible she'll get released from the train window as soon as we pull away from the station."

"Don't be such a spoilsport," she admonished, peering in at the bird in the basket. The pale, opalescent colours at her throat shimmered in the darkened space like a sprinkle of fairy dust. In fairness, Olive was willing to concede that this probably wasn't her most auspicious idea, but it wouldn't hurt anyone, either. George wasn't going off to war—not yet. He was headed to an RAF airbase outside of London. If anyone suspected he was harbouring a stowaway, he need only get rid of the evidence. Poppins would handle herself just fine. She was Olive's best bird, and their last chance to thwart the censors, their last bit of mischief for a very long time.

She bobbed her head, feeling no compunction about sending her along. "Watch over him, Mary Poppins," she murmured, "and fly home safe." Olive fastened the basket closed and shifted her attention to George. "She has enough feed and water for a couple days, and there's paper and a bit of lead in the canister attached to her leg. Send me a joke, preferably inappropriate. A limerick would be even better." She managed a watery smile as all around them, teary mothers and sweethearts were clinging to their young men in uniform, dreading the moment when they'd have to say their final goodbyes.

George nodded, looking as if he could see right through her brave front. "I'll miss you, Olive." His voice was reassuringly steady as he engulfed her in a tight hug, careful to hold the basket clear. Too soon, he pulled away but stood still, staring down at her. Grinning, he made a fist and clipped her lightly on the jaw. "If anything has prepared me for this, it was tagging along in your wake. You're as domineering as any commanding officer."

"You're already a hero, George," she said crisply before planting a hard kiss high on his cheekbone. "Remember that and don't go daredeviling about." Her eyes burned against the tears.

"What's it to be, then?" he asked with amusement. "Am I a spoilsport or a daredevil?"

"Obviously, it depends on the situation." She pursed her lips primly, patiently, the way she'd always done when hoping to get her way. "Don't get cocky," she added as he hoisted his duffel one final time, the precursor to goodbye. "It affects your aim," she reminded him.

"I'll remember that." He nodded, then shot her a grin as the porter called the all aboard. "You know we would have made a great team," he said, walking backwards, away from her. "Me at the controls, you as the gunner."

"The best," she agreed, a new lump in her throat. If it weren't for that pesky royal proclamation that forbade women from operating deadly weapons during wartime, they would have been inseparable. The king was evidently inclined to turn a blind eye to everyday life in the country—she'd been firing a rifle since her tenth birthday. She'd shot down her share of falcons, the natural enemy of pigeons, but the Nazis, a much more dangerous predator, had been deemed off-limits for women. No matter if they *were* crack shots. "Make sure you find someone almost as good," she instructed, swallowing with difficulty. There wasn't time to tell him she intended to get as close to manning a gun against the Germans as she possibly could.

"Will do," he said, putting a hand up in one final goodbye. "Keep an eye on Mom and Dad and Gillian for me, would you?"

Olive nodded solemnly—she could picture them, sitting around the breakfast table, having already said their goodbyes. They were the sort to get on with things. She wasn't nearly as self-possessed, a fact her mother had considered a particular shortcoming. As he turned and walked the remaining steps to the corner, she kept her gaze riveted on the vulnerable strip of exposed skin at the back of his neck, just above his collar, until he disappeared from view. She locked her knees to resist running after him and turned away, abruptly taking hold of her handlebars.

Barring any unforeseen circumstances, Poppins would likely be back that very afternoon, but Olive had no way of knowing when she'd set eyes on George again. A fist of worry lodged in the centre of her chest.

As she stood, disheartened, her eye caught on a tall, lithe woman exiting the station, her luggage gripped tightly in hand. She moved with a sinuous grace, clad in wide-legged grey trousers and a trim jacket the colour of eggplant, a curlicue pattern of embroidery adorning the shoulders. Her red-gold hair was cut short and stylish under a dark blue beret cap with a rakishly turned brim and a fanciful ribbon flower of cream and gold. Olive's eyes followed distractedly. There was something familiar about her, but it wasn't until she'd angled her head at a passing gentleman, revealing the coquettish slant of her eyes and the mischievous pout of her lips, that the mystery was solved.

It seemed Violet Darling had finally come home.

A prick of curious interest pierced the numbness that was rapidly settling over her, but Olive couldn't be bothered to give it her attention. She was too busy wheeling her bicycle back toward the village, trying not to consider that her best friend had just boarded a train that would shortly be steaming out of the station in the other direction. As her steps carried her down the lane, her vision blurred with tears. She could feel a great gaping void cracking open in her chest, and it was quite clear that if she was going to make it through this war, she was going to need to fill the gap quickly. Luckily, she had a plan.

Olive heard the news stories on the wireless every evening. If the Allies were going to come out on the other side of this war victorious, everyone had to do their bit. For her stepmother, that meant the Women's Institute and its ceaseless schemes and fundraisers. For her father, she could only hope it meant a relaxed perspective on his beloved pigeons, work as usual as a veterinary surgeon, and the relative safety of the Home Guard. And for Jonathon, their resident evacuee, who had arrived unexpectedly and rooted himself so thoroughly in their lives that they'd be loathe to see him go, it entailed a thriving victory garden, an enviable salvage collection, and ever-changing plans to thwart a German invasion. As for Olive, she held on to a rather desperate hope that her part in the war would defy expectation.

She'd been halfway through her studies at the Royal Veterinary College in London when the school had been evacuated to Berkshire. News from home hadn't been encouraging: her stepmother Harriet was bravely, if rather distressingly, waging a worsening battle with multiple sclerosis, and her father was struggling to keep up with the demands of his busy animal surgery. So, she'd decided to come home.

As it turned out, he'd been in particular need of someone to rout the steady stream of villagers who'd been spooked into thinking their pets could not weather the war and therefore must be humanely dispatched. She had cajoled, badgered, and bullied as necessary and was relieved to have been mostly successful. There *were* now two extra cats prowling about the lodge, much to the irritation of the pigeons, but the sight of them never failed to lift Olive's spirits.

It was these little victories, more than anything else, that had brought the war into sharp and jarring focus and sparked in her a sense of urgency for something just out of reach. She'd been fidgety for months, knitting imperfect grey socks, baking grey bread, and assisting with all manner of tasks under mostly grey skies. All of it had left her feeling helpless, resentful, and vaguely guilty. It hadn't endeared her to the ladies of the WI, either. She expected they'd be much relieved to see her focusing her efforts elsewhere, particularly as she intended to follow the lead of Winston Churchill's youngest daughter.

Mary Spencer-Churchill had been interviewed on the wireless the previous evening, talking of her work for the Auxiliary Territorial Service, in which she served on a mixed-gender battery in Hyde Park. When the prime minister had authorised women to help operate the anti-aircraft guns, his daughter had signed up to serve in the ATS that very day. As Olive sat, rapt with attention, curled up on a leather wingback in her father's study, Miss Churchill had outlined the opportunities for women as spotters, rangefinders, and predictors. They could do absolutely everything, it seemed, except fire the guns. Thoroughly exasperated by such rampant unfairness, Olive was nonetheless willing to overlook it, and she had promptly imagined herself amid the noise and commotion of a gun emplacement in London or farther afield.

Caught up with excitement and patriotic fervour, she'd found she had no one to confide in. Harriet had gone up to bed shortly after dinner; her father had fallen asleep in the chair across from her; and Jonathon had been engrossed in the latest Bigglesworth story, lying on his stomach before their sad little evening fire. Probably for the best: her father would surely have objected to such a spontaneous decision. If she were to convince him, she'd need to plan her argument, being careful to downplay the risks involved while emphasising her aptitude and the need to do her bit. So, she'd switched off the wireless, planted a distracted kiss on her father's downy head, rumpled Jonathon's tousled locks, and climbed the stairs, her thoughts fractured and fizzing with the enormity of change on the horizon.

She'd had to bite back the words a moment ago with George— there had been more important things to say, and nothing was settled yet. But it would be; she was determined that it would be.

An unexpected gust had her clapping her free hand over her hat, lest it go tumbling along the river. At the same moment, the train's whistle sounded as its engine churned into motion, on its determined way to London. Rather than turn around, Olive walked on, resolved to get on with things.

Well aware that war was a study in distraction, she stopped to peer in the window of H. Ware, Chemist, at the much-diminished display of cosmetics, perfume, and other ladies' toiletry items. She heard the snick of the door opening just beside her. Before she could turn, she was unceremoniously thrust forward and nearly tumbled over her bicycle.

"This is a shop," a clipped voice informed her, "not a museum, Miss Bright. Kindly move yourself out of the way."

Olive rallied and turned to find Miss Verity Husselbee glaring daggers. Her silver-chestnut hair was neatly rolled and tucked beneath a forest-green felt hat, her wide-set hazel eyes were slightly squinty beneath downturned brows, and her nostrils were flared with affront. She was outfitted in camel-coloured trousers, a belted tweed jacket, and well-worn boots, a pair of binoculars hanging from her neck, as if she was off to hike the Inner Hebrides instead of simply planning to terrorise a village.

Olive was in no mood for a verbal lashing, particularly an unwarranted one. She glanced pointedly at the CLOSED sign on the door in question before answering glibly, "Given that the shop doesn't open for another hour, I thought I *was* safely out of the way. Then again, I hadn't expected to confound a burglar before breakfast."

Miss Husselbee snorted her displeasure, looking and sounding rather like her father's fusty old piebald. "The door," she said haughtily, "was unlocked. Naturally, I stepped in. I was thinking only of efficiency, a quality, it seems, Dr Ware does not value particularly highly." She glanced irritably back at the windowed door through which she had sailed a moment ago, then speared Olive with a pointed look. "I wouldn't trust him if I were you."

Content to be distracted, Olive promptly propped her bicycle against the building's inky blue exterior. Miss Husselbee's nerve was the stuff of legend, and villagers were often to be found whiling away an evening at the pub telling tales—real and imagined—of the woman's inarguable cheek. Olive's favourite involved a facetious encounter with Herr Hitler, in which she denounced his moustache as an impotent caterpillar with delusions of grandeur. While the beastly little German's reach may not yet have extended to Pipley, the village had been waging a quiet war with its very own tweedy autocrat for quite some time.

The only daughter of a long-dead local magistrate and his hawkish wife, Verity Husselbee lived alone at Peregrine Hall on the outskirts of the village, along the banks of the River Lea. She had a strong sense of the proper way to do things and a compulsion to impose her will on others in the interest of the greater good. Naturally, this tendency was not generally well received.

Her habit of wearing binoculars didn't help the situation. Miss Husselbee claimed she kept them on hand for birdwatching, but the villagers suspected a more nefarious intent. Her seemingly innocent umbrella was resented in equal measure, as she had a habit of tapping its ferrule on the pavement whenever someone's comment or behaviour prompted even a whiff of disapproval. The rat-a-tat of her approach was as effective as an air-raid siren, causing villagers to whip around corners and dodge into shops in a desperate attempt to steer clear of notice.

Olive had long suspected the bluster was prompted by loneliness. Certain a loft full of avian friends was the answer, she'd taken to accosting the older woman whenever she had a pigeon in tow. Unfortunately, the busybodying had carried on, but Olive

liked to think Miss Husselbee took secret pleasure in the camaraderie.

Olive's mother hadn't got along with the older woman, but
Harriet had forged a special bond with Miss Husselbee. Her
stepmother had been walking home from the village on an au-
tumn afternoon and had collapsed some distance from the lodge.
Frightened by her suddenly worsened condition, she'd begun to
panic. And then she'd heard the approach of a familiar umbrella.
As Harriet told the story, Miss Husselbee had promptly taken
charge, conscripting a trio of Girl Guides with an empty trek cart
to assist. Within moments, Harriet had been tucked carefully
into the cart and was being pushed along the lane, accompanied
by a retinue of followers, all of them singing cheery songs—Miss
Husselbee, evidently, the loudest of them all. Since the rescue,
the two women had become fast friends, and Miss Husselbee
would often pop in to check on Harriet's condition, the pigeons,
and, to his utter exasperation, the state of Olive's father's surgery.
Olive had taken to calling her the Sergeant Major, but never to
her face.

"Why shouldn't I trust him?" Olive whispered sotto voce,
linking her arm with Miss Husselbee's, as if the pair of them was
thick as thieves.

"All sorts of reasons," said the older woman, extracting her
arm from Olive's grasp. "And I couldn't possibly discuss them
with you. Loose lips sink ships, Miss Bright, or haven't you been
paying attention?"

"Clearly, Dr Ware is keeping everything shipshape," Olive
said, continuing with the nautical theme, "otherwise he wouldn't
be so tediously secretive." She offered an exaggerated wink for
good measure.

"Don't be impertinent, young lady," Miss Husselbee demanded, her frown lines settling in comfortably. "I'm certain
Harriet would want you to heed my warning."

Olive relished her response. "I rather doubt it, given that she's
the reason I'm darkening Dr Ware's doorstep."

The umbrella came down with a violent thump. "Sometimes I do believe you're intentionally dense, Miss Bright." Her brow folded in on itself, a great big wrinkle of disapproval. Her gaze flicked to Olive's bicycle. "Pigeons are resting today, hmm?" she said, managing to infuse the question with disapproval.

"As a matter of fact, I've just seen Poppins off on the train with George." Olive didn't bother to hide her satisfaction, her smile daring the Sergeant Major to question the decision.

A grouchy sound elicited from behind tight lips. "I suppose she's the best of all of them." There was the barest hint of curiosity in the words, but it wasn't truly a question.

"She's my favourite," Olive said stoutly.

"If she's anything like her namesake, she'll manage." With a decisive thump of her umbrella, she turned away, adding over her shoulder, "Carry on, Miss Bright. And do let me know when she's back."

With Olive's gaze trailing behind her, the older woman charged off down the lane. Feeling punchy, Olive saluted her retreating form. Such was the nature of her conversations with the Sergeant Major: maddening, with a twist. After a moment, she spun on her heel and rapped smartly at the door before nudging it open a crack. If Dr Ware was already in the shop, recovering from Miss Husselbee's intrusion, perhaps Olive could engage him in a commiserating chat and casually hint her way around to picking up Harriet's order early to save herself another trip.

"Hullo, Dr Ware," she called sunnily.

"Yes, yes. Come in." His tone was only mildly exasperated.

Not needing any further encouragement, Olive stepped into the neatly compartmentalised shop. As always, her eyes ranged rather giddily over the rows of carefully labelled bottles, jars, and canisters lining the back wall in a colourful assortment of blues and greens, then swept along the glass display cases and paused at the enormous mortar and pestle of Carrera marble and the tall druggist scales, both of which took pride of place on the wooden countertop. A quiet shuffle drew her eye farther back, into the corner of the shop. Dr Ware was sitting at the little desk behind the counter, his spectacles only slightly askew, as he eyed her with weary patience. The table lamp gave his skin a sun-warmed, slightly jaundiced appearance and his eyes an artificial twinkle. In truth, he looked resigned and a trifle dishevelled, his papers gathered haphazardly into unwieldy stacks. She felt a twinge of guilt for interrupting him. He'd worked in the Department of Biochemistry at Oxford years ago, but to her, he was simply the village purveyor of throat lozenges, rose-petal lotion, and chocolate bars, even if they were in short supply these days. By the looks of things, he hadn't given up his research entirely.

"Good morning, Olive. I see you've survived the skirmish."

Meeting his sardonic gaze, she realised he was referring to her run-in with the Sergeant Major. "And lived to fight another day."

He rose and came around the desk and along the counter to stand across from her; he was only inches taller, but his broad shoulders seemed to fill the space. She smiled, noting the silk handkerchief in his shirt pocket and the gravy-coloured stain on his collar. His shirtsleeves were rolled to the elbow, exposing forearms covered with pale curly hair; and his hands, propped on the counter, were capped by nails bitten to the quick. "When she stormed out of here, I wondered who'd end up on the receiving end of her ire. I should apologise." With a sharp shake of his head, he pulled off his spectacles. He spared a moment to rub ruthlessly at his eyes before finally pulling his hand away to offer her a bleary smile.

"Of course you shouldn't," Olive insisted, feeling freshly guilty. He looked entirely spent, and the day had barely begun. "You're not even open yet, and we've pushed our way in. You've every right to be in a temper. I'm leaving right now so you can get back to your work." She glanced curiously toward the corner that was glowing in the lamplight.

He glanced backwards. "No need. My concentration is shot in any case." Distractedly, he plucked the handkerchief from his pocket with the flair of a magician and rubbed its pink silk over the lenses of the spectacles he still held in his hand. He looked much younger without the owlish lenses, his grey eyes sharper, less distracted. It was as if a mole had nudged its way from the ground to stare blinking into the light of day. His age was a mystery, and Olive wondered suddenly whether he was old enough to avoid being called up. Perhaps the Sergeant Major had suspected he might be dodging his responsibility and had tried to press him for answers. Momentarily caught up in a nebulous conspiracy theory of her own making, she didn't see him slip his glasses back on or tuck away the handkerchief. "She was irritated with me. That's why she was behaving like a harridan."

Blinking herself back to reality, Olive ran her fingers over the polished wood trim of the display case, not wanting to be off just yet. "She can be quite insistent on getting her way, and seeing how difficult that is these days, I expect she's inclined to be more testy than usual." She flashed him a mischievous glance. "Don't tell me you were out of wart cream?"

"No, no. Fully stocked," he said, too distracted to realise the suggestion had been in jest. "It was answers she wanted, not remedies."

Olive nodded in understanding. "It must be extremely difficult to diagnose suspicious symptoms accurately." She suppressed a shudder at the very thought of Miss Husselbee's medical maladies.

He shook his head, somewhat flustered now. "No, no, nothing like that. And I couldn't possibly discuss other customers." He smiled awkwardly but took a step back from the counter, shoving his hands in his pockets. She heard the crinkle of paper, and he stilled, a hunted look in his eyes, as if he'd been caught out wearing a hairpiece. He promptly yanked his hands out again and busied himself straightening a box of combs on the counter. Curious now, Olive leaned confidingly closer.

"She did say you were being entirely too secretive—" His

elbow jerked violently and collided with a depressingly empty canister of humbugs. They both reached to steady it, and Olive said quickly, "But don't worry. You're in good company. We're all doing our bit."

Now he really looked harried and eager to get away, but before she could speak, he remembered. "I have Mrs Bright's vitamins and anticoagulants right here." He turned, pulled open a drawer in the cabinet behind him, sorted through various paper bags, and retrieved one, which he handed over.

Sensing she was about to be shuffled out the door, she changed tack. "You look as if you could use a distraction, Dr Ware. Harriet tells me there's a dearth of male participation in the village play." She lifted her eyebrows, smiling encouragingly. "Perhaps you could . . ."

"I'm afraid not," he said, his tone now dismissive. "I've no time to spare. I wouldn't be suitable in any case. Have a good day, Olive." Before she could reply, he had moved to gather the stacks of paper that littered his desk, squeezed behind the little chair, and unlocked the door that stood just beyond it and led to the back room and his living quarters beyond. Without a backwards glance, he slipped through and tapped the door closed behind him.

Olive stared, blinking, after him, wondering if he was coming back. He'd left the door to the shop unlocked, and anyone could barge in at any moment—that should have been only too obvious.

"Thank you, Dr Ware," she called. "I'm sorry to have bothered you so early. I'll just let myself out."

No answer—not even a peep.

Was he hiding back there? From *her*? Much as it pained her to agree with Miss Husselbee, he *was* being oddly mysterious. Curiosity surfaced and swirled, but she tamped it forcibly down and stepped out of the shop into the steadily warming air of early morning. It was nothing to worry over and no business of hers. He was tired and flustered and feeling a touch pernickety—quite rightly, too. The Sergeant Major had stuck her nose where it didn't belong and been thwarted for her troubles. In other words, it was business as usual in the village.

Except that George was gone.

Gripping the paper bag against the handlebars, she climbed onto her bicycle and was poised to push off when Henrietta Gibbons came around the corner, pulling a weathered blue trek cart whose wheels looked like they were holding on by sheer force of will. There was a pillowcase tucked into a corner of the cart, its folds tenting and shifting as if by invisible hands.

"You're out early, Hen," Olive said. "Doing your good deed for the day?"

Henrietta Gibbons, Girl Guide—as she'd taken to introducing herself to everyone she met—was an auburn-haired eleven-year-old with the manner of royalty, despite her homely nickname. She paused her progress.

"You could say that," she allowed.

Exasperated, Olive pressed, "Truthfully?"

The girl considered. "Is it still a good deed if you're getting paid?"

"Not *as* good."

She shrugged accommodatingly. "I've hours left to fit in a bona fide."

Olive's gaze flicked to the pillowcase. "Who's paying you, and for what?"

"Dr Ware wanted mice."

Olive frowned. "Why?"

"He didn't say. I didn't ask. But at two for a shilling, how could I refuse?" She glanced back over her shoulder. "I caught four." Her smile was one of delighted triumph.

Not feeling equal to the task of questioning her further, Olive said, "Well done, then," and walked on as Hen swept past to rap on the chemist's door. She wondered if the Sergeant Major knew about the mice.

She resumed her bicycle and coasted through the village. Her eyes strayed unerringly toward the noticeboard, which was crowded with a calendar of events, various adverts, and the colourful placard that took pride of place. The Daffodil Dance was only two days away. The mere thought of it prompted Olive to start pedalling in earnest.

As she rode home, admiring the glorious spring green, she thought of her mother, who had been an ambulance driver in France during the Great War and had later died of tuberculosis. Olive couldn't imagine a life more tragically cut short. Her mother had been so vitally, fervently alive, flitting like a butterfly between projects and causes. She'd left her daughter to nurture her own independence, and Olive relished the chance to follow in her mother's marvellous wake. Serena Bright was a shining star, tireless and charming, but those very qualities often overwhelmed her. Then she would retreat to the dim privacy of her bedroom to face the merciless headaches that stole over her, and Olive would be dispatched to the chemist for her tablets. She'd spent countless hours lingering outside the door to her mother's room, hoping to be let in, but her mother was never anxious for her company. When Olive did see her, she was skittish and irritable, shirking the sunlight and drawn into herself. And as the months passed, and her mother began to slip away more and more, now quite dependent on her tablets, Olive took refuge in her memories. The sickness, when it came, seemed almost inevitable.

Olive was certain her mother would have appreciated her desire for a more active role in the war. A volunteer position that would put her on the front lines and engage her efforts in the defence of Britain. Or at least as close as was possible for a woman. She would have understood that Olive wasn't scared to go, but rather was afraid not to. Most of all, she'd know instinctively how best to convince Rupert Bright that this was what his daughter needed to do, despite his predictable misgivings. But Serena

Bright had been gone a long time, and Olive's stepmother was a different sort of woman entirely.

When her mother had been in the final, painful throes of her illness, the hospital had dispatched Harriet Vickers. Her brisk, efficient manner, cheery disposition, and indomitable spirit had been precisely what was needed, and by the time Serena Bright had slipped away, Olive and her father had become quite irrevocably attached. It had been only a matter of months before her father decided to marry again, and free of the long shadow cast by her mother, Olive had guiltily basked in the lustre of Harriet's warm accessibility. Resentments had flickered over the years—when Olive's memories would shift in favour of those long-ago crystal-bright days when the world had seemed to spin giddily around her mother—but they had quickly faded, like a cinema reel played out.

Harriet worked tirelessly for the war effort, but she had no aspirations, for herself or her stepdaughter, beyond the WI, and she likely wouldn't condone anything inherently risky. With the best of intentions, she might even tender a comparison between mother and daughter, prompting Olive's father to come stodgily down on the side of caution. As far as the ATS was concerned, Olive was very much on her own.

Long before coasting through the gate, she could hear the raucous chattering of the little birds in the hedgerows that bordered the lane. Her father had renamed the ancient hunting seat Blackcap Lodge, and Olive thought the new title suited the sprawling Tudor-style dwelling perfectly. It hinted at long-ago hunting parties, warm fires, adventurous rogues, and cosy bunk rooms. The reality, that it had been named for the little dark-headed warblers that came in situ, was irrelevant.

As if she'd conjured him, her father appeared right in front of her, a tall, barrel-chested man, his once blond hair silvering with the same grey that had lately begun to overrun the bushy tangle of his eyebrows. He stood beneath the blossoming cherry tree in the side yard, scuffing mud off his boots while his Welsh corgi, Kíli, nosed in the hydrangea bushes. Hearing the crunch and pop of her wheels on gravel, the dog backed out of the shrubbery to trot in her direction.

"Coming or going?" she called to her father, sliding off the bike before it came to a full stop. She leaned down to rub behind the dog's ears as its little nub of a tail twitched eagerly.

"Going, I'm sorry to say. A swollen fetlock takes precedence over a leisurely breakfast. As it should," he added with a nod. "So, I'm off to the Donnelly farm. But Harriet would love some company, I'm sure." He winked at her and squatted to rummage about in his surgeon's bag, making certain he had everything he required.

Her stepmother would no doubt try to press her into spending the morning knitting, and she couldn't bear it. Not today.

After a moment, he said distractedly, "George get off all right?"

Propping her bike against the side of the old barn he'd outfitted as a surgery, Olive pressed her lips together, nodding, relieved that the rawness of her emotions had scarred over a bit. She could blame only her distracted state of mind for the words that tumbled out on the next breath. "I sent Poppins with him."

Her father straightened, his brow furrowed in confusion. "You're not serious . . . ?"

She squirmed, wishing she hadn't said anything. He probably wouldn't have noticed, anyway. Poppins was one of her pigeons, and with racing postponed for the duration of the war, she'd taken full charge of the loft.

"I didn't want him to have to go off alone . . ." Her voice sounded irritatingly sullen.

He rubbed a rough hand over his face before pinning her with a glare. "Are you out of your bloomin' mind?" His face began to redden as exasperation fired his blood. With a muttered curse, he began to pace, prompting Kíli to respond with a choreographed crouch-and-bounce ballet, which was generally ignored. "What if the Pigeon Service picks today to visit? How do you imagine they'll take to the news that you've sent one of our best racers out on a lark?" Before Olive could respond, he roared, "Quit that, you ill-mannered brute!" The dog had apparently nipped his fingertip, hoping for a bit of attention. Even now, the squat little thing wasn't cowed, well aware that Rupert Bright's bark was much worse than his bite.

The Pigeon Service was no doubt well aware of the same; they simply couldn't be bothered to tolerate either. But she couldn't very well say that.

"None of this is a game, Olive," her father said, shooting a disapproving glance in her direction. His eyes were tired, and his face had thinned over the past year, the skin having slackened at his cheekbones and jaw, which was currently roughly shaven and grim.

"I know that!" She nearly shouted the words, unable to stop herself. "How can you think I don't know that? He went off this morning, one step closer to taking his turn against those hateful Nazis, and there's every chance that one day soon he'll be shot right out of the sky . . ." The last word crumpled out of her. She clipped her mouth shut, fighting down the lump that had returned, noticeably bigger than before, to the base of her throat.

His manner changing abruptly from ferocious disapproval to brusque understanding, her father stepped toward her, placed his hands on her rigid shoulders. "You mustn't think like that, Olive. George wouldn't want you to think like that." Reaching up to run the pad of his thumb over her cheek, he added, "What on earth's happened to your fighting spirit, my dear?"

"I suppose the knitting and gardening aren't keeping it particularly sharp." She sounded mulish, even to her own ears. "I'm sure it'll be back on track soon enough," she added cryptically, determined to speak to him that very evening.

"You always did want to be smack in the centre of things," he said softly. "Just like your mother. Sometimes, my dear, it's more courageous to be the one left behind."

Olive searched his face, wondering if there was more to that quiet certitude than was prompted by this particular moment.

"Now, don't go telling the pigeons I said that." His ruddy cheeks rounded in amusement at his little joke, and she turned to glance wistfully towards the dovecote, which was standing sentry a little ways from the house, like a turret displaced from the top of a castle wall. Hexagonal in shape, ringed with leaded-glass windows, and crowned with a cupola, it was ridiculously fanciful. But it was equipped with everything the birds could want. Even now, three of the creatures were sunning on perches high above the ground, their quizzical, intelligent eyes scanning the spring-softened countryside. She wondered ruefully if they spied any errant NPS officials.

"They're not coming," she said, her tone flat. She hadn't voiced her suspicions even to George, but the reality had been worrying her for some time. "Too much time has passed."

Her father immediately understood, making her wonder if he'd come to the same conclusion on his own. "I've offered," he huffed, dropping his hands. "I can't very well help it if the National Pigeon Service doesn't appreciate the sort of standard we adhere to. It's why we're champions, by God." His voice built to a crescendo but quickly calmed as his gaze skimmed her face. "I suspect the War Office will put a bit of pressure on the NPS before too long. The situation is too critical." He wrung his hands distractedly. "The Bright loft is known for fast, smart birds with good instincts and fighting spirit."

"I know," she said, the tightness in her chest loosening slightly. She was suddenly desperate for a cup of tea. "So, you can understand why I couldn't help but send one with George. He'll be sending her home soon enough, but it makes my mind easier, knowing she's with him."

He was silent for a moment before absently patting her on the arm. "Yes, well. Don't lose hope, Olive. They'll come. You'll see." He glanced sternly down at Kíli and hoisted his surgeon's bag before adding, "I'd best get on with things. You go in and eat your breakfast. See if you can bring yourself to knit a sock or two." He winked at her and walked down the drive, whistling for the dog, who went hurtling after him, churning up a low trail of dust.

With a deep sigh, Olive skirted the barn and slipped under the lacy pink overhang of the cherry tree, shortcutting the path to the dovecote. After retrieving the key from its uninspired hiding place beneath a large moss-covered stone, she unlocked the door and stepped into the dim interior, with its familiar earthy tang.

As she tipped her head back to admire the pale sunbeams filtering in through the pigeonholes far up in the cupola, a little flicker of warmth kindled in her chest. "Good morning, Bright young things." Corny it might be, but it always made her smile. She lifted the heavy lid on the bin of pigeon feed and stared down at the ever-dwindling supply. With the bulk of crops reserved for human consumption, there was little available maize, peas, wheat, or barley left for pigeons. What there was had been reserved for lofts that had been vetted by the Pigeon Service to provide birds for the war effort.

Scooping some feed into the long, shallow trough on the floor near the far wall, she glanced up at the numbered nesting boxes tucked into the lime-washed walls, wondering if the birds had any sense of how dire their situation was becoming. A svelte white hen with red-rimmed eyes scrutinised her from a box at eye level. "You needn't look at me like that, Queenie. I'm doing everything I can." The hen was clearly reserving judgment, and Olive wished she could offer something more definitive, but this was war, and certainty was as common as citrus—which was to say there was none to be had. She hadn't tasted—or even glimpsed—an orange in months.

"Rest up," she said, encouragingly, replacing the scoop and

sealing the bin of food. As her gaze ranged over the dovecote's inhabitants, her thoughts flashed back to the fairy tales she'd devoured as a girl. Here they all were, locked away in a tower, waiting to be saved. Well, in truth, they were waiting for a chance to do their bit in this war. She snorted, startling a young grey that had wafted closer, likely ready to eat. "We don't need a hero, ladies and gents," she said briskly. "Because we are going to save ourselves."

After giving them all a jaunty nod, she walked through the door, pulled it closed behind her, and relocked it with the key. As she dropped the key back into its hiding place, she murmured quietly to herself, "I just need to figure out *how* exactly we're going to do that."

Chapter 2

"You're not the sort of girl who lets herself feel helpless, Olive. And certainly not hopeless."

Olive started, her gaze flicking to the lemon-yellow chaise in the corner and the piecrust table beside it, against which leaned a polished cherrywood cane. The room had been empty when she'd slipped inside, not quite ready for breakfast or company. As she'd stared blindly out through the parlour's French doors, into the back garden, gently raking her nails over a neatly embroidered pillow and thinking hard, her stepmother had made her cumbersome way to the chaise, arranged herself comfortably, and turned on the wireless. Olive now realised it had been droning on about what to eat and how to prepare it for some time. It felt as if she'd managed to squeeze an entire day's worth of emotions into the two hours since she'd crawled out of bed.

"George is doing his duty, and you can do no less," Harriet said, clasping her fingers over the pearl affixed to her earlobe. Her stepmother, Olive knew, spoke from experience. She'd long managed the Bright household with high spirits and brisk efficiency, but lately her condition had demanded she carry on from a windowed corner of the parlour with her favoured ruby-red afghan draped over her legs. Her tiresome battle with multiple sclerosis, long manageable and unchanging, seemed as if it might now be beginning in earnest.

"It's not at all fair that women are always the ones left behind," she continued, dropping her pen into the cradle of the book open on her lap, "but I like to think it's because we are more steadfast, willing to carry out all the little jobs that are entirely necessary but quite beneath the notice of most men."

Harriet's sable hair was styled in an impeccable chignon, the shock of white near her right temple giving the style a rakish, modern flair. Paired with the clever glint lurking amid her calm grey eyes, and the wry twist of rose-coloured lips, her entire demeanour exuded self-sufficiency, giving not the slightest indication of her ever-expanding need for assistance. Olive's decision to step into the fray was not without its pitfalls. How would Harriet manage without her? And what of the pigeons? She'd be going against her father's wishes, and Jonathon would once again be left behind.

As the wireless marched on in its programme schedule to *Take Your Choice*, a medley of music from records pulled seemingly at random, Olive couldn't help the sigh that escaped her.

Harriet suddenly reached out, and her hand fumbled with the catch of the jade enamelled box on the little piecrust table. Inside, Olive knew, was a neat little phalanx of cigarettes. Mostly they remained untouched—in reserve—until her stepmother's defences were down, her nerves particularly frayed, or her symptoms depressingly debilitating. The paper bag from the chemist sat where Olive had left it, crinkled and ignored on the table, beside the little box.

"The best thing you can do now is carry on, keep busy, and have faith that every effort, no matter how small, is helping the cause. And to that end," she began, her lips curving into a mischievous smile that didn't quite match the harried look in her eyes, "I've put your name in for the WI's latest undertaking. It was unanimously agreed that your veterinary expertise made you an ideal candidate to chair this particular scheme." As Olive digested this news, Harriet selected a cigarette and flicked her elegant gold lighter to flame.

Olive opened her mouth to protest her suitability, given that she had every intention of going off to join the ATS, then popped it closed again. No one knew her plans. Now, more than ever, it had become imperative that she speak to her father the moment he got home. She'd simply have to stave off her stepmother's expectations until then.

Oblivious to the warring thoughts tumbling about in Olive's head, Harriet had closed her eyes to enjoy the first few puffs of her cigarette. As they fluttered open again, she said, "Having refused a part in the play, I decided you'd have plenty of time to be in charge of the Pipley pig club we're starting."

Olive nearly scoffed. Harriet had basically volunteered her to raise an indeterminate number of piglets for the sole purpose of supplementing the village ration. It would be a grim job of mud, manure, and pig slop that eventually led to butchering. "*Marvellous,*" she agreed, wondering if Harriet was paying close enough attention to register the ringing tones of sarcasm.

"See, you *do* have a flare for the dramatic. You would have been wonderful in our little production of *Pride and Prejudice.*" She spared a wry glance for Olive, then turned to look out into the garden. Her fingers, so often busy turning balls of yarn into socks, were now still, a mere prop for her cigarette. Olive ran her fingers over the legs of her trousers, her thoughts in a dizzying pendulum of go-stay.

No longer able to sit still in the silence, she stood abruptly and crossed to the doors to let in some fresh air. She leaned against the doorjamb, relishing the feel of sunlight streaming across her face. It had been a long, cold winter.

"Violet Darling came off the train this morning," she said, without turning.

"Did she indeed?" The response was appreciatively stilted, a full measure of curiosity infused into every word.

Miss Violet's recent years may well have been shrouded in mystery, but her younger sister, Miss Rose, was a veritable open book, a particularly apt comparison given that she happened to be the village librarian. The sisters were in their thirties, only a decade or so older than Olive, but she'd used the honorific since childhood, and it was second nature now. Over the years, the story of the Darling sisters had been much discussed, altered, and exaggerated until it resembled a tale worthy of Hans Christian Andersen.

Unable or unwilling to manage the pair of them when their mother died, their father, Maverick Darling, promptly sent for his sister, their aunt Felicity. Cast as the evil stepmother of the story, she was consumed by her own maladies and comforts and was ill equipped to care for two young girls, leaving them to take refuge in books. Miss Rose turned to classic literature, while Miss Violet found immense pleasure in lurid novels and thrillers of all sorts.

Over the years, their reading material informed their behaviour. Rose grew into a quiet, intellectual young lady devoted to her books, while Violet could best be described as a rambunctious pleasure seeker who was entirely too friendly with too many boys. Hoping to head off what she imagined was the impending ruin of a well-bred young lady, Miss Husselbee (the fairy godmother of the tale, at least by her own estimation) took Violet to task. Or tried to. Violet ignored her outright and flagrantly carried on. Enter Emory Hammond, the charmingly handsome, sun-kissed stepson of Lord Murchison, whose estate bordered Miss Husselbee's. He came to stay the summer after Olive turned twelve—Harriet's first summer in Pipley—and made a habit of driving his snappy little motor car through the village and over the hills at dangerous speeds, the wind whipping through his hair, the sun glinting off his roguish smile. He'd wave jauntily at the poor unfortunates he left in his wake, and Olive couldn't help but wave fiendishly back. He was not at all what he should be, or so she was told. No doubt that was precisely why she developed the most awful crush on him and was devastated when she discovered that Violet Darling had lured him away.

The two ran off together in late August of that year and had been absent from their lives ever since. It was well known that Violet had made a name for herself writing the sort of lurid novels she'd enjoyed as a girl, and the gossips were quick to surmise that her own story did *not* have a happily ever after. In fact, the theories of the pair's whereabouts tended to be laced with grim tragedy: sunk on a transatlantic crossing, dismembered by a lion in Africa—or a tiger in India—fated to live a dusty, forgotten existence in Australia or the American West. The appearance of a new novel every few years did nothing to stifle the conjecture. But now, here was Violet Darling, home again. Or rather, Violet Hammond. Where Emory might be was anyone's guess.

"Leave it to Violet Darling," Harriet said, in quiet appreciation. Olive shifted to face her stepmother, waiting for the rest of this ambiguous statement. Harriet blinked, realising she had a rapt audience, and switched her cigarette to her left hand, then took up her pen in her right. "She's swooped in to save us feeling sorry for ourselves. Now we'll all feel superior instead," she said wryly. She tapped her pen against the book, considering. "I don't suppose I should ask her to play Kitty or Lydia—that might set us off on the wrong foot. But perhaps Elizabeth? Dare I risk the scandal?" Harriet had been tasked with the thankless job of writing a workable script and assigning the much-loved and much-loathed roles to willing participants. Olive suspected the resultant squabbles could very well outlast the war.

There was a step in the hall, and Jonathon appeared, coming through from the kitchen. But he lingered on the threshold, one last mouthful of breakfast keeping him silent as his jaw worked in earnest.

He was of medium height, the crown of his head coming to Olive's chin. But she was tall, and judging by his lanky frame, he had a good bit of growing yet to do. His dark hair, while neat, was in need of a trim, and his eyes, a coppery brown, seemed always to be warring between darting curiosity and wary uncertainty. Barely there freckles marched straight over the bridge of his nose, and his smile, when it flashed, exposed teeth that were slightly too big. He was wearing a school blazer, a maroon jumper, and navy short trousers that exposed all manner of cuts and scrapes.

"Good morning, Jonathon," Harriet chirped, her smile edging out the distracted arrangement of her features.

"Morning, Harriet," came the quiet reply, and Olive watched as a tinge of pink crested the tips of his ears as he came farther into the room. Her nose twitched at the scent that clung to him, and she raised a hand, to lay it lightly against the lower part of her face, as if in quiet contemplation.

Jonathon Maddocks had been living at Blackcap Lodge for nearly four months—he'd come just after the new year. And while he had made new school chums in the village and was a natural with the pigeons, he still seemed skittish at home, as if he believed one false step would mean a second relocation on the heels of his first.

His arrival had taken all of them by surprise. With his father away in North Africa, his mother, a flighty school chum of Harriet's, had been utterly overwhelmed and had promptly packed her twelve-year-old son off to Pipley for the duration while she retreated to a private sanatorium in the Scottish Highlands. And despite their best efforts to make him feel welcome, Jonathon clung to his quiet shyness. In a flash of inspiration, Harriet had given him responsibility over their victory garden, such as it was, and he'd taken to the task with gusto. He'd managed to charm every gardener in the village with knowledge to share, and Olive had high hopes of surplus produce and a splendid variety in the months to come.

Olive had quickly found she quite liked having Jonathon around. With Lewis gone—and now George—he was her most constant companion. "No complaints from Miss Fen or your school-mates on the lingering effects of your morning activities?"

His brow furrowed. "I'm only stirring the compost."

"Never mind," she said, guessing his teacher was too polite to comment. Olive had kept away from the back corner of the garden ever since Jonathon had begun feeding the towering heap as assiduously as if it were a pet dragon. "Anything to report? Hints of an onion, maybe?"

"Not yet," he said, a mischievous light flickering in his eyes. "But I do have a few surprises up my sleeves." He paused, but it was clear he wanted to say more, and after a moment, it came flooding out of him in an excited rush. "Hen and I went foraging yesterday and met a Land Girl called Iris Wells, who said that she and two others are digging up the tennis lawn at Peregrine Hall to put in a whopper of a vegetable garden." Not even wanting to stop for breath, he sucked in reserves and barrelled on. "Hen and I plan to go round to see Miss Husselbee after school to ask if we can help." Pride and purpose shone on his face, lifted his chin, straightened his spine.

Hen had attached herself to Jonathon the moment he'd stepped off the train from London as an official evacuee. Ostensibly, she was following Guide protocol, showing him around and making him feel at home, but Hen invariably had ulterior motives. Olive recognised the intrepid look in the girl's clear green eyes. Her own mirror had reflected a similar glint each morning, before she'd fetched George from his father's garage and they'd set off together on the day's adventures. Hen may have been a year younger than Jonathon, but her wing, it seemed, was already sufficiently capacious, as he'd been quickly and efficiently hustled under it. Olive had yet to hear him complain; George hadn't, either.

"Well, that sounds quite promising," Harriet allowed, before adding, "However, I don't want you to get your hopes up. Miss Husselbee can be a bit . . ." She glanced to Olive for assistance.

"Prickly?" Olive supplied. *Suspicious*, she thought, thinking of Dr Ware. "Uncharitable?" She was warming to her theme.

"That's plenty. Thank you." Harriet's cultured tones smoothed over the slightest pettiness, a quality that made her a godsend to the WI.

"She's all right," Jonathon said, shoving his hands into his pockets. "She gave me a cutting from a broad bean plant trailing up the wall of her kitchen garden. I've planted it beside the sweet peas, and it's shooting right up." He picked at a loose bit of skin on his thumb. "Besides, she's already promised us some paper for our salvage collection. We need to go by and pick it up."

Olive had a sudden thought. "If the lime gravel border is going, as well, perhaps she'd let you collect a cartful for the pigeons. They're getting short on grit and will need it more than ever if they're left to forage for seeds." Olive spoke lightly, not wishing to dwell on the pigeons any more than she already had.

"And if it happens that Miss Husselbee doesn't need you," Harriet said cheerily, "Olive might like your help with her new endeavour." Jonathon tilted his head curiously. "She's to head up our pig club."

"A *pig* club," Jonathon said blankly, eyes wide. "Golly, how did you get suckered into that?"

The question was spared an answer by another sliding step in the hall. They turned as one toward the doorway, through which Mrs Battlesby shortly appeared, feather duster raised to swipe the lintels. "If you're having breakfast, Miss Olive, you'd best get on before I do the washing-up," she said with a wink.

The housekeeper had a mild tick, whereby her right eyelid occasionally, inadvertently, closed for a long blink, a motion indistinguishable from a wink. Rather confusingly, she also tended to make pointed comments, which she capped off with a knowing wink from the same eye. As a result, people were forever pondering the intention of that fleetingly closed eye, while Mrs B remained entirely oblivious.

Brisk and brown-eyed, her hair a tumble of frizzing brown curls fading to grey, Mrs Battlesby handled the cooking and cleaning, and various other assorted jobs that none of the rest of them took an interest in, and managed to be done in time to walk back home in the afternoon to repeat the same manner of tasks in the cottage she shared with her husband, Archie Battlesby, a veteran of the Great War, who'd never fully recovered from the tendrils of mustard gas that had seeped down into his trench. Mostly, he kept to himself, but as a member of the Home Guard, he'd lately been spending his time preparing the village and its environs for the possibility of a German invasion. Olive had always found him brusque to the point of rudeness, and he had a disconcerting habit of following a person's movements with only his eyes—like the subject of a baleful portrait painting in a Gothic novel. She found it unsettling in the extreme.

"Coming, Mrs B," she said, not wishing to miss her share of bacon, no matter how meagre it was sure to be. Breakfast was rather a pale shadow of its former self now that rationing limited a second helping of bacon and a truly decadent slather of butter and jam, but the limits on tea were particularly maddening. As far as Olive was concerned, the tragic situation of teatime on rations would have been reason enough to go to war if Chamberlain hadn't already engaged them.

"When you're ready for school," Olive said to Jonathon, "I'll walk with you. I'm meeting Margaret to write letters to the Friendless Serving Men, and I've offered to help decorate the hall for the dance." Normally, she was gung-ho for any sort of village entertainment—it was a much-needed break from the tedium when so many other simple pleasures had been stripped away. But now things would be different. With both of them perpetually unattached, she and George had always paired up for the dances, any romantic curiosity between them having been summarily squelched by a single kiss three years ago and the resultant snorting laughter. Clearly, she was going to have to get used to going alone.

This particular dance was a tradition in the village, held every year on the first Friday in May, when wild daffodils carpeted the neighbouring woods and trailed along the hedgerows, a profusion of sunny faces popping open to welcome spring. When she was younger, she and the other girls had woven the flowers into crowns with twists of ivy and lengths of ribbon; they'd stuffed themselves with cakes and punch, then whirled until their dresses frothed around them. Exhausted, they'd trail home after their families under a star-filled heaven, the whole world heady with the scent of spring. Her mother had loved any excuse to get dressed up; she was lovely and charismatic and always the centre of attention.

"Olive?" Harriet's voice filtered through her memories, and Olive blinked, coming back to the moment—the reality that nothing was the same as it had once been. With a wrinkle of concern now marring her brow, Harriet shifted forward. "If you're passing the library, do stop in and tell Rose I'm very much looking forward to meeting her sister. Perhaps you could casually suggest that the Darling sisters are perfectly suited to play a pair of Bennet sisters." Her eyes twinkled with mischief as her shoulders dropped back onto the chaise.

Olive shot her a look of exasperation. She was happy to run errands, balking only when they involved an element of cajolery on behalf of her stepmother's schemes. "Fine, but only because I have a *legitimate* reason for stopping." She pushed off the door-jamb and elaborated as she crossed the room to follow Mrs Battlesby back to the kitchen. "Monsieur Poirot unmasked the murderer in *Death on the Nile* last night, so it's on to the next case."

It had been Miss Husselbee who'd introduced Olive to Agatha Christie's Belgian detective. The Sergeant Major had taken *Peril at End House* from the library and not cared a jot for the antics of "that frivolous little man," so when Olive, fresh home from London and rather dispirited, had made a pest of herself with the toys being sorted for the jumble sale, Miss Husselbee had pushed the book into her hands and shooed her away. Olive had taken herself off to the churchyard and had read for hours in the shelter of the old yew tree. When the shadows had grown too long and even squinting hadn't been sufficient to make out the words, she'd tucked the book into her pocket and walked home through the village, looking askance at everyone she passed, her thoughts crowded with suspicion.

Unlike Miss Husselbee, Olive found she had rather a soft spot for M. Poirot: his unflinching determination to do what must be done, tempered by his many little absurdities—those moustaches! She had quickly caught up on all his adventures to date and was now working her way through them all over again, trying to pinpoint the clues that would eventually lead to the gathering of suspects and the thrilling unmasking of the murderer. Poirot was by far her favourite of Mrs Christie's clever sleuths, although the back-and-forth shenanigans of Frankie and Bobby in *Why Didn't They Ask Evans?* made Olive sentimental for past adventures with George.

Harriet was well aware of her stepdaughter's penchant and often teased her about her little Belgian friend. Now her eyes rolled in amused exasperation as another wisp of smoke escaped her. "You hardly need a book, darling—we have our own little mystery right here."

Olive stopped in her tracks. "What is it?"

Harriet cut her eyes around at her stepdaughter. "Where has Violet Darling been all this time? Where is her husband? And perhaps most interesting of all, why has she come back?"

"I suspect the answers are rather straightforward and won't require an investigation or prompt a murder. So, I'll need to live vicariously," Olive said wryly. "Oh," she said, turning back, "you'll need to find another Mr Darcy. Dr Ware is too busy."

"And I was so hoping he'd agree," Harriet said consideringly, already deep in thought, as Olive reached the doorway.

As the wireless switched to the jaunty harmonising of the Andrews Sisters, Harriet called after her, "And if you could drop the spare accumulator at Forrester's Garage, I'd be ever so grateful. Thank you, darling."

Olive groaned inwardly.

Olive had carted the family's spare accumulator to Forrester's to be recharged at least once a week since the war had started. No one—least of all her increasingly immobile stepmother—wanted the wireless to fall silent. But for once, she barely noticed the twinge in her shoulder as the battery dragged at her side; she was distracted by a new, burgeoning sense of responsibility, a fierce impatience to get on with things. It was as if, with George leaving, the clock had begun to spin faster, its ticking becoming louder and more insistent, a persistent reminder that it was high time she volunteered. Officially. Doing real work, making a solid contribution to help win the war. The trouble was, she felt tethered to Pipley like a barrage balloon.

Sighing, she took a moment to appreciate the beauty of Hertfordshire in the spring. The greys and browns of winter had, at long last, been vanquished by a downy blanket of spring green, speckled with the sunny yellow of daffodils and the luminous violet of wild bluebells. It was good to remember that life carried on—all the best parts of it—even when it seemed as if hope was gradually giving way.

The insistent buzz of an aeroplane sounded suddenly in the companionable silence, putting Olive instantly on alert. Moving closer to Jonathon, poised to take his arm, Olive braced for the possibility of an air-raid siren. It didn't come. Instead, they stood still, watching one of their own, a Vickers Wellington, bisect the sky above them, heading west.

"Now that George has gone"—Jonathon's already quiet voice

was dampened further by the drone of the engines far above them—"are you planning on leaving, too?"

She looked at him—he very deliberately wasn't looking at her—and her shoulders dropped.

"I think I need to," she said quietly. "Don't you? It's a joint effort, after all, and I'm not contributing here, not really." In fairness, every one of her responsibilities *could* be taken up by someone else, whether it be her father, Jonathon, Mrs Battlesby, or the women of the WI. It wouldn't be convenient, and it would likely not be easy, but it could be done. As things were, she was entirely dispensable.

He was silent. No empty protestations for the sake of her feelings.

Bear up, Olive. You wouldn't want that in any case.

"You won't even miss me," she said, bumping his shoulder with hers. "Too much to keep you busy. You'll have to care for the pigeons, you know. Or do the best you can, anyway." She'd write a letter, requesting that the Bright loft be given fresh consideration, but beyond that, it was out of their hands.

Jonathon turned toward her, his face slack with worry.

She gave his shoulders an encouraging squeeze, the string bag that held her library book bumping gently against his arm. "And don't worry about this business with the NPS. Pigeons are extremely resourceful. With you watching over them, they're bound to do just fine."

They had reached the edge of the village now and were walking along the river, the chattering redwings in the nearby hedgerow volubly conducting business of their own.

"Maybe you'll be posted to one of the services stationed nearby." Jonathon sounded optimistic, and she couldn't blame him. He was a protective, sensitive soul and was liable to worry if he couldn't keep an eye on her himself.

Olive thought it best to shy away from the honest answer, that she rather hoped to be posted somewhere a bit more dangerous, and was poised to agree with him as she switched the battery to her other hand. But in that in-between moment, a high, crisp voice reached their ears, coming from the other side of the brick wall that edged the riverbank, just over the footbridge.

"You cannot possibly think to hide this information from the vicar."

Bafflement stole over Olive's face as she strained to hear the response. Unfortunately, she had no luck discerning individual words amid the whisper-hissed reply. Given that it prompted a familiar, cracking thump, it seemed unlikely to be accommodating.

"That's Miss Husselbee," Jonathon said in hushed tones redolent of both respect and uncertainty.

Having been the cause of that umbrella thump that very morning, she nodded in recognition and tried to decide what to do. Should they stay put and risk eavesdropping on a private, and very awkward, conversation, or walk on and risk a direct confrontation?

"It is very much my business," Miss Husselbee began again, forestalling any decision on Olive's part. "A person's sordid past is the business of any good citizen." Another punctuating thump.

Olive's eyes flared as she wondered whom Miss Husselbee might have cornered with such an accusation. *Sordid past?* Her mind boggled.

"What's *sordid?*" Jonathon had leaned in so close that his breath tickled her ear.

"Shameful." They shared a look.

"Golly," he said, subdued.

The second voice, lashing out, louder now, shook them still. "For once in your tedious little life, mind your own business."

Olive took hold of Jonathon's arm; she knew that voice.

Miss Husselbee naturally ignored the suggestion. "I knew the moment you set foot in the village that you'd be trouble, and it's rare that I'm mistaken."

"You know *nothing* about me," came the scathing retort, "and you had better not spread your spy-gathered stories any further."

"Don't presume to threaten me, young lady. Only one of us can claim the moral high ground, and it certainly isn't you."

"How is it," the voice said tightly, "that you've not yet been murdered in your bed?"

Olive and Jonathon stood rigid with shock, as if listening to the latest instalment of *Lights Out*.

Olive could well imagine the rolling of Miss Husselbee's hazel eyes. "Leave it to you to be melodramatic about the whole affair. I have found you out, and it is my duty to ensure that you do not deceive someone who has placed his trust in you."

"Stay away from him, or I'll—" The words were bitten off: either her plans were too unspeakable to utter or she hadn't yet settled on a punishment worthy of such a betrayal.

Judging by the frosty harrumph, the older woman wasn't cowed and had simply walked on.

Caught in the middle of a secret half revealed, Olive was fretting and distracted when Jonathon tugged her sleeve. As they stepped onto the bridge, a woman had emerged from behind the wall and was quickly turning away to walk briskly in the opposite direction. Olive stared after her, her thoughts echoing Jonathon's quiet words: *It's Margaret.*

Wednesday, 8 January 1941
Peregrine Hall, Pipley
Hertfordshire

The weather has been particularly disagreeable these past few days. However, I still manage to venture forth from the Hall at least once a day, swaddled in scarves and sturdy tweed. My reasons are partly self-serving—the fresh air and exercise are invigorating to both body and spirit—and partly altruistic. Someone must keep a sharp eye on the goings-on in this quiet corner of Britain, and I consider myself more than equal to the task.

We are beginning to hunker down on the home front as that beastly Hun marches across Europe, wreaking havoc and hate. More of our boys have joined up, but an even greater number of new faces have joined the ranks of our little village. Over the past several months, we've had a steady trickle of evacuees from London and Southampton, my favourite among them a boy of twelve, who's proven himself a stalwart young fellow despite the irresponsible antics of his mother. I admit I'm considerably less impressed with the woman who has somehow managed to ensnare our young vicar. If I believed in such nonsense, I'd say she's bewitched him. For there is something about her that sets me the wrong way. A shortage of silk stockings, and the girl coats her legs in gravy browning! It requires only a single hungry dog to show her the error of her vainglorious ways; surely one will soon step up to do its duty. The other newcomers have, as yet, done nothing to call attention to themselves, either good or bad, but time will tell.

V.A.E. Husselbee

Chapter 3

"I wonder what went on in her sordid past," Jonathon said ghoulishly as they walked on. He appeared relatively unaffected by the whole exchange, but Olive's thoughts were in a whirl of confusion. "It looks like this is *another* mystery," he said excitedly. Before she could answer, he went on, "Could she be a secret agent?" She shot him a quelling glare just as he turned to climb the steps to school. He'd managed only two before he turned, his eyebrows climbing, and said, his voice quiet with awe, "Or a *double* agent." He clearly required no response, because with a flashing grin, he hurtled up the remaining steps and disappeared through the windowed door, his olive-green socks sliding lazily down his pale, thin legs.

"It's nothing," she said to no one at all, not entirely convinced. Margaret had sketched in her past with broad strokes, but what had been left unsaid? For the second time that day, the Sergeant Major's tongue wagging had sent her thoughts into a spiral of suspicion. Beastly woman!

Margaret had been modelling ladies' stockings and undergarments for a London department store when the Blitz started—a fact she'd already confided to the vicar, who also happened to be her fiancé. After too many consecutive nights spent in damp, overcrowded air-raid shelters, holding her breath as the bombs screamed down, she had decided to evacuate. With her father dealing with Nazi U-boats in the Atlantic and her mother long dead, she'd shown up in Pipley, somewhat at loose ends. Her aunt Eloise had dragged her along to the WI's weekly knitting parties, where she and Olive had quickly become fast friends, bonding over their clumsy-fingered efforts.

Judging by her friend's blistering reaction, Miss Husselbee had somehow uncovered something more. Something Margaret wanted kept quiet. Or else she was creating drama for its own sake, and Margaret simply wasn't in the mood to put up with it. It wouldn't be the first time the pair had butted heads. With any luck, the matter could be cleared up that very afternoon, over a cup of tea and a quiet, calming chat. If nothing else, her friend could turn the whole thing into a riveting letter for some unsuspecting soldier.

Her string bag had wrapped itself around her wrist, and as Olive let it unwind, her book paddling around in a circle, it struck her that the surreal conversation between Margaret and Verity Husselbee was exactly the sort that might take place in a Christie mystery. She scoffed. Whatever the trouble, it certainly wasn't anything worthy of murder.

Although according to Poirot, cold-blooded, deliberate murder was motivated by gain, jealousy, fear, or hate. Judging by the feelings of much of the village toward Miss Husselbee's meddling ways, she might be a bit at risk. The bad luck of it was that the Sergeant Major was effectively the Miss Marple of the village—ferreting away little bits of gossip and then bringing them to bear on the guilty parties—although she tended to be much more strident about it. Who, then, would solve Miss Husselbee's murder?

Olive shrugged dismissively. If it came to that, *she'd* do it— she'd learned a good bit from Poirot's order and method. He'd started out somewhat haphazardly, in her opinion, in *The Mysterious Affair at Styles*, but by *Murder on the Orient Express*, he was marvellously intuitive and efficient.

Moments later she'd rounded the corner into the gravelled yard of Forrester's Garage, conscious of a callus forming on her middle finger, under the handle of the accumulator. Her boots scuffed loudly as she pulled up short, her heart hitching as she stared at the coveralled man bent over the yawning hood of a battered green Wolseley. It was silly really. It couldn't possibly be George, but she felt the aftershock just the same: an awful sense of emptiness low in her stomach. George had worked for his father before going off to train for the RAF, and she could always find him tinkering under the hoods of a rotating collection of automobiles. But no longer.

She took a deep, stuttering breath and walked determinedly past the car, nodding at Tommy Marin, who'd peered over his shoulder at her, his cheek smeared with grime. Squinting into the relative darkness of the garage's twin bays, she scanned the shadows for George's father. She found him settled on a stool beside a wood stove, patching a bicycle tyre by the light of a lamp. He was hunched and rumpled, and he hadn't shaved. She inhaled deeply as she approached, hoping for a whiff of lavender soap amid the pervasive scents of rubber and gasoline. George had always smelled of lavender soap, and Olive was feeling rather mawkish. But despite multiple sniffs, she couldn't detect even a hint of it—Mr Forrester smelled of something else, which she couldn't quite place.

Judging by the shift in posture and the quizzical frown from Mr Forrester, she was making a cake of herself. She stepped clumsily backwards and bumped the accumulator against her knee. Biting back a curse, she smiled, her mouth tight with pain, and glanced down to see if any acid had leaked onto her trousers. "Morning, Mr Forrester."

He nodded. "Your repair holding up?"

A few weeks ago, she'd shamefacedly wheeled her mangled bicycle into the garage after a collision with a signpost. She'd been tracking the flight path of a promising yearling as he'd made his way home from a launch at Hertford Castle, and not watching where she was going. She'd come away without injury, although George, who'd popped out from beneath a lorry like magic when she'd rolled in, had seen fit to work her pride over pretty well.

"Perfectly," she told him.

He nodded and aimed his chin at the glass-encased accumulator dragging at her right hand. "You were just in Monday. It's not lost its charge yet, has it?"

The accumulator would run the wireless for at least a week, but her father had insisted they keep a spare, always charged and ready. "Not yet, but Jonathon would be lost without Mr Middleton's gardening programme," she said, poking fun at the BBC Home Service.

Mr Forrester seemed not to have heard any but the first two words. Olive understood. She wasn't in the mood for conversation, either, but one had to carry on.

"Shall I put it with the others?" she asked.

When he nodded, she skirted a jumble of old bicycle wheels, some warped, others missing spokes, all depressingly flat, to the sturdy wooden worktable against the back wall of the garage. The table was divided: on the left were the batteries that needed charging, and on the right, the ones ready to be picked up. Olive hoisted the beastly thing, being careful not to tip it, lest any acid drip. After turning it so that her surname, marked in white paint, was displayed, she pushed it back from the edge.

"How's Lady Camilla bearing up?" she asked solemnly. Olive hoped George's mother's grace and good humour would carry her through the fearful uncertainty of sending her only son off to complete his flight training.

"Well enough," he said gruffly, using his pocketknife to cut a length of patching tape before tucking the roll back into his shirt pocket. Olive understood what remained unspoken: *As well as can be expected*.

"Right," she said, not knowing what else to say. But then, figuring it couldn't hurt, she leaned closer, lowered her voice, and admitted with a shy smile, "I sent a pigeon along with him."

His head came up to rake her with a suspicious glare. "I don't want him in trouble."

Olive's smile cracked as she stared at the angry caterpillar brows that had inched together over his nose. His eyes were bloodshot, and his cheeks stained a ruddy pink. "There won't be any trouble." She shook her head, wanting to dispel any whisper of uncertainty. "He'll have released her before anyone even knows she's there. Besides, these days, pigeons are war heroes—they may as well be mascots of the RAF." Her smile was surely too wide and too bright, but he wouldn't notice, because he was staring down at the bicycle tube caught between his knees.

"Well," she said finally, breaking the silence, which had grown awkward. "I'd better be off." She shifted guiltily, poised to hurry away, but with her shoulders sagging under the weight of their shared worry, she turned back. "George will be all right, Mr Forrester. He's brave and smart, and he's got plenty of experience getting out of scrapes."

The phone rang then, shrill in the darkened garage. He lifted the receiver but didn't put it to his ear, eyeing her with pointed dismissal. Eager to be away, she spun, her heel skidding slightly on an oily patch, and strode quickly back across the yard and around the high holly hedge. Alone again and free of the accumulator, she swung her arms and hummed a little tune, wondering if absolutely everything was destined to be awkward now.

Rather conveniently, the lending library was tucked into the south-facing corner of the village hall. Maverick Darling had made his fortune in the mills and then had donated the funds for both the library and the village hall. And while half of the building had been requisitioned the previous year by the Women's Voluntary Service and the Home Guard, the remainder continued to be put to regular use for meetings, lectures, and knitting circles, as well as organised games of whist, rummy, and badminton. The concerts, amateur theatricals, and dances, put on more frequently since the onset of the war, were highly anticipated and well attended, a much-needed respite from the constant worry and uncertainty that plagued them all.

Olive slipped through the door and stood, her arm curled behind her, her hand still gripping the knob, as the peaceful silence and cosy warmth of the room settled around her like a hug. She took a deep breath, the crisp newness of spring fading under the layered scents of paper, leather, and lemon oil.

Miss Rose was, as always, tucked behind the broad wooden librarian's desk, hunched over the pages of the book open in front of her. In the dim lighting, she seemed pale as a watermark behind the delicately framed spectacles linked to a chain around her neck.

Olive took in her Peter Pan collar, dowdy cardigan, and the long, elegant fingers resting on the navy blue wool sleeves. While she couldn't see them, Olive felt confident that the desk hid a plain brown tweed skirt and sensible shoes. It was always the same. Olive had often felt that when Violet had gone off, she'd left Rose trapped, Pipley's very own Sleeping Beauty, locked away forever in a life of dreary monotony. Although, in fairness, no one would call her a beauty.

Her hair was forever scraped into a severe bun that stretched the youthful, freckled skin of her face and highlighted slightly bulbous eyes as unfathomable as dark treacle. Her nose was a touch too long, her lips were too wide, and her teeth were rather a jumble. Her expression, as ever, was patient and reserved.

"Hello, Olive." Rose rarely raised her voice beyond a quiet murmur, even on the high street. She'd clearly adapted to a life in the library. "May I help you with something?"

"Morning, Miss Rose," Olive said, approaching the desk. Her

gaze settled on the miniature bouquet of wildflowers corralled in a jam jar before shifting errantly to the book claiming pride of place. With a brittle smile, the librarian leaned forward, crossing her arms lightly over its pages.

Olive slid her borrowed book forward. "I'm looking for another Christie mystery." Propping her hip beside the delicate cluster of red campion and pignut, she added, "I've a mad crush on Hercule Poirot and his little grey cells." She tapped her temple with her index finger, but when it became obvious that Miss Rose was completely distracted by the invasion of her personal space, she slipped her hand awkwardly back down again and fisted it at her side as she stood up straight.

"I see," said Miss Rose, peering up at her over the rims of the spectacles she used for reading. "I prefer Miss Marple, but to each her own." Despite the broad-mindedness inherent in the words, the awkward shift in Miss Rose's gaze seemed to indicate that Olive's preference for a little Belgian with an egg-shaped head over an upright British lady was entirely perplexing. "I believe we have several of Mrs Christie's novels on the shelf right now, if you want to check."

Olive couldn't help but compare Miss Rose, rather uncharitably, to her glamorous sister. Not yet ready to broach the topic of Violet Darling, she drifted toward the shelf of mysteries that lined the wall beside the window. Her finger skimmed the neat row of spines before coming to a stop on the perfectly cosmopolitan *Murder on the Orient Express*. She plucked it from the shelf, feeling rather in the mood for an adventure by train. After quickly settling on a Georgette Heyer novel for Harriet, she approached the checkout desk.

"Success," she said.

Miss Rose reached for the books, and Olive watched in silence as she stamped out the correct date on the library cards—one for the book and one for the record—before sliding the selections back to her.

Tucking both into her bag, Olive said coyly, "I was at St Margarets station this morning, seeing George Forrester off to flight school." Peering up at her, Miss Rose schooled her features to exhibit polite interest. "I thought I recognised Miss Violet . . ."

The librarian's lips curved into a bland smile. "It's very likely you did," she said, lacing her fingers in front of her in a move that clearly said, *Will there be anything else?*

Olive had no idea why Miss Rose was being so close-mouthed on the topic, but she refused to be deterred.

"You must be so pleased to see her after all this time. Did you know she was coming?"

The fingers clenched. "I had a telegram a few days ago."

"Do you suppose she'll be staying through the end of the war?" Olive pressed.

"I suspect. But Violet is unpredictable. You are probably old enough to remember, but surely you've heard the gossip?" There was no rancour in her tone, but her eyebrows lifted in the barest challenge.

Olive let it pass. "Harriet's never met her, you know," she said conversationally. "When I mentioned Miss Violet was home again, she thought it might be rather fun for the two of you to be Bennet sisters together." She smiled encouragingly.

"Let me guess. She was thinking Mary and Lydia?" Her tone was heavy and resigned.

"Elizabeth was mentioned," Olive allowed.

Miss Rose slipped her glasses from her nose and gazed hopefully at Olive. "Elizabeth is a wonderful part. I'd have to think—" Her eyes shifted distractedly away and then flicked eagerly back again. "Has Mr Darcy been cast yet?" Her fingers fidgeted, smoothing the pages of the book in front of her, which, judging by the diagrams, appeared to be some sort of biology textbook.

Olive blinked, uncertain how to proceed. Clearly, Miss Rose was under the impression that Harriet wanted her and not her sister for the role of Lizzy Bennet. Harriet was going to murder her, but she really didn't want the responsibility of dashing any hopes today. "I did just put a bug in Dr Ware's ear," she confided, not bothering to admit that it had crawled right out the other.

The librarian flushed, her pallor flooding with patchy colour.

Eager to be done with the subject and on with her business, Olive said, "Will Miss Violet be at the dance?"

Miss Rose was too distracted to answer immediately, but as the silence grew, she started out of her reverie. "I beg your pardon." She shook her head slightly and straightened her spine. "I rather doubt it. When I mentioned it, she was quick to inform me that without canapés, champagne and, most importantly, *men*, there's little reason to bother." It was distinctly odd hearing Miss Rose use the word *men* in that context. Then again, a casual mention of Dr Ware had sent her into a veritable tizzy.

"Well, that's a shame. But she's bound to discover that even a bit of entertainment is better than nothing." Olive took a step back. "On that note, I'm off to decorate the hall."

Miss Rose stood and smoothed the familiar tweed skirt. "I'll go with you." She pulled a little wooden sign from her top desk drawer, then walked to the door in her sensible shoes, latched it, and propped the sign against the window frame. Olive had been thwarted by that sign often enough to know it read BACK BEFORE LONG.

Together, they walked to the back of the library, through the tidy kitchen, and out into the main hall. Olive couldn't help but smile as her eyes ranged over the comforting space—it had played host to so many good memories, all of them overlaid with the astringent tang of vinegar and the homey scent of lemon oil that came of clockwork cleanings. Arched metal girders spanned a high ceiling over a polished honeyed wood floor, a floor that bore the varied markings of its storied history. The sage-green wainscoting was the perfect backdrop for all occasions, and the diamond-paned leaded glass windows added just the right amount of sparkle.

At the far end, screens had been positioned to separate the

requisitioned space from the area kept in reserve for village use. She could see slivers of darting movement on the other side—volunteers wrapping bandages or packaging up parcels for prisoners of war. On this side, George's mother, Lady Camilla Forrester, and Miss Winifred Danes were already beginning to move the chairs from their current sewing-circle grouping, to ring the tables at the edge of the room, thereby clearing space for the dance floor.

Of an age, the two women were opposites in almost every respect, and it always amused Olive to see them together. Miss Danes was petite and curvy, her ample hips and bosom cinched to a trim waist as if by a string. Her hair was still a dark chicory brown, her cheeks were round and flushed, and the faint odour of sugar clung to her even now, months after it had gone on the ration. It was rumoured she'd worked as a secretary to an affluent businessman who'd died under suspicious circumstances and left her a sizeable inheritance, but rumours could rarely be trusted. She lived alone in a comfortable cottage and had a brother—a rather greasy individual—who came often to visit. In contrast, Lady Camilla was tall and slim, with long, elegant limbs and striking cheekbones. She walked with a brisk sense of purpose, her corn-silk hair always twisted neatly into a chignon and her clear green eyes snapping with intent. The only daughter of an earl, she'd been a socialite before her marriage; now she was a wife, a mother, and the stalwart president of the Pipley WI. She was efficient, tireless, and skilled at the sort of witchcraft that kept one's lipstick unsmudged and one's hair unmussed. Olive gazed enviously at Lady Camilla's cobalt-blue skirt and crisp white blouse, its pin tucks and mother-of-pearl buttons, and wondered how they might stand up to pigeons, accumulators, pigs, and dirt. Sighing, she splayed her hands over nubby trouser–clad hips for a moment before getting to work.

"The more the merrier," called Miss Danes. "It's rather tedious to always be rearranging the chairs."

Lady Camilla offered a tight, distracted smile and ran a hand along the upsweep of her hair, then fingered one of the marcasite combs tucked neatly at the base of her neck. She'd likely already been subjected to various petty complaints before they'd arrived.

"Has Harriet, by any chance, made the final casting decisions for the play?" Miss Danes went on, switching topics. "I honestly don't understand what's taking so long—several of the characters may as well be living right here in Pipley. Margaret would make a lovely Jane Bennet, and Rose is a perfect Mary," she said point-edly.

Olive winced. Miss Rose had turned slowly from the glass-fronted cupboard that housed the WI's china set, tablecloths, and paper lanterns to stare blandly at Miss Danes.

"If Harriet is typecasting," she said sweetly, "I think you can look forward to playing Mrs Bennet, Winifred." The words were said without obvious malice, merely delivered as unavoidable truth, and all eyes turned assessingly toward Miss Danes, who began chuffing with embarrassment. The tables had been effec-tively turned, and Olive bit her lip at the efficiency of it all while Miss Rose briskly cleared her throat. "Should I bother with the spring bunting," she called to the room at large, "or should we simply resign ourselves to Miss Husselbee's favoured red, white, and blue?"

As if her ears had been burning with the fire of village contro-versy, the woman in question swept through the outer door, hold-ing a deep rectangular basket, the inevitable umbrella hung over her forearm. Two other ladies trickled through in her wake: Lil-lian Crabbleton, an exceedingly shy girl of sixteen, whose mother had probably sent her along, and Mrs Spencer, who always wore a hat with a flower tucked in its brim. Today it was a wilted sweet pea. Having caught the gist of the question, Miss Husselbee was already simmering with righteous indignation.

"*Resign* is entirely too passive, Miss Darling. We should ac-tively *embrace* patriotism in all its forms. Britain is, I need not remind you, at war," she said stoutly, settling the basket on the nearest table in order to put the aforementioned decoration into immediate use and thus quell all further discussion.

"If it isn't Lady Catherine de Bourgh," Miss Rose murmured, her lips curving in a subtle smile as she laid a stack of pale yellow tablecloths on the closest chair. Olive suspected she hadn't been meant to overhear, and quickly carried off several of the table-cloths to get to work. Barely a moment later, Miss Rose an-nounced, "I've had an idea for a raffle," her voice stretched beyond its usual library bounds.

The other women glanced at her curiously, while Miss Hussel-bee frowned slightly, holding the Union Jack bunting against her chest, as if about to belt out, "Rule, Britannia!"

"Whoever donates the largest sum," Miss Rose continued, fo-cused on her audience, "wins the right to decorate the hall for the next dance in a manner of his or her choosing." Clearly, Miss Rose was in a mischievous mood, and Olive, for one, was quite enjoying it.

The murmurs had barely begun when they were ruthlessly cut off.

"Fustian," Miss Husselbee said dismissively. "A village event is not within the purview of a single individual. It should always be a joint effort, intended to buoy friendship and solidarity." Every other woman in the hall stood still, her eyes flitting and rolling at the irony of that statement. When no one voiced an ob-jection, Miss Husselbee nodded smartly, grasped the back of a chair, and dragged it across the floor with a hideous screech, holding the bunting out before her.

When she'd reached the far side, Miss Danes spoke up. "Put to a vote, I suspect Miss Darling's idea would garner more sup-port than you might imagine, Verity." Her rosy cheeks puffed out slightly as she pressed her lips into a tight little moue. She was clearly uncomfortable defending one nemesis against another, and so, quickly busied herself once again with the task of moving chairs.

Gripping the edge of the wainscoting for support, Miss Husselbee climbed onto her chair and gazed down on them all, her particular focus reserved for Miss Danes. "That *you* would be in support of the removal of such a symbol of patriotism does not come as a particular surprise, Winifred." She pressed her shoulders back, tipped her chin up haughtily, and looked down her nose. A vein popped out on Miss Danes's forehead, and her face suddenly bore a marked resemblance to a ripe pink gooseberry.

"I don't know what you mean," she said, her voice cracking with embarrassment.

"Don't you?" was Miss Husselbee's ready reply.

"I'm quite certain I don't," Miss Danes snapped.

Olive was moving from table to table, smoothing the wrinkles from each cloth as vigorously as if her efforts could smooth the tensions from the room. Lady Camilla, who had crossed the hall to collect the rest of the tablecloths, now darted an assessing glance between the two women who suddenly seemed at daggers drawn. For a moment, Olive thought she'd let the quarrel run its course—these squabbles were entirely commonplace— but with a swift intake of breath, she swept selflessly into the fray. "I think perhaps what Miss Darling and Miss Danes are suggesting is that a little variety might boost our spirits and morale quite as efficiently as the patriotic bunting, which," she hurried to add, "is certainly a favourite of us all."

"I am as strong a proponent of boosting morale as anyone in this village, but not at the expense of patriotism. Once patriotism is thrust heedlessly aside, treasonous behaviour is wont to slip in, in its place."

A tittering rose up among the women scattered throughout the hall at the use of a word they all found shocking.

"We are a far cry from treason, Verity," Lady Camilla said lightly. "The Daffodil Dance is a village tradition in peacetime and in war. We are all simply trying to make the best of things."

"Not all of us," Miss Rose murmured cryptically. Olive was

quite taken with this new side of the librarian—perhaps having her sister back in the village had brought her out of her shell.

Miss Husselbee's lips curved into a superior smile. "Miss Danes will likely be bringing a cake for the refreshments table." Speared with a challenging glance, Miss Danes could only nod in assent. "I would suggest that any of you questioning the potential for treason in this village should have a slice of it." She harrumphed from her perch on the chair and turned away to begin hanging the bunting.

Every eye, widened in shock and uncertainty, had shifted guiltily toward Miss Danes, whose gooseberry colouring had ripened dramatically. Wincing, Olive snapped a cloth over the table in front of her. Normally, she and Margaret would have been communicating volumes with the gratuitous use of rolling eyes and twitching brows, but her friend hadn't shown. They'd arranged to meet at the hall and then walk to Margaret's house for the midday meal and an afternoon of letter writing, so her absence was curious, to say the least. Although, after the conversation she'd recently overheard on the riverbank, it wasn't at all surprising that her friend had kept away.

But to miss an accusation of treasonous baking!

In all likelihood, it had been prompted by a suspicion that Miss Danes was using more than her ration of sugar or butter, or even chocolate. And perhaps she was—it wasn't entirely uncommon for villagers to dabble in black-market goods. Her father had boasted quite happily of the extra petrol coupons he'd managed to lay in, in the face of Harriet's recently reduced mobility. Olive knew the practice shouldn't be encouraged or condoned, but it seemed rather a tame infraction, all things considered.

They all worked in silence after that, Miss Husselbee charging around the perimeter in solitary determination, dragging her chair behind her, while the rest of the volunteers finished decorating the tables: two long ones positioned near the kitchen to hold refreshments and a bevy of round ones flanking the dance floor. Mrs Spencer had brought four coffee cans crammed full of daffodils, which grew en masse in the woodland beyond her garden, and they tucked generous bouquets into jam jars to set in the centre of each table.

Olive was admiring the hall's dark, elegant bones, enlivened by sunny shades of yellow beneath the delicate paper lanterns and stalwart swags of patriotism, when she turned to see Miss Husselbee peering into the string bag she'd left hanging on a chair. Rolling her eyes, she walked over, wondering if she dared accuse the old harridan of snooping.

"May I help you?" Olive said sweetly.

"No need," came the Sergeant Major's ready reply. "I was curious about your reading habits. And I wanted to make sure you hadn't snapped up something I'd hoped to get myself."

And if I had? Would we be facing off at twenty paces?

She didn't say the words, but they fairly hummed in her ears.

"I've read the latest Georgette Heyer, and Christie isn't my cup of tea," Miss Husselbee said dismissively. "I've had to go a bit farther afield than our little library collection for a certain novel that I'm finding particularly true to life." Her eyes were trained on Miss Rose, who seemed unaware of the attention. Irritated at being ignored, the Sergeant Major huffed loudly.

The vicar chose that moment to pop his head into the hall, prompting a second huff. Much more, Olive thought, and she'd sound like a steam train.

Leo Truscott had come to the village just after the start of the war and had quickly charmed the lot of them, with one notable exception. Miss Husselbee remained suspicious of him, certain he was trying too hard to be liked. The news, little more than a month ago, of his engagement to Margaret Middleton had further reinforced her disapproval. Leo took it in his stride, but Margaret bristled with indignation whenever she was nudged into company with the woman.

As Olive watched, the ladies quickly closed ranks around the handsome vicar. His glance up at the miniature Union Jacks amid a chorus of twittering was a dead giveaway as to their topic of conversation. "You've all done a wonderful job transforming the hall for the dance," he said, his deep, rich voice carrying to all corners of the hall.

"Will we see you at the dance, Leo?" Mrs Spencer asked, her handbag looped over the hand that warmly pressed his.

"I wouldn't miss it," he answered. "And I confess I'm looking forward to the offerings at the refreshment table as much as the dance itself." Flashing a grin that looked distinctly devilish, Leo detached himself from the doting group and headed in Olive's direction. He was about six inches taller than she was, a lofty six feet two, with plenty of muscle to flesh out his bones and hair the colour of wildflower honey. She and Margaret had discussed his attributes at considerable length.

Smiling warmly, he said, "I'm afraid Margaret needs to postpone your afternoon together." His manner was always eloquent and forthright and tended to make her feel quite virtuous.

Olive frowned. Mags had already skipped out on decorating. Now it was to be the letter writing, too? "Did she say why?" Her forehead crinkled in concern as she bent to smooth an errant wrinkle in the nearest tablecloth.

He shrugged. "She said only that she didn't feel up to it today and could I carry along her regrets."

"All right. I suppose I'll see her at the dance, then. That is, if you're willing to share her," she teased.

"This week's sermon is to be on cultivating a giving heart," he said with a wink. "The writing process will ensure that particular virtue is at the forefront of my mind." He gave her shoulder a friendly squeeze before slipping back out of the hall.

Olive had only a moment to consider the implications of Margaret's absence.

"That man is not what he seems."

Startled, she swung around to find Miss Husselbee standing behind her with pursed lips and raised brows.

"I disagree. He *seems* kind, understanding, knowledgeable, and hard-working. And all evidence confirms it," Olive said tartly.

"That's exactly what he *wants* you to think," came the ready response. "He's entirely too approachable. We could all do with a bit of fire and brimstone to get the blood flowing and put the fear up our backs."

Met with no reply, Miss Husselbee huffed and stalked out of the hall, hot on the vicar's heels. Poor man. Utterly exasperated, Olive stuck out her tongue at the retreating figure.

The rest of the ladies gathered their bags and baskets, preparing to depart now that the hall was perfectly turned out for the dance, but Miss Rose had returned to the breakfront. She had carefully tucked away the sheets of tissue that had separated the tablecloths and was pulling out the punchbowl. Cups and plates had been arranged on the refreshment table, and tomorrow afternoon, ladies would parade in with cakes and sandwiches arrayed on their best serving dishes, but Miss Rose was always in charge of the punch.

Olive crossed the room to speak to her. "Well, it looks as if Miss Husselbee has got her way again," she said, gazing down the length of the hall, newly draped with the usual bunting.

Miss Rose followed her glance. "And not a one of us surprised."

"I don't mind it," Olive admitted, suddenly imagining what it would be like to leave this all behind—the bickerings and the sameness—to begin war work away from home.

"If Violet was here, she'd be ripping down Verity's bunting and putting up the yellow just for spite." Miss Rose gripped the punchbowl so tightly that Olive could see the whites of her knuckles. "Never tell her I said so, but Violet is not so very different than Verity, their ages notwithstanding. Both of them full to bursting with sheer bloody-mindedness." She seemed almost to be talking to herself, but the moment was quickly gone with a half-hearted curve of her lips.

"We're all fortunate to have your steadying influence and sensible outlook," Olive said.

"Yes, well," she said distractedly, twitching the hem of the tablecloth in front of her. "Violet has a long shadow, and she's always needed a minder. I slipped rather naturally into that role, and when she left, I found myself rather hemmed in by expectations. I used to wonder if anyone would ever see past them," she said quietly, blushing quite prettily—and rather curiously.

Olive felt the truth of those words on her own account. With any luck, that would all change very soon. "So, *show them*," she urged, lightly squeezing the librarian's arm. "The world is in an uproar as it is—I suspect there's not one of us who will emerge from this war unchanged—so you may as well take advantage. Let them see who you really are and what you're capable of."

It could have been Olive's imagination, but she thought Miss Rose stood a bit taller. "There *is* someone . . . ," she started, raising a hand to the hair tucked up at the base of her neck. But seeing Olive's brows raised in curiosity, she balked. "Perhaps I will. But right now, I'd best get back. Duty calls." She turned and made to hurry back through the kitchen, leaving Olive to stare after her.

Miss Rose could do as she pleased, but Olive had already resolved to take her own advice.

Chapter 4

Her afternoon unexpectedly free, Olive set off home, using the solitary walk to plan her argument for enlisting in the ATS. In the distance, she could make out the faint explosions sounding from the grounds of Brickendonbury Manor. Some days, they popped like firecrackers; others, they more closely resembled the low rumble of rolling thunder. And afterwards, dark smoke curled stealthily into the clouds, like secrets slipping into obscurity. She'd been close enough a few times to see everything first-hand—and the craters left behind—but it was all meant to be kept secret. Signs were posted, and the grounds patrolled, so she'd had to sneak past and keep to the trees, no longer welcome to roam the property. Just another change wrought by the war.

Olive quickened her steps at the thought that Poppins might have already returned home, eager to have a message from George, no matter how silly. As she turned to walk through the open gate, her gaze strayed to the birds that loitered atop the dovecote, but they were indistinguishable at such a distance. The pop of gravel had her twisting around in surprise to see an official-looking black Austin coasting to a stop just behind her, its engine abruptly cut. Olive could see two men behind the windshield, and as she watched, they exchanged a few words before folding open the doors and stepping into view.

They both looked to be in their late twenties, dressed in rumpled trousers, scuffed shoes, and jumpers fraying at the cuffs. But where the driver was dark haired, his face shadowed by a plaid flat cap and impending stubble, his cohort had shiny copper-coloured hair, bright eyes, a snub nose, and a friendly, open countenance.

"If you've come to see my father, he's not at home," she said with a smile, but the driver seemed to pay her words little attention. His gaze had flicked toward the dovecote, same as hers, before settling silently on her.

Her face, she knew, was still winter pale, particularly against the raw red bloom of her lips. She had a habit of tucking them roughly between her teeth whenever something was worrying her, and lately her whole world was a worry. She watched his gaze range over her muddied boots and trousers, the chapped hands settled on her forearms, and her wild curls. She'd replaced the scarf she'd worn earlier with a pair of tortoiseshell combs, but they weren't managing the task any better. She looked away first, shifting her attention to the other visitor, who was currently tracing lines in the gravel with his boot, as if he could happily while away the afternoon that way.

"We'd like to have a look at your pigeons," the driver finally said, his voice a low hum that skimmed over her skin.

She blinked at them, momentarily stunned. The Pigeon Service had finally sent someone—two someones—to assess their birds and officially add the Bright loft to the list of pigeoneers committed to the war effort.

It's about bloody time.

"*Of course*, you can see the pigeons," she said, stepping toward them. "You've certainly taken your time in getting here—we've been expecting your visit for *months*. I'm Olive Bright, by the way." A surge of relief burst through her. Things were going to be tickety-boo.

With a startled look at his cohort, the copper top stepped forward. "Danny Tierney," he said, giving her hand a warm, hearty shake.

Olive noted the Irish lilt to his voice and blurted, "Has the Irish Homing Union joined with the NPS in supplying pigeons for the war effort?" Ireland remained staunchly neutral, but Olive was optimistic that their fanciers would side with the Allies.

His gaze slid guiltily sideways, but before he could answer, the darker man moved forward and gripped her hand, his shrewd gaze suddenly sharpening as his fingers tightened on hers. "You've been expecting us?"

"Not you particularly, of course," she said, tugging her fingers from his. She smiled blandly. "Seeing as I don't yet know your name."

"This is Jameson Aldridge," Mr Tierney said. "Don't mind him. He tends to get right down to business, pleasantries be damned."

Here, she thought, were the perfect Darcy and Bingley. Ruthlessly tamping down her frivolous thoughts, she hurried to welcome them.

"No worries. You're here now. I'll show you around." She turned to lead them toward the dovecote, giddy with excitement. The timing was brilliant. Were he home, her father might throw a wrench in things, making demands and lording the Bright reputation over the committee members, but with him away, she could convince them to certify the loft—even grovel if she had to. The War Office needed the Bright pigeons, and she needed to know, before going off to join the ATS, that they'd be all right.

"We completed the paperwork months ago," she said, just a hint of reprimand in her voice. "It's high time you showed up.

Our birds have been yearning to get their assignments and get to work." She was laying it on rather thick, but Mr Aldridge's dead-pan demeanour was throwing her a bit. She was eager to get the matter taken care of and have him rumbling away again down the drive.

But first she'd show off her birds, every one of them a testament to her considerable experience breeding and training racing pigeons. She'd pull out the trophies only if she thought it might make a difference, and she wouldn't worry at all about deciphering Jameson Aldridge's inscrutable behaviour unless he seemed skittish with regard to their certification. "I admit I haven't heard your names before, which surprises me. The racing world is relatively tight-knit, and my father knows everyone."

Olive rummaged beneath the yew hedge beside the door to the dovecote, unearthed the key from its hiding spot, and slid it into the securing padlock. "Necessary reinforcements against snakes and rats," she said, nudging her boot against the iron plating at the base of the door until it swung wide. "And poachers," she added, holding up the key.

"Welcome to the Bright loft." Pride was ringing in her voice. But there was a hint of desperation there, as well, which she hoped they couldn't hear. "I recommend you take cover."

There was a built-in wooden bench just inside the door, with storage under the seat. She propped it open now and pulled out a brimmed hat, which she settled neatly on her head as she did a quick scan for Mary Poppins. Her shoulders dropped slightly as she realised the bird hadn't yet returned.

As the men moved past her, Mr Tierney readily accepted a hat. Mr Aldridge was evidently unconcerned with the threat posed to his own cap. Both men had tipped their heads back, and their gazes were spiralling around the interior of the little building. Olive tried to imagine seeing it through their eyes: the intricate lattice of wooden rafters that rose to a cupola on the roof, the numbered nesting boxes tucked into one wall, the inverted V forms, on which curious pigeons were perched and staring, the tidy arrangement of breeding pens, and the serviceable gravel floor, on which sat troughs for food and water.

"The nesting boxes are all lime washed to prevent the spread of germs and disease, and we're scrupulous about cleaning the loft twice a week."

Neither of them exhibited the slightest hint that they'd even heard her little spiel, so shrugging, she tipped the bench seat closed again and settled in to wait. No doubt this vetting process would take a bit of time.

"Bright birds . . . ," Tierney said with a little smirk. "You have to admit, Aldridge, they sound quite clever."

Aldridge clearly didn't feel compelled to admit any such thing; he didn't even respond, so intent was he in his perusal of the loft. Olive wasn't used to dealing with anyone of Mr Aldridge's particular intensity, and the effort was beginning to wear.

"Of course they're clever," Olive insisted. "And all named for characters from children's literature."

A white tiger-grizzle pigeon chose that moment to slip through a hole in the cupola and, with a magnificent fanning of wings and tail feathers, glided gracefully down, stretching its legs to land on the top rung of a wooden ladder propped against the far wall.

With her visitors momentarily distracted by the dramatic entrance, Olive took the opportunity to sweep her eyes over Mr Aldridge's surly profile. His jawline was angular, almost hard, and his cheekbones were prominent. His dark hair curled around his ear, hiding one end of a faded white scar that snaked dangerously down towards his chin.

"That's Hook," she said abruptly, wondering about that scar. "Captain Hook. So named for the black grizzling near his eye." She circled her finger before her corresponding eye until she realised no one was looking her way.

"A pirate pigeon," Tierney said, with a flash of teeth. "Just the sort of bird we're looking for."

Perhaps spooked by the exuberant tone, Badger—another grizzled white—launched from his box. As he reached the rafters, he was directly above Mr Aldridge. Quite possibly in tune with Olive's mood, he chose that moment to relieve himself. The good news was that the pellets were demonstrably healthy: firm and army khaki in colour; the bad news was that each of them struck his head before bouncing off to join the scattering on the floor.

The man stilled, and Olive bit her lip to keep the corners of her mouth respectably restrained. From the corner of her eye, she could see Tierney trying, and failing, to stifle a snicker.

"I did offer you an alternate hat," she said prettily as he turned to look at her, pulling his cap from his head.

The glimpses she'd had of dark hair, tucked away, had been just the tip of the iceberg. In the soft shafts of sunlight spearing through the dovecote, his wavy mop of hair seemed the colour of devil's food cake, and his eyes, previously shadowed by his cap, were a clear grey blue, sheltered by hooded lids and long, curled dark lashes. Classic Irish colouring made him striking, but there was too much geometry in his face. It was all sharp planes and angles, including a curious kink at the bridge of his nose. He reminded her of a ghost from her past, a man who'd been both a thorn in her side and a short-lived romantic interlude before he'd joined up and effectively disappeared from her life. As he levelled his gaze on her face, she couldn't help but feel relieved that his physical appeal was effectively counterbalanced by his stony reserve and disgruntled disapproval. Flirting with an NPS committee member charged with vetting their loft would have been entirely inappropriate; luckily, he'd efficiently dispatched all temptation. As if to corroborate that decision, he turned abruptly away from her and wiped his cap against a clean spot on the wall before settling it back on his head.

"Occupational hazard," he said brusquely, still glancing around him, perhaps newly curious about the healthiness of the birds and the suitability of the loft. It was unfortunate that this surprise visit hadn't fallen on a day she'd scraped down the walls and cleared the floor of the inevitable droppings, but she couldn't very well be expected to keep the dovecote pristine for months in anticipation of an impending visit. Mr Tierney, she noticed, was checking the bottom of his shoes.

"Once upon a time, their diet was a mix of beans, peas, winter corn, and barley or rice, but with the shortages, we've had to improvise. We're running rather low on feed in general, so your visit comes as a great relief." *Don't sound desperate!* She was quick to remind herself that it hardly mattered. Mr Aldridge certainly knew that if he denied them approval, they were going to be in dire straits.

"What's the maximum distance your birds have covered in a single flight?" he asked abruptly.

She straightened. "Around five hundred miles."

"Average speed?"

"Poppins is our fastest bird and has been clocked at eighty-five miles per hour, although average speed is closer to fifty."

Tierney let loose a long, slow whistle. Aldridge quietly lifted a single brow, and something flickered in his eyes. She suspected it was disbelief, and it set her hackles up.

"The difference factors in weather conditions, wind speed, and the pigeon's efficiency in getting its bearings."

Aldridge let that pass. "Which one is Poppins?"

Her self-righteous indignation promptly shrivelled, cringing in on itself as worry crowded forward. It took her a moment to rally, but she lifted her chin, not quite meeting his eyes. "Not here at the moment, I'm afraid." She offered no further explanation, hoping he'd leave it at that.

For only the third time in the ten minutes they'd spent together, she had his full attention. Mr Tierney's was similarly piqued, and she found herself facing down two very different pairs of eyes.

"Where is he?" Aldridge asked.

Murder. "As it happens, Poppins is a hen," she croaked, stalling for time.

"*Mary* Poppins," Tierney asserted, looking askance at his companion, his tone mildly reproachful.

"Is that relevant to her current location?" Aldridge said dryly.

Olive ignored his tone as the pulse fluttered worriedly at her throat. She swallowed with difficulty. "As Hook and Badger have just demonstrated, the birds are free to come and go as they please to a certain extent."

"So, you're saying she's out on her own reconnaissance?" he pressed.

Olive couldn't decide whether he was testing her or simply teasing, and the not knowing was entirely exasperating.

Olive considered her options, her heart urged into reckless beating by nerves and uncertainty. There *was* some measure of truth to his interpretation of the situation. "In a way." She lifted her gaze to his and determined not to blink, no matter what his reply.

"So, if I were to wait," Aldridge said carefully, "with the intent of examining the loft's fastest bird, how long do you estimate it would take?"

Tierney's gaze volleyed curiously between the pair of them.

Crackers! She had no idea when Poppins would make her way back to the loft. It all depended on when George decided to let her go—it could be two minutes from now or two days.

"It's rather difficult to predict and dependent on all sorts of things. As I'm sure you're aware." She tried smiling and felt her attempt bounce right off him.

"Right." His gaze held hers; his was heavy, calm, and implacable. Hers merely felt hunted. She suspected he could carry on for hours, perhaps *days*, but a telltale twitchiness was beginning to overtake her. Judging by the scrutiny in his gaze, he suspected some version of the truth and was even now trying to break her, and while that should have been the only incentive necessary to hold the line, she could feel herself beginning to crack. This visit was immensely important, and with Poppins absent, it was beginning to feel precarious.

And then he blinked. A second later he turned away, and her lungs flooded with relief. Olive eyed the open doorway, as if by staring hard enough at the periwinkle sky beyond, she could make Poppins appear. It wouldn't be any use talking of other birds at this point, many of which had placed in numerous races. He knew he'd caught her at some deceit, and it was clear he had his own agenda.

While she'd been distracted with worry, Aldridge had approached one of the nesting boxes, eyeing the preening blue cock poised in the opening. Reaching for the bird, Aldridge seemed to hesitate, but as with everything else where this man was concerned, she couldn't be sure. Listing slightly to the side, lifting herself on the toes of her boots, she attempted to see around his broad shoulder as he examined the bird. When he turned, she rocked back on her heels, feigning composure.

"That's Fritz," she informed him.

"Oldest lad of the Swiss Family Robinson," Tierney guessed, beaming with approval.

She smiled distractedly, staring at the long fingers splayed over Fritz's folded wings, lacing under his chest. Aldridge was literally keeping him at arm's length. Her gaze shifted quizzically between the pigeon and the man before settling objectively on the bird.

His eyes were bright and clear of discharge; his chest was thick; his back broad. His wings, tucked tight against him, were layered with smooth, silky feathers, and his feet were clean. She nodded, pleased with Fritz's smart showing coming on the heels of Badger's bad manners.

Aldridge brushed his finger against the aluminium ring circling Fritz's left foot.

She opened her mouth to explain that it was used for identification, embossed with letters and numbers signifying the bird's number, year of birth, and loft, but quickly shut it again. He already knew all that.

"It seems you have quite a mix of breeds," he said, setting the bird back in its nesting box. "Are they all homing pigeons?"

A wrinkle formed between her brows. "This is a racing loft, Mr Aldridge. These birds are bred and trained to find their way home when released in an unfamiliar place, hundreds of miles away. This makes them ideal for war work. Isn't that why you're here?"

He flicked a glance at her, and she had the impression he was keeping something from her. "How many have experience flying long distances?"

"All but the young birds and those in their second season. We don't send them farther than seventy miles in their first season and two hundred and fifty in their second."

He abruptly changed tack. "The paperwork submitted to the NPS indicated a Rupert Bright as the owner of the loft."

The question was implied, and Olive was acutely aware of its importance. Her father had a reputation for being an expert on racing pigeons, but that reputation came with qualifying adjectives, including *brash* and *bullheaded*. It was up to her to downplay those bits and convince Mr Aldridge of her father's absolute willingness to do whatever was necessary to support the war effort. Even if it meant relinquishing control of his precious birds into the hands of the military. If push came to shove, there'd be no other choice.

"Rupert Bright is my father," she said, choosing her words carefully. "But as I mentioned, he's out at the moment. He's a veterinary surgeon and away from home much of the time."

"Is he the one responsible for training the birds?" Aldridge said.

"Not anymore." He'd propped his shoulder against a clean spot on the wall and crossed his arms over his chest, watching her closely. Her gaze flicked to Tierney, who was peering into nesting boxes and attempting awkward birdcalls. Olive bit her lip. "I've done the bulk of it, going on seven years."

His face didn't register surprise at this information. And more curiously still, not a flicker of disapproval, either. "And the breeding?" he queried.

"I've handled much of that, as well." Olive crossed her own arms and glanced down at the tips of her boots. "I was at the Royal Veterinary College before the war"—her chin went up— "and I've taken full responsibility for the pigeons since I've been home."

He eyed her for an uncomfortable moment, making her itchy with uncertainty. "Are you working for the war effort in any official capacity? WVS, Land Army?"

"Not currently, but I have plans," she said, poised to launch into a giddy explanation.

"They'll keep," he said abruptly. She clamped her jaw shut, stunned at the utter gall of the man. Oblivious, he shrugged off the wall. "For now I think it's time we were honest with each other."

A prickle of unease grew in her stomach, and she began to fear that her decision to send Poppins off on a mission of her own might have undermined any chance for the rest of the birds to make a real difference. One look at Tierney confirmed that he could offer nothing more than a sympathetic smile. Aldridge was the man in charge.

Silence quivered between them, punctuated only by the occasional cooing or flapping of wings from the spectating birds, a regular theatre-in-the-round. After an insufferable several moments, in which the prickle grew into a thorny thicket of dread, she opened her mouth on an admission of guilt.

"The National Pigeon Service isn't coming," he said dryly. Her mouth popped shut. "I'm not here to offer you accreditation."

Olive stared at him, conscious of a subtle weakening in her knees. He'd yanked the rug out from under her, and her world was rocking uncomfortably. Her gaze shifted between them— Tierney looked guilty, and Aldridge, grim—and shock settled heavy on her heart. She should have realised—and would have if she hadn't been so over the moon at their arrival—the NPS was unlikely to have young, able-bodied men at their disposal. They were surely staffed by men her father's age or older. She'd made a snap assumption, and they hadn't corrected her.

"Who are you, then?" she asked, her voice level. Void of the anger coursing through her.

"I've read the paperwork on the Bright loft," Aldridge said. "Your father has evidently made quite an impression on those in leadership positions at the NPS. I believe the words *inflexible* and *insubordinate* were used with some vehemence with regard to Mr Bright."

Her cheeks flushed, but he barrelled on, once again staving off any response she might have made.

"It doesn't matter in the slightest what they think," he said, dismissing her umbrage as distractedly as he might wave away a second cup of tea, "if you are willing to consider an alternate opportunity." He paused a moment to let the words sink in. "Our organization has an immediate need for pigeons, and we've got approval to vet your birds and loft on our own, outside the purview of the NPS and their committee."

Her eyes shifted to the door and narrowed with exasperation. "Oh no you don't, you ill-mannered brute." In the moment before she moved, she noticed the startled look on Aldridge's face and silently praised Remus's impeccable timing. He'd skulked through the doorway without bothering to glance in her direction and was now poised to prowl behind the men, who were likely wondering why she was advancing on them in a half crouch. "Pardon me"—she lunged between them—"while I get rid of him." She held the hissing tabby up for their inspection, and Aldridge shirked violently away. Tierney grinned knowingly at his partner.

"He's actually a very nice fellow—if you're not a pigeon," she told them, dumping the cat out the door and pulling it closed behind him. Turning back, she smiled blandly. "You were saying?"

Aldridge seemed to have recovered himself. "I can guarantee that our offer is the only chance your birds will have to assist with the war effort."

She crossed her arms as her stomach flip-flopped with impinging dread. "You clearly hold all the cards, Mr Aldridge," she said tightly, "but you're going to have to let me see your hand. You can't possibly expect my father and me to make a decision with no information."

"Can I trust that you won't reveal the nature of this conversation to anyone, even if we cannot come to an arrangement?"

Olive bristled. "Of course."

Aldridge nodded to Tierney, who stepped toward her and pulled a folded sheet of paper from his pocket. "We'd like you to sign to that effect," he said, handing her the paper, along with a pen.

As her eyes scanned the words, a familiar urgency gripped her. She'd felt so helpless with the war so far beyond her reach, but suddenly, here it was, in her own dovecote. She flattened the copy of the Official Secrets Act against the nearest wall, scribbled her signature on the appropriate line, and handed pen and paper back to Tierney.

He smiled, a mischievous glint in his eyes. "We work for Baker Street, Miss Bright—"

Olive interrupted before he could go on. "Don't tell me.

You're Sherlock," she said, looking pointedly at Aldridge before swinging her gaze back to Tierney. "And you're the all-suffering John Watson."

"It's a fitting comparison in more ways than you might think," said Tierney. "But in truth, we call it Baker Street because it's even more top secret than everything else these days. Only those of us on the inside know the organization's true name—and we're not meant to use it."

"I suppose the pigeons will be Irregulars?"

"Oh, I think we all fill that role to a certain extent," Tierney said with amusement.

Aldridge took over. "It's been determined that pigeons might be of some benefit to our various operations. In communications with the NPS, your name came up. Given that none of us can boast any"—here he paused awkwardly—"*pigeon* experience, any arrangement would need to involve your continued care and maintenance of the birds." He raised his brows pointedly. "And all of this is naturally contingent on your birds being as impressive as you would have us believe," he added, qualifying the statement.

She had a sudden flash of insight, and a spark of irritation fired in her blood. "This visit hasn't been about the pigeons at all, has it? You've been assessing *me* since the moment you drove up."

"Don't take it personally," he urged. "If you're to work for Baker Street, you'll need to get used to all manner of these little tests."

She glared at Aldridge. "I should have known you weren't NPS," she muttered. "Your knowledge of pigeons is laughable."

The pair of them looked at each other, no doubt believing they'd played their parts with aplomb.

Olive's lips twisted wryly. "You don't know the first thing about these birds or their abilities. And you were clearly worried Fritz might pee on you."

Tierney barked out a laugh, but Aldridge twisted his head sharply to the side, obviously disappointed in himself.

She narrowed her eyes as a thought suddenly occurred to her. "Your secret operations are based out of Brickendonbury, aren't they?"

That caught their attention, and Tierney quickly sobered.

"What do you know about Brickendonbury?" Aldridge demanded.

Thrilled to momentarily have the upper hand, Olive answered casually, "The entire village knows it's been requisitioned for the war effort, and they've all heard the explosions. Not everyone has seen them up close, though." She lowered her voice conspiratorially and flashed them an impish grin. "The ones that go off in the moat are my particular favourites."

"Mine too," Tierney agreed with a wink. He deflected a dark look from Aldridge with a dimpled grin, then added, "I'd say she seems round about perfect, all things considered."

Aldridge gazed at her calmly, but a muscle worked in his jaw. "Brickendonbury is three miles from here," he said, "on a private road sheltered by a dense line of trees. You seem to know rather a lot about goings-on that have been intentionally kept secret from outsiders."

"You wouldn't believe how often I get underestimated," she said confidingly. Aldridge tipped his head back, as if marshalling his patience, and Olive took pity on him. "In order to train the pigeons to home properly, condition them for long races, and improve their flying times, I need to release them from various points at varying distances from the loft. Brickendonbury has always been a good starting point."

"Right." He nodded, thoroughly exasperated. "To answer your question, yes, our operations are being run out of Brickendonbury, otherwise known as Station Seventeen."

"What sort of operations are they?" A little thrill zipped through her at the thought of being officially in on the secret.

The question prompted a hitch of a smile from Mr Aldridge. "Secret ones." Seeming to understand the exasperation such an answer was likely to inspire, he added, "The details of an operation are shared only with the personnel involved in its ultimate success or failure." As she opened her mouth, he tacked on a final clarification. "As far as you're concerned, they're secret."

"Naturally," she drawled, refusing to show her disappointment. "Are you the ranking officer? Or is that a secret, as well?"

He smirked. "No. The man in charge has a better sense of humour, a diabolical imagination, and a flair for the dramatic."

What a pity he didn't come instead.

"Captain Aldridge *is*, however, the officer in charge of acquisitions," Tierney said pointedly.

Captain, is it?

"Let me guess." Olive was no longer under any illusions. "That would include my birds."

"Aye. And you, as well," Tierney confirmed.

When her eyes widened in unconcealed shock, Aldridge hurriedly clarified.

"What Mr Tierney means is that I would be your liaison with Baker Street and Brickendonbury."

"I'm not entirely comfortable forming a liaison with you, Captain Aldridge." A rough cough emanated from Tierney, but she went on, "It would be better for everyone if you spoke with my father."

"No," Aldridge said abruptly. "Respectfully," he continued, "we'd like to avoid the aforementioned inflexibility and insubordination." He paused, scanning her face. "By your own admission, you've been running the loft for years—your racing record stands as recommendation enough. We're willing to bring you in as our pigeoneer, in a mutually beneficial arrangement," he said pointedly, "providing you can manage to keep it secret." He slapped his cap against the leg of his trousers, the picture of nonchalance.

"You may want that word with my father, after all," she said. Her lips curled into a sour smile as she marvelled at his high-handedness. "I'm not nearly the paragon of virtue you might imagine." His gaze said he could well believe it.

"It is, of course, your decision, but if you reject our offer, it's unlikely your loft will survive the war. As I said, the NPS is not coming, and our offer will not be extended to your father." With an unexpected touch of empathy, his voice softened as he continued, "If you'd been officially vetted, the NPS would have collected your birds for deployment by the RAF or the army. You'd never have known where they were being sent or on what purpose."

"Yes, well, at least I'd be certain that wherever they were going, their importance to the war effort would be understood and appreciated." She glared at him. "With you," she continued harshly, "they're liable to be involved in explosions set off by Irregulars who don't fully grasp their potential."

Feeling much harangued, she sighed and reached up to rub her throbbing temple. She needed a moment to grasp the nature of the situation before her. Everything was topsy-turvy: the NPS wasn't coming, and it seemed Baker Street was here instead. They wanted *her*, as well as the pigeons, which meant her plans for shooting down Jerries would fizzle and die before they'd ever had a fighting chance. And if she agreed, all of it would need to remain a secret, which meant she'd have to lie. How could she possibly engage in such a betrayal? This was her father's loft. How could she conspire to send his pigeons off to war without his knowledge or permission?

"If I agree, can you guarantee feed for the birds?" she asked, peering at him from beneath her hand. "Otherwise, it's a deal-breaker, I'm afraid."

He nodded sharply.

Olive's teeth worried her lower lip. That assurance wouldn't have been nearly enough for her father, but the fact that Captain Aldridge could offer it was a huge mark in his favour.

"Can you provide a certificate of exemption?" Equally as important as the feed, that paper would ensure that in the event of an invasion, her loft would be saved from destruction. Without it, birds and loft would be destroyed to prevent them being used by the Germans.

Once again, he nodded. "There does remain one small detail before we can determine if this arrangement has any chance of success," Aldridge said, interrupting the clamour of thoughts vying for attention in her head.

"That's wildly optimistic," she said acidly, "but do tell."

"You've not yet held up your end of the bargain." She blinked in confusion, but after a frustrating pause, he clarified, "I'm going to need to know where exactly Poppins is and when she'll be back."

Sunday, 24 September 1939
Peregrine Hall, Pipley
Hertfordshire

Like countless of her pigeons before her, O.B. has flown back home again. The war has put a halt to her studies at the Royal Veterinary College in London, and now she is endeavouring to keep busy wherever help is needed. But it's quite clear, at least to me, that she is biding her time. Before long, she'll almost certainly volunteer for one of the women's auxiliary services.

Her father won't like it, but he'll bear up, as we all must. Surely, he'll understand that after all the war stories her mother told, she will feel compelled, likely even obligated, to live up to that legacy. I've often wondered if I should have spoken up long ago. There are times when you stumble over the truth, quite by accident, and you must decide what's to be done with it. In this case, I'm not entirely certain I made the right choice. There is still time, however. Perhaps I should reconsider the matter.

For now, O.B. is preoccupied, waiting for the Pigeon Service to come calling. We have all heard her father's stories of the pigeon heroes of the Great War and know what good those birds have done and will do. I daresay she'd be better off drawing inspiration from those birds as she struggles to find her way through these harrowing times.

V.A.E. Husselbee

Chapter 5

Thursday, 1st May

Hearing the latch behind her, Olive spun around to stare, slack-jawed, at the narrow frame silhouetted in the loft's doorway. "Jonathon!" Her outburst startled a few of the birds, prompting them to take up new positions amid the loud flapping of wings. She waved him in. "Hurry and shut the door. Remus is lurking." He did as instructed and turned shyly back, eyeing the visitors with open curiosity. "How long have you been standing there?" she demanded.

"Long enough to hear that the NPS isn't coming."

"And Brickendonbury?" Olive suggested.

"Yes, that too." As Aldridge swore, Jonathon added, "If it helps, I'm still bally confused."

"It doesn't," Aldridge said brusquely. Catching Tierney's eye, he gestured for the paper Olive had signed earlier and the requisite pen. Both were handed over, and he approached Jonathon as he unfolded the document. Olive moved to stand by the boy's side. "You've heard enough that I'll need your signature, certifying you won't speak of any of this to anyone."

Jonathon peered down at the page he'd been handed. As he realised the importance of the document in front of him, his eyes flashed up and bobbed between the two men. Unable to conceal the awe in his voice he said, "Are you here on official war business?"

"The less you know, the better," Aldridge said sternly.

Jonathon looked crestfallen, but he took a moment to scan the page and then bent to carefully sign his name beneath hers.

"I disagree," Olive said consideringly.

His jaw rigid, Aldridge silently plucked the document from Jonathon's hands, clearly wondering what he'd done to deserve being involved with this circus. Judging by his contemplative expression, Tierney seemed to be blessed with an open mind.

"If I agree to a liaison," Olive began, "then all of it—the odd comings and goings, the pigeons gone missing, not to mention the sudden, miraculous appearance of feed—will either need to be explained or kept secret. My father will be a particular challenge. He is quite keen on the pigeons and liable to look in on them at any moment of the day." Her mind boggled even as she considered the intricacies of the deception.

"You're a resourceful girl—I'm sure you'll think of something."

She narrowed her eyes, not at all certain he'd intended the statement as a compliment.

"It would be one thing if I lived alone. It's quite another to deceive two curious people living under the same roof, not counting the one coming in daily to cook and clean, who happens to be as tenacious as a badger. It would be nearly impossible to carry off without an accomplice."

"An accomplice?" The disbelief was back in the captain's eyes.

"A sidekick," Olive clarified. "A right-hand man, so to speak."

"Sure, and she's right, Aldridge. She cannot do it alone."

The captain rubbed a hand roughly over his jaw, exasperation writ large in every line of his body.

Jonathon mustered his courage and spoke up. "I know all about war pigeons, how they can get through, flying hundreds of miles home, when a wireless breaks down. I've been hoping this lot get their chance to be heroes, and I'd like to help if I can." He stopped just short of saluting, and Olive smiled fondly at him.

Before Captain Aldridge could reply, a distant voice sounded from the drive.

"Ho, ho, I do believe she's back."

With a sick sense of déjà vu, Olive realised it was only a matter of seconds before her father joined them in the dovecote. Jonathon still stood in the doorway, his face a mask of uncertainty. A glance at their visitors showed that Tierney had thrust his hands in his trouser pockets and Aldridge had donned his soiled cap and was pulling it low over his eyes, both of them having instinctively shifted toward the wall.

The door swung wide once more, amid some muttered grumbling, and her father appeared and fussily shooed Jonathon out of the way. "If I'm not mistaken"—his gaze landed excitedly on his daughter—"our girl's come home! I saw her approach, so she should be heading in at any moment."

As he suddenly caught sight of their visitors, his brow beetled in confusion. "Who are you?" he demanded of Aldridge, who was nearer the door.

Nervous urgency whipped through Olive. She hadn't formally agreed to an arrangement, but if her father had reason to be suspicious, it would be over before it had even begun. Needing desperately to fill the silence, Olive parted her lips, her mind blank; then, in a rush, the lie came to her, perfectly formed. "This is Jamie Aldridge." She flicked an admiring glance in his direction. "He's asked me to the Daffodil Dance."

A sound closely resembling a snort emanated from Mr Tierney's vicinity, and he promptly bent forward, raising a fist to his mouth.

"I see." Her father glanced between his daughter and her date for the dance, eyes narrowed. "And are you planning to go with him?"

Olive blinked, soundly caught in her own trap. Her throat felt thick and uncooperative, but the answer finally came. "Yes, of course."

Her stomach roiled with conflicting emotions. As if everything else weren't enough, now she'd embroiled herself in an imaginary entanglement with Captain Aldridge. What had possessed her to call him Jamie? In fairness, he had encouraged resourcefulness. She wondered if he was second-guessing that decision now.

"Who's this he's brought along, then?" her father demanded.

"Danny Tierney, sir," came the ready reply. "I already have a date for the dance."

"Right," her father said, eyeing him quizzically. "Rupert Bright." He shook each of their hands in turn. "These are my birds." His gaze swept proudly around the dovecote. "Although my daughter," he added wryly, "has come to view them as very much her own." He winked at her then. "And I suppose they are."

As Olive watched, her father tipped his chin down and clasped his hands behind his back, stepping farther into the loft. She was well acquainted with her father's lord-of-the-manor moods. "Know anything about pigeons, lads?"

"A very little," Tierney said cautiously.

"They've already been instrumental to the war effort, did you know that?" His chest was puffed out proudly in the tweed hunting jacket he wore out on calls.

Tierney, she'd quickly learned, tended to defer to Aldridge on all matters, and it was the latter who answered, albeit somewhat unwillingly. "I'd heard they've had some success."

Her father's lips curved ever so slightly at the corners. It was a look Olive recognised well: he was prepared to school these two young strangers on the noble pigeon, and he planned on enjoying it immensely. He sidled closer. "The King himself keeps a loft at Sandringham," Rupert Bright informed them. "Pigeon racing is a hobby of his, as it was for his father and grandfather before him, and now the young princesses have caught the bug, as well. The royal line started with a pair of pigeons, gifted by King Leopold II of Belgium." He brought his chin up, pausing to let the prestige sink in. "They've won their share of races, and in a true demonstration of patriotism and solidarity, a few of those royal birds have been offered in service in the Great War as well as this latest debacle. I'll have you know—"

They were saved a continued lecture by the arrival of Mary Poppins, who chose that moment to slip in through the dovecote's cupola and lower herself gracefully among them, as if drifting down beneath an open umbrella. Olive smiled, a flutter rising from her stomach to her chest until it feathered out on a sigh of relief.

Her father hopped spryly forward, lifted Poppins from her perch and, with quick fingers, deftly slipped the tiny canister from her leg. Holding it up for Tierney and Aldridge to see before handing it over to Olive, he said proudly, "See that? She was released heaven knows where but returned unerringly to her home loft, message intact." He set her beside a tray of water on the floor and beamed down at her. "Did you know pigeons are the only birds that don't need to tip their heads back to drink?"

Poppins knew they were watching her and took the attention as her due. She was, inarguably, a pretty bird, with her pearly white chest, heart shaped like a dove's; her wings marked with distinctive grey-blue bars; and the iridescent colour at her throat. But more importantly, she was a champion. Olive was glad to have her back and had just extracted the message she'd carried when her father's thundering voice startled her into dropping it.

"With the proper oversight, these birds would be pivotal to the war effort, but the Pigeon Service wants only to snatch them away and shuttle them into service without anyone knowledgeable enough to manage them."

Olive crouched to retrieve the paper, gritting her teeth as the tirade rolled on.

Here was the stubbornness Captain Aldridge had spoken of. Her father knew full well that the army had conscripted experienced fanciers to train airmen and soldiers how to handle and care for the birds; his determination to stay involved was simply a matter of pride. "I've half a mind to write to Churchill himself and see what we can do about this infernal situation. It's damned irresponsible to let these pigeons waste away in the country when they could be saving the lives of His Majesty's forces, to say nothing of our Allies on the Continent." He glanced up sharply. "What do you think, Aldridge?" Olive recognised the light in her father's eye—he was ready to pounce on an answer he didn't like.

"You make a good point, sir." Aldridge's steady voice and agreeable reply diffused the fraught feeling that had settled over her.

"Of course I do," her father grumbled, peering around at the birds huddled in nesting boxes and perched like spectators on any available ledge. "Carefully bred racers like these, trained for distance and speed, can make a world of difference. These are champions, son."

As if suddenly remembering, he turned to Olive and said brusquely, "Well? Come on, then. Read it out. Not something private, is it?" His gaze swivelled quizzically to Captain Aldridge.

"No, of course not," she protested. She felt her cheeks flame in front of all those staring male eyes and busied herself unfurling the scrap of paper between the thumbs of both hands.

1ˢᵗ May, 15:00
RAF Brize Norton

Dear Olive,
    Once again, it seems you have me dancing to your tune. Poppins gave me no trouble on the journey, and several of the chaps on the

train were keen to offer her bits of biscuit and rub the rainbow at her throat for luck.

Olive couldn't help but smile at this.

I'm sure you're wondering why she's so late in coming back. I had to stash her for a bit when I reported for duty, and then rumour got around that I'd brought a stowaway, and of course everyone wanted to come and have a look. Plenty of chaps were ready to underestimate her, being small and rather reserved, but I talked her up a good bit—and you, as well. When it came around to the business at hand, she did what needed to be done, clearly determined to demonstrate how wrong they'd all been to doubt her. You would have been proud of the cheer that went up for her when she got her bearings and set off for home.

Naturally, you'll be curious about her flying speed, so you'll be glad to know I asked the conductor at Hanborough Station for the distance back to London: it's right at sixty miles. Add another ten or so for the bus ride to the airfield, and the twenty-five from Pipley up to Paddington, and you're at ninety-five miles. But Poppins will have shortcutted some of that distance, so you'll need to rely on your maths to figure the final number.

It's a bit gusty here, and rain is likely imminent. I feel sorry for the old girl, but she's in training, right? Soon she'll be flying tougher missions than this. We both will, once everything gets organised. Seems the commanding officers are still working out where to send us all. The Luftwaffe have been using green pilots for target practice, so there's talk of sending us on to airfields out of reach.

Olive felt the grip of worry clutch her heart and throat. *How much farther out of reach?* Realizing this wasn't the time to worry over it, she pressed on.

I'll write when I'm able, and you do the same. Let me know that Poppins made it and when the NPS comes calling. I'll keep all her latest fans updated with the news.

Yours ever,

George

For a fleeting moment, Olive stared at the neat little lines on the curling page, wondering if it had occurred to her best friend that being stationed beyond the enemy's reach put him squarely out of hers, as well. She shook her head, clearing it of those thoughts. Uncertainty, risk, privation—all were part of their lives for the foreseeable future. Self-consciously aware of her abrupt silence, she glanced up before checking her watch.

"It's just past four now, and if we round down a bit to account for a more direct route, the maths are actually quite straightforward. Somewhere between eighty and eighty-five miles in an hour, in less than favourable conditions. Well done, Mary Poppins," she concluded, beaming at the new arrival.

"Yes, indeed," her father agreed, gazing at the bird, who was now rooting around for food. "Good to have her back and ready for when the Service finally gets around to us," he said, with a wink for his daughter. "Only think what she could do for the war effort." With a blustery grunt, he turned, his gaze touching on each of the men in turn. "What about you two?" he asked.

"Sir?" This from Aldridge, with Tierney looking on expectantly.

"You're not a couple of conchies, are you?" His brows were already beetling with judgmental curiosity.

Olive stilled, wondering how they might answer such a question.

Aldridge went on. "The official word is that I'm medically unfit for active service, so I've been consigned to desk work," he said. Olive wondered if she'd imagined the little flicker of shame in his gaze. She couldn't help but be curious as to the truth of that statement, not to mention whether he was even a captain.

"Ah," her father said grimly, scuffing his boots in the gravel.

"Tierney here has been called in as an instructor," Aldridge said, his gaze now settled deliberately on Olive.

"Is that so? I suppose the specifics are hush-hush." Rupert Bright looked almost giddy.

"Exactly, sir." Tierney was obviously content to have Aldridge field all questions on the matter.

Olive's eyes widened as she tried to reconcile this information with the mischievous, flame-haired man, who promptly shot her a raffish wink. She supposed it was entirely possible that all of it was a whopper of a lie.

"Of course," her father muttered, with a final, curious glance at Tierney. "I have a son stationed in Greece. Last we heard, he was in the mountains, somewhere around Delphi, but that was months ago." His voice was matter of fact, but Olive could hear the strain running beneath the surface. Before any of them could comment, he said briskly, "Well, then, carry on." Sparing a final glance for Poppins, he dropped his hand on Jonathon's shoulder before walking swiftly out of the dovecote.

When the crunch of footsteps had faded up the drive, Aldridge broke the silence, his lowered voice threaded with exasperation. "The village dance? That's your cover story?"

Having expected this reaction, Olive had prepared her reply. "That little fib neatly deflected any and all suspicion that the pair of you might be here about the pigeons, which, I believe, was the whole point. Besides, I thought you encouraged resourcefulness?" She propped her hands on her hips and waited.

Mildly cowed, he muttered, "When is the dance?"

"Tomorrow," she informed him, relishing the startled expression that tumbled over his face.

"How do you plan to justify our connection after that?"

"Assuming I'm willing to put myself and my pigeons at your disposal?" she asked archly.

"Obviously," he said dryly. It was ridiculously easy to imagine him in knee breeches and cravat, arrogantly informing her that her pigeons were not handsome enough to tempt him, and she almost smiled.

"I'll think of something, Captain Aldridge. Don't you worry." After a moment's consideration, she added, "I should probably call you Jamie, so you're used to it. Dad is liable to have told Harriet and Mrs Battlesby by now, and by this time tomorrow, the entire village will know you as Jamie. You don't mind, do you?"

"If you'd fancy it, I could—" Tierney was cut off sharply by a dark look from Aldridge.

"When will I have your decision?" he asked, refusing to answer either of them.

"Tomorrow. You can pick me up at seven," she said sweetly.

"How soon can you have birds ready to fly out?" he asked, determinedly formal.

The question took her by surprise—everything was happening so fast, and very nearly beyond her control. "It would be easier if I knew—" she began.

He sighed wearily. "There's nothing I can tell you, Miss Bright. Consider yourself flying blind."

Olive wondered if she'd misheard. Was it possible he was making a joke, albeit a bad one? It seemed unlikely, as that would indicate he possessed a sense of humour, which hadn't been in evidence before now.

Gritting her teeth, she answered. "I assume you're planning to send them to France or beyond." His expression gave away nothing, so she soldiered on. "For such a distance, I'd like at least a week." She refused to elaborate on principle. "Not to mention the feed you've promised."

"Fair enough. In exchange, I'd like to take the letter with me to double-check the distance and conditions."

She'd been intending to read the message over again when she had a moment of privacy, but it seemed even that was beyond her control. Her jaw tightened as she relaxed her fingers to expose the tiny canister nestled in her palm, the message from George curled beside it.

Aldridge reached out, ignoring the letter in favour of the canister, and held it between his finger and thumb.

"Where did you get this?" he asked, his tone equal parts curiosity and accusation.

"Don't worry," she said sourly. "I haven't engaged in any illicit arrangements with any other government agencies. It's left over."

"From the Great War?" Tierney said, eyeing the tiny capped metal cylinder.

Olive nodded. "My father is a member of the National Union of Racing Pigeons and friends with a great many fanciers across the country and abroad. A member of the Pigeon Service in the Great War gifted him a few spares, and we occasionally put them to use sending messages for fun."

Aldridge grunted something unintelligible and scooped up the letter.

"Your messages will be in code, won't they?" Jonathon said, sounding breathless with excitement. "To guard against the Germans reading them?"

"That's right," Aldridge agreed. "It's best to take precautions, even if their chances . . ." Here he trailed off, as if belatedly realising that conveying a lack of trust in the birds probably wasn't in the best of taste, particularly in their own loft.

At twenty-two, Olive already had a lifetime's worth of experience defending herself, and her birds, to close-minded individuals, and even though *they'd* come to *her*, it seemed this was to be no exception. She smiled thinly and spoke crisply. "It was my mother's idea to raise pigeons. She was an ambulance driver on the Western Front in France in the Great War and had gone off shift one day, after hours spent transporting men with heartbreaking injuries to the nearest field hospital. A nurse came bustling through with the news that one of the surgeons was operating on a pigeon." Aldridge's gaze slid sideways—guiltily, she thought—but hers never wavered. "The bird had come in covered in blood, blind in one eye, with a bullet through the chest, and its leg nearly severed. Wounded as it was, it had flown twenty-five miles to deliver a message that saved almost two hundred soldiers. The surgeons managed to put her well enough to rights, and after that, my mother was simply in awe of them, because how could you not be?"

Tierney's jaw was suddenly working as if he had a piece of toffee stuck in his teeth, while Jonathon merely stared at her, clearly hoping for more details but savvy enough to know that they could wait.

"I suppose, then, that I should prepare myself to be awestruck," Aldridge allowed.

"Yes, do that," she said, her voice steely.

With the hint of a smile lurking at the corners of his mouth, Aldridge tucked the confiscated letter and canister into his pocket and gestured to Tierney, who nodded at Olive, rumpled Jonathon's overgrown locks, and slipped out into the late afternoon sunshine. Olive stared at the man remaining, his eyes once again shadowed and unreadable. She couldn't imagine what had prompted her to call him Jamie; the name conjured an image of someone friendly and approachable, and he was neither. On second thought, she realised that assessment wasn't entirely accurate. In between the moments of brusque interrogation and disgruntled exasperation, she'd seen something—the barest glimpse—of the sort of man he might have been if circumstance hadn't caught hold of him. His eyes looked like there was a bit of wild in them, tamped fiercely down. In another life, they might have been friends.

Whatever expression crossed her face during this silent reverie was enough to have him barking an abrupt goodnight.

Before she could stop herself, Olive called lightly after him, "I do hope you know how to dance."

His stride faltered on the threshold, but he didn't turn. Instead, he quickly resumed his determined march out of the loft.

As she watched him go, it struck her that the way things were, friends was not a possibility.

Chapter 6

Olive was pacing her room, her fingers fidgeting unceasingly as her skirt swirled around her. She'd been smugly self-assured when Aldridge had questioned the lie she'd told her father, but having spent the past hour getting ready for the dance, she was positively fraught with nerves.

Initially, she'd considered her impromptu resourcefulness a stroke of pure retaliatory genius. By introducing him as her date for the Daffodil Dance, she'd put him soundly in his place, while ensuring that he would be forced to endure an uncomfortable evening pretending he was fond of her. Her head had been clouded with triumph in the early moments, but later, the reality had brought her thumping down like a turnip. Thanks to her spiteful dealings, she now had a date for the dance who not only refused to carry on a normal conversation but also seemed, inexplicably, to dislike her. Heaven knew, she'd not given him a justifiable reason for such an attitude—not yet, at any rate.

On the bright side, his presence should stave off any requests that she help serve the punch. And she wouldn't be stuck going alone. She rubbed at the spot just above her right eye where her pulse was starting to pound its way into a headache.

Memories of a not so long-ago relationship had already begun to shade her expectations for this one. Perhaps that was unfair, but life, she'd learned, rarely was. Captain Aldridge was rather disconcertingly like Liam; both proudly sported a brusque demeanour, dark hair, and hard jaw. She and Liam Barlow had been first-year veterinary students together, and while she'd been eager and effusive, he'd responded with haughty contempt. That had lasted until she'd bested him on exams and earned a coveted spot as a research assistant, working alongside him. At that point, his arrogance had given way to grudging respect and, shortly thereafter, desire. It had been her pleasure to tease him quite mercilessly before finally giving in.

She was her mother's daughter and, as such, had never subscribed to the idea of separate standards for the sexes, and certainly not to the outmoded notion that her future should hinge on her chastity. So, she had seduced him when she was good and ready and had enjoyed the pleasure of his company for a fleeting few months.

He'd joined up in the early days and bidden her a fond farewell. There hadn't been a letter in all that time. She much preferred to think he'd got over her—the alternative was too bleak. Now, here she was, feeling distressingly as if she was starting all over again. But this was entirely different and would absolutely not culminate in seduction.

Moving purposefully in front of the mirror, which was in dire need of re-silvering, she stood straighter, smoothing down the full skirt of her favourite dress. It was a couple of years old already, worn to plenty of dances but still stylish, deep aubergine, with a gathered bodice and a sweetheart neckline that set off her mother's pearls. She needed only a slick of lipstick.

Just after war had been declared, Harriet had gone up to London to get some early Christmas shopping done ahead of the rationing. At the time, cosmetics companies had been focused on patriotism and not yet constrained by shortages. She had bought Olive three lovely tubes of red lipstick in a shade called Auxiliary

Red and had murmured in her ear as she'd opened them, "War-paint." Olive had used the lipstick sparingly since then, saving those tubes for the days when she'd don a uniform and proudly do her bit. She thought of Jameson Aldridge, of his dark eyes banked with secrets and judgment, and of his fleeting half smile, and she decided that tonight she could use a bit of that confidence-inspiring red. For luck, forbearance, and self-restraint. Certainly not because he reminded her of a man she'd once fancied herself in love with.

She traced the colour over her lips, then stepped back and capped the tube with a click before checking that her dark curls were still pinned in place. The little clock on her bedside table confirmed what she already knew: it was time to go down. Her father had left with Harriet and Jonathon a bit ago; her step-mother liked to arrive early and take her time getting seated, not wanting her illness to detract attention from what she termed "more important things." "I confess," she'd said coyly earlier that afternoon, another cigarette trapped between two elegant fingers, "I'm very anxious to meet your young man."

Olive had answered without thinking. "I'm not feeling the slightest bit possessive, so it's likely nothing will come of it."

Harriet frowned in confusion. "If you can't even muster the enthusiasm for the dance, why ever did you agree to go with him?"

Caught out, Olive hurried to shore up the deception, struck by how all-encompassing an arrangement with Captain Aldridge was likely to be. "He's fine," she started. "Definitely handsome, but entirely too serious. We've too much of that already." She looked across the room to see Jonathon watching her, his face carefully impassive. Needing a moment alone with her thoughts, she went to the kitchen then and sat distracted over a cup of weak tea as Mrs Battlesby bustled around her, alternating snippets of gossip, nonsensical murmurings, and bits of well-meant advice. Not a single word had sunk in.

Rousing herself from those errant thoughts, she dropped her

gaze to the blurred photograph on her dresser. Her mother's dark hair and round face were familiar, but the skirted uniform, too-large overcoat, and driving goggles perched atop her head seemed to belong to another person entirely. A person who existed a long time ago, in another war, whose legacy she still hoped to live up to.

"You mustn't ever take no for an answer," her mother had instructed after Olive had been turned away at the gatehouse of Stratton Park School for Boys. "Meet adversity head-on." She'd raised an eyebrow then and looked pointedly at her daughter. "And, my dear, you'll find that adversity is almost always a man. Charm, convince, or outsmart him. Otherwise . . ." She'd shrugged. "He'll get his way instead of you." So, she'd trooped back to Brickendonbury, found her illicit way onto the grounds, and bearded the headmaster in his den. A week later, she had become the first—and only—girl to be enrolled at Stratton Park. The smug smile this accomplishment had brought to her mother's lips was icing on the cake. But that advice was no longer cut and dried, and adversity was once again breathing down her neck. Well, not literally—not yet.

Turning away, Olive twitched the blackout curtain aside to peer through the window, and her eyes lingered on the crescent moon hanging in the night sky, seemingly festooned with cobweb clouds. Below, the countryside was under a blanket of velvet darkness, still and quiet. As she watched, a pale shaft of light took shape along the lane, shifting and wavering as a hulking shadow crawled along behind it. The beam swung round, darting in through the gate, spreading shuttered light over the gravel.

Her heart bucked in strong, nervous beats as she slid her feet into heels, grabbed her cardigan, and hurried down the stairs, hoping she could slip out before Kíli sensed an intruder, abandoned his spot on the study's Axminster carpet, and tore through the house, barking out dire warnings.

She was past the cherry tree before he'd even climbed out of the car. "Ready," she called, her eyes struggling to adjust to the darkness as she hurried toward the passenger door. He didn't answer, and she stopped still, hovering uncertainly, as his silhouette skirted the bumper, rounding the car. It could have been anyone approaching in the dark, even a German soldier. She was pondering whether the heel of her shoe would make an effective weapon when he finally spoke.

"I see that." The low burr in his voice sent gooseflesh furring over her arms, and she shivered. Captain Aldridge reached around her to open the passenger door, and with a deep breath, she slid into the car.

Neither of them spoke until they were backing out of the drive.

"Why are you in such a tearing hurry?" he asked, the heat of his arm, propped on the seat back behind her, lifting the hairs on her neck.

She shrugged. "It's not a date. It's a ruse, and we're both in on it, so why waste time?" She looked over at him, but other than the line of his profile, the dark gave nothing away.

"I assume that means you've decided?"

Olive didn't pretend to misunderstand him. In truth, she'd thought of little else since the previous afternoon. She'd had a great deal to consider and wanted to be sure that she took all of it into appropriate account.

The offer extended by Captain Aldridge had, in effect, fractured her life into slivers of individual importance, and she'd been trying to fit them back together into some semblance of a whole. She was determined that their pigeons should contribute to the war effort—it was surely what her mother would have wanted. And if Aldridge was to be believed, his offer was their only chance for both service and survival. It would also be an opportunity for her father to make an impact in this war, in an admittedly roundabout way, but she couldn't discount the importance of that. As desperate as she'd been to step outside the cocoon of this village, to make her mark, and do her bit, making the decision to leave had been heart-wrenchingly difficult. Convincing her father to let her go would likely prove to be even more so. The loss of her mother had devastated him, and now he was similarly helpless against Harriet's deteriorating condition. Losing her, even for a time, would be a tremendous burden on his heart and mind.

But if she agreed to stay on as pigeoneer, she would be abandoning her carefully considered plans. Having imagined herself an indispensable member of a crack team, doing critical tasks in the face of impending danger, Olive considered training pigeons at home little different than knitting jumpers or raising funds for the Red Cross. The worst that could happen would be a good tongue-lashing from Captain Aldridge, and she had no qualms about her ability to handle that particular consequence. She wanted to be *involved*, not kept in the dark by a man who put little stock in her abilities. Rather than living up to her mother's legacy, and proving she was just as competent as a man, she'd be resigning herself to being thoroughly underutilised and unappreciated.

And then there was the inherent deception. She would be expected to carry on with her life, such as it was, while engaged in a top-secret agreement with a government organisation. Her pigeons would be doing the war work, and she'd be left to arrange the cover-up. Her life would be one great fraud, built on lies of all sorts and necessarily lonesome.

With the subtle shifting of the clouds, it seemed as if the moon had been blotted out with a great drop of ink, and the aptness struck her mightily.

Her brain had been a teeter-totter of uncertainty until she'd realised there was really no decision to make. Someone had been confident enough in her abilities to request her assistance. To offer it would wreak havoc on every aspect of her life, and yet how could she refuse? This was for Britain, for soldiers and airmen—for *all of them*. Training pigeons was such a little thing, a small part of what she was truly capable, but getting her birds into the hands of the men keeping secrets inside Station XVII could be pivotal to the war effort. *This*, evidently, was her bit. There was only one acceptable answer.

"I'll do it," she told him, a bittersweet smile curving her lips, as the car crept silently into the darkened village. The barely discernible silhouette of the hall emerged on their left, its charming windows shrouded into obscurity with blackout cloth.

"You don't sound particularly pleased," he said, killing the engine.

What did he expect? In a matter of hours, she had lost her Watson to the RAF and had, rather ironically, been demoted to keeper of the Irregulars. She had every cause to feel the way she did. "Perceptive of you." That was all he'd get from her on the topic. She deserved a few secrets of her own.

"I suppose your attitude is your own business as long as you get the job done. Speaking of which, a couple of Baker Street agents from Station Fifteen are flying out tonight. We try to schedule the drops during a full moon to give them a fighting chance at finding their way, but this time they'll have to make do. I've got the go-ahead to send a pigeon along as a trial run."

She whipped around and tried to focus on a face that was little more than a murky shape looming beside her. "Tonight?" she demanded in a hissed whisper. She'd had no time to prepare for this.

"Four hours from now," he confirmed. "Is there a problem?" His clipped tone gave her the answer. He wouldn't be sympathetic to any she might present.

"I suppose I'm not allowed to go along for the drop-off?"

"No."

"Naturally."

"Luckily, you're my date to the dance, so we'll get our fill of each other long before that."

"More than," she agreed with a forced smile and a sprightly tone as they climbed out of the car. "Is it always going to be like this? No details, no notice?"

"Yes and no. You'll still be in the dark, but you'll have a bit more warning."

"Yes, *sir*," she said before stalking stiffly away from him, toward the dance music filtering out into the night. She was painfully aware of a tightness clutching her chest and recognised it as helpless fury. She was to be kept ignorant of relevant details that would otherwise direct the selection and preparation of birds for the long-distance journeys they would undertake amid potentially gruelling conditions.

An idea began to take shape, glowing like a firefly in her mind. Captain Aldridge might be adamant about keeping her in the dark, but he'd hinted that his commanding officer was rather more open-minded. She felt certain she could do her job more effectively if she knew a bit about the intended operations. Brickendonbury was a sprawling estate and had, until recently, been the home of Stratton Park, a preparatory school for boys. Not so long ago, she'd been welcome in those halls—a student herself. Perhaps it was time to meet the latest inhabitants.

Her words drifted to him on a whisper. "You said you weren't the officer in charge. Who is?"

He was silent a long moment, but as they neared the doors of the hall, he murmured, "What are you up to?"

"Is there a problem?" she quipped, turning innocently to face him in the shadow of a boxwood hedge.

"I suspect there will be."

"I've been told I'm a resourceful sort of girl," she said sweetly. "I can probably find out on my own."

He cursed and ran a hand over his jaw. The doors beside them suddenly pushed open, letting the warm yellow light and a gorgeous clarinet solo loose into the night. A man in uniform, whom Olive didn't recognise, emerged, tugging the hand of Eileen

Heatherton, a particularly nosy switchboard operator. Grinning, the pair hurried around the corner, trailing laughter in the dark. The doors fell closed behind them, but in the shrinking shaft of light, Aldridge was watching her, his blue-grey eyes seemingly glowing in the meagre light. No doubt he was wondering if he'd made a grave error in hitching his wagon to her star.

"If you're going to cause trouble, perhaps we'd be better off finding another fancier."

"Trust me, Jamie," she said, smiling through gritted teeth, "you won't find a better pigeoneer."

"Fair enough," he conceded. "The CO is Major Boom. He's responsible for most of the explosions, so watch yourself and behave," he said lightly, moving closer. "Now, are you ready to go in?"

Feeling as if he was deliberately thwarting her, she countered irritably, "Are *you*, Jamie?" before taking a deep, steadying breath. And another. Damn if he didn't smell deliciously of aniseed.

"If you're coming down with a cold, make sure not to get too close," he said abruptly, peering at her as if he might catch the offending germs in the act of jumping ship, so to speak. Olive glared and resolved not to take another whiff.

Without a word, he pulled the door open with one hand and laid the other against the small of her back. Turning to get a look at him in the full light, she couldn't help the tiny frisson that skittered over her skin. His shoulders were distractingly broad in his khaki dress uniform, but his jaw, as ever, was tight, and his eyes were cautious and remote. He looked as if a date with her wouldn't necessarily be preferable to a firing squad. She grabbed his hand and tugged him onto the dance floor, determined to have a little chat. If they were going to perpetrate a deception, then they could jolly well make a good job of it.

A Victor Silvester record was slipped onto the player, and she shifted closer, one hand in his, the other gripping his shoulder, and began to move. He gazed down at her, a hint of a smile cracking his grim façade, and she tried to pretend the feel of his hand skimming warm against her waist wasn't the least bit distracting.

"Shall I lead, or will you?" he asked dryly.

"Your choice," she said. "But if it's going to be you, you might at least pretend you like having me in your arms. I can't be the only one upholding this charade."

Mischief darkened his eyes, and a rather devastating smile curved his lips as his hand pressed her closer. Feeling beaten at her own game, she beamed up at him.

"Now," she said primly, "we need to circle the room, making certain everyone gets a good look at you. I figure we'll tell them you work at Brickendonbury—very hush-hush, of course—and that you found me trespassing with a basket of pigeons." The corner of her mouth hitched. "I charmed my way out of trouble, and here we are."

"Entirely believable," he murmured near her ear. It was impossible to tell if he was serious.

She slid her gaze to look at him, relieved to see that some of the grim tension had leeched out of him. Her eye caught on his scar, and without thinking, she raised a finger to touch it where it curved over the hard line of his jaw. He flinched imperceptibly, and she tucked her fingers into a fist and laid it against his shoulder. "How did you get it?" She shouldn't have asked, but she was desperate for some sort of connection. An opportunity to recast him in a role other than that of disapproving stranger so as to make this tremendous undertaking a bit less nerve racking.

"It's not something I talk about."

"Why not?" she pressed, not willing to give up so easily.

"You're rather contrary, aren't you?"

"Yes, I am rather," she agreed unrepentantly.

He rolled his eyes even as his hand tightened at her waist. He was back to being irritated.

"I did warn you, you might not like working with me," she

said, looking away from him to rake her gaze over the couples crowding the dance floor. "I don't see Mr Tierney and his date."

"He doesn't have a date," Aldridge said shortly, and she felt oddly as if she'd failed her first test.

As Olive tamped down her frustration at having to work with someone so bloody disagreeable, she kept her head on a swivel, alternating between beaming beatifically at the man beside her and catching the eye of every gossip-prone woman in the room. Mr Battlesby, wearing a Home Guard armband over the sleeve of his suit jacket, was eyeing her knowingly, as if he was onto her deception. With a weak smile, she spun Aldridge into a turn, only to be rewarded with a muttered curse.

The hall looked lovely, hung with lanterns and the familiar patriotic bunting, the happy faces of daffodils smiling from every table while dashing men in uniform from a nearby training base swayed alongside local girls doing their level best to keep up morale with lipstick and drawn-on stocking seams. Olive took a moment to sigh with appreciation. She hadn't got around to dragging Liam to a village dance, but here she was with Aldridge. Sneaking a peek at him from beneath her lashes, she conceded that as long as he wasn't talking or glaring, being caught up in his arms, whirling around the room, was tolerable—pleasant even.

When the song had swept to its conclusion and the scattered couples had shifted apart, clapping in appreciation, Olive navigated the pair of them off the dance floor to the corner where Harriet was holding court, her eyes snapping with curiosity. Sitting beside her, Jonathon was tearing through a serving of pudding that smelled warmly of cinnamon.

"Delighted to meet you, Mr Aldridge. I'm Harriet Bright, Olive's stepmother."

"It's actually Captain Aldridge," Olive corrected. "But he won't mind if you call him Jamie." She tugged gently on his arm, a mischievous gleam in her eye. "Why don't you sit down and have a little chat, and I'll get us some punch. This is your chance to rest a bit before I drag you back to the dance floor." Without waiting for a reply, she dodged away, having no compunction about leaving him to fend for himself in what would surely be a merciless interrogation.

Olive took her time, skirting the dance floor, scanning the crowd, and offering distracted smiles wherever they seemed to be expected. When she spotted Margaret, tucked away at a table on the other side of the room, she doubled back and came up behind her, the words ready on her tongue.

"If you want to break a date with me, you should have the guts to do it yourself," she teased.

Margaret was one of those fortunate girls whose crying jags finished with her eyes wide and dewy and her cheeks delicately flushed, and it seemed Olive had caught her on the tail end. Despite her friend's distress, Olive couldn't help but admire her cinema-star good looks, complete with clear grey eyes, patrician nose, high cheekbones, and perfectly coiffed honey-gold curls, all of it made more alluring by firecracker-red lips. Her dress was also red, patterned in a blue-and-white flower print, with a neat line of buttons up the front.

"Who's made you cry, Mags?" Olive asked quietly, pulling out the chair beside her and laying her hand on her friend's arm.

Margaret sniffed and reached for her clutch, then unsnapped it to fish out her compact. Peering at herself in its little mirror, she pressed the powder puff to the skin beneath each eye, plumped up her lips, and tucked away a few stray hairs before folding the compact away and turning her attention to Olive.

"The shop is murder on Fridays," she complained. She worked at Pratten's Grocery and regularly complained that her time off barely balanced the exhaustion of dealing with people on a daily basis. "You wouldn't believe how many people accused me of hoarding onions. Onions! Utterly ridiculous. If I'm going to hoard something, it'll be lipstick and cigarettes."

"Sensible," Olive said, not for a moment believing the excuse. "And yesterday?"

Margaret's jaw tightened, and she snapped her clutch closed with a violent motion. "I didn't come to the hall, because I didn't trust myself not to *throttle* that woman." Her voice had turned steely, and her nostrils flared in fury.

"Miss Husselbee, do you mean?" Olive said, playing coy.

"Well, naturally," she said lightly, her voice cracking with strain. "Wretched woman." She propped her elbow on the table and pressed her fingers to her temple, as if she could rub out a headache with a little focused effort.

"You've managed to abstain until now," Olive pointed out. "From the throttling, I mean. What's changed?" Clearly, something had, but she wasn't ready to admit she already knew the half of it.

Margaret's eyes glossed over with tears as she pressed her fingers against her breastbone. It was a moment before she spoke, her closed lips quivering, as if holding back words better left unsaid. "She's seen one of the adverts from the years I was working in London." She dashed away a tear that had started to fall, her lips curving self-deprecatingly. "She said some nasty things, that's all." Her eyes flicked to Olive's and away again as she swallowed down emotion.

"But you know quite well that Leo's already told you it doesn't matter in the slightest." She squeezed Margaret's arm.

"I know, I know. It *doesn't* matter. Perhaps I was foolishly naïve to hope that no one would find out, but can you imagine the tittering if they all find out the vicar's wife has posed in her knickers? I can't let that happen." She shook her head vehemently. "I can't."

The vicious words of warning that had slipped so easily from her friend's lips echoed in Olive's mind, seeming entirely too dramatic now that she knew what had provoked them. Then again, Margaret wasn't the first person to overreact to Miss Husselbee's self-righteous pronouncements. The older woman had a knack for setting people's hackles up.

"I'm sure Leo knows the precise line of scripture to put her squarely in her place," Olive said with a glance back across the hall. Leo Truscott was dancing with Mrs Battlesby, whose eyes were closed, her face wreathed in contentment.

A sob tore through Margaret, bringing Olive's gaze whipping back around. "There must be something else," she insisted, covering her friend's hand with her own.

"It's Leo."

"Don't say he's been brainwashed by the Sergeant Major," Olive said in disbelief.

"He's thinking of joining up." She swiped her cheeks with her handkerchief and gazed beseechingly at Olive. "And while I admire his sense of duty and his determination—you know I do—I can't bear the thought of him going." Leaning closer, she spoke into Olive's ear. "I'm trying to discourage him, but it's not working, and I've been having rather . . ." She paused, steeled herself, and went on. "Wicked thoughts."

Olive smirked. "Well, that's certainly nothing new."

Margaret huffed in exasperation. "I don't mean that sort." She glanced quickly around before clarifying in a whisper, "Treasonous thoughts." Her eyes were huge and pleading, heavy with guilt and uncertainty.

"Tell me," Olive insisted urgently.

"I daydream about kidnapping him—actually tying him up—because he'd never go along with it otherwise," her friend said defiantly, her chin tipped stoutly up. She sniffed prettily. "I know it's cowardly, but I can't help it. I can't lose anyone else."

With a sigh of relief, Olive said carefully, "Miss Husselbee doesn't know about this particular wickedness, does she?"

"Of course not! I haven't even talked to Leo about it. But what am I going to do?"

"Let me think on it—but don't do anything rash in the meantime," she said quellingly. She really couldn't expend any effort worrying about this peculiar development right now. Next, Margaret would be asking if she could stash her fiancé in the dovecote for the duration.

Olive turned, in search of Aldridge. He was precisely where she'd left him, smiling politely as Harriet chatted gaily away, seeming to offer an occasional shy word in response. He quite looked the part of a striking young captain interested in keeping company with her stepdaughter. Olive's lip curled at the irony. She wondered if Harriet was fooled. When she turned back to Margaret, her friend's lovely countenance had been transformed by a mask of furious hatred, which appeared to be directed at Miss Husselbee, who was currently poking Dr Ware in the chest. Pretending not to notice, Olive stood and stepped in front of her friend.

"I promised someone a glass of punch. Shall I bring you one, as well?" She focused on smoothing her skirts, more certain than ever that she'd caught her friend in a lie. "There's no alcohol in it, but you could pretend," she teased, forcing a smile.

"No, I couldn't," Margaret said emphatically, the mask gone. "I'll be fine. A regular pillar of British womanhood."

Seeing the lines of strain at the corners of her mouth and the smudgy shadows under her eyes, Olive would have lingered, but Leo would be back soon, and she couldn't very well leave Aldridge alone for the entire evening. If she didn't pretend a bit of infatuation, they'd be washed up before they'd even started. She'd already lectured him on that very topic.

So, she said only, "That's the spirit, Mags," and turned to move away, vowing to broach the mysterious subject with Miss Husselbee instead. Lord, help her.

"Olive," Margaret called, her voice turned lilting and suggestive, once again familiar, "I'm going to want to know all about that dishy officer of yours." The apples of her cheeks rounded prettily. "Bring him into the store. If I like him, I'll find him an onion," she said, winking.

Olive smiled mysteriously and slipped away, having no intention of doing any such thing.

As she approached the refreshment table, positioned against the windows at the end of the hall near the kitchen, Olive stared at the array of cakes and sandwiches without truly seeing them. Her thoughts were still distracted with Margaret and Leo. After a moment, she glanced up to see Miss Husselbee standing a few feet away. Dressed in a tweed skirt suit and a green felt hat with a duck feather tucked into its band, she was carving a sliver from a fluted honey-coloured cake, her mouth frozen in an angry grimace. Recognizing the distinctive blue of Miss Danes's stoneware beneath the cake, Olive frowned. If she didn't have a secret of her own to keep under wraps, she would make an effort to quell the inevitable accusations, but she *did* have a secret, and she couldn't afford to risk Miss Husselbee's beady-eyed attention. Although the thought of the Sergeant Major facing down Jameson Aldridge was certainly tempting.

She turned deliberately away, happy to direct her focus toward the other cakes. All the usual suspects, it seemed, except one. It stood out, distinctive in its appeal, topped with a lustrous layer of pale white icing. Someone must have saved a month's worth of sugar rations. Olive felt a flutter of excitement to be the first to cut into it, and after selecting a plate, she bent to the task.

"I wouldn't if I were you," a sultry voice drawled over the din of music and conversation.

Olive glanced up, the serving knife poised just above the smooth sweep of butter and sugar, to see a woman propped on the windowsill behind the punchbowl, the folds of blackout cloth making it appear as if she was sitting for a portrait. She looked utterly out of place and was very clearly not enjoying herself—she couldn't even be bothered to raise her eyelids past half-mast—but she looked rather magnificent. Olive couldn't imagine how she'd not noticed her before.

She wore a silk pantsuit the colour of forget-me-nots, the loose drape of the bodice gathered into a yoked waist above roomy trousers. Several gold chains encircled her neck, each of them hung with a single pendant. One was a filigreed timepiece; another, some sort of hieroglyph; the third, an opal medallion. A stack of bracelets clinked at her wrist as she raised a cigarette to dark red lips.

Here was the prodigal Darling. She was no Rose, but there were definite similarities of feature—the straight, narrow nose and wide-set blue eyes, the pale skin and subtly pointed chin. Yet it was as if Violet had got first pick of the lot, and Rose had been left to cobble herself together from what remained. Then again, perhaps the difference was that Violet clearly took significant pains to set hers to best advantage.

"Why not?" Olive asked, tearing her eyes away to scrutinise the cake.

The woman slipped a hand into her pocket and retrieved a folded tent of pale cardboard, which she carefully placed beside the cake. It read SPAM CAKE, WHIPPED POTATO ICING.

Olive recoiled, her eyes flicking up accusingly. "Why would you hide that important information?" she demanded.

Miss Violet shrugged her elegant shoulders. "I decided to have a little fun. It's dreadfully dull in here, isn't it?" she said, glancing around. "But I told you, didn't I? Before you could make the ultimate sacrifice. At least as far as cake is concerned." She spared a contemptuous look for the deceitful creation. "Who knows what might be mixed up in there? Beets? Turnips? If canned meat isn't strictly off-limits, then clearly the standards have been breeched." She dropped back down onto the sill.

Olive cringed at the possibilities. "Who made it?"

"Clearly a heathen. Or someone with a childish sense of humour. Beyond that, I've no idea."

Pale thumbprint biscuits, their centres glinting glossily with jam, sat clustered on an adjacent plate. "I assume these are safe?" Olive said with mock seriousness as she reached for one.

With a sharp shake of her head and a shiver that nearly had Olive snatching her hand back, Miss Violet said, "I abhor raspberries," and drew twitchily on her cigarette.

Olive shrugged, selected one, and took a bite, relishing the summery flavour of the berries. "Where's Miss Rose?" She turned and scanned the crowd as she popped the rest of the biscuit in her mouth.

"Laid up with a headache, I'm afraid. If she weren't truly suffering, I would never have agreed to fill in," she said, leaning forward to take up a pair of tongs, which she used to push the plate of thumbprint biscuits farther down the table. "Thankfully, she'd already made the punch." A thirsty young couple dashed up at that very moment. As Olive looked on, Violet shrugged languidly off the sill, slopped some punch into two cups, and sent them on their way with a disinterested smile.

"You're Violet Darling." Olive caught herself. "Sorry, Hammond. Welcome home. I understand you've made rather a success of yourself as an author."

Miss Violet started at the question, and her lips parted in what looked like shock, but she quickly recovered. "Two out of three," she said, her lips quirked at the corners, "and never both at the same time." As Olive was working this out, she added, "In the interest of privacy, as well as professional integrity, I use a nom de plume."

Olive waited, unconsciously leaning closer as curiosity got the better of her. When nothing more was offered, she tentatively inquired, "And do you ever reveal it?"

A smug little smile had settled on Miss Violet's lips, while her cigarette, propped on bended elbow, hovered inches away, hazing the air with curls of silver-white smoke.

"If it isn't the viper in the nest!" Olive started at the strident tones and shocking words and turned to see Miss Husselbee glaring daggers at Violet Darling. She was rather relieved not to have merited a notice. "You may have fooled the rest of them," the Sergeant Major continued, her nostrils flared indignantly, "but I have found you out."

"I haven't the slightest idea what you mean, Miss Husselbee. Although Rose did mention you were in fine form yesterday, spouting wild accusations. Presumably, this is more of the same?" Olive now noticed pencil-thin lines creasing the pale skin around Miss Violet's eyes and mouth, as if Miss Husselbee had cracked into her façade.

"Do not trust a thing this woman tells you," Miss Husselbee instructed Olive, her fruity tones sounding even more austere than usual. "She is not at all what she seems." Her lips puckered tightly, but with another look at Olive, she demanded, "Why are you brandishing that serving knife, Miss Bright?"

Miss Violet answered for her. "She's got cold feet with regard to that cake, and rightly so, in my opinion."

Miss Husselbee stared down at the unbroken circle of cake, then up at each of them in turn.

"It's made of Spam," Miss Violet said, distaste lacing her voice, "and some malicious soul has 'iced' it with potatoes."

"You need a bit of backbone, young lady," Miss Husselbee said, defying her own warning about trusting Miss Violet. Shooing Olive out of the way, she snatched up the knife. She cut herself a healthy slice, took up her fork as if it were a spear, and proceeded to eat with gusto. Miss Violet watched with raised eyebrows, and Olive, her lips pressed tightly together, was unable to look away.

When all that remained were crumbs, Miss Husselbee dabbed the corners of her lips with a napkin. "Well done indeed and quite what Woolly had in mind."

Olive narrowly avoided rolling her eyes. Only Verity Husselbee would refer to the Minister of Food, Lord Woolton, by such a name without irony.

"Who did you say was responsible for this delicious creation?"

"I didn't," Miss Violet replied almost languorously, "because I haven't any idea. It was sitting there, pretty as you please, when I showed up to man the punchbowl. I'm hardly to blame if its dubious origins have made it utterly unapproachable." She eyed Miss Husselbee askance, adding dryly, "Until now, that is."

Miss Husselbee harrumphed, then set down her plate and fork with a clatter. A feline glitter stole into her eyes. "I daresay your notion of blame is very different from that of the rest of us, but no matter. I will see to it personally that you're held accountable for your transgressions." The words crashed down like the knell of doom. At least that was Olive's impression. Miss Violet seemed to take them in stride. With a final warning glare at Violet Darling, Miss Husselbee stalked away, barrelling through the dancers, sending various couples spinning off in other directions.

Olive stared blankly after her.

"I'd forgotten her dramatics," Miss Violet said, then drew contentedly on her cigarette as she watched the Sergeant Major's progress through the room. She glanced at Olive, her lips forming a twisted sort of smile, as she tapped her ash onto the abandoned cake plate. "I can remember catching a beautiful orange butterfly and pinning it to a strip of wood bark to keep in my room. You'd have thought I'd shot one of her precious hounds. She lectured me quite tediously on destructive tendencies, God's creatures, and frivolousness, of all things." A sharp laugh escaped her. "I still have that butterfly, although I've since had it mounted and put under glass. And I took my own revenge—that beastly woman met a gruesome end in my first published novel. There were many detailed drafts, as I was quite determined that she should suffer, and the whole process was deliciously cathartic." She smiled then and looked quite normal despite her rather sinister admissions. "I see I shall have to take care now that I'm back under her watchful eye."

Her laissez-faire attitude was mind-boggling. If it had been Olive accused, she would have chased after the woman, demanding specifics. "You really have no idea what she's talking about?"

Miss Violet shrugged. "She could have stumbled over any number of little indiscretions in my past, but I hardly see why they'd be of interest now. Besides, I've done nothing I regret." Her eyes looked distant for a moment but quickly refocused. "No doubt this is simply a new tactic to try to weasel me under her thumb. Her efforts didn't work all those years ago. They won't work now," she added grimly.

Olive felt a hand at her elbow as Miss Violet's eyes sparked suddenly with new interest. She turned to see Captain Aldridge staring down at her, exasperation plain in his eyes. "I thought you were getting punch," he said tightly.

"I was. I am," she gabbled, fighting the flicker of irritation that threatened to pull her brows into a frown and urged her to shake her arm free of his grasp.

Miss Violet filled a pair of cups and shot Olive a knowing look. "You better go, darling. He looks better than anything you'll find on this table."

There was no stopping Olive's blush as they accepted their cups of punch and nodded their thanks. Aldridge took her elbow and manoeuvred her away from the table, obviously seeking a private word.

"What took you so long?" he demanded, heat sparking in his eyes, as he cornered her near the kitchen.

"What does it matter? You had a reprieve from the dancing, which you quite obviously were not enjoying."

"You're right. Being alternately interrogated by your stepmother and lectured by your father was infinitely preferable. At one point, I was almost coerced into playing the role of Mr Darcy in the village play," he retorted.

Olive grinned at his sour tone, liking him more for it, and made a mental note to grill Harriet later for any details she might have gleaned. "It wouldn't have stretched your abilities too significantly," she said wryly.

He gave her a crushing look, which she ignored, sipping her punch and bobbing her head in time to the music as skirts flared like pinwheels of colour on the dance floor. Her gaze was caught by Winifred Danes, making her determined way toward Harriet, no doubt hoping for a hint at the play's cast list, which her stepmother intended to post on the village noticeboard the following day. Olive winced; in the absence of willing men, several of the roles had been assigned to women. Miss Danes would be playing George Wickham.

When she spoke, it was without turning her head. "I admit, this cover story cannot possibly justify your future visits to the dovecote. Looking at the pair of us, no one would believe we have romance on our minds."

There was a muttered curse as he set his still full punch cup down on a nearby table.

Hers was abruptly wrenched away and deposited beside it. Gripping her now empty hand in his, he began to weave through the crush of bodies, and she could do nothing but follow along. Aldridge pushed open an outside door and, after tugging her through, let it fall closed behind them. The darkness felt smothering after the light, bright hall, and as he drew her around the building and under the shadow of a towering silver birch tree, she worked herself into quite a mood.

"If you're looking for some privacy to deliver another lecture, we can go back inside. It's plenty noisy."

"I'm not, but now you mention it, the idea isn't without merit."

Olive crossed her arms over her chest, fed up with the whole evening and irritated that he'd managed to ruin the dance for her. "Carry on, then. It's clear I'm going to have to get used to these little chats."

He stepped closer, looming over her in the dark; it was unnerving having him so close, being unable to see his face. Then again, having him close was unnerving enough. "I dragged you out here because when a man is smitten with a girl, he tends to be rather desperate to get her alone."

His voice dragged a shiver over her skin, and she blinked in the darkness, momentarily disoriented. "Right," she croaked, her good sense returning with a mortifying swoop. Clearing her throat, she stared down to where her heels were sinking slowly into the dirt. "We'll just stand out here for a bit and fool them all."

"Do you have a better idea?" he demanded, his tone mildly exasperated.

Her fingers tingled where she gripped her upper arms, shivering in the cool night air, and for an awful moment, she couldn't think of a single thing to say. She shrugged. "You could tell me about your scar."

He was silent for too long, and Olive wondered if she'd pushed him too far. But then, that lilting voice swam out of the dark. "Why do you need to know?"

She sighed. "I just want *something*." Dropping her arms, she took a step and promptly tripped over a tree root. It was impossible to see anything, but somehow, he found her arm, catching it before she tumbled to the ground. Despite his hand, she felt suddenly, desperately, as if she was flailing, but she shook free. Her voice rising, she said, "If I'm not to be allowed to join the ATS, not to be allowed to work in a battery, aim the guns, and shoot down the bloody Germans, not to be allowed to talk to *anyone*, I'd like to feel a bit of camaraderie with the person who may as well be holding me hostage!"

"Olive—" His voice was no louder than a murmur, so he wasn't to blame when another voice called sharply from the road.

"Who's back there?"

Aldridge reacted instantly, nudging her backwards until she was propped neatly against the smooth bark of the tree trunk. When he shushed her, ever so quietly, she could barely discern his voice from the shiver of breeze through the leaves above her. Olive's stomach clenched with worry and guilt. She was too outspoken, too impatient, too *loud*. She was going to be furious with herself if she'd undermined their tenuous connection.

Footsteps rustled in the grass, and Aldridge propped his hand at her waist, his eyes staring fiercely into hers. Memories of dark corners and roaming hands swept through her. Once he'd found her willing, Liam had taken advantage of every opportunity to get her alone—those sharp-edged moments a fervid reprieve from their days of intense focus and studious behaviour. She took a shallow, gasping breath and braced herself for a kiss—one more layer to the ruse—as he leaned into her. But it was his hand that closed over her mouth. Her heart stumbled in shock, and her pulse pounded a raucous rhythm at her throat. His palm was rough and hot on her cheeks, and her trapped breath a humid reminder that he didn't trust her.

When the torch flashed on, it showed only as a halo around his head. His eyes hadn't shifted their focus, and even in shadow, she was close enough to read the warning there. A harassed grunt drifted toward them from somewhere behind him, and the beam swung away, plunging them back into near darkness. "You'd best be gettin' along now," came the voice, sounding rather far off.

Neither of them moved, and as the light faded, Olive fought to steady her breathing. He waited until the night resumed its symphony—the tentative chirp of crickets, the silky sound of long grass swaying in the breeze, the low hoot of a faraway owl—before he dropped his hands and shifted the weight of his body away from her.

"Well, that's settled, then." Olive's words came out in a harsh whisper as she disengaged herself from the tree. She smoothed out her skirt, unable to meet his eyes. Her palms felt uncomfortably clammy.

"Settles what?" Aldridge seemed intent on scanning the darkness for other lurkers.

"Assuming one of us was recognised, news of our passionate tryst will shortly be spread throughout the village."

"Shall we go in now?"

"No," she said, crossing her arms emphatically and refusing to move. "I want to know about the scar."

She was being childish, she knew, but she felt utterly shortchanged. George was gone, someone had brought a Spam cake to the dance, Aldridge refused to give a bloody inch, and a kiss had been snatched almost directly from her lips. Not that she'd wanted or expected one—Aldridge was entirely too crusty and condescending to inspire such a desire, to say nothing of the fact that a kiss would have been entirely inappropriate. But she'd been frazzled, worried, and utterly gobsmacked in the past two days. Having his lips slam down on hers for one long moment would have been incredibly freeing. At the very least, it would have given him a taste of her frustration, most of which could be laid squarely at his feet. But the moment had passed—his lips would have likely proven as intractable as his will in any event—so it would have to be the scar.

"We talked about this," he said, warning in his voice. His silhouette was subtly limned by the barest hint of moonlight; his face, dark. She could imagine his eyes and mouth any way she wished, instead of frowning with disapproval.

"Did we, though? I think not," she said sweetly. "I think I asked and you refused. That appears to be my lot in this war, at least for the foreseeable future. But tonight, right now, I'm putting my foot down."

"I'm beginning to think you're *very* like your father, Miss Bright."

"A compliment, Captain Aldridge? You shock me," she said tartly.

"Fine," he said, moving closer, crowding her back into the shadows of their birch tree. "But don't think you can make a habit of this sort of ultimatum. Pigeons or no pigeons, I'll cut you loose, and the lot of you can fend for yourself."

She waited, silent, her eyes drifting to the vacant sky, where little wisps of clouds veiled the stars.

"Fifteen October, London was at the mercy of the Blitz. I was working late and got word that Finchley Road had been hit. My sister shared a flat at the end of it with three other girls. They all worked in one of the canteens." Olive's heart clutched guiltily, and she suddenly, desperately hoped the story had a happy ending. "A great many buildings had been hit, and I was praying they'd made it to the Anderson shelter. Turns out they had." He paused a moment, and Olive suddenly didn't want him to say any more, but she couldn't bring herself to stop him. "Ironically, their building was unscathed, but the shelter had taken a direct hit, and all four of them were gone."

Olive sucked in a silent breath, staring wide-eyed at the looming shadow of him. "I'm so sorry."

"I'll have to tell you the rest, or else you won't be satisfied."

Tears welled in her eyes, guilt shamed her, but she didn't speak. She'd pushed him too far, and he'd never stop now.

"I sat down on the curb, even though the sirens were still screaming, and the Luftwaffe was still tearing up the sky. I couldn't move. And then a parachute bomb drifted down a few roads over, and it was as if the world exploded. I was blown backwards, scraped the side of my face on a broken garden wall. That bomb must have killed at least fifty people, and I came away with a scrape on the jaw. It'll never be worth talking about."

She reached up to swipe at the wetness on her cheeks. "I don't know what to say, except that I shouldn't have pushed."

"Turnabout is fair play," he replied, his voice betraying not a hint of the grief he must still be feeling. "I know quite a lot about you, Miss Bright. If we're to be partners of a sort, you deserve to know something about me." He must have realised she'd have another question ready on her tongue, because he was quick to add, "And now you do," officially shutting down any further confidences. At least for now.

She nodded, not willing to push her luck, and blinked back the moisture in her eyes.

"Shall we go back to the dance, before your reputation is in tatters?"

"Yes, let's. And no more resting on your laurels. I'd like to dance. And I'm not leaving without a proper slice of cake." She wondered if anyone else had been brave enough to taste the Spam cake—or been tricked into it by Violet Darling.

Tuesday, 22 April 1941
Peregrine Hall, Pipley
Hertfordshire

I'm sure I need not say that I do not condone black-market activities as a general rule. If the government and Lord Woolton have decided that certain items should be rationed for the good of the country, then far be it from me to question their intentions.

I also do not condone exceptions for particular individuals—we should all be held to the same standard, if for no other reason than to instill a sense of camaraderie. But when that noble intention is undermined by individual isolation, brought on by a progressively debilitating disease, then an exception should, and must, be made. Whereas the rest of the members of the Pipley WI would willingly walk or cycle to meetings and other village functions, H.B. is bereft of that option. I'm very much afraid she'll shortly need to rely on crutches or, worse, a wheelchair. I truly hope it doesn't come to that. And I will defend R.B.—and G.F., as well—to the authorities myself if either should be brought up on charges of using unauthorised petrol coupons for her benefit. I hope I speak for the entire village when I say that we stand ready to do whatever is necessary to assist with each new challenge on this long and difficult road. Even if it makes criminals of us all.

On an unrelated note, I have a suspicion that W.D. might be involved in something untoward. She has been acting rather superior of late, particularly as concerns her sponge cake. I fully intend to investigate.

V.A.E. Husselbee

Chapter 7

Captain Aldridge was a better dancer than George, and having readily accepted her challenge to taste the pariah cake, Olive suspected he was more of a daredevil, as well. But when she'd dragged him back to the refreshments table, the entire cake had disappeared; nothing remained but the sad little tented sign, not even the plate. Olive had stood in stunned silence, entirely impressed with the village's collective backbone. Miss Violet, she was quick to note, had also disappeared.

"I should still get credit," Aldridge said when they were back in the car, slinking along the inky black lanes.

"I'm afraid that's not how we do things around here," she said officiously. "You have to do the deed to get the glory."

"I'll remember that." His voice was quiet, but she could hear the amusement lurking beneath.

As much as she'd dreaded spending the evening with him, the irony was, she'd been more trouble than he. But she didn't regret her outburst, no matter how childish it might have been. Neither did she regret pressing him for the story behind his scar. As unpleasant as it had been, it seemed to have inspired an easiness between them.

As he effortlessly manoeuvred the car around the bends in the road, the low, slatted beams of the headlamps raked over the hedgerows, and tiny glowing eyes reflected eerily back, sending a ghostly little shiver along Olive's skin.

"Don't forget I'll need a bird tonight to take to the airfield, and I'll let you know when we need them for our own missions," Aldridge said quietly.

Crackers! She'd forgotten about tonight's little test. "Very well. I'll do my best to prepare them without benefit of any relevant information."

"Excellent," he said, irritatingly chipper, as he turned the car through the open gate of Blackcap Lodge.

She narrowed her eyes at him. "Do you happen to know the secret behind a pigeon's innate ability to find its way home? Even if released in an unfamiliar location, hundreds of miles away?"

"Instinct?"

"In part, yes. They're also very intelligent. But neither of those explanations accounts for their motivation to brave harsh weather, predators, and exhaustion, flying at full speed to get home." She paused a moment, wondering if she'd piqued his curiosity. It was impossible to tell. "While the young cocks might cat around a bit, for lack of a better term, pigeons tend to mate for life. And they don't like to be away from their partner."

The car coasted to a stop. "Are you saying you breed a cock only with a single hen?" The disbelief was clear in his voice.

Optimistic that he might have been somewhat affected by her sentimental explanation, she was abruptly flustered. "Well, no, but—"

"I suppose, like the rest of us, they're expected to lie back and think of England."

Seeing her expression, he let out a deep, rolling laugh that sounded as if he'd lured it out of hibernation, and she promptly groped for the door handle. "I think we've reached the limit of each other's company for one night, Captain Aldridge."

He killed the engine. "So, we're back to Captain, are we? It's becoming uncommonly difficult to keep up." She could hear the amusement lingering in his voice.

A shadow crossed the low beam of the headlamps he'd not yet extinguished and had the pair of them starting in surprise. Jonathon was hunched in on himself and ghostly pale, his dark eyes squinting against the light.

Aldridge was as fast as she, the pair of them swooping down on the boy where he hovered near the hood. "What is it?" they demanded in unison.

There was just enough light to see that his eyes were wild and he was shivering violently. She ran her hands over his arms, then finally let them fall to grip fingers that were like icicles. She propped him against the bumper, still holding one of his hands, and noticed the subtle sheen of perspiration on his brow.

"What is it, darling? Are you feeling ill?" She was pressing the back of her hand against his forehead when he finally spoke.

"I found a body." His voice was high and clear, as if he was fighting free of feelings that threatened to engulf him.

Aldridge started violently on Jonathon's other side, but Olive relaxed slightly at this explanation and put up a hand to still his urgency. Jonathon was a sensitive boy and viewed each of the birds as a beloved pet. When Tavi, named for Rudyard Kipling's precocious mongoose, had died a few months ago, he'd been devastated. Aldridge waited, rigid as a tension wire.

"It must have been distressing to find another one so soon," she said gently. There would be time later to worry over the cause of death.

In a voice like the edge of a knife, Aldridge said, "What do you mean, another one?"

"For heaven's sake, they're pigeons, and while it comes as a shock—"

"It's not a pigeon," Jonathon cut in, his voice cracking with strain. "It's a *person*."

Olive's exasperation evaporated, to be replaced by patent disbelief. "Are you quite certain?" She gripped his hand tighter, instantly realising what a stupid question it was. He had lived through the Blitz and must have seen his fair share. She swallowed. "Of course you are." A frisson of shock skipped up her spine. "Who is it? Do you know?"

"I'm afraid it's Miss Husselbee," Jonathon croaked.

Olive gasped. "But it can't be. We just saw her at the dance." She turned desperately to Aldridge. "I don't know if you spoke to her. She was in tweed, with a duck feather in her hat. She was probably prosing on about patriotic duty." Her voice caught on the last words.

There was recognition in his eyes, and something else, shock perhaps, and Olive wondered what had put it there.

"Where is she?" he demanded, his voice sharp.

"Beside the yew hedge near the dovecote," Jonathon replied quietly.

Aldridge strode off with silent steps. In the pale light from the headlamps, his broad shoulders exuded a sense of unrelenting competence.

Olive turned back to Jonathon. "Are you all right? We'd better go along, if you can manage it." At his nod, she gently pulled him off the bumper. "What are you doing out here all alone? Why didn't you go and fetch someone?"

He seemed to waffle a moment. "I was waiting for you to get home," he admitted. "Captain Aldridge said everything's to be kept secret . . ."

Olive considered this. It wouldn't have occurred to her that a dead body near the dovecote came under the jurisdiction of the Official Secrets Act. Nor that it should involve Captain Aldridge. Because why should it? It didn't matter. He was here; they were both here now. She urged Jonathon to go on talking as they walked.

Home from the dance, he'd come straight out to check on the pigeons and heard a strange sound coming from the shadows just beyond the door. Naturally, he hadn't wanted to get any closer without a weapon. Olive just barely resisted taking him to task on this point, and he forged on with his story. Armed with a garden hoe, he had stepped around the corner and found Miss Husselbee lying on the ground, her hands swatting limply at the air. He'd dropped down beside her, but there was nothing he could do.

Beside Olive, he sniffled quietly, clearly relieved to be done with the grim retelling.

"Oh, Jonathon, how horrible for you." She threaded an arm, now felted with goose pimples, through his, imagining his worry and helplessness as he waited with Miss Husselbee in the dark.

By this time, they'd navigated the darkness well enough to reach Aldridge, who had surged up from his crouch beside the body. "She was alive when you found her?" he demanded roughly.

The pair took a faltering step back at the intensity of his reaction, and Jonathon looked chastened. Olive gave Jonathon's arm a reassuring squeeze, not bothering to hide a flash of annoyance. But Aldridge, looking intently at Jonathon, missed it altogether.

"Yes, sir."

"Did she say anything?" he asked, his voice low and urgent.

Olive felt the boy's body go tense beside her. "N-no," he stuttered. "Nothing."

"You're certain?" Aldridge pressed. She could tell by the set of his shoulders that his obdurate manner had returned full force. As if the past few hours never existed.

Again, that little flutter skimming through Jonathon's thin form, there and then gone, like a damselfly touching down.

But he shook his head sharply. "Yes, sir." The waver had left his voice, and he stood straighter. It occurred to her that he was taking his new job as assistant pigeoneer very seriously indeed.

"Good lad." As Aldridge clapped him on the shoulder, Olive slid past them and bit her lip. As she stared at the crumpled shape on the ground, her heart began to pound out its objections. "Are you quite sure she's . . . ?" she said, her eyes darting to Aldridge.

He gave a single, solemn nod. "Don't touch her," he bossed.

"Don't worry," she snapped, kneeling down and instantly regretting the instinct. The ground beside the body was wet. Ignoring her newly damp dress and chilly knee, she peered down at the village termagant, startled to find the woman's eyes wide and staring and her cheek smeared with moisture. Miss Husselbee's hat had tipped backwards when she'd fallen, and her fingers lifelessly brushed the handle of her umbrella while its black folds fluttered limply in the light breeze. Her legs, wrapped up in thick stockings beneath her sturdy tweed skirt, were arranged at an awkward, uncomfortable angle. Olive couldn't help but think that it all looked so very wrong.

She gave her head a firm little shake, exasperated with the turn of her thoughts. It seemed her penchant for murder mysteries had left her prone to sinister imaginings. But as her mind darted from one recent memory to the next, each involving Miss Husselbee, she stilled, suddenly a bit worried.

Margaret, facing exposure and lashing out. Violet Darling, slandered and casually chatting about murder. Winifred Danes, publicly accused of black-market dealings and full of rage. Not to even mention Dr Ware's odd behaviour. But surely it was all the typical village melodrama. It couldn't possibly be more than that. *Could it?*

An unhealthy odour reached her nose, and with sudden realisation, Olive struggled to stand, getting her heel caught in the hem of her dress. She felt a hand under her elbow and allowed

Aldridge to help her up. Turning to face him, she said, "She's been sick right here."

"Yes, I know," came the brusque reply.

"And here was me thinking you might have let on before I landed in it," she retorted. Determined not to be distracted by his lack of chivalry, she pressed on. "This doesn't make any sense. She was absolutely fine not an hour ago and is . . . was," she said soberly, "as healthy as a horse." Olive felt the words tumbling out of her, coming too fast. "She was always prosing on about the healthy habits that had led to her robust constitution and lifelong reprieve from the pokings and proddings of doctors."

"And?" Aldridge had not yet let go of her arm, and the tone of his voice hinted that he was waiting expectantly for her to reach the same conclusion he had.

She glanced at him, wondering if she should voice her suspicions—her fears. "I think . . . ," she started, then tried again, this time channelling Hercule Poirot. "I think there is a strong possibility that she may have been . . . poisoned." She had been going to say "murdered" but then had remembered the puddle of sick. Olive's stomach rolled distressingly, and she desperately hoped she was wrong.

The grip on her arm tightened ever so slightly before he released her. "As it happens, I agree." A surge of satisfaction welled unexpectedly in Olive's chest as Jonathon's mouth dropped open in silent shock. "She's not in the habit of coming for a visit at this time of night, is she? I thought not. It's possible she ingested something that caused her to feel disoriented or suffer hallucinations along with a sick stomach. She has no apparent injuries, and if you're to be believed, no real health concerns. This all makes a strong case for poison." Olive wrapped an arm around Jonathon and squeezed his shoulder. "The police will determine the official cause of death, but if it's murder, we'll need to eliminate the possibility that it might be connected to the work being done at Station Seventeen."

"Murder?" Jonathon breathed.

"How could it possibly be connected?" Olive demanded, incredulous.

"It doesn't strike you as odd," Aldridge said tersely, "that a dead body has shown up virtually on your doorstep the very day you agree to supply pigeons for top-secret operations instrumental to the war effort?" Looking dispassionately down at Miss Husselbee, he added, "We can't rule out the possibility that she was a spy—or involved in something nefarious."

Olive goggled at him. "A *spy*? No." She shook her head vehemently. "You couldn't possibly be more mistaken." The thrill it gave her to say those words was invigorating. "Nevertheless, Jonathon and I will be more than happy to assist."

He made a noise between a laugh and a curse. "No need. Baker Street will handle the matter."

Olive glared at him, her breath steaming out between them in the chilly air. When she spoke, her voice was honeyed and calm. "Why don't you go and warm up in the kitchen, Jonathon. I'll be there in a moment to make you a cup of cocoa and ring for the police."

The boy shifted his feet but made no move to depart.

"Was there something else?" she asked quietly.

"Could you walk me?" he said in a shallow voice.

Immediately contrite that they'd mentioned murder in his presence, Olive wrapped her arm around his shoulders. "I'll be back in a moment," she told Aldridge, her voice hard, before leading Jonathon away.

As soon as they were out of earshot, the boy pulled to a stop. "She did say something," he told her in a whisper, his eyes wide and fathomlessly dark.

Startled, she spoke without thinking. "Miss Husselbee?"

Nodding, he confided, "She said, 'Serena.'"

The look in Jonathon's wide, solemn eyes convinced her she hadn't misheard. "I see," she said slowly. "All right. That's certainly curious."

"I figured you might not want me to mention it in front of Captain Aldridge."

"Right you are. It's surely no concern of his, but *I'm* certainly curious." She laid a hand lightly on his head and affectionately tousled his hair.

"Goodnight then," he said and headed off with no argument, his thin shoulders set in a stolid line and his hands jammed rigidly into his pockets, no doubt relieved that his role in the unexpected tragedy was at an end. At least for tonight.

Olive stared after him, wondering what reason the Sergeant Major might have had for uttering her mother's name. After a moment, she turned and walked back to Captain Aldridge to pick up where they'd left off.

"As you don't require my assistance," she informed him crisply, rubbing her arms against the chill, "perhaps I'll investigate on my own."

He levelled her with a warning glare. "It's best to leave the matter to the authorities."

She met his eyes and, in a cold, clear voice, replied, "I am stuck in this village for the foreseeable future, conscripted into all manner of WI schemes while supplying pigeons on the sly, not to mention conducting an extremely improbable flirtation with a certain broody captain. If I'm to make it through this war with my sanity intact, I need something else. Searching for clues to a murder should do perfectly well."

Standing over Miss Husselbee's body in the cold dark was more than enough to have tears pricking at her eyes and a great ball of regret forming at the base of her throat. With telegrams coming every day to inform desperate mothers that their sons would never come home, it was absurd that this one unexpected death made her feel as if her world had been upended.

Despite her gruff exterior, Miss Husselbee had always been rather soft-hearted when it came to the Brights. She'd never batted an eye at Olive's pigeon antics, often volunteering to cart a bird along on her travels or supplying a small sack of snails plucked from her garden plants. When Harriet's condition had been diagnosed, Miss Husselbee had rallied to her side, willing to assist whenever necessary and undertake any task her friend could not. She hadn't deserved to die this way.

A sigh escaped his lips as he raised a frustrated hand to the back of his neck. "Then perhaps you'd like to search the body?"

The offer was made with a gallant flourish of his arm, but she wasn't entirely certain how to interpret the largesse. Glancing warily down at Miss Husselbee, she whispered, "For what, exactly?"

"Impossible to guess, my dear Watson."

She was thankful suddenly for the darkness; his sarcasm was quite enough without her being subjected to the amused quirk of his lips, as well. And it wasn't the time to tell him that she was unused to playing the role of Watson.

"Isn't that a job for the police?" she asked.

"If an inspector performs the search, do you suppose he'll share his findings? This is our best chance of gathering what information we can. But we'll need to be quick about it. I've left the headlamps on—your father could happen along at any moment—and you've promised Jonathon a cup of cocoa." His voice still held a note of urgency, but his tone was lighter, almost teasing.

Pressing her fingers against her palms, trying to prepare herself for the task, Olive stepped closer and crouched beside the umbrella. A scurry in the nearby hedge was quickly silenced by the answering call of an owl some ways off. Predator and prey. Staring down at Miss Husselbee, she wondered anew at the circumstances that could have resulted in her death, and simultaneously wished she was wearing gloves. Biting her lip, conscious of Aldridge waiting and watching, she let her hand hover for a brief moment over the still form while she mustered a bit of fortitude.

"Christ!"

The explosive hiss had Olive yanking her hand back as she half sprang, half stumbled up from her crouch, her gaze flying to Aldridge. Her heart hammered against her ribs as her eyes darted wildly in confusion.

He was staring distastefully down at something on the ground beside him. She squinted into the dark. "What is it?" she demanded nervously.

"It's a *cat*." He injected the word with a full measure of contempt.

Olive wilted with relief, then immediately recovered, propping an exasperated hand on her hip. "For heaven's sake, Aldridge. What is your objection to felines? Or is it animals in general?" she said, wondering if this might explain his apparent dislike of the pigeons.

"It's cats," he said through gritted teeth, eyeing the harmless creature. The animal didn't seem the slightest bit put off by his dislike, judging by the way it was butting its head up against his trousers. Aldridge was manfully enduring, his whole body clenched. "They're so—" He seemed to be running through a compendium of unflattering adjectives, only to find them all lacking. "Unpredictable."

Grinning, Olive said, "That's Pandora. She's one of the barn cats. It seems she's found your Achilles heel." A hysterical laugh bubbled up from somewhere inside her, and as she let it out, it shuddered into a painful hiccupping sob, which she stifled with a hand clapped to her mouth.

Aldridge detached himself from the cat with an oath, skirted Miss Husselbee's body, and wrapped a comfortingly warm arm around Olive's shoulders. She wanted to turn her face into his chest and inhale the spicy scent of him, to block out the circumstances just for a moment. But he wasn't George or her father. He was a veritable stranger, and a disapproving one at that. A moment's vulnerability would not stand in her favour.

She pulled away from him. "Don't worry. I'll protect you from the little kitty." She plastered a wide smile on her lips and dutifully resumed her position beside the body.

She lifted the green felt hat from those moonlit-silvered curls, then slipped her fingers carefully along the edge of the band, dislodging the duck feather, and ran them over the inside lining. Finding nothing, she felt a bit silly but pressed on, nonetheless. Rather gratifyingly, her search uncovered a veritable treasure trove of items in the deep pockets of Miss Husselbee's blazer, each of which was laid carefully on her prone torso.

The right-hand pocket held a folded cotton handkerchief, a key hanging from a length of blue cording, and a silver whistle. In the left, she found a miniature notebook, bound in camel-brown leather, and a short sharpened pencil, which stabbed itself smartly under the nail of her index finger. Her colourful curse took Aldridge by surprise. Resisting the urge to suck on her finger, she delved a second time and unearthed a trio of coins and an empty candy wrapper that smelled pleasantly of peppermint. She took a deep whiff, hoping to hold other scents at bay.

Once she'd finished with the blazer, she ran her hands lightly over the blouse beneath, then down over her skirt, searching for further clues. Finding none, Olive scrambled up, holding the little leather notebook. She brushed her fingers roughly against the skirt of her dress, saying dryly, "I'll leave her undergarments to you."

Aldridge squatted beside the body and tripped his index finger over her finds. "I don't think that's necessary."

"You clearly didn't know Verity Husselbee. She could have all manner of things hidden in there. What *are* you doing?""

He'd levered Miss Husselbee up on her side and run a hand along beneath her. Now he pivoted on the balls of his feet to stare up at Olive. "Leaving no stone unturned, so to speak." He divvied her possessions back between the pockets and stood, putting out his hand for the notebook.

Olive didn't want to relinquish it, having not yet had a chance to look through it. "She was a bit of a busybody," Olive said, lowering her voice respectfully. "It's likely only a list of grudges and grievances. Then again, it could be a log of bird sightings—blackcaps and wrens, the occasional kingfisher. Or perhaps it's a bit of both and we've all been given code names. I'm probably the Pigeon," she babbled.

"You seem to be going into a curiously talkative state of shock," he said wryly, gesturing again for the notebook.

"*I* rummaged through her pockets," she informed him archly. "I should get first crack at it."

"I disagree, Miss Bright. And I'm not leaving without it." He plucked the little volume from her fingers as she stared at him in confusion.

"You're not going to take it," she demanded, feeling suddenly panicked as he slipped it efficiently into his pocket.

"Weren't you, only a moment ago, intending to abscond with it yourself?"

Olive bristled at his tone. "No," she protested, "I only wanted to look at it."

"I see," he said disbelievingly. "As you said yourself, she's dead under suspicious circumstances, and secrets are hard currency. I need to find out if her death touches us in any way." He paused before adding, "I'm taking it."

For a brief moment, Olive considered appealing to him with Miss Husselbee's last word, but she didn't yet know what it meant herself, and he didn't need an additional reason to mistrust her.

He was watching her, waiting for her reaction to this gauntlet thrown down. Was he questioning her willingness to do whatever was necessary—even if it went beyond the bounds of the law? It was a fair question. *Was* she willing? She was rather surprised to discover that the answer came easily. No matter how frustrating and mysterious he was, she was inclined to trust him. She would just have to hope that any clue that might lead back to her mother was sufficiently cryptic in nature as to elude him. Not that she suspected anything untoward—her mother had been dead for more than ten years. The fact that Miss Husselbee was a collector of secrets—particularly naughty ones—was surely irrelevant.

"I won't say a word," she said carefully as they began walking slowly out of the shadow of the dovecote, lured by the twin beams of his motor car. "But I want a look at the notebook myself when you're done. And I want your promise that you'll keep me informed of any details relevant to her death." The light struck the whites of his eyes as they rolled sideways with frustrated exasperation.

"Is that all?" he said, feigning indulgence.

"Stop being so bloody high-handed." She was in a temper now—he seemed to bring it out in her. "You've been trying ever since we met to scuttle me out, and it's a waste of both our time." She rounded on him and looked him squarely in the eye. "I have a better chance than you of finding out who killed her."

There was a beat of silence, and Olive tipped up her chin and crossed her arms over her chest, unwilling to back down.

When he spoke, his voice was dismissive. "It doesn't matter—"

"Of course it matters," she insisted hotly, stepping closer.

"That's not what I meant. I was merely pointing out that it is neither of our responsibility to find out." He paused, and she could hear the amusement in his voice when he added, "But humour me, Miss Bright. Why would you assume you'd be a more capable sleuth?"

"Plenty of reasons," she snapped, raising her hand to tick them off, thumb already in position. "I've lived in this village my whole life, and I know its history, written in a thousand little grudges, arguments, and triumphs. Miss Husselbee was right in the middle of all of it." Her index finger joined the thumb. "I've lived so long outside the bounds of expectation, no one bats an eye at anything I do or say." Middle finger up. "I'm clever," she said defiantly, fully expecting him to protest, "and good at deductive thinking. Better than all the boys at school." She smirked, "Odds are, better than you." Her ring finger made four. "I'm rather a stickler for fair treatment"—she swallowed—"and I want to be certain justice is done." With the addition of her pinkie finger, her splayed palm was raised between them, as if to ward him off, but she took another step toward him. "Miss Husselbee was a . . . fixture. A friend. She was important to me and my family. It's personal." She dropped her hand. "So, you would be wise to take advantage." Suddenly conscious of how close they were now standing, she became aware that her last words might well have taken on a different meaning entirely. She poked him sharply in the chest for good measure.

"Be careful what you wish for, Miss Bright."

"Do we have a deal, Captain Aldridge?"

He held her gaze for a long moment before deigning to answer. "As long as you understand that as far as Baker Street is concerned, everything is still top secret. *Damn it*!"

"Don't tell me the cat's come back?" she said with a superior smile.

His arm shot out, twisted, and she caught the flash of his watch in the light from the headlamps. "Very funny. Go get the bird. I can just make it if I go now and drive without any care for my own personal safety."

"Just so long as you get the pigeon there in one piece," she quipped. "Give me the torch."

For once, he didn't argue. In an impressive show of efficiency, she had the door to the dovecote unlocked and a bird in hand in less than a minute. With Aldridge trailing her, she strode quickly to the barn, leaving him to wait outside as she slipped in to retrieve a wicker carrier. She was murmuring to the bird as she stepped out again but stopped abruptly as she faced Aldridge.

"This is Hook," she said wryly. "You met him once before and seemed entirely unimpressed. We're confident he can change your mind." Her voice was deliberately light.

"Ring up the manor as soon as he's back," he said as she ran her fingers skilfully over the pigeon and slipped him into the carrier before handing it over. "I'll be waiting for your call."

"Just what a girl likes to hear," she teased as he walked away from her at a brisk clip. "I enjoyed dancing with you," she called quietly after him. "It's a shame we can't always be on equal footing."

"I suspect you'd run rings around us all, Miss Bright," he said, already swallowed up by the shadows along the drive. A moment later, she heard the engine and the subsequent roar as the car hurtled into the night.

To say she was shocked would be to put it mildly, but the quiet admission from her reluctant partner in crime was nothing compared to Mrs Battlesby's startling revelation the following morning.

Chapter 8

"Verity Husselbee was an inveterate spy." Mrs Battlesby thumped the greyish dough she was rolling out on one end of the kitchen table to punctuate the statement.

Olive sat up with a start. She'd been slumped over her breakfast at the other end, her mind muddled with sleep and questions, and quite possibly the onset of a cold. "What on earth do you mean?"

She nodded toward Olive's plate. "Most folks would count themselves lucky to have farm-fresh eggs instead of that sickly grey substitute." Her eyebrows rose pointedly, and she stayed silent until Olive dutifully lifted her fork and was chewing her first mouthful.

"While I wish it hadn't been Jonathon who found her, poor mite, I can't say as I'm surprised someone did." She peered surreptitiously at Olive but needn't have bothered: her audience was captivated. Turning the disc of dough, she went on, "It was only a matter of time."

"What do you mean, spy?" Olive remembered her reaction to that very suggestion the night before and now narrowed her eyes in disbelief. "Was she working for the government?" Olive pondered this revelation. How had she missed something so tremendous? She pictured Miss Husselbee as an agent of the Crown, her brusque, no-nonsense manner, ready binoculars, and vicious umbrella skills now seeming a perfect fit. Could *this* somehow be the connection to her mother?

Mrs Battlesby cut ruthlessly through her imaginings. "Oh, no. Nothing so important as that. Can you *imagine*?" She snorted derisively.

"A spy for whom, then?" Olive pressed curiously, fidgeting in her seat, her breakfast entirely forgotten.

"Keep eating, dear," Mrs Battlesby insisted. As Olive shovelled in the remainder of her eggs and chased them down with tepid tea, the housekeeper beamed and turned her attention back to the dough. "That one spied for no one but herself. Although she was quick to tell you she was keeping tabs for Mass Observation," the housekeeper informed her in haughty tones. "Thought it justification for all manner of snooping." The table was shaking with the vigorousness of her feelings on the matter, and her lips had puckered in agitation.

Olive frowned. "I'd forgotten about that."

"No reason for you to remember." Mrs Battlesby shook her head, adding, "Count yourself lucky you've not yet managed to do anything interesting."

Neither Mrs Battlesby nor Miss Husselbee had ever met Liam. Olive smiled slightly and said, "But Mass Observation is meant to be a chronicle of mundane events, like summer dances, prize-winning cucumbers, and twisted ankles. A little glimpse of life in Britain, strictly for research purposes."

The housekeeper raised a flour-dusted arm to wipe her brow. "Verity was more interested in ferreting out the secrets that people prefer to keep hidden . . . babies born too soon after the wedding, girls having affairs with married men"—she clucked her tongue—"all manner of broken commandments." Olive digested this information as the housekeeper went on. "I expect she thought putting her busybodying to work for Blighty was down-right noble. Setting it all down to be sent off in monthly instal-ments and read by heaven knows who all." She shook her head. "It doesn't bear considering."

"She wasn't necessarily recording *everything* to be sent off to Mass Observation."

"I s'pose not. But everyone in the village had to know it was a possibility. And there are some for whom that could mean trou-ble." The housekeeper looked up, her brown eyes snapping as her index finger divined itself toward Olive. "Verity Husselbee has chased the devil down the wrong path at last."

Keeping a mental inventory of everyone's shortcomings and missteps was one thing; documenting them for Mass Observa-tion was quite another. The old martinet might have stumbled onto someone committing criminal—even treasonous—acts, someone who'd decided to eliminate her rather than risk expo-sure. A shiver ran over her skin as Olive remembered the rage in Margaret's voice, but she deliberately ignored it. Her friend had explained all that, or had tried. There was, surely, something her friend was leaving out, but it certainly wasn't murder. Besides, poison wasn't her style. If anything, Margaret would have clawed the woman's eyes out.

Jonathon had scratched at her bedroom door much too early with the news that the police had officially deemed Miss Hussel-bee's a "suspicious death." It was not the most auspicious way to wake up. Her stomach had clenched, her thoughts had caromed sufficiently to whip up a headache, and her attitude had quickly turned as grim as the cloud-laden sky. It certainly seemed as if the woman's holier-than-thou attitude and brazen score keeping had somehow got her killed. More precisely, *poisoned*.

Olive's lower lip slipped worriedly between her teeth. Jona-thon's information hadn't run to specifics, but remembering the puddle of sick she'd had the misfortune to kneel in, Olive sus-pected the contents of Miss Husselbee's stomach would prove very interesting indeed. She glanced at the pale yellow dregs on her plate and promptly shoved it away, bile rising to her throat.

Mrs Battlesby clearly felt they'd exhausted the subject of Verity Husselbee and was now prattling on with fond memories of bacon and, ironically, a pet pig she remembered from childhood. Olive offered an occasional murmur of curious attention as she sipped her tea and allowed her thoughts to run on.

She'd been rather baffled and, admittedly, a little concerned by the mention of her mother, but it was entirely possible that Miss Husselbee's last uttered word had merely been the product of a delusional mind and a long-ago memory jarred loose. Alternatively, Jonathon might have misheard or confused the word amid the shock of the moment. If she consigned it to coincidence or circumstance, other questions rose quickly to the fore, the grim countenance of Captain Aldridge—it was once again impossible to think of him as Jamie—hovering alongside them in her thoughts.

What if Miss Husselbee's presence at Blackcap Lodge *was* significant, related somehow to Olive's recent involvement with the enigmatic entity known as Baker Street? What was really going on at Brickendonbury? Had she unwittingly put her family in danger? She frowned, wishing she could discuss everything with George, but writing letters back and forth wasn't at all the same. Like it or not, she needed to have another chat with Captain Aldridge, and this time, she would have to demand a few additional details. He wouldn't be keen on sharing, though, which was all the more reason to investigate Miss Husselbee's death on her own. She imagined her little grey cells crackling with anticipation. It was also possible they were crackling with self righteous glee at having information Aldridge didn't.

It was entirely satisfying to cast him in the role of the bumbling Hastings, while she was determined to be as meticulous as Poirot. Order and method were key. The village was awash with viable suspects, dodgy behaviour, and possible motives. It would be easy to get bogged down in the sheer numbers. She would just need to focus. As she channelled the little Belgian detective, her finger ranged consideringly over her upper lip. After a time, it occurred to her, with a start, that she was stroking an imaginary moustache to rival Poirot's. Relieved that no one had caught her out, she hurriedly tucked her hands into her lap. A moment later, with a secret smile, she stood up from the table and pressed a kiss to Mrs Battlesby's cheek, having resolved to do something interesting for a change.

By Saturday afternoon, it was obvious that Captain Aldridge was avoiding her. She'd telephoned the moment Hook had shown up in the dovecote—quite exhausted from his flight over the Channel, but none the worse for wear—and been told by the FANY answering the phone that she would relay the message. She hadn't mentioned that in her eagerness she'd ignored his directive and extracted the rice paper curled inside the canister strapped to Hook's leg. He'd clearly been expecting as much. The message wasn't encoded and, in fact, mentioned her by name. It had no doubt been written after they'd found Miss Husselbee's body and planted before Hook had even left the airbase. The audacious missive read, *If we're to be partners, I need to be able to trust you. Do better, Miss Bright.* The flush of shame had mingled with the heat of irritation, but she'd been forced to concede he'd won that round. He'd made his point, but if he pressed the issue, she fully intended to pretend absolute ignorance.

By Sunday afternoon, he'd yet to put in an appearance, and Olive was tired of twiddling her thumbs. She'd written to George, telling him of the dance, Miss Husselbee's death, and her suspicions regarding the Spam cake, but the effort had only left her more frustrated. She refused to mention Captain Aldridge as a romantic interest, and the truth behind their "liaison" was strictly off-limits. For a long, horrified moment, she wondered what she was going to do when George came home on leave. How could she possibly explain him? It didn't bear thinking about, which left her freshly frustrated with the captain.

She'd given Aldridge the benefit of the doubt, but he'd obviously never had the slightest intention of keeping her informed. She was disappointed but not surprised. He might have Miss Husselbee's notebook, and the connections and credentials to obtain further details from the police, but she was flush with village gossip and potential clues. "He can keep his secrets," she announced to an audience of thirty or so marginally attentive pigeons. "I'll ferret out my own." With a sharp nod, she stepped up beside the blue cock that Aldridge had selected for his farcical examination. "Look sharp, Fritz. It's time for a little exercise," she said, tucking his legs neatly between her index and middle fingers and slipping him into a carrier.

With questions and hypotheses frothing at the edges of her brain, Olive had convinced herself that a visit to Peregrine Hall was her best course of action. The police had surely been and gone, and while Detective Sergeant Burris might be a friendly sort of chap, he wasn't likely to share their findings. It was entirely possible, however, that they'd missed something, and it definitely couldn't hurt to look.

As she stepped out of the dovecote with her avian companion, her thoughts flickered immediately to George, then Jonathon, and even absurdly to Aldridge, before she yanked them back under control. She didn't require a sidekick—Aldridge would never consent in any case. And while she was perfectly capable of going alone, Fritz would provide a ready-made excuse if anyone questioned her presence on the grounds. Her birds had been accessories to all manner of trespass over the years, so it was only natural to have one along on this endeavour. Her lips quirked—Poirot wouldn't approve. Then again, as far as detective skills went, Fritz was likely to prove at least as useful as Hastings ever had in finding the killer.

The killer.

She stilled beside the barn. She'd come to grips with Miss Husselbee's sudden, unexplained death, but her mind had not yet truly accepted the idea that someone she knew had, quite recently, done murder. Abruptly, her surroundings distilled: the delicate white flowers seemingly trapped among the blackberry canes tangling at the gate, the plaintive mewling of the barn cats skulking through the grass, the low trill from the carrier basket, signifying Fritz's impatience to get on with things. Her current plan involved a solitary bike ride along a mostly deserted river path to Peregrine Hall, where she intended to poke about for evidence that could incriminate someone in this terrible crime.

With a grim twist of her lips, she conceded that the person in question might *actively* object to such a plan. *Actively* perhaps meaning violently. It was possible she was putting herself in considerable danger. She let that sink in for a moment before dismissing the concern. She was relatively confident she could talk her way out of suspicion, having had a long history of success with that tactic. *Eccentric* and *peculiar* were the words most often used to describe her behaviour, and she'd long ago discovered the ambiguity could be used to her advantage. It was unlikely anyone would suspect the real reason for her visit to Peregrine Hall, but if they did, it would surely be dismissed with a shake of the head and a roll of the eyes. However, as a concession to George, who wasn't there to stop her, she resolved to be extra cautious. Willing to leave everything else to chance, she set off.

Soon she was peering out of the wood that bordered the hall, her gaze skimming over the expanse of what had once been a carefully mown lawn sloping down to the river. Now it was a mess of turned earth. The Land Girls had apparently already begun converting it into a vegetable plot, but a quick look around suggested they were elsewhere today. Olive shifted her gaze toward the hall. It was handsome but without frill, three stories, capped by a grey slate roof, with a stately portico over the door and a modest forecourt. A terrace occupied the corner where the main house met the modest east wing, and several tables and chairs filled the space. There were no cars parked in sight, and no movement behind the windows.

She left her bicycle stashed in a tangle of bramble, and carting Fritz along for cover, she stepped onto a narrow strip of remaining grass, then ranged her gaze up to the sky and over the landscape, as if assessing flight conditions. She strode quickly up the steps to the terrace and ducked out of sight behind a low garden wall, half expecting a cry to go up. When nothing happened, she peered through a topiary potted in a concrete urn, her eyes darting nervously around the grounds. Head cocked, she listened intently for any noises from the house.

None were discernible, further confirmation that the police had already carried out their investigation. She skulked to the nearby French doors and peered through the windows. Having been invited to Peregrine Hall for the odd garden party and purposeful tea, she was familiar with the flow of the rooms. The drawing room was empty, but the doors wouldn't budge, so she slipped along the terrace to try the ones leading into the library. Also locked.

The effort of swivelling her head in all directions was making her dizzy, so she stepped off the terrace into the shelter of the kitchen garden and dropped thankfully onto an iron bench set into the curve of a holly bush. Fritz had remained appropriately silent. Biting her lip, she considered the merits of going round to the front of the house and knocking on the door. Under normal circumstances, she felt certain she could talk her way in, but the police had probably instructed the housekeeper not to admit any visitors without approval. Picturing the round face of DS Burris shaking his head with an indulgent chuckle, she promptly abandoned the idea and growled in frustration.

In support of her continued efforts to keep her wild curls in a semblance of order, her hair was chock full of pins, and she wasn't unskilled at picking locks, but the French doors had sounded as if they were bolted to the jambs. *What now?* She stared down at the basket beside her.

"This is where you fall a bit short in the sidekick department," she informed Fritz in a whisper. "I could use a brilliant idea right about now." The pigeon stayed expectedly silent as Olive stared at the neat garden rows spread out before her, sown with lettuce, broad beans, and English peas. Her stomach growled as her eyes flared with inspiration. She hopped up and hurried along the cypress border, hunting for the kitchen door.

When she found it, she tipped her head close, listening, but could hear nothing over the infernal thump of blood in her ears. If someone was hanging about, she'd need a ready excuse for barging in. Unfortunately, one hadn't yet occurred to her, so this was, admittedly, a trifle risky, but what choice did she have? Her hand hovered over the doorknob, and as she grasped it, a sound rose up right beside her, a sort of ghostly chuckle. Olive yanked her hand away, recoiling several steps, even as she realised it was only Fritz, likely complaining at being cooped up too long. Or possibly offering a belated opinion. There was definitely something to be said for working alone.

"I'm not particularly happy with it, either," she groused, "but we can't keep skulking around. Have a little faith." She tried the knob, and the door swung silently open on well-oiled hinges, thereby allowing her pins to stay safely tucked into her curls. Beaming, Olive darted inside.

Moments later, she was tapping the door to the library closed behind her and turning the key in the lock, having met no one on her trek from the kitchen. As she moved into the room, her gaze went instantly to the French doors, and she confirmed that they were indeed bolted shut. She took the precaution of crossing to draw the deep blue curtains against them, on the off chance that someone else might be inclined to snoop. With that done, she settled Fritz and his basket on a little table beside the unlit fireplace, giving him a clear view into the room. Knowing the Sergeant Major's strong sense of moral rectitude and responsibil-ity—to say nothing of her strict rules of order—Olive felt certain that her contributions to Mass Observation would have been written out in this room. As such, she deduced, any relevant clues were likely to be found here.

The room was very much like her father's study, but with sub-tly feminine touches. The floor-to-ceiling shelves were lined with books, an occasional bust or knick-knack tastefully arranged amid the volumes. The desk had elegant turned legs and a pair of ceramic spaniels guarding one corner. In another, tucked into an ornate gilt frame, was a photograph of Miss Husselbee as a child, posing with her parents, each of them stiff and unsmiling. A typewriter sat in the very centre, an electric lamp positioned just behind it. Olive switched on the light and stared down at the Parsons chair, upholstered in a forest-green brocade. Its upright back was nearly flush against the edge of the desk, and she could envision Miss Husselbee's arched eyebrow daring her to pro-ceed.

With an oath, she dragged it back and moved to sit down, her foot skimming over something on the dark red patterned carpet. She picked it up and settled it in her palm. It was a tarnished brass button bearing the crown and anchor of the Royal Navy. Wondering if it might be a clue, she giddily slipped it into her pocket, then seated herself carefully in the chair and com-menced her search, starting with the top right-hand drawer. At the front was a thick sheaf of paper for the typewriter. Deter-mined to be thorough, she lifted out the entire stack and flipped through it, hoping to find a clue tucked between the pages: a cryptic message, a mysterious cipher key, or a copy of the Sergeant Major's will, significantly altered the day she died. Un-fortunately, her efforts yielded only a mocking puff of air, which fanned over her face as blank white pages arced past. Her shoul-ders slumped slightly as she replaced the paper. Tugging the drawer farther open displayed a box of envelopes and a spare typewriter ribbon.

Olive tugged on the handle of the small, shallow middle drawer just as Fritz's patience wore out. A sudden flapping of wings, startling in the silence, had her heart plunging in fright. Once he had her attention, he clucked in churlish irritation. Her eyes slitted in frustration. "Give me a moment," she insisted before hastily rummaging through a collection of letter-writing paraphernalia. Her hand stilled over a pair of postcards farther back. Both were addressed to Miss Verity Husselbee, one from the Isle of Skye, the other from Monte Carlo, both written as if from a template: *It was a rather gruelling (tedious) journey, but we've made it. Weather is chilly (warm), but we've stumbled over an old acquaintance (school chum) and look forward to catching up....* Both were signed "Yours very sincerely, H&H." Olive stared at the postcards, which were dated decades past, and suspected that such sterile missives might conceivably be from the upright couple in the frame. She placed them gently back in the drawer, a stab of pity slowing her movements.

The top left-hand drawer yielded nothing more interesting than a book on birding, a folded map of south Hertfordshire, and a paperback novel. She paged quickly through the latter, which appeared to be Gothic in the extreme. This must be the one Miss Husselbee had referred to. Written by Lila Charmant, it was titled *A Lady Avenged.* Olive tried to imagine the Sergeant Major taking refuge from the self-imposed rigidities of her daily life in these pages and failed miserably. Chiding herself for wasting time on fanciful thoughts, she dropped the book back beside its avian fellow and slid the drawer closed.

She laid her hands on either side of the typewriter and drummed her fingers on the desk. She glared at the trim little machine. A single sheet of paper sat at the ready, only an inch exposed above the ribbon, as if Miss Husselbee would momentarily swoop in to record the scandal of this very trespass. Olive ran her fingers over the metal keys, imagining the funny jumble of letters being pressed into words. Typing was not among her credentials.

What would you have to say, Miss Husselbee? What advice would you give an amateur sleuth like myself? Would you criticise me for dragging a pigeon into my scheme or warn me against trusting a man spooked by cats? Perhaps I would agree with you on both counts.

Distractedly, she fiddled with the typewriter's platen knob, turning it forward, then back, watching the sheet of paper scroll hypnotically up and down, as she considered the repercussions of banging out her frustration on the little keys. But the thought scuttled guiltily out of her head the second she realised the page wasn't blank. After rolling the entirety above the ribbon, she read it carefully.

Friday, 2 May 1941
Peregrine Hall, Pipley
Hertfordshire

I have lived in this village my whole life, and while there will always be wickedness and little immoralities, I've never had reason to be truly horrified by the behaviour of someone of my acquaintance. But just recently, I have discovered that there is one among us—I hesitate to even put down the initials—who has fallen quite irreparably from grace. The situation is even more distressing given the current state of affairs. As a country, we are fighting against the evil that would invade across the Channel, yet here it is among us, insidious, festering. I must decide what to do.

Olive's eyes had grown progressively wider the farther they'd travelled down the page. Now it seemed they might pop out of her skull. This had surely been the beginning of a diary entry for Mass Observation. Dated the day of her death, it hinted at something so huge that it was beyond Miss Husselbee's considerable experience at taking villagers to task. She'd rolled her thoughts back into the typewriter to give herself time to consider, and that little bit of caution had worked to Olive's great advantage.

Everything else, it seemed, had been collected and taken away, whether by the police or the staff, it was impossible to tell. No newspapers or magazines had been left behind, and not a single slip of paper lay in the bin. She'd found no other typed pages, and a quick search of the bookcases had uncovered no additional pocket journals similar to the one found on the body. Mrs Battlesby had said the Mass Observation diaries were submitted in monthly instalments. While this was likely the first entry for the month of May, what of her April efforts? Could they have been sent off already?

Olive tapped her finger against her lips, thinking quickly. It was possible Miss Husselbee's notebook would hold a key to deciphering this unfinished entry—and possibly identifying the murderer—which meant her next step was convincing Aldridge to let her have a look at it. Her lips curved into a slow, satisfied grin. She'd found something all on her own—something significant, she was certain of it. A bona fide clue. Sparing only a moment to consider the possible repercussions, she rolled the single sheet of paper from the typewriter, folded it neatly, and tucked it deep inside her boot. She comforted herself with the knowledge that Hercule Poirot would have likely done the same, had he been the boot-wearing sort.

On impulse, she pulled open the top left-hand drawer once again, pulled out the paperback novel, and tucked it into the pocket of her jacket. She couldn't help but be a little bit curious.

Done searching, she stood and positioned the chair just as she'd found it, pausing for a moment to consider whether to continue her search upstairs. The clue she'd discovered hinted that the Sergeant Major saw to the business of spycraft and Mass Observation in this very room. It was probably better not to risk it. With a little zing of confidence fizzing through her veins, she scooped Fritz from his spot by the fireplace, twitched the curtains back into place, and slipped through the door to the hall.

Getting out wasn't quite as easy as getting in. She heard voices and was forced to kill a bit of time waiting for them to fade off in an indeterminate direction while praying Fritz would stay quiet. But before long she was hurrying back across the lawn, dodging behind statues and hedges wherever possible, in her haste to reach the shelter of the wood.

"I'd say you've kept up your end of the bargain," she said, carefully lifting Fritz out of his carrier. "More or less." She ran a finger over the silky-smooth feathers of his chest. "Remember to watch for hawks," she lectured before tossing him into the air with a practiced motion. His wings beat mightily as he rose above her, and she watched as he wheeled in a wide circle, getting his bearings, before heading off in the direction of Blackcap Lodge. Olive stared after him as he flew over the river and the trees beyond, leaving her quite alone.

If Aldridge wouldn't come to her, *she* would go to him. She'd fully intended a visit to Brickendonbury to introduce herself to the commanding officer at any rate. Two birds, one stone. Given the clarity with which she could imagine George's scoff and eye roll, it was almost as if he was right there beside her.

"Jamie is going to be bloody furious," she murmured. The corner of her mouth hitched in perverse anticipation as she yanked her bicycle from the brambles that held it upright and turned it toward Brickendonbury.

Thursday, 5 October 1939
Peregrine Hall, Pipley
Hertfordshire

It is perplexing to me how a well-meant, perfectly useful suggestion can be met with such ferocious opposition. I merely suggested to A. B. that the holly bush bordering the lane in front of her cottage would benefit from a ruthless cutting back. You would have thought I'd been referring to the woman's toenails, although I suspect the same could be said of those, as well. That holly bush is particularly menacing whenever a lorry is trundling past. There's simply no room to step onto the verge without getting trapped in a thicket of sharp-tipped leaves. I've had stockings ruined, hair disarranged, and my cheek marred by a raffish-looking scar, all due to that rapacious shrubbery. But A. B. isn't even a trifle sympathetic. "It'll be cut back when Mr B gets round to it," she says. Which is to say, perhaps not at all. She coddles that man, whereas it is my opinion that he could benefit from a regular schedule and rigorous responsibility. It is widely known that he was caught up in a cloud of mustard gas during the Great War, and he's never shaken free of it, poor man. It's left him with sullen silence and a dodgy mind. Letting him run round the countryside in the Home Guard, with the notion that he's the last line of defence against the Germans, is bound to test his sanity. Mark my words.

V.A.E. Husselbee

Chapter 9

Sunday, 4th May

As the wind streamed through her hair and whipped at her skirts, her thoughts seesawed wildly between resolute confidence and anxious uncertainty. For the first time since the war began, she felt a sense of purpose, as if she'd taken hold of her own destiny. Finding a really good clue had made a world of difference. That little success had served to remind her that she was clever, tenacious, and bloody resourceful. It had fired her imagination, bolstered her confidence, and urged her to march right up to the men in charge at Brickendonbury and tell them she wanted to do more—no matter how unnerving the prospect might be. Gripping the handlebars a little more tightly, she narrowed her gaze against the beams of green-gold sunlight streaming across the lane and stood on the pedals, pumping harder, eager to get on with it.

She'd planned to pedal past the main entrance to the property and instead find a more obscure entrée onto the estate, through the woods or one of the adjacent farms. But that was before she realised there were no guards posted at the gatehouse. Security had been entrusted to a wooden barrier and a sign instructing visitors to keep out.

Olive stopped her bicycle across the road, in the shade of an elm tree, straightened her shoulders, tucked a few flyaways back into their pins, and mentally rehearsed an introductory speech. Confident she could concoct a pigeon-related excuse without an actual bird, she stood on the pedals and crossed the road.

Her heart was thumping dully in her chest and her legs pumped in slow motion as she cautiously skirted the barrier and glided up the drive, past the gatehouse, with its shadowed windows and eerie quiet. She glanced around warily, but it seemed there were no guards lurking about, eager to send her on her way. So, with a wide grin and a jolt of confidence, she pedalled down the familiar drive, fully intending to walk right up to knock at the manor's front door.

She would remember that moment for a very long time.

Her eyes were closed, the breeze skimming over her skin, when the bicycle jolted beneath her. As her eyes flashed open in confusion, the peaceful spring afternoon exploded all around her. Furiously loud reports, close at hand, had her arms jerking in shock, twisting the handlebars in a manner that had the bicycle cringing in on itself. With her balance off-kilter, she began to tip and couldn't right herself, and she went down hard on one knee. Momentum sent her sprawling, scraping her elbow, her shoulder, and the palms of her hands, as the cacophony kept on. She recognised the sharp sting of panic clawing its way into her and fumbled to disentangle her legs from the twisted bicycle frame. Once free, she clasped her hands against her ears, pressed her cheek ever farther into the sharp bits of gravel, as the firing barrelled on overhead.

It was a fearsome tempest of sound, and Olive wanted desperately to crawl away, to find shelter, but it was impossible to tell which direction was safe. So, she stayed very still and wilfully tamped down her panic to make room for a burgeoning fury. When it finally stopped, her palms had been imprinted with countless tiny stones, and her jaw was sore from grinding her teeth. The sudden absence of sound was deafening, like being plunged underwater, and in the aftermath, her mind couldn't make sense of things. She had righted her bicycle and was standing, staring bemusedly down at the stark red blood streaming from cuts on her hands and knees, when she noticed a cluster of men hurrying toward her. All at once they were crowding around her, as if she were a curious specimen in a lab, talking both to her and each other, seemingly baffled by the entire situation.

"Are you all right, Miss?"

"Her injuries look relatively minor, but we'll need to get her patched up."

"Good God! The spigot mortars weren't rigged for girls on bicycles! What does she mean by riding through here, merry as you please?"

"Bloody hell! There are signs to keep people out of here. Do you suppose she can't read?"

Words and faces swam out of the haze of shock, blurred, and ran together as she blinked, trying to get her bearings. Someone took her arm, and someone else slipped her bicycle from her limp grasp. A frenzy of questions, muted and unintelligible, so as not to reach her ears, were exchanged among the men.

Despite the general confusion, she felt compelled to announce, "Of *course* I can read," in ringing tones. Then again, the whole world seemed to be ringing.

"Miss Bright." The voice snapped her out of the fog with an almost Pavlovian response. She stood straighter, wincing only slightly in the process, disengaged her arm from the gentle grip of a man with thinning brown hair, dark eyes, and an aquiline nose. Gritting her teeth, she plastered a smile on her face as a familiar cap hove into view.

"I don't particularly want to talk to you, Captain Aldridge," she said sweetly, her mouth insufferably dry. Naturally, he'd been Johnny-on-the-spot for her mortifying fall from grace, and she was in no mood to be on the receiving end of a lecture delivered by smugly quirked lips. Anything she wanted to tell him could damned well wait.

Stifled laughter was drowned out as a short, stout man in an officer's uniform stepped forward. He had a cherubic face, a wispy head of hair, and round spectacles, through which he eyed her critically. "You know this girl, Aldridge?"

"She's the fancier, sir," he said, coming to stand in front of her, his critical gaze ranging over her. Olive was fully aware that she must look a fright; she could feel her hair pulling out of its pins, hanging in clumps around her face, but she couldn't be bothered to fix it.

"Pigeoneer," she countered tartly.

He conceded the point with a single raised eyebrow. "Olive Bright, pigeoneer"—he paused, as if still resistant to make the introductions—"meet Major Boom, commanding officer of Station Seventeen."

She took a deep breath, schooled her features, and put out her hand. "I've been hoping to have a word with you, sir."

The CO seemed startled, his eyes roving over her uncertainly. "Yes, well, I thought I'd put Aldridge in charge of you. He did say you have a fair bit of bottle." His eyes twinkled. "Come up to the house, and we'll have a little chat once the FANYs have had a look at you. We need to make sure you're fit to ride back out of here," he added wryly.

"I'll take care of her, sir," Aldridge said, prompting Major Boom to spin on his heel and stride back the way he'd come.

Olive felt a warm hand grip her upper arm. "Are you out of your bloody mind?" he muttered.

She turned to look at him, exhilarated by her success, if still a bit overwhelmed by the shock of it all. His eyes shifted over her face, then darkened as they settled on the grin curving her lips. With an oath, he dug into his pocket for a handkerchief and handed it over.

"Well, Lady Resourceful, I'll be curious to hear how you explain your face, which is bleeding rather profusely, by the way, from a cut at your temple, not to mention the hole in your jacket and your skinned knees."

"I'll try not to involve you," she said drolly, digging her finger into a jagged hole at her elbow. She sighed and used the handkerchief to dab gently at the stinging spots on her cheek and forehead, indulging in a few furtive sniffs. It smelled comfortingly of aniseed balls.

His grip gentled, and they walked slowly up the drive, falling behind everyone as they all returned to whatever it was they'd been doing. More than one man glanced curiously back at them, but not a single one lingered, except for her escort. Olive wondered suddenly if Mr Tierney was about somewhere, but she didn't imagine Aldridge would appreciate the question.

"You could have been seriously injured, you know." His voice had taken on its brusque, lecturing quality.

"Well, if I'd *known* what was in store, I certainly wouldn't have charged up the drive," she told him.

"I suppose that's something."

"What on earth do you mean booby-trapping the lane that way?" she said angrily. "Any number of curious individuals, children in particular, could wander through the gates. Someone could be seriously injured, to say nothing of a heart attack."

"They were blanks, you know."

"Obviously." There had been several long, panicky seconds when she hadn't known. "And yet I still find myself walking away with all manner of cuts and scrapes."

"Would it surprise you, then, to hear that you're the first trespasser to set off the spigot mortar, shoot up the grounds, and draw out a welcoming committee? Everyone else seems able to read the signs and follow the rules."

She looked coolly at him and finally said, "I regret having made such a dramatic entrance. But if I hadn't come this way, you can be sure I would have found another way in."

This answer prompted him to rub a rough hand over his face

and look away. Olive couldn't help but notice that his jaw looked painfully tight. "This is a serious operation, Miss Bright. And your flagrant disrespect for rules and protocol does not inspire confidence or trust. It is, in fact, the sort of thing that gets people killed. Or at the very least, dismissed from service."

They'd cut across the lawn, walking in the shade of enormous oak trees, and finally come in view of the manor house. Olive gazed soberly up at the stuccoed white, crisp and stark against the varying shades of spring and evergreen. Its jumble of architectural details reminded her of a carefully pieced scrap quilt, none of it matching, all of it working beautifully. Its two-storeyed line of windows was broken by a stone porte-cochère at the centre. Beyond that soared a broad square tower, crowded with masonry and ringed with a balustrade. She wondered what the view of the countryside must be like from up there.

"I suppose I deserve what I got," she said, then sniffed once more before handing back his now bloodied handkerchief. "But you didn't hold up your end of our bargain," she finished stoutly.

"I didn't what?" To his credit, he tucked the handkerchief back in his pocket.

"We agreed to share information regarding a certain *murder*." Olive infused the final word with a bit of ghoulish excitement and felt instantly guilty. "*I* dug through her pockets and found the notebook. *You* carried it off, with a promise to share information, and then went radio silent. Trust works both ways, Captain Aldridge." Before he could muster a response, she ploughed on, fuelled by self-righteousness. "You've left me to my own devices and have no idea what I've been doing."

"I have *some* idea," Aldridge said, a sardonic twist to his lips. "I'd venture the entire estate is aware of you at this point."

She ignored that. "Would it surprise you to hear that I've been prowling about in Miss Husselbee's library?"

His fingers gripped her more firmly as he pulled her to a halt. "That's the dead woman?"

She nodded, anxious to sit down. Her knees were starting to pain her. "I found something, too."

He swore, but any lecture he had planned was unavoidably postponed as he ushered her through the front door and into the hall, which was a bustle of activity.

A blond pixie, wearing the smartly belted army-tan FANY uniform, detached herself from her position behind a desk and hurried toward them, her curious eyes darting first to Olive but quickly settling on Aldridge.

"Can you get her fixed up, Liz? Then bring her along to Major Boom's office?"

"Yes, sir," the blonde said smartly, her tone rather at odds with the adoring gaze she trailed after him as he walked swiftly away.

"You look a little rough, sweetie," she said confidingly once he was safely out of earshot. "I don't know what happened to you, but if it got you an escort by Captain Aldridge, I'd say it was worth it."

Olive snorted, her lips twisting into a grimace, as her gaze trailed after him. She noted the set line of his shoulders and the tight clench of his fists.

Liz wrapped her arm around Olive's waist and tugged her in the opposite direction. "That man gives me the most delicious shivers. He doesn't even need to speak. Those eyes, those shoulders, that little thing he does with his lips . . ."

Olive stared down at her, wondering if Liz was having her on. What little thing he did with his lips? Frowning? Scowling? She couldn't imagine either inspiring the sort of fascination that Liz seemed to be harbouring toward the man.

Realizing it didn't matter in the slightest, she switched her focus to her surroundings. It had been several years since she'd been inside the manor house, and while its bones were intact, it was obviously changed.

Liz led her into a room at the back of the house, which had been repurposed into a makeshift nurses' station. Six empty cots, made up with crisp white linens and woollen blankets, were lined up along the cherrywood wainscoting, and an impressive stock of medical supplies was arranged on metal carts lined up near the windows.

Liz pressed her down onto the nearest cot and efficiently fetched the requisite supplies—gauze and bandages, antiseptic and scissors. "Lie back and rest for a moment," she insisted, firmly pressing her fingers into Olive's shoulder blades with an unexpected wiry strength.

"I really don't think I need—" Olive started, resisting.

"Don't worry," Liz said, nudging her back down and settling herself on a stool beside the cot. "It'll only take a few minutes. He'll wait. He clearly wants to talk to you."

Liz seemed torn between excitement and mild jealousy. Her mind sufficiently boggled by this alternate view of Captain Aldridge, Olive looked away from the gold-flecked green eyes and watched the quick efficient hands, which had started snipping dressings and sticking plaster to fit her myriad injuries. The dreamy sparkle in Liz's eyes had dimmed, replaced with clarity and focus, as she set to the job before her.

"Have you been here long?" Olive asked.

"At the manor?" She considered. "It'll be a year in June."

The sting of antiseptic splashed lavishly onto her cuts had Olive screwing up her face and fighting down a flurry of cursing. When the worst of it was over, she resumed her questioning. "Are there a lot of injuries to deal with?"

"Not usually." She was pressing a square of gauze to Olive's temple—one that would require a darn good explanation. "But I'm not strictly a nurse. They have us FANYs doing all manner of odd jobs—whatever's necessary. I much prefer the evening shift . . . dancing and parlour games, keeping spirits up and flowing." She flashed a grin of straight white teeth, complete with pointed incisors, and affixed the dressing and sticking plaster to Olive's temple.

Olive was desperate to ask for details but knew Liz must be constrained by the Official Secrets Act, as well, so she didn't bother. Major Boom would decide soon enough if she was to be let in on the secrets of Brickendonbury Manor. Lost in her own thoughts, she settled into silence as Liz finished patching her up. She was swinging her legs over the side of the cot when another patient sauntered in, holding a hand up to stem the flow of blood from his nose. The bright red looked even more garish against a mane of coppery-coloured hair.

"I wouldn't have thought you'd be visiting me so often, what with being the instructor and all," Liz said, with a teasing little twist of her lips.

"I figure if they can get one over on me, then I've got them ready, haven't I?" Danny Tierney's eyes, full of mischief, sobered when he looked past Liz to Olive's bandaged face and knees.

"What happened to ye? And what're ye doing here?" he demanded, his Irish stronger than Olive remembered.

"I'd hoped to convince Major Boom to let me in on a few secrets," she admitted, sliding off the cot to stand stiffly, "but getting shot off my bicycle by a booby-trapped round of blanks might have been the wrong way to go about it." She lifted an eyebrow. "I'm guessing I shouldn't bother asking what happened to you."

"You two know each other?" Liz asked, nudging Tierney onto the cot Olive had vacated, twisting her head to look at him. "You're determined to have the most interesting nose in the building, aren't you? One more break and it might be a different shape altogether."

"Is there a prize for that?" Tierney asked.

"We met briefly a few days ago," Olive told her. "I figure it's all right to admit that, seeing as we're all in the belly of the beast, so to speak."

Liz glanced curiously at Olive as she pressed several squares of folded gauze to Tierney's nose. "I'll need to go to the kitchen to get some ice for the swelling."

"And I suppose I'm ready to face the firing squad," Olive said, straightening her shoulders.

"Aldridge?" Tierney asked with a crooked grin.

"Yes." He would, at the very least, be first.

"I'll take you over," Tierney volunteered. With a glance at Liz, he added, "I'll come back for the ice. I promise."

"I can drop her on the way," Liz insisted. She had a hand on her neat arrangement of curls and seemed to be trying to check her reflection in a round mirror on the far wall. Olive wondered if Aldridge had any idea the sort of effect he was having on this girl.

"I wouldn't recommend it. He's likely in no mood to be friendly," Tierney said, indicating Olive with a flick of his gaze. Both women rolled their eyes, and Tierney tugged Olive away.

"Thank you," she called over her shoulder before leaning into Tierney to murmur, "You know she—"

"It's painfully obvious to everyone but him," Tierney confided.

Major Boom gave the object in his hands a measured twist, then leaned forward and carefully set it on the edge of his desk, directly in front of Aldridge. It looked to be a short, barrel-bottomed cousin of an everyday Thermos, complete with smooth brown cap, which was marked in grease pencil with a series of letters and numbers. A quiet, rhythmic ticking now filled the silence.

"That will go off in five minutes," Major Boom announced.

Olive felt certain she hadn't heard right, and her brow wrinkled in confusion. *Go off? As in explode?* Her gaze shot to Aldridge, but he seemed unfazed. In fact, his face in profile was expressionless, beyond a subtle lift at the corner of his mouth. No doubt, after her recent experience on the drive, he expected her to react poorly. She wasn't about to give him the satisfaction.

Bravely ignoring her twinge of uncertainty, she widened her smile and switched her focus back to Major Boom. This would likely be her one and only chance to convince the powers that be that she would be more useful *in* the know than out of it. No matter how much Captain Aldridge was determined not to trust her.

"The FANYs do a fine job keeping us all right as rain," said the head of Station XVII. "You're looking much improved, Miss Bright. Do you need a drop of whiskey to settle your nerves?" he offered, pulling open the bottom drawer of his desk.

"No thank you, sir. I've quite recovered." Her gaze slid distractedly over the untidy surface of his desk, which was littered with screws, pencils, and wire of varying gauges. Teetering on the near edge was a condom packet. Olive dropped her gaze and promptly noticed another on the floor at her feet. Schooling her features, she glanced curiously at the round-faced commanding officer, but the ticking proved too distracting, and she couldn't help but wonder what she'd let herself in for. It hadn't occurred to her to plan her arguments, and now she couldn't think, her thoughts consumed by the unassuming device, which might very well explode in . . . How much time had already passed?

The CO seemed to be experiencing no such worries, his arms resting casually on his desk. "Perhaps you were unaware that Captain Aldridge is my adjutant here at Brickendonbury, which means that he's acting on my authority." He eyed her critically, his fingers steepled.

Olive stayed quiet, fairly certain she could feel Aldridge shooting a telepathic "I told you so" in her direction. She didn't turn but flicked a peripheral glance towards the corner of the desk and resisted the urge to tip up the little watch face pinned to her jumper.

"But on occasion," he went on, "I find him a bit more cautious than the situation calls for. Make no mistake, we are in a dickens of a situation, and if you ask my opinion, embracing the unexpected is our best chance to come out on top." He leaned forward in his chair and, with his voice lowered confidingly, declared, "You, my dear, are entirely unexpected."

"Thank you, sir," Olive said, hoping this was the correct response. She couldn't help but feel buoyed by possibility. She sat forward nervously, wondering if this was yet another test. Her head was starting to ache, and she wanted nothing more than a strong cup of tea far away from ticking devices and critical eyes, but she needed to bear up and present a competent, determined front. She drew a deep breath. "I'm flattered that . . . Baker Street"—it felt distinctly odd using that identifier—"approached me to provide pigeons for operations critical to the war effort." She swallowed, her gaze flitting away from Major Boom's gentle, encouraging demeanour toward the little device, which had begun to look ever more threatening. She could feel her heart rate rising and her pulse beat beginning to thrum at her throat. "However," she said tightly, "Captain Aldridge is quite firm on the point that the entire business is 'need to know.'" Now she did flick a glance at him. "And rather adamant that I don't."

Major Boom chuckled, but Olive pressed on, not caring that she was hurrying, stumbling over words, possibly even gabbling.

"But, sir, I respectfully disagree. Keeping me at arm's length, and very much in the dark, causes problems and creates obstacles. If I'm not given the details of a mission, how can I select the best-matched birds or tailor their training? My impromptu cover story cast Captain Aldridge in a romantic role, and I'm not at all certain that it can hold up." Olive hoped the man in question noted the barb. "Particularly with the current friction between us." Another sharp sideways glance at the little device, which seemed suddenly to loom large in the room.

"And finally," she said, the pitch of her voice rising as the words tumbled urgently out of her, "unless the tide of the war begins to turn, I expect women will be conscripted before too long." She paused, and a little smile hovered for a moment before flitting away again. "As it stands, my involvement with

Baker Street is to be kept a closely guarded secret, so it won't offer any sort of excuse. I'll be expected to sign up. Whether it's factory work, the Land Army, or the ATS, I won't have time for pigeons. That responsibility will fall to my father."

As she paused, she realised her pulse now matched the infernal ticking, as if she herself was poised to explode.

"And as I understand it"—she heard the quaver in her voice and struggled to keep it steady—"my father is considered somewhat of a liability. Which means your arrangement with our loft would be at an end." She leaned in, fighting her own frustration. "I believe our pigeons can make a difference. They are champion racers, brilliant homers—every bit as accomplished as their pedigree and racing history would lead you to believe." She paused for breath, knowing that if her next words didn't convince them, she'd failed in her reckless mission. "They are not, however, self-sufficient. And while I am prepared to do whatever's necessary, their ultimate success depends on the pair of you trusting me more than you currently seem to."

She desperately hoped her little speech hadn't come across quite as self-important and melodramatic as it had sounded. Flicking her gaze to the corner of the desk, she raised a hand to the plaster on her forehead; it had begun to itch.

Up until now, Aldridge had remained silent, but now he spoke up, his tone wry with disbelief. "And in deciding to trust you, we're to overlook the fact that you pedalled past the posted signs warning everyone to keep out?"

Damn the man! Hadn't she been punished for that little indiscretion quite enough already?

"Perhaps," she allowed, her voice tight, "I was overeager and a bit foolhardy in coming here, but there was no other choice. My liaison has proved to be quite mulish and dismissive of any input I offer."

Aldridge snorted, but Major Boom's face remained impassive as he rolled what appeared to be a large ball bearing back and forth between his fingers, shifting his gaze between the pair of them. Olive ground her teeth and felt her jaw harden into a rigid line. She wasn't about to back down. The fact of the matter was, they had come to *her*, had asked for her despite the disadvantage of familial affiliation. In theory, that should factor in her favour, and yet, as the ticking laboured distressingly on, she grudgingly conceded that she could not claim the upper hand in this conversation.

Olive flattened her hands on the tops of her knees to suppress the fidgety bouncing of her legs. Neither man seemed even remotely concerned that five minutes had surely dwindled down to nothing, but Olive's pulse was all but roaring in her ears.

No longer concerned about saving face, she was poised to crawl beneath the desk, but the older man moved first. With his free hand, he hefted the unassuming little device and, with all the casualness of tossing a ball to a dog, flung it through the open window. It had just cleared the hedge when it exploded into a rollicking fireball, which spun out over the lawn, and somersaulted down the slope, to break the smooth blue-green surface of the moat.

Olive jerked violently in reaction, the memories of her ambush on the drive still uncomfortably fresh. Outwardly, she recovered quickly—long before her frantic pulse would return to normal—just before Aldridge slid his gaze in her direction, his sharp eyes assessing. Both men remained imperturbable. When no one spoke, Olive was left to ponder whether that sort of recklessness was commonplace or if it had simply been an exhibition for her benefit. It likely wouldn't behove her to mention it either way, so she waited, a brittle smile tugging at the corners of her lips.

Major Boom let the ball bearing roll away from him until it lodged itself between the handles of a pair of pliers lying atop a roughly cut strip of metal that appeared to be somewhat tangled in a ball of twine. He laced his fingers and focused his spectacled gaze solemnly on her face.

"Quite right, Miss Bright. I do see your point. You've come to us mostly vetted, your father a well-respected veterinary surgeon with decorated service in the Great War, and your mother, Captain Aldridge tells me, a member of the First Aid Nursing Yeomanry, working on the front lines as an ambulance driver."

Olive felt a familiar spark of pride zip through her and sat up straighter. "Yes, sir. My mother was considered something of a hero in her unit, and I hope to live up to her legacy."

Aldridge's pencil was scraping busily over a page in his notebook, but she ignored him.

"Of course," said Major Boom, a kind smile spreading over his features. "You have an admirable pedigree and an impressive array of accomplishments in your own right." He pulled a sheet of lined paper towards him, then tipped his head to run his spectacled gaze quickly over it. Once done, he laid it neatly in front of him before raising his eyes to meet hers. "The only female accepted at Stratton Park School for Boys, right here at Brickendonbury Manor, long-time assistant in your father's surgery, prodigious experience in the breeding and training of racing pigeons, and a brief stint at the Royal Veterinary College, which was"—here he tipped his head down again—"unfortunately cut short when the Germans went on the warpath."

Olive lifted her chin, her breathing settling and her heart rate bumping back to normal.

With a glance at Aldridge, he came to the denouement. "I'm willing to take a chance on trusting you with more responsibility and the details of these missions, Miss Bright, if you're willing to take a job here as a FANY."

A thrill shot through Olive, and she sat eagerly forward in her chair, pressing her lips together to keep from babbling with excitement and thereby prompting him to rescind the offer. Major Boom had paused, letting that news sink in, but when she would have answered—a calm, measured reply—he ploughed on.

"As far as anyone outside of Brickendonbury is concerned, you're a regular girl, with all the responsibilities of the rest of them. And mind, we will expect you to pull your weight in that regard. You'll need training, but that can wait until this pigeon business is ironed out a bit. It's important that we get right on that, Miss Bright." He rubbed his chin, seemingly deep in thought, then suddenly stood, sending his chair rolling backwards on its castor wheels. Aldridge rose also, and she followed suit.

"Thank you, sir," she said, beaming at the round face, the twinkling eyes, and the little pinked ears. She'd already forgiven him the nerve-rattling explosive.

He brought his attention back, as if from somewhere far away, blinked, and offered a distracted smile. "Right, then. Aldridge here will handle the rest. Any questions, any problems, he's your man." He pulled a rag from his pocket and wiped it back and forth under his nose.

Judging by the captain's palm-up gesture, that was their cue to leave, and she preceded him to the door. Major Boom had begun muttering to himself, and Olive glanced back the moment he mentioned pigeons.

"I wonder if they could carry miniature explosive charges . . ."

Her attention was so diverted that she collided with a suave-looking man who was passing in the hall. He caught her by the shoulders to steady her.

"*Pardonnez-moi, mademoiselle*. The fault is entirely mine." His accent was French, and his eyes were deep chocolate brown, fringed in thick, dark lashes.

"You can let her go now, Casanova," Aldridge said drily just behind her.

The man, whose wiry strength was well hidden beneath an olive jumper and utility trousers, stepped back, slipping his hands innocently into his pockets.

Olive smiled distractedly at him and let herself be led along by her crusty companion. After a moment, she tugged on his arm, pulling him to a stop in the centre of the hall. "He can't possibly be planning to endanger my birds by arming them with bombs," she snapped accusingly.

People detoured around them: FANYs garbed in smart belted jackets and skirts, carrying folders or cardboard boxes of supplies, men dressed as Casanova had been, looking rather shabby due to the varied holes, scorch marks, and grease stains marring their clothes. Many of them were chatting in languages she didn't recognise, and some sported painful-looking bruises. She frowned, her curiosity further piqued.

"He won't," Aldridge insisted, taking her by the elbow. Olive released the breath she'd been holding and hurried to keep up with his long strides. "The logistics would be impossible." He forestalled any comment she might have made by adding, "There are a thousand other things you could, and probably should, be worried about. Don't waste time on that one. He has countless new ideas every day. The vast majority fade from his mind at the first hint of failure." He turned and met her eyes, held them until he was certain his meaning was clear. She and her birds would be expected to prove themselves. Otherwise, they'd be promptly dispatched to make way for someone or something that would.

As they reached the last door on the right, he gestured her in. A map of Europe covered one wall, with coloured pushpins marking various points in France and Belgium, and a pair of filing cabinets stood sentry in the far corner, beside a window that looked out over the east lawn.

They stood staring at each other as he shut the door, each, no doubt, braced for a difficult discussion. He looked frustrated, whereas she felt as if the day's wounds were being healed by licks of triumph.

"You might as well sit down," he said, walking around her to settle into the chair behind his desk. Instantly, one mystery was solved. On the edge of the desk sat a candy jar half full of aniseed balls—no wonder he smelled like liquorice. Whereas the massive desk in Major Boom's office was crowded with clutter, this one had nothing out of place. Olive had a rebellious desire to muss something, merely to watch his reaction. With effort, she mastered it but refused to abandon it altogether, planning instead to hold it in reserve. She sat primly to face him.

He'd propped his elbow on the arm of his chair and shifted his head so that he could rub a hand over his lower jaw. "You talked a good game in there—a little patriotism, a little extortion—all of it with a bloody plaster stuck to your head. Quite literally." The last was delivered with an amused scoff. When Olive made to protest, he held up a weary hand, and she popped her mouth shut again, narrowing her eyes. "He was charmed, quite utterly. You didn't even flinch when the bomb went off, and I will admit that very few men who march through that office can say the same."

Olive had a sudden, desperate need to know if he'd been one of that number, but she didn't ask. Judging by the look in his eye, he had expected the question and was marginally surprised that she hadn't voiced it. She thrilled in even the tiniest victories where he was concerned, no matter how absurd.

"You may have convinced him to take you on," he continued, "but don't believe for an instant that he won't frog-march you off the estate himself if you're argumentative, insubordinate, or just plain badly behaved."

Glancing down at her hands, fisted in her lap, Olive could no longer contain her frustration. "*Why*," she demanded, whipping her head back up to meet his eyes, "do you have to be so starchy, stuffy, and bloody severe? You didn't want me here, but here I am. *Not*, as you might imagine, to make your life difficult, but because someone believes I have something to offer. Isn't that what this war is about? Bridging the gaps in every way possible, finding solutions in the unlikeliest of places, trusting each other to do the right thing? All of us are fighting this war in countless little ways. I want the chance to do something bigger. That's why I came. Why I skirted the warning signs on the drive." She winced at the memory. "Admittedly, not my best idea," she murmured sotto voce, earning a wry grin from Captain Aldridge. "Why I endured the relentless, entirely menacing ticking of a homemade bomb less than two feet away from me, until I could stand it no longer and was ready to dive behind the desk rather than risk being blown to smithereens."

He shot her an assessing glance but didn't reply.

"If you're looking for an enemy in everyone you meet, Captain Aldridge," she told him rather huffily, "then you'll have a much harder war to fight than the rest of us."

He exhaled sharply and stared down at his desk for a long moment before meeting her eyes. "I would say you might as well call me Tupper, but seeing as you've got your heart set on Jamie, why don't you stick with that?"

"Tupper?" she asked, eyebrows shooting up.

"We all have code names on the estate, the officers and agents at any rate."

Olive scoffed. "If the entire village knows your real name, why do you need a code name?"

"The entire village *doesn't* know my real name," he said carefully.

She stilled, narrowed her eyes. "Aldridge isn't your real name?"

Holding her astonished gaze, he swung his head like a pendulum, one corner of his mouth edging up a bit more with each change in direction. Olive couldn't deny that smug suited him— he was as devilishly attractive as he was exasperating. "Afraid not. Neither is Jameson. And Jamie isn't even close."

Olive took a moment to consider this new information. Then she sat forward, lifted the lid of the candy jar, and selected an aniseed ball. Then she carefully replaced the lid, sat back, and popped the candy into her mouth. His expression didn't change, but Olive imagined there was a tick she couldn't see.

"Why all the subterfuge?" she asked frankly, her words only slightly garbled.

"If one of our agents should be captured . . . tortured for information, we don't want the enemy to be able to identify any other agents or officers."

"I see," she said soberly.

He seemed uncomfortable in the sudden silence and quickly broke it. "I have a more traditional code name than most, for the purpose of liaising with civilians, as well as other government departments." He paused, then added, "Jameson was a Scot, making Irish whiskey. It's just the sort of misdirection we encourage around here. Although some of the men—Tierney in particular—don't like its formality, so they devised an alternate."

"I think I'll stick with Jamie," she said. "Although Tupper has a certain appeal."

"I come from a long line of sheep farmers," he said dryly.

Remembering how difficult it had been to get him to relinquish the story of his scar in the darkness behind the village hall, she didn't press, certain she wouldn't have any success while they were seated squarely on opposite sides of that tidy desk.

"They were clamouring to call me Mutton," he added.

"I suppose with a name like Tupper, you've developed something of a reputation with the ladies," Olive said, biting the inside of her cheek. He coloured a flattering shade of rosy pink. "Or are all the code names here similar in theme? I met Casanova already."

"That's not a code name," he said abruptly, "rather a nickname bestowed by one of the FANYs after an . . . incident. His code name is Pimpernel." At Olive's look, he merely shrugged, then cleared his throat. "Now, shall we get on with things?"

Olive held up a finger. "Are you even a captain?"

"Rest assured, Miss Bright. That part is real."

Her lips twisted ruefully. "Was the bomb your idea?"

He seemed taken aback by the suggestion. "Why would you think that?"

"You've made no secret of your opinions, Jamie." The name was said pointedly, as they were making a new start. "You don't have much regard for the abilities of my birds or my disagreeable attitude and flippant mouth. Maybe you wanted to see me squirm."

A mask suddenly came down. His eyes, a moment ago lit with wry amusement, now looked flat and angry. "Miss Bright," he said, with an edge to his voice that lifted the hairs at the back of her neck, "my personal feelings for you and your pigeons are of no consequence. Men with far greater authority and military expertise than I have given the orders. My job is merely to ensure that they're followed. It is not, under any circumstances, to harass you for my own amusement."

"I'm sorry," she said, suddenly feeling as if she'd offended his honour. The admission should have settled the matter, but the words niggled at her in their ambiguity, and she couldn't help but wonder what his personal feelings might be. *It doesn't matter. Focus, Olive.*

"Besides," he continued, "I bloody hate those homemade bombs. It's honestly all I can do not to toss them out the window as soon as he arms them."

Olive's eyes widened, and she leaned avidly forward. "But why does he?" she demanded. "Arm them, I mean?"

"He's a bit of a menace." He said this with obvious admiration. "A genius mind, but a menace all the same." Aldridge extended his arm and distractedly nudged the third report from the bottom in a stack of ten or so back into alignment. Olive bit back a knowing smile. "The CO is a consummate inventor, with considerable military training in explosives, which is why he was chosen to run Station Seventeen."

Olive's eyebrows rose with eager curiosity. "So, Baker Street is developing and testing new explosives for the armed forces?"

"Yes, but not all of that is happening here," he replied. "Baker Street is the code name for a rather widespread organisation under the purview of Mr Churchill himself. Explosives and other weaponry are being developed at Station Twelve, whereas Station Seventeen is dedicated to sabotage training"—he raised an eyebrow—"one aspect of so-called ungentlemanly warfare." He frowned at the cup holding his pencils and stretched out a finger to nudge it ever-so-slightly to the left. "However," he went on before Olive could interrupt, "the CO keeps up his hobby and likes to keep the rest of us on our toes. Thus, the explosives."

"That might justify their presence on the lawns or in the moat, but not in the offices, where they might put people at risk," she insisted.

"I can assure you, no one is ever at risk. The CO has an uncanny knack for knowing the second a fuse will run out."

"I'll take your word for it," Olive said, not at all mollified. "He doesn't do it very often, does he?"

"He pulls out one of his 'pets' for every training class. But don't worry. You're not a trainee."

"But I need training," she reminded him warily.

"Not the sort we specialise in here." With a sigh, he rose, adding, "It might be easier if I just show you."

She stood and, as he opened the door, inquired, "Do I even want to know why there are condoms scattered about his office?"

"I don't know," Aldridge said cagily. "Do you?"

Chapter 10

Sunday, 4th May

The ride home was exhilarating, and not simply because she felt triumphant. And vindicated. And the tiniest bit smug at having thwarted Captain Aldridge's best efforts to keep her out of it. That all would have certainly been worthy of a spontaneous whoop of joy, but the loan of a motorised Welbike had been the icing on the cake. With her bicycle disastrously mangled from the spigot mortar, and herself covered in cuts and scrapes, Aldridge had evidently been moved to pity. Which was how she found herself buzzing along the empty roads of the estate, with permission to take a shortcut home.

Aldridge had promised to bring her bicycle around in the car the following day—along with the much-awaited pigeon feed—then drive her to Forrester's to drop it off for repairs. Until she had the use of it again, she'd been offered the loan of the collapsible motorbike, which had been designed by someone in the Baker Street organisation. She'd asked no questions, merely accepted with alacrity. Now, bumping smartly down the lanes, she strove to get her story straight before dinner.

She was to tell her father and Harriet that one of the girls working at Brickendonbury had got pregnant and been sent off.

They needed someone to fill in quickly and were willing to give her a chance on Aldridge's recommendation. She was to do secretarial work but couldn't discuss it, having been required to sign the Official Secrets Act. This would be an extension of the pre-existing cover story, which they'd been instructed to maintain as long as possible.

While her father, at the very least, was aware of the occasional explosions on the grounds of Brickendonbury, she was forbidden from revealing that the manor house was now a school for industrial sabotage that included lessons in machinery, demolition, and silent killing. She sobered, a chill crawling over her skin, at the memory of Aldridge casually walking her across the lawn to watch Danny Tierney demonstrate various ways to incapacitate an enemy, first with a faceless muslin mannequin trussed up in a German uniform, and shortly thereafter, opposite a sober-faced volunteer sporting visible bruises. In the wake of that business, the detonations had, ironically, felt rather cathartic. But she couldn't admit to any of it, nor to the fact that she'd be trained in radio communication, ciphers, nursing, and mission preparation. They wouldn't have any idea what she was getting up to in the halls of her old school.

They'd touched on her role as pigeoneer, as well. Aldridge had shown her the specially designed containers—each equipped with its own parachute—that would drop the pigeons into occupied territory alongside the agents. He'd also shared the brief packet of instructions Baker Street had issued for the use of carrier pigeons. Despite the need to add a few minor notes in the margins, an effort that had prompted an inscrutable look from Aldridge, she'd felt more optimistic about the entire endeavour than she had thus far. The remaining preparations would all be up to her.

Jonathon, it had been agreed, was to be kept in the dark as much as possible, fed bits of information only as necessary. Being deemed assistant pigeoneer was probably one of the great thrills of his young life, but telling him any more than was strictly necessary could jeopardise their arrangement.

As she turned through the gate of Blackcap Lodge, the Welbike spitting up gravel behind her, she realised with a colourful curse that she'd entirely forgotten her intentions regarding Miss Husselbee's notebook. Initially frazzled by being shot at in the lane, subsequently thrilled at the opportunity to sign up as a FANY, with additional responsibilities, and finally distracted by all that was going on under her nose at Brickendonbury, it had utterly slipped her mind. She'd simply have to wait until the following day. In the meantime, perhaps there was an opportunity for a bit more sleuthing. It occurred to her that Miss Husselbee could have already mailed the April diaries back to Mass Observation. A quick stop by the post office would determine whether those pages were now officially out of reach. Otherwise, she'd need to find them. Their absence *must* be a clue.

Jonathon ran around the side of the barn, no doubt drawn by the puttering roar that had announced her arrival. His eyes boggled. "Where did you get that?" The words were loud in the sudden silence as Olive killed the engine. "And what happened to your face?"

Olive touched the plaster at her temple. "Captain Aldridge loaned me the bike, and the other is a long story. Quick, go and tell Harriet it's only me, so she doesn't get up and come looking—and don't mention my face. I'll meet you in the dovecote in a moment." Grinning like a hooligan, he took off running for the house.

She rolled the Welbike to the far corner of the barn and leaned it against the wall. Humming to herself, she tramped around to the dovecote, shut the door firmly against any prowling felines, quickly clapped a hat over her tousled locks, and surveyed her troops. A moment later, Jonathon tumbled in, and the door slammed behind him.

"Harriet said to tell you she'll be eagerly awaiting the details," he said in a rush.

"Naturally," Olive said with a cagey smile. "Now, what do you want to hear first?"

Eventually, they got around to the details she'd squeezed out of Aldridge regarding the pigeons' first mission, with departure scheduled for the following Sunday night. They had a week to get the birds prepped and ready.

"They're to be parachuted into Southern France. That puts the flight home at around five hundred miles."

What she didn't tell him was that they'd be dropped near Pessac, just outside of Bordeaux. She'd need to look at a map for a more accurate calculation, but the estimate would do for now. Olive's gaze darted from perch to nesting box as she began to narrow the field of candidates.

"They'll be dropped in the early morning hours, so with any luck, the first will be released in full light. All the birds are going to need to be trained in night flying, but we can't worry about that for this mission. There's simply no time."

"They don't know how to fly at night?" Jonathon asked, eyes boggled.

"They know *how*," she clarified. "They are disinclined to do so. We'll need to make it worth their while," Olive said with a wink.

She paced the circumference of the dovecote, her hands behind her back, as she spoke aloud, half to herself, while Jonathon stood beside the ladder. "This mission is a test," she said quietly, "and in order to convince Baker Street to continue our arrangement—and supply the birds with much-needed feed—we'll need to make a strong showing. Careful selection is paramount."

The birds had always been freshly evaluated before every race, she and her father gauging their speed, endurance, reliability, and general health before choosing which ones to enter. Going forward, there would be additional considerations, and the full responsibility of selection would fall on her shoulders. She suspected these missions would all involve parachute drops into occupied Europe, likely Belgium, Holland, or France. That meant the return flights would be arduous and fraught with peril. The birds would face vicious winds off the Channel, ruthless natural predators, and enemy fire, because the Germans were well aware of the importance of carrier pigeons, and snipers were instructed to shoot on sight. It was imperative that she choose carefully and prepare those selected as best she could in the time available, which was liable to be severely limited.

Before the war, she and her father would often hold little training races of their own. They'd each select a bird and drive off for the day in whatever direction they fancied. After a picnic peppered with boasts and predictions, the birds would be launched into the air for the great race back home. Harriet was the official, unbiased referee and in charge of recording which bird showed up first. More often than not, Olive's pigeon edged out her father's, but he was a good sport about it. Mostly.

Olive smiled at the memory. Petrol had been first to be rationed, and now there wasn't any to spare for pigeon flight training. Occasionally, she'd send a bird with someone heading to London or to visit family in Yorkshire or Suffolk, but even that seemed too capricious with all that was going on. That left her bicycle, and she could ferry a pigeon only so far under her own power. She was struck with a rallying thought. Perhaps Aldridge could be convinced to make her an extended loan of the Welbike and throw in a petrol allowance, as well. It wouldn't be an easy task—his acceptance of a pigeoneer into the ranks of Baker Street was already stretching the limits of his tolerance. Olive grinned to herself, confident that she could convince him. And success would be worth every bit of mulish objection she'd have to endure.

A motorbike would greatly benefit her birds' training regime. She'd be able to transport them much farther afield, which would provide a vastly expanded proving ground for their homing capabilities and endurance training. It would also facilitate night training—so long as she could see well enough in the dark with the headlamp dimmed and shuttered. The whole village knew the NPS hadn't come calling—and her pigeon training efforts had, of necessity, ground to a halt—but in her new role as a FANY, it was entirely possible she could justify these mysterious jaunts and thereby deflect suspicion, quell village gossip, and keep her father squarely in the dark.

Jamie is not going to like this one bit.

Olive bit her lip. "I *really* need to settle on what to call that man," she muttered, skimming the soles of her boots over the gravel as she glanced up at Jonathon. "It's bad enough we're keeping secrets. We don't need to complicate matters any further. He makes it so difficult, though. I can't possibly call him Jamie when he's behaving like the lord of the manor, which is probably why I keep reverting to Captain Aldridge." A quirked grin had cropped up on Jonathon's face. "Right," she said briskly. "Let's make a start."

By all appearances, the occupants of the loft were ignoring her, busily tending to their mates, their nests, or their stomachs, but she wasn't fooled. Pigeons were forever curious, and as Olive slid her gaze from one to the next, considering each in turn, their eyes watched her carefully.

"What do you think, Poppins?" Her favourite hen was pacing in her box, her head bobbing rhythmically. "Should we let a few of the boys have a try?" The bird didn't seem particularly agreeable, prompting Olive to add, "I'll pencil you in as an alternate." Her gaze panned the loft. "We need three good racers. First- and second-season birds can be eliminated, and we don't want to choose any of Father's favourites, or else he's bound to notice and make things difficult."

In the centre of the top row of perches, clearly intent on showing himself to advantage, Fritz gazed down at her. "What about Fritz?" Olive said, glancing narrowly at Poppins. The two had mated the previous year and were quite devoted to each other, but also ferociously competitive. "He clocked some impressive racing times before the start of the war." Jonathon inched closer to him, staring up. "He's a big bird and quite strong," she went on. "His size could give him a considerable advantage in overcoming any potential headwinds over the Channel." She glanced at Jonathon. "What do you think?"

"Agreed," Jonathon said solemnly. Olive smiled fondly at him.

A bit of a scuffle on the ground beside her had Olive flicking a glance at Badger.

"You want to throw your name in the ring, is that it?" she said with a twist of her lips.

"He did survive the falcon. He's a right scrapper," Jonathon said encouragingly. He'd asked to hear the story many times since she'd first told it. It had bolstered his respect for these humble birds.

While Fritz was a veritable show bird, beautifully formed in unmarred blue, Badger was a scrawny, gimpy grizzled white. But he was a survivor. She'd seen him go into a free-fall spin when a peregrine falcon had closed in behind him, talons extended with brutal intention. Badger had escaped without a scratch and had flown home to court a pretty grey hen named Wendy.

Olive considered. "It's a fair point. The ability to outmanoeuvre a predator twice his size to carry a message home could mean the difference between life and death for Badger *and* the operatives that would depend on him."

"Maybe even Britain herself," Jonathon said soberly.

Nodding, Olive agreed. "He's officially on the list."

She settled on the bench as her eyes roved over the rest of them, some standing in profile, eyeing her warily, others peeping in and out of the pigeonholes in the roof, oblivious to her decision-making.

"Lancelot?" Jonathon suggested.

"Too risky. He's young and hasn't settled with a mate yet and could well decide not to make the journey home if a flirty mademoiselle crosses his path."

"Of course he'd come back," Jonathon insisted stoutly.

Olive shrugged. "We can't take the risk that he might live up to his namesake. He just needs a bit of time."

With two strong beats of his wings, a red-chequered cock flapped up from the floor and landed beside her on the bench. He bore her scrutiny with preening pride.

"What about Aramis?" Jonathon suggested, eyeing the bird critically. "He's got camouflage colouring." That was true to a point. White birds could be more easily spotted by the enemy—and its sympathisers. "Now that he's mated with Roberta, he'll be eager to get home again."

Jonathon was almost fizzing with excitement, and Olive knew he'd be thrilled to have chosen one of the three birds to be sent. But she needed to consider carefully. She scooped up Aramis, ran her fingers over his breast and wings, examined his feet, and looked into his eyes. He had won several shorter races and had been in training for a longer one when his chance had been snatched away.

"You're looking fit, Aramis. Ready to do your bit?"

"One for all, and all for one," Jonathon said eagerly.

Grinning, Olive opened her hands and gave the bird a little toss. "Fair enough. Fritz, Badger, and Aramis will be the three pigeon musketeers. And Poppins will stand ready to assist." She promptly sobered, fully aware that she might very well lose more than one of these birds.

Barring any health concerns that might come to light with a thorough inspection, Olive was confident all four birds could handle the flight from Pessac, France, and would clock in impressive times, but she'd need to get them back in racing shape quickly. They hadn't been trained with any consistency or regularity since before she left for the Royal Veterinary College, and now they'd have to do it all in secret. Her father would naturally be suspicious of any sort of rigorous training unless she was able to come up with a plausible explanation for their no longer dwindling supply of pigeon feed.

A short, sharp whistle sounded from the drive. Her father was home, calling to Kíli to hurry along through the gate. Not quite ready to share her news, and unwilling to subject herself to a fresh diatribe on the NPS, she laid her index finger against her lips, winked at Jonathon, and slipped out of the dovecote, cut through the garden to the kitchen door, and hurried up the back stairs. Safe in her room, she beelined for her mother's photograph, giddy all over again. If she wasn't to be allowed to leave British shores or man a gun in support of the war effort, then her new role as a FANY was surely the next best thing. She was carrying on her mother's legacy in this small way.

She knew the stories by heart, even so many years later—her mother had never tired of recounting her thrilling days as a FANY. Amid cold and mud, infection and fear, Serena Bright had thrived, relishing those fate-tempting, shiver-inducing moments that shifted the balance amid the maelstrom of death and destruction. As a young girl, Olive had taken it all for granted, but lately, thinking back over the details, she was staggered by the tales of her mother's accomplishments. Olive had barely managed to get past the Brickendonbury gates unscathed to volunteer her services on the home front. She sighed and slid her index finger along her mother's smiling face. "I hope you'd be proud of me," she whispered.

"What happened to your head?" Rupert Bright demanded from across the table.

Olive, who'd been poised to announce that she was now, officially, working for the war effort, felt her shoulders droop with the distraction. Before coming downstairs, she'd pulled away the plaster and arranged her hair to cover the gash, but clearly not well enough. "It's nothing," she said, lifting a hand to feather her fingers over the spot and instantly realising her error.

"And your hand?" her father prompted, concern crowding

over his features. Jonathon, who already knew the details, kept his head down. Harriet glanced up curiously in the act of scooping a serving of parsley potatoes.

Olive focused on the raw flesh on the inside of her palm. "I fell off my bicycle on Mangrove Lane," she said calmly. Truthfully. Which, at that moment, felt an enormous relief. "Something shot out of the trees and startled me, and I went over, hit my head on a rock, and scraped up my hands and knees." She curled her fingers and dipped her hands beneath the table, smiling at the eyes staring back at her and adding an innocent shrug for good measure. "My bicycle took the brunt of the fall, but Jamie lent me the use of a little motorbike to get back home, and he said he'll take the bike around to Mr Forrester for me."

"Did he?" Harriet said, with a knowing smile. "Such a nice young man."

Olive nearly laughed out loud. While he might be a young man, Captain Aldridge wasn't the least bit nice. At least as far as she could tell.

"What were you doing over on Mangrove Lane? Those military types don't take kindly to trespassing, my girl. No matter what you think you're entitled to do."

"As a matter of fact, I had business at Brickendonbury."

"Did you now?" her father said. His voice was teasing, but his eyes were wary.

"Yes, and I have some news."

"It won't interfere with the pig club, will it?" Harriet inquired, slicing neatly into her sausage and cabbage roll.

"No," Olive said flatly. She'd forgotten the pig club.

"Don't say you've heard from the NPS?" was her father's guess.

She shook her head, feeling a pang of guilt to be squelching the guarded optimism in his voice. With a sideways glance at Jonathon, she exhaled a deep breath and announced, "I've signed up as a FANY."

Her father had just shovelled a mouthful of food through his lips and now choked out a response. "You've *what*?"

Olive set down her fork. She'd known this conversation would be difficult, but she'd had lots of practice with difficult over the past few days. In fairness, it had been weeks. Months. And it wasn't about to get any easier anytime soon.

"Jamie . . . ," she started, lowering her gaze and schooling her voice to sound self-conscious, "Captain Aldridge knew I wanted to do something more for the war effort than I'm doing now." She glanced at her stepmother as she clarified. "Something more than a scheme. So, when a position came open at Brickendon-bury, he suggested I come in for an interview."

"The projects undertaken by the WI are instrumental to the war effort," Harriet reminded them all in a tone she used to rally support and donations for those very endeavours.

Before Olive could respond, her father swooped in with plati-tudes. "Of course they are, my dear. No one could possibly argue the counterpoint." Then he turned to his daughter to demand, "What sort of position?"

Olive felt the heated flush, prompted by the impending lie, begin its slow rise from the base of her neck. "Officially, I'm to be a secretary, but in reality, I'll be more of a dogsbody, or a driver if I'm lucky."

"Wouldn't they prefer someone skilled in those sorts of tasks?"

Olive rolled her eyes. "I appreciate the vote of confidence, Dad, but I think I can handle it. And you needn't worry. I'll be trained."

"But you'll be wasted there! All your schooling—none of it was preparing you to be a secretary. There'll be no one to help me in my practice. I would have had a hell of a time delivering all those calves without you—to say nothing of the pigeons." He looked round the table, at each of them in turn. "Not to mention the pig club," he hastened to add as his gaze touched on his wife.

Her stepmother laid a hand on her father's arm. "I suspect she won't be a secretary for long, Rupert. As long as she needn't demonstrate her knitting skills, I feel certain she's destined for a greater role. Just like her mother." She winked at Olive, whose smile suddenly felt etched in place. She couldn't decide whether Harriet's comments were innocently reassuring or shrewdly perceptive.

Wanting to shift the conversation, she said, "I told them all about the work both of you did in the last war, and all you're doing now. I thought it might bolster my chances." She hadn't really, but in fairness, they'd known plenty already. "They were very impressed with Mum, too, her being a bona fide hero of the ambulance corps, with plenty of daring evacuations to her credit."

Rupert Bright's demeanour instantly shifted from bushy-browed frown to slack-jawed stillness. His shoulders went rigid as he quietly demanded, "You told them about her?"

"Yes. Why shouldn't I?"

"No reason," he said hurriedly, with a sharp shake of his head. "Yes, well, her accomplishments are irrelevant. What matters is that they realise what a prize they have in you."

"Thanks, Dad," Olive said, wondering if the shivery feeling that clung to her insides was due to unexpected emotion or cringing worry at lying to her father.

"So, you rode in, happy as you please," he inquired, "took a tumble on the drive, then got interviewed and accepted on the spot?"

"More or less," she said, happy to leave the spigot mortar out of it. "They patched me up, as well."

"Hmm. Is it official, then? When are you meant to start?" Her father clearly wasn't yet ready to embrace this unexpected turn of events. Heaven help her if he ever found out about the pigeons.

"It's official," she assured them all. "My training starts next week. That'll give me plenty of time to make a start on the pig club and maybe finish that pair of socks that's been languishing."

Harriet's smile was wryly amused. "Wonderful."

"You're certain you'll be safe working there?" her father pressed sceptically. "There's plenty of talk in the Home Guard. Several of the men have been out on patrol and heard mysterious explosions coming from the grounds."

"I'll be fine," Olive insisted. "I'm not to know any details of that sort, but it's clear that they're all very conscientious about it. All the necessary precautions are being taken. I won't be in any danger." Worried that her cheeks had pinkened at the memory of her explosive chat with Major Boom, Olive took a sip from her water glass.

Harriet spoke up. "I know you're a very capable girl, but I hope your Jamie isn't putting undue pressure on you."

Her Jamie? It was really too ridiculous. They could barely hold a conversation without one of them seething with frustration. But she couldn't very well protest.

"Don't worry," she said with a broad smile. "I'm entirely capable of pushing right back."

"You've demonstrated that well enough, my girl," her father said with a gruff shake of his head. "I suppose we'll all have to get used to not having you around as often."

He seemed glum, but it was a small price to pay. At least he'd raised no objections, despite being a little out of sorts with the whole business. The trouble was, he knew only the half of what she'd actually be doing. She took a bite of her supper, carefully not meeting anyone's gaze, as she envisioned herself walking a narrow tightrope far above the village green. After several long moments, her father's voice startled her out of her reverie.

"I stopped in at the Fox and Duck for a quick pint on my way back from the O'Connors' farm this afternoon. I chanced to speak to the constable."

Olive rested her arm heavily on the table, her fork cradled, forgotten, in her hand, as her heart thudded dully in her chest. It had been only hours since she'd trespassed, venturing into Peregrine Hall in the hopes of finding some clue to the Sergeant Major's suspiciously sudden demise. And in the time since, she'd forgotten about her entirely. Forgotten that less than forty-eight hours ago, she'd been rummaging through the pockets of a dead woman. Forgotten she had found a lead and had fully intended to follow it, with Aldridge's cooperation. She felt suddenly ashamed as she waited for her father to tell them the rest.

A glance showed her father running his tongue over his teeth, a habit he had when trying to gird himself to say something he'd rather not. His features were heavy with emotion, and Harriet had stilled, clearly braced against the worst. "The results of the post-mortem indicate that Verity Husselbee died of poisoning."

"I think that's what we feared," Harriet said sadly. "She was in marvellous good health. It would have been hard to imagine it could be anything else. But what could have poisoned her? Not something she ate at the dance, surely. Otherwise there would have been other . . . tragedies. Do you suppose she could have had one of those rare allergies?" She was babbling, a clear indication of how thoroughly this news had affected her.

Rupert Bright turned his head slowly toward his wife, his face grim.

Instantly, Olive knew. "It was the Spam cake, wasn't it?" she blurted.

Each of them started, and round the table, three heads swivelled to look at her. Her father's eyes narrowed curiously, and he carefully demanded, "How did you know that?"

"I didn't know." Olive swallowed, already feeling the tears beginning to prick against her eyes. "But no one seemed to know who'd made it, and it disappeared with only a single slice served. Who else but Miss Husselbee would willingly eat a pudding made of tinned meat and potatoes?" She shuddered. "Whoever wanted to kill her went about it in a diabolical manner."

Harriet was quick to object, her voice brisk. "Don't be silly. Verity may have been overly outspoken, but she was harmless. No one wanted to kill her. It must have been some sort of accident."

Her father cleared his throat meaningfully. "Harrington found digitalis in her stomach, my dear, and she's not been taking it for her heart."

Harriet's frail-looking hand swept up to cover her lips as her eyes widened in disbelief.

"What's digitalis?" Jonathon said, finally speaking up.

Olive stood and collected the dishes, her mind beginning to buzz with suspicion. "Digitalis is from the foxglove plant. If prescribed in the right quantities to patients with weak or irregular heartbeats, it can help stabilise the condition. But if administered in an incorrect dosage, or to individuals with healthy hearts, it can be fatal." She plugged the sink, ran the water over the dishes, and left them to soak.

"Did you learn that at veterinary college?" Jonathon asked.

"As a matter of fact," Olive said, coming back to her chair and fixing her gaze on Harriet, "I learned all about it at a WI meeting here in the village. We had a visiting lecturer from Oxford University. He explained how there'd been a shortage of the drug since the beginning of the war and requested our help in restoring the supply. He described in great detail how to handle and dry the leaves of the foxglove plant to ensure they could be made into effective medicine. And shortly after that, we formed a collection party. We donned our gloves, took up our baskets, and spent a week harvesting foxglove leaves as part of the Oxford Medicinal Plants Scheme."

Jonathon's eyes had widened ominously.

Harriet hadn't spoken, but Olive's father murmured, "I'd forgotten all that."

"Are you familiar with the foxglove plant?" Olive asked Jonathon.

"I'm not sure."

"It's easiest to identify in the summer, when it's blooming. Rather a showy number, with spikes of trumpet flowers mostly in shades of purple and pink or even white. We had no shortage of leaves to dry, as the plants were growing wild along the lanes."

"Better to avoid it altogether," her father suggested, prompting a nod from his young charge. "But I believe we're getting somewhat off topic." He rubbed his fingers over his forehead so vigorously, the skin folded into fleshy wrinkles. "As difficult as it is to believe that Miss Husselbee's umbrella has thumped its last, it's harder still to accept that someone could have done this intentionally."

They were all silent, lost in their own thoughts, until her father spoke again.

"There's to be an inquest Wednesday morning. They've agreed to allow me to appear in lieu of Jonathon." Beside her, Jonathon dipped his head, his face having paled sufficiently to set his freckles into stark relief. Her father turned his gaze to the hunched figure. "We'll go over your story once more, and that will be an end to it."

Olive rubbed a hand briskly over the boy's back. "Chin up." He was likely remembering his moments alone with Miss Husselbee as she lay dying, being the one entrusted with her last word. Poor chap. "Does anyone want pudding?" she said, her gaze shifting to the sticky mound waiting on the counter. Mrs Battlesby's creations were valiant at best.

"I'm suddenly feeling rather queasy," Harriet said, pushing her chair back. Her father rose and helped her to her feet. No doubt she'd realised that one of her close friends—a member of her beloved Institute—was likely to have done this horrible deed.

The pair had taken only a few awkward steps, her father's arm banded tightly around Harriet's waist, when he bent to sweep her into his arms. Olive and Jonathon stared as Harriet tipped her head against her husband's shoulder and let herself be carried from the room.

Olive raised her eyebrows at Jonathon. "What about you?"

"I'll try it," he said gamely. "I can always fish out the sultanas if the rest of it's awful."

"That's the spirit," she said and set the steamed cinnamon pudding on the table beside him.

He took up the spoon, carved out a large piece, and settled it on his plate. Then he turned and glanced behind him, very obviously needing to confirm that they would not be overhead, before jutting his chin toward her and whispering, "Are you going out early tomorrow morning with the four musketeers?"

"Yes, I suppose so." An outing at dawn would be her best chance to avoid the gossips. "It'll be chilly," she said abruptly.

"Are you taking the Welbike?" Jonathon pressed. Olive considered. It would be faster, but considerably louder, perhaps drawing unwanted attention at that hour. She should have been expecting the follow-up question. "Can I come along?" The colour was back in his cheeks, and he held his fork like a trident, each tine spearing a sultana. She couldn't help but smile. It would be a tight squeeze, getting all of them onto the motorbike, but they were nothing if not resourceful.

She nodded emphatically. "Of course. You're my right-hand man."

"With the pigs, as well?"

Olive bit back a curse. She'd been deliberately pushing the pig club from her mind, but she knew she couldn't escape it. She forced a bright smile. "You're joking, right? I wouldn't even *want* to do it without you."

She let Jonathon enjoy the glossy, sticky pudding, a bit of the sauce having already adhered to his cheek, while she tackled the dishes and marvelled at the drastic changes a few days had wrought.

She bit her lip, rather embarrassed to have got so caught up in the shock and scandal of Miss Husselbee's death as to envision herself as something of an amateur sleuth. Her mother's name, the last word on the dead woman's lips, had been entirely unexpected, and she'd understandably been curious. Add to that the fact that she'd been rather coincidentally on the scene for a great many suspicious circumstances. Clues and questions had niggled at the corners of her mind, prompting her to action, and she'd had the very best intentions, but why had she ever imagined she could do more than the police? Enough. She had a fair amount on her plate as it was. Tomorrow she'd have another chat with Margaret—for her own peace of mind. She didn't really suspect her, but her friend's past was somewhat of a mystery, and then there were her dodgy answers and odd behaviour. She'd get to the bottom of it, and then she'd turn over the clues she'd collected to the police, including, with any luck, the notebook Captain Aldridge still had in his possession. Although it wouldn't hurt to check in at the post office for the missing Mass Observation diaries, just in case. After that, it would be up to the authorities to turn up any additional clues and determine who had poisoned the Sergeant Major. She had responsibilities of her own to get on with, and she wasn't equipped to solve a murder.

Poirot, with his meticulously waxed moustaches, his tremendous ego, and his order and method, would never have allowed his life to become so thoroughly disarranged, she thought, yanking the stopper from the drain. Miss Marple, on the other hand, as a woman and a villager, would certainly relate. Miss Rose, she decided, may be onto something.

Tuesday, 11 June 1940
Peregrine Hall, Pipley
Hertfordshire

When the secretary of the Pipley WI suggested inviting a guest lecturer from the Department of Botany at Oxford University to one of our meetings, I assumed we'd be getting a lecture on vegetables: which varieties provide the most yield, which are the hardiest, etc. Having been encouraged to raze our flower gardens and grow for victory at the start of the war, it's entirely understandable that we were all shocked to be lectured on some lesser-known benefits of certain flowers.

Living in a country village, naturally all of us present were well versed in the many natural remedies to be found in plants. But the scheme proposed by Dr James was considerably more involved than collecting a bit of chamomile for a soothing tisane. It seems there is a shortage of certain medicines, and he's devised the "Oxford Medicinal Plants Scheme" to supplement the supply. We were all quite committed until he informed us we'd be foraging for foxglove. Imagine our consternation—foxglove is quite poisonous! With a bit of clarification, Dr James managed to set our minds somewhat at ease. Evidently, if given at the correct dosage, the dried leaves can be quite rejuvenative for individuals with particular heart conditions.

So tomorrow we're to gather in the hall, and our collection party will troop off with baskets and pruning shears to wrestle the spires of foxglove into a worthy cause. Dr Ware was quite supportive of the idea and has volunteered to come along, as well. I do hope everyone remembers to wear gloves; otherwise this scheme could well end in tragedy.

V.A.E. Husselbee

Chapter 11

Jonathon got off to school Monday morning with bright eyes, pinkened cheeks, and thoroughly chapped lips. They'd covered miles on the Welbike, with Jonathon clinging like a monkey to her back. All four pigeons had been released, and Olive and Jonathon had come home to find them all returned, waiting patiently for their breakfast.

"Don't let on that you've been up for hours, buzzing around with some fly boys," she reminded him with a wink.

"And a couple of girls," he added, then flashed a mischievous grin before quickly tucking it away again.

Olive watched him dart up the steps, trailing his gas mask, before she turned to walk back toward the post office, trailing her own. Hoping to dodge curious questions from her father and Harriet, she'd decided to leave off using the motor and instead had pushed the Welbike to the bottom of the hill below Blackcap Lodge and back up again on their return. Between the fatigue and the numbing wind that had buffeted her face over the miles, she was dragging, and there was still a long day ahead. In addition to the tricky conversations and the compulsory gas mask training exercise she'd need to endure, there would, unavoidably, be pigs. What she wouldn't give to settle into a cosy chair with a Christie mystery, but even a hot cup of tea would be nice.

Margaret, she knew, would be helping to clean the church this morning before work, but Olive fully intended to pin her down as soon as she'd finished at the post office. She turned her collar up against the wind and hurried.

She was back out in the damp chill ten minutes later. After waiting for the other customers to finish their business, she'd stepped to the counter, cornering the twittering Mrs Petrie, and launched into a whispered monologue on the ever-popular topic of Miss Husselbee.

It had been such a shock to find her near the dovecote—Jonathon had been first on the scene, but she'd been close behind him. Knowing Miss Husselbee to have been in robust good health, and having herself knelt in the sick, she'd thought instantly of poison, of that odd Spam cake at the Daffodil Dance. And then, just yesterday, they'd found digitalis in Miss Husselbee's blood—foxglove. Olive had met Mrs Petrie's gaze and enunciated the last word slowly, for full titillation effect. Then she'd nodded solemnly and proceeded to lie outright.

"The police," she said, "suspect Miss Husselbee's Mass Observation diaries might reveal a possible grudge or resentment that could have led to her murder." The word hung between them: *murder*. The inquest hadn't yet determined murder, but Olive was certain, and as incentive, it was too good to pass up. "But they haven't found the diaries," Olive said eerily. Mrs Petrie's eyes couldn't possibly have been wider if she'd said, "Bodies." "Do you know what I think? I think she might have already mailed them off, hoping to stave off the killer."

Mrs Petrie blinked several times, as if coming out of a trance. Her head twitched. "No, they must still be somewhere in Pipley. Miss Husselbee hasn't been in to mail a parcel in weeks, although she was in a few days ago to pick one up." She propped her elbow on the counter and leaned closer. "Maybe she's hidden them, as an insurance policy." She gasped suddenly, jerking up-right and still, her eyes darting erratically. "Or perhaps the mur-derer has already got to them."

Olive slumped, her lips twisting in disappointment. That was precisely what she was afraid of. It was still possible that Miss Husselbee's notebook would help decipher the last words she'd written for Mass Observation, and thereby identify her killer; they could certainly hope.

"You have the makings of an amateur sleuth, Mrs Petrie." She winked conspiratorially, and before another word could be said, she slipped out the door.

Now for the hard part.

Olive sat on a bench beside the river with a view of the church gate, having every intention of waiting for her friend to emerge. She could have slipped into the nave and helped Margaret dust the statuary and tidy the hymnals, but she had decided that a conversation touching on murder should probably remain out-side. So, she waited and shivered and imagined what she would say. By the time Margaret came striding out with a tug on her jacket and a swirl of her skirt, Olive was ready to blurt her ques-tions, decorum be damned.

She ignored Margaret's start of surprise as she strode up and linked arms. Her friend's stiff comportment and ghost of a smile made it seem as if Olive was escorting a hostage as they walked back to the cottage Margaret shared with her aunt Eloise. And, in a way, it was; she fully intended on inviting herself in for tea and letter writing.

"We're due for a make-up," Olive reminded her. "You can-celled on me the day before Miss Husselbee was murdered."

"*Murdered?*" she gasped, her eyes looking hunted.

Olive hustled her down the lane and behind closed doors.

It wasn't a good day for decorum.

Moments before sitting down across from Margaret at the

kitchen table, Olive glanced in the hall-tree mirror and noted that her eyes were oddly bright, her cheeks uncharacteristically pink, and her smile a caricature of its usual self. She wondered if her friend had noticed the outward signs of her discomfiture.

Judging by the focused expression on Margaret's face as she poured out their cups of tea, it seemed unlikely. Such was their ritual: indulging in a few quiet moments to pretend that some things carried on, unspoiled, in honour of the men for whom they penned encouraging letters. Men who were fighting for decency and humanity. They pretended not to notice the weak tea and the rapidly dwindling supply in the biscuit tin.

Olive accepted her cup of tea and waited politely for Margaret to take up her own. Then she pounced. "There's something I need to tell you."

Margaret pounced right back, leaning in excitedly as her eyes widened in avid curiosity. "It's about your mysterious someone, isn't it? The tall, handsome officer from the dance."

Olive had forgotten all about her friend's desire for a good gossip on the topic of Captain Aldridge. She would have preferred he not intrude in her life more than was strictly necessary, but men, particularly those of the broad-shouldered, chiselled-jaw variety, were not the sort of detail that Margaret readily dismissed.

Considering her options, Olive decided it would be easiest to go tit for tat. She curved her lips into a shy, secretive smile and said, "Not exactly, but I'm willing to offer a trade."

Her friend's answering smile flashed mischievously. "I'm engaged to the vicar, sweeting. There are no more tall, dark strangers for me." True enough—Leo's locks were paler than Margaret's own.

Olive took a sip of tea, stalling for time. Then, carefully setting her cup in its saucer, she winced in self-conscious apology before coming straight out with it. "I overheard your conversation with Miss Husselbee. The day before she died."

Margaret's easy smile slipped slowly from evidence. An unconvincing replacement promptly appeared beneath a rapidly blinking, shifty gaze. Olive waited without saying another word. "I wish you hadn't," her friend finally said, her shoulders dropping in weighty resignation.

"It was awkward," Olive admitted. "Jonathon was with me, and neither one of us could imagine what could have possibly provoked either of you to have spoken so fiercely."

Margaret's mouth flattened, her cheeks hollowing with the shifting of her jaw. But still she didn't speak, distractedly fiddling with the tea things on the table between them.

"And now she's dead," Olive said into the silence. "And I, for one, believe she was murdered."

"Surely not," Margaret insisted.

Olive shrugged. "The inquest will be the official word, but the circumstances of her death are extraordinarily suspicious, and no shortage of villagers are relieved to see her gone."

Margaret didn't answer, and Olive was beginning to feel mildly frustrated when her friend's eyes suddenly flashed wide in understanding. "Hold on . . . Is this your way of inquiring whether *I* had something to do with her death?" An acceptable reply had not yet occurred to Olive when Margaret barrelled on again. "Do you honestly believe that if I'd wanted to kill her, I would have poisoned her with *cake*?" A half laugh escaped her, and Olive thought it sounded forsaken.

Margaret speared her with a hard stare, and Olive hurried to reply. "I don't. I don't think that." She really didn't. A person would have to be mad to do something like that. Or desperate. The pad of her finger moved hypnotically over the embroidered flowers on the tablecloth as she thought back to that day. Margaret had definitely sounded desperate.

"I was angry—furiously angry." Her friend's fingers had clamped over the tiny silver locket that hung just below her collar. Olive was relatively certain she hadn't imagined the little gulp of sadness that had punctuated that protest. "But I didn't want her to die. I just—I didn't want anyone to know about the adverts."

Olive stared at her friend in disbelief. "But what did it really matter if everyone knew you'd modelled for ladies' catalogues? It's not as if it was gentlemen's magazines." Olive slanted a glance at her friend. "It wasn't, was it?"

"Surely that's not the question I'm to answer in exchange for details about your date to the dance," Margaret said wryly.

"Er . . . only if the answer is yes," Olive said, wincing at how horribly inept she was at this sleuthing business.

Margaret frowned. "I don't follow." Then the light dawned, and Olive cringed, braced against her friend's feelings of betrayal. "You don't believe me," she said flatly.

Sighing, Olive propped her forearms on the table and leaned in. "I think there's something else you're trying to keep secret, and I wish you'd tell me what it is."

"Why should I?" she asked, her tone and expression mulish. "Presuming I have something to tell."

Olive's own shoulders dropped. "Someone else might have overheard, and if they don't know you like I do, I imagine they'd peg you as a prime suspect. If you're investigated by the police, your life in London will no longer be a secret."

Margaret's lip quivered, and her gaze shifted angrily away, stubbornness holding her rigid.

Feeling like a heel, Olive tried to back-pedal. "I'm sorry, Mags. Truly. I didn't mean—" She took a breath and started again. "I know you had nothing to do with Miss Husselbee's death." Cringing, she went on gently. "But if there *is* something else, it's bound to come out. I only want to help you."

"I appreciate that," Margaret said, mustering a brave smile, "but, really, there's nothing." But of course, there was.

She raised her teacup to her lips, her eyes locked on Olive's over the rim. When she set it down again, the lines of her face had smoothed out and the twist of her lips spelled mischief.

"And now that I've answered your question, it's your turn. Where did you find him, and how long do you plan to keep him?"

Olive tried to downplay everything, which was rather simple, because absolutely nothing was going on with Aldridge. *Jamie*. At least nothing Margaret would have been interested in. Being a devotee to romantic novels and their cinematic counterparts, she was determined to have what she termed "lurid details." Which was how Olive found herself engaged in a quarter of an hour's embellishment. She outlined her first meeting with the man— he'd seen her carting pigeons around and been curious. She gushed about their date to the dance—he was an excellent dancer and a marginally better kisser. And finally, she extolled the details of their time spent together since—long conversations, considerable flirting, and a number of heated moments. It was as close to the truth as she could manage without giving anything away. Margaret certainly didn't need to know that the heated moments were the angry sort, and as such, she was thrilled with this progress. Unfortunately, she was particularly interested in discussing his physical attributes, which Olive had resolved to try not to notice. She'd worried it would only make things more awkward than they already were.

As quickly as possible, Olive turned the conversation to the new job she'd be starting the following week. Margaret was gratifyingly impressed.

"All of it is frightfully exciting—particularly your proximity to your handsome captain. It's just a shame you'll have to wear that dingy brown uniform. I wouldn't be at all surprised if a sour old warden had designed it to resemble a burlap sack."

"I think it looks smart," Olive said defensively as they rummaged for paper with which to write their letters.

Margaret considered, her head tilted. "Brown does suit you."

Not certain the words could be interpreted as a compliment, Olive didn't bother responding. Brown did suit her. There wasn't much to be done about that.

An hour later, having written their quota of letters to the

Friendless Serving Men and shared a cosy meal of cheese and potato dumplings, they set off to the green for the training exercise. The entire village was out en masse, everyone made vaguely anonymous by the rubberised masks with their bug-eyed goggles and drain-like snouts. The children had been let out of school early and were dodging about, ignoring everyone in authority. And the daffodils were flowering carelessly underfoot.

As they all waited for the Home Guard to stop arguing amongst themselves and get on with it, Olive's distracted gaze stuttered to a stop on the tall, masked figure whose careful, measured movements were so familiar. She'd hurried towards him until the truth, realised after three dull thuds of her heart, pulled her up short. It wasn't—it couldn't be—George. Flushed with fervent hope quickly dashed, and with private shame at her own naïve imagination, she turned her head away as the object of her perusal, Mr Forrester, leaned his head toward the publican, Mr Framingham, for a private conversation.

Gillian Forrester popped up just beyond her peripheral vision and asked eagerly, "Is your dishy captain here somewhere?" Olive turned to see the girl scanning the crowd.

Her mother, standing beside her, chided, "Really, Gillian."

"He's not here," Miss Danes answered. "I'd recognise him straightaway—those shoulders are a dead giveaway." Her plump hand was laid on her plump bosom. "Wherever did you find him?"

Olive was tempted to say she'd run him down with her bicycle, but knew she didn't dare.

"He found *her*," Margaret cut in, relishing this little bit of private knowledge. Naturally, this sent a wave of intrigue through the clustered group.

"So, it was *you* who asked *him* to the dance?" Miss Danes queried.

Lady Camilla pressed her fingers to the back of her neck, where her neat upsweep was surely being mussed by the mask. She was clearly determined to cling to decorum amid a sea of gossipy, goggle-eyed creatures.

"No, he asked me," Olive lied smoothly from behind the layers of rubber and asbestos that covered her mouth. "He'd seen the poster on the village noticeboard."

"He seems to have got more than he bargained for," said a voice from behind her.

Startled, Olive turned and found herself staring disconcertingly at yet another gas mask, but this one was whimsically topped with a wide-brimmed straw hat, a cobalt-blue scarf tied at its crown. A belted caftan and flowing trousers hinted that the newcomer was none other than Violet Darling. So, too, did the timid figure of Miss Rose, half hidden behind her, readily recognisable in her Fair Isle jumper and lace-up library shoes.

"Gossip abounds," she went on sweetly. "I understand that he was with you when you found Miss Husselbee's body outside your pigeon loft."

A collective gasp went up.

"*Was* he?" Gillian said excitedly, clearly having got hold of the wrong end of the stick. No one else cared that the pair might have been trysting in the dark; curiosity had shifted from romance to death.

"He was," Olive said shortly.

"Lucky for him, he arrived in the village too late for the woman to prowl about in his private business."

"Violet, don't," Miss Rose said quietly. She laid a quelling hand on her sister's arm.

"Oh, leave off, Rose," she said with a vicious motion. "I can't be the only one who breathed a sigh of relief to hear it was finally over. The years she spent watching and listening for every little mistake, jotting notes and keeping track like an earthbound Saint Peter." Her lips curved ever so slightly. "Well, no longer."

Only a few steps away, a cluster of men were gruffly arguing, and beyond were the carefree calls of children, but there was a sudden hush over their little group. Gillian had stepped closer to her mother.

"You won't admit it," Violet went on, "none of you will, but I rather suspect there are enough of us to have formed a club. What fun those meetings would have been." She tipped her head back on a hollow laugh. "We've all heard it was poison that killed her. Someone must have administered it. Someone who is, even now, hiding behind a mask, breathing with happy relief." She paused, eyeing them each in turn. "I'll leave you with a shocking truth. It wasn't I." With that final salvo, she whirled and, with their eyes trailing her, walked to the opposite side of the green to sit beside Harriet.

"Well, she doesn't pull any punches, does she?" Margaret said admiringly.

"For all her faults, the woman is dead," Miss Danes said sharply. "She deserves a little Christian charity. And I, for one, certainly didn't kill her, no matter what she dared accuse me of."

"It would seem," Margaret said slowly, "that there's a terrifying truth to what Miss Darling suggested. It certainly makes one think." After a pause, she added, "I hear she's to be our Lizzy Bennet."

"I'm not certain Harriet was cut out for the responsibility involved in casting this play," Miss Danes snapped.

"Oh, I don't know. I rather think she tapped into our true natures," Lady Camilla replied. According to Harriet, she'd been delighted with the role of Lady Catherine—and even more so at having Miss Danes cast as Wickham.

Before Miss Danes could bluster a response, Rupert Bright called out abruptly over the din. "All right now. We're ready to start the drill."

It was then that Olive noticed that Miss Rose had slipped quietly away. She'd accepted the role of Mary Bennet without argument.

It was over almost as soon as it began. A bonfire had been built at the edge of the green, and the Home Guard now stood waving rugs on its far side in an effort to send the billowing clouds of smoke toward the cluster of villagers, most of whom patiently bided the exercise. There were, of course, the exceptions: those who hadn't quite got the hang of tightening the straps of their masks and fell into coughing fits as the smoke overcame them, and those—mostly children—who attempted to navigate the murky environs, extending their arms out in front of them like Frankenstein's monster as they slunk slowly through the man-made fog.

In those few, otherworldly moments, with her head swimming in a private cloud, Olive reviewed what she'd discovered. She was forced to admit that despite Margaret's abject refusal to share the secret that had prompted her ugly confrontation with Miss Husselbee, she believed her friend's protestations of innocence. Similarly, Violet Darling's bold admission of relief at the Sergeant Major's death didn't fit the modus operandi of a murderer. Every bit of new information led her to further questions. It couldn't hurt to take a quick peek through Miss Husselbee's notebook before it was turned over to the police—if she could ever manage to get her hands on it. Curiosity was pricking at her as fiercely as the desire for justice. She may not have been much liked, but Verity Husselbee hadn't deserved such a horrible, harrowing death.

As the smoke dissipated and the masks came off, a good number of villagers headed for the Fox and Duck. Harriet, however, was among those ready to be off. Olive could see that her thin frame, even supported by her husband, was entirely too wobbly. She camouflaged it well; with her ready smile and a tailored dress in a cherry-red and white print, Harriet perpetrated the elaborate illusion that the disease was no match for her typical aplomb. She'd be boosted into the lorry used by the Home Guard and ferried back home, but once safely ensconced in her parlour, with no one the wiser, she'd collapse in exhaustion and reach for her little enamelled box. Olive couldn't help but feel a mild sense of relief that she wasn't going off somewhere far away.

Leo sidled up beside her, his gas mask tucked under his arm and his hands thrust deep in his pockets.

"She's getting worse, isn't she?" he asked, following her gaze to Harriet and her father.

"Little by little. But she's managing," Olive said, glancing up at him.

His dog collar was softened by a camel-brown cardigan, patched at the elbows with ovals of tweed. Paired with the spectacles he now needed to review his sermons and the church accounts, he had the look of an armchair scholar. Margaret had been prompt in appending her assessment: an armchair scholar with the physique of a university oarsman. Olive tucked her tongue into her cheek at the memory of that gossipy afternoon on the little island in Pipley Pool, the pair of them sheltered behind the green curtain of its languid weeping willow. But she quickly sobered, her thoughts routed by her friend's recent suspicious behaviour.

Glancing around, she saw that Margaret was chatting with Gillian Forrester, the pair likely bemoaning the travails of wartime glamour. She had a few moments at least, and she decided to take advantage. She linked her arm with Leo's and tugged him away.

"I'm a bit worried about Margaret, though."

"You're not the only one," he admitted, his frown pulling at the corners of his eyes. "But there's no use trying to grill me for information. She hasn't confided in me."

Olive nodded once. "So, no confession of murder." Leo turned sharply in alarm, prompting her to add, "Ignore me. Miss Husselbee's sudden death has me on edge as much as Margaret's stubborn refusal to confide in me. I've been reading too many Christie mysteries and have been fancying myself an amateur sleuth." Feeling punchy, she leaned closer and said, "Shall I add you as a suspect?"

The question prompted a deep frown to overtake his typically placid face. "Why would you ask that?"

"Margaret's told me you have hidden depths." She imbued the words with teasing curiosity.

He coloured. "I don't think murder is what she was implying." In a low, solemn voice, he added, "Is it official, then? It really was murder?"

"No, not yet," she admitted. "But you can consider yourself crossed off my list. And you needn't worry. I don't suspect Margaret, either. It's honestly difficult to suspect anyone."

"Of course it is. Even in the midst of war, it's demoralizing to think of one person taking the life of another."

"You're right," she said with a sad smile. Leo was gazing over her left shoulder, and she turned to watch Margaret's approach.

"Hello, darling," her friend said, going up on her toes to buss a kiss over her fiancé's cheek, which promptly rounded in delight. But his eyes, as they met Olive's, were troubled.

She could offer only an encouraging smile. "Well, I'm off, then," she said, having caught sight of someone with whom she wanted a word.

"Dr Harrington," she called, walking quickly across the green. "May I speak with you?" The older man turned to glance back at her and then waited politely as she approached.

"Not sick, are you?" he said dryly, peering down at her from under his trilby hat, his gruff demeanour made more approachable by the flash of a dimple.

"No, nothing like that," she assured him, falling into step beside him. "How's Dotty faring?" she asked, her lips curving at the thought of the energetic Jack Russell terrier.

"She's doing just fine, and Mrs Harrington is pleased to have her as a companion." When his wife had insisted they couldn't keep the little dog in the early days of the war, he had been devastated and had declared himself in Olive's debt when she'd managed to change Mrs Harrington's mind. "And what can I do for you?" he asked shrewdly.

"I wanted to ask you about Miss Husselbee."

Dr Harrington would have been the one to examine her, making him the ideal person to answer her questions. He eyed her quizzically, his lips twitching below his moustache, as if poised to deny her.

She hurried on. "We've just been so distressed by her death, and finding her, in such a state, at the Lodge. Jonathon, poor dear, said she was confused and disoriented. She'd been sick." Remembering those bleak, horrible moments sent a shudder through Olive.

He sighed resignedly. "Yes, well," he said, briskly, "those *are* symptoms of foxglove poisoning, which, I'm sure you know, was the result of the post-mortem."

"And you're certain that's how she died?" It was an impertinent question; her only excuse was a desperate desire to escape the horrid reality of murder. Dr Harrington seemed to understand this and did not take offence.

"Digoxin isn't typically included in an autopsy toxicology screen," he told her, "but I have several patients being treated with it and thus some experience at recognizing the effects of the drug. Verity Husselbee was the picture of health, with no complaints of the heart, and yet she died of that organ's failure. Curious, I thought."

Olive nodded her understanding and said quietly, "It can't have been an accident, can it?"

"I tested her blood, and there were elevated, toxic levels of several cardiac glycosides, all of which are present in the foxglove plant." He leaned closer. "In addition," he added delicately, "there was the vomit, a known side effect of foxglove poisoning. It was a . . . er . . . reflux of a Spam and potato cake, which, I understand, was served at the dance. It would appear the cake had been dosed quite heavily."

"But the whole village was at the dance, and Miss Husselbee is certainly no wallflower. Someone should have noticed she was ill, shouldn't they?"

She must have sounded guilt ridden, as the question prompted the doctor to lay a gentle hand on her shoulder.

"The symptoms likely didn't manifest straightaway, and they might very well have come on quite gradually as she walked home or, rather, off. Her appearance at Blackcap Lodge could be the result of hallucinations or a general state of confusion caused by the poison."

Olive didn't bother to mention Miss Husselbee's final word; it seemed likely it was merely an adverse effect of the poison.

"I must be off," Dr Harrington said briskly. "If you have other questions, come along to the inquest with your father." He tipped his hat and started off again, his gas mask tucked carefully under his arm.

Olive stared after him. There could be no doubt now: murder had been done. The inquest would simply make it official.

Hearing footfalls behind her, she turned to see Captain Aldridge walking towards her through the daffodils, his face a mask of aloof detachment.

Chapter 12

Despite her uncertainty, Olive flashed a wide smile and rose on her toes to kiss him on the cheek. "Hello, Jamie," she said brightly, catching his eye and daring him to follow her lead. Rather shockingly, he took her free hand, laced his fingers with hers, and pulled her toward the river. She felt cold, her thoughts bleak, and the warmth of his callous-roughened hand was surprisingly comforting.

The New River glinted a shimmery blue-gold in the sun. It had rained the night before, and the ground was criss-crossed with muddy tracks, but the grass was a dizzying spring green, with wildflowers scattered throughout. Olive let herself imagine, just for a moment, that the war was over and life, back to normal. And then she promptly stilled, horrified that she might have accidentally given Captain Aldridge's hand a happy squeeze.

"You weren't here for the training exercise, were you?" she said abruptly, hoping he hadn't overheard the gossip pertaining to her "dishy captain," particularly her contribution to it.

"Thankfully, no. I'd only just arrived when everyone dispersed. Was that the doctor you were speaking to?" he said, nodding after the retreating form of Dr Harrington.

Deliberately ignoring his question, she asked, "Where did you come from? Don't tell me you walked from Brickendonbury."

He waited a moment to respond, perhaps wondering if he should press her for an answer, and finally said, "I left the car in the wood near the lodge and came down to the village when I realised no one was about. I brought the feed, as promised, and your uniform."

Now she did squeeze his hand, without a hint of self-consciousness. No matter what Margaret had to say on the matter, Olive was thrilled at the opportunity to don a FANY uniform and get to be doing official work, whatever it might be.

He reached into his inner jacket pocket and pulled out a trim leather volume. "And this, as well."

Her eyes widened. "Is that the notebook?" She'd never really got a good look at it in the dark. It had been pulled from Miss Husselbee's pocket and handed over straightaway.

"It is. And I've tucked the message from your friend inside."

Her startled gaze flew up to meet his steady eyes, which now seemed more blue than grey, as she tugged the notebook from his grasp. She fanned through the pages to quickly reach the bookmarked page. With a glimpse at the thin paper marked with George's precise handwriting, her heart kicked over, but she quickly tamped down her mawkish reaction, eager that he not see. "What did you find out?" she said, glancing up at him. A little thrill shot through her veins at the possibility of another clue, no matter that she was officially done with sleuthing.

"Nothing useful. The good news is, the woman appears to have had no connection to Baker Street or Station Seventeen whatsoever."

"That may be, but I'm certain there's something here that points to her murderer."

"If it *was* murder," he said pointedly, "the police will be looking for the most likely suspect." Olive opened her mouth to protest that there was a village worth of suspects, but it seemed he wasn't quite finished. "And from what I understand from Jonathon, your friend is suspect number one."

She'd been flipping through the pages, scanning the short-hand notes written in the Sergeant Major's neat script, but now her head jerked up. "Margaret?" she demanded, the pitch of her voice rising. "What on earth did he tell you?"

"That they argued about your friend's sordid past," he said dryly. Olive suddenly wanted to slap him.

"She is *not* a murderer." Never mind that intuition wasn't a precisely compelling argument for the defence.

"Really? Do you have a better suspect in mind?"

Olive stared at him, at the unruly waves of dark hair, the steady, knowing gaze, and the mocking tilt of his eyebrow, suddenly aware that cluing him in on the Mass Observation diaries and the medicinal plants scheme would serve no purpose. Miss Husselbee's sudden and unexpected demise didn't touch him— not really. He didn't know any of the players in this particular drama, and he fully expected it would play out exactly as it should, without any help from the pair of them. George would have listened to her theories and tagged along to the occasional burglary, and Olive realised she'd been harbouring a buried hope that Captain Aldridge might, somehow, fill the void he'd left behind. It was too naïvely optimistic of her. They were entirely incompatible—he would never be curious for curiosity's sake, never be reckless or daring or bold. Confiding in him would lead only to disagreements and frustration.

"Not one I'm willing to share," she said, her jaw painfully tight.

He eyed her for another long moment before replying. "Suit yourself. I doubt you'll make heads or tails of the rubbish in that little book. Just see that when you're done, you turn it in to the police."

"*Me?*" she demanded, thoroughly exasperated. "Am I to always be left to talk you out of trouble?"

His eyebrows went up, and in a startling change of pace, his lips broadened into an amused smile. "You report directly to me, Miss Bright. Or had you forgotten?"

"I hadn't forgotten, Captain Aldridge," she said tightly. "It would be impossible for me to do so, as you're determined to exert your authority at every opportunity."

His teeth flashed then, straight and white. "Aren't you supposed to be calling me Jamie?"

Ignoring him, she stepped closer and raised her index finger to poke him in his very solid chest. "I did not yet report to you when you decided to remove evidence from the body of a poisoned woman and withhold it from the police." She felt compelled to add, "Except, perhaps, on matters concerning pigeons." She then indulged herself in one more poke, for good measure.

He grabbed hold of her finger and tugged, setting her off balance and putting them very close indeed. "You're not entirely innocent, *Olive*," he said quietly, his voice an Irish purr that sent goose pimples down her spine. "*You* removed the evidence, and you did nothing to stop me from carrying it off. You, my darling, are an accessory," he said, releasing her finger and then flashing another toothy grin, this one decidedly triumphant. Before she could protest—it was a toss-up whether the endearment or the accusation was more startling—he leaned in again, quick as a flash. His lips brushing the hair at her temple, he whispered, "Just do it. And don't pretend you'll have any trouble. We both know differently."

"Yes, *sir*," she said coldly, tucking the notebook out of sight and jamming her hands into her pockets.

They walked in silence for several long moments, and Olive watched the finches dart in and out of the hedgerows, letting the birdsong calm her thoughts. A movement on the other side of the river caught her eye: a couple sat on the bench opposite, tilted toward each other and speaking softly. She slowed her steps as she realised the cosy pair was Dr Ware and Miss Rose, their movements tentative and rather awkward, their sidelong glances sweet and shy. Not wanting to intrude, she laid a rigid finger to her lips and tugged her companion into the shadow of the nearest tree.

She peered curiously around the trunk and beamed at Dr Ware's freshly combed hair and cherry-red handkerchief and Miss Rose's primly buttoned pale blue cardigan and neatly arranged skirt. It was adorably obvious that they were as sincere in their affair as she and Aldridge were disingenuous. They were perfectly suited. *This* was romance, sweet and hopeful; it did her heart good. Miss Rose must have been referring to Dr Ware when she'd confided that there was someone she hoped could see her true self. The Sergeant Major's accusations swam into her thoughts, but Olive quashed them. Dr Ware couldn't possibly have parlayed his absent-minded, thoroughly endearing innocence into any sort of intrigue. They'd barged into his shop before it was even open and taken him unawares. What had looked like shifty behaviour was likely just frazzled exasperation. He'd wanted a few moments of privacy to work on his formulas or read the latest scientific journal, and they'd interrupted. His reaction had been thoroughly justified. The contented smile that had settled over her face faded instantly at the voice in her ear.

"Which one of them is on your list of suspects?" He was peering past her, his jaw, beside hers, already darkening with stubble.

"Oh, hush," she said irritably. She took hold of his arm and dragged him off. She tried to smile, as a concession to their cover story, but she suspected she managed only a grimace. Why couldn't Tierney have been the pigeon liaison and Aldridge the killing instructor? It seemed a much better fit.

As if sensing her frustration, he began whistling out of tune.

"Must you?"

"That depends. Am I allowed to talk now?" He seemed in rather a good humour.

Olive gestured expansively for him to proceed.

"There are a few things we need to discuss, and seeing as there's no one about to eavesdrop, now's as good a time as any." When she didn't reply, he pressed on. "We're going to need a bigger pool of pigeons." He was quick to clarify. "That is, if this first mission is successful and it's decided that we'll continue to use the birds."

She turned slowly to look at him. "Let me get this straight. You're suggesting that I encourage my birds to breed in the hope that, at some future date, Station Seventeen *might* require their services."

"I wouldn't expect it requires too much encouragement, does it?"

Olive glared. "And how exactly," she said tightly, "am I expected to feed all these extra birds if it's concluded by some narrow-minded individual that they are not worth the trouble?" She spied Mr Beamish approaching along the path just as Aldridge slipped his hand around hers. Without missing a beat, she arranged her face to express the sort of shy happiness she imagined she could conceivably be feeling if her fingers were linked with those of someone who didn't behave like an utter blockhead where she and her pigeons were concerned. She then added quietly, "To say nothing of how I might explain this glut of young birds to my father when, as far as anyone knows, I have no way to feed them and no reason to encourage amorous activities."

When the scent of mothballs and perspiration had trailed off behind them, they dropped each other's hands and shifted apart as if magnetically repelled.

"Olive," he said calmly. "*This* is what you signed up for. This job requires you to be resourceful, to find a way of making people believe what you want them to believe so that they don't suspect the truth." He stopped walking, and she pulled up short beside him, rather startled at his solemn expression. "I know I don't need to ask if you can handle that, so I'll ask instead, Are you committed to doing what's necessary?"

Olive had wilted a bit, feeling abruptly ashamed to have complained about such trivial difficulties when so many across the Channel were making tremendous life-altering sacrifices every day in the face of Nazi occupation. Having Aldridge deliver the lecture was all the more demoralising. But pride snapped her resolve smartly in place. "Of course I am. The fact that I've agreed to head the Pipley Pig Club should be all the proof you need," she said, her voice heavy with sarcasm. "*Murder*," she muttered, turning and setting off at a brisk pace back toward the village. She didn't even bother to check that Aldridge was following her. "The piglets are being delivered today. I need to go look them over and make sure everything is shipshape."

Expecting him to object, she was surprised to find him amenable and grinning. "There's no shortage of code-name possibilities for you now, is there?"

"I don't need a code name," she snapped, striding briskly. "I'm not an officer *or* an agent."

"But the Brights are pigeon famous. Or so I've been led to believe," he teased, easily keeping pace. "We wouldn't want the Germans coming to look for you."

"Why not? Jonathon and Hen would likely relish the chance to dispatch them."

"Hen?" he said sharply. It was almost comical the way he could switch between personalities; one moment he was teasing and mildly charming, and the next he was abrupt and thoroughly suspicious. She wondered suddenly if he'd ever been an agent—before he'd been deemed medically unfit. If their relationship were different, she would ask him. But she'd been put dispassionately in her place enough times to know the way the wind blew, and she wasn't in the mood for the chill just now.

Olive held up her hand to stave off a peppering of questions. "Henrietta Gibbons. She's a friend of Jonathon's—a Girl Guide. We've not told her anything we shouldn't, and you don't need to strong-arm her into signing the Official Secrets Act, although I'm sure she'd dearly love to." When his eyes narrowed in either suspicion or confusion, she went on. "The pair of them are thick as thieves, with plans for sabotaging a Nazi invasion that would make your hair stand on end. But as far as you and I and the country are concerned, they're harmless." She smiled thinly. "Now," she finished, "shall we get back to business, or is it time for me to bat my eyelashes at you again?"

Olive could have been mistaken, but it looked very much as if Captain Aldridge was blushing. For some reason, that made her impishly happy. With a brusque clearing of his throat, they were back to normal again.

"Right. I assume you're on schedule with the first round of pigeons?" He paused for Olive's nod of confirmation, then went on. "I'll pick them up Sunday morning, we'll get them crated up, and they'll go out from RAF Stradishall around ten in the evening."

"I want to see them off," she said stoutly.

Watching his lungs expand in preparation for an all-suffering sigh, she cut him off. "Is there a chance you might politely consider my argument, or would you rather just dismiss the idea out of hand?"

"Have at it," he said with a magnanimous gesture. But it was ruined when he quipped, "But it's unlikely your argument will sway me."

"How fair-minded of you," she retorted. "Let me ask you this. Have any of the agents been trained to handle pigeons or been instructed how to care for them?"

"Not yet, but if—"

"If this mission goes well, then perhaps you'll look into it?" she said before sighing and starting over. "Like any animal, these birds will perform at their greatest capability if nurtured and trained. They have been trained," she said bluntly. "They will be as ready as it is possible for them to be, but they deserve a bit of consideration. Don't think me overly sentimental. I know the risks. Some will be injured, and some may never return to the loft. But given an opportunity to reduce those risks—to ensure the birds are well rested, to reduce their anxiety at being away from their mates and young, and to assure proper handling as they're loaded into the crates—I'd be a fool not to request it. And as someone invested in their longevity and the success of this mission, you'd be wise to encourage it." She crossed her arms and levelled him with a look, primed to parry every objection he laid before her.

He didn't answer immediately, which prompted a cautious optimism—even the fact that he was considering her request was more than she would have expected. After an interminable silence, broken only by the drone of an aircraft flying somewhere behind the trees, Aldridge ran a rough hand through his windswept hair, gave vent to a frustrated oath, and settled his steady gaze on her. "I'll pick you and the pigeons up at eight o'clock at the edge of the wood. You'll be home quite late, although I expect you'll have no trouble coming up with an excuse," he said dryly.

Her face warmed with a grateful smile, and she stopped just short of throwing her hands around him for an impromptu hug. Instead, she slipped her arm through his and made to tug him along the river path, wondering if she could sweet-talk him a little further. The little thrill that whipped through her with each negotiated success was enough to smooth over the brusque attitude that Aldridge seemed to think was required for efficient dealings. Willing to play the game, she endeavoured to be politely subordinate as he reviewed the expectations and instructions for their own private pigeon service.

By the time they'd reached the empty plot behind Forrester's Garage, she'd even convinced him to let her hold on to the borrowed Welbike for a bit longer—in the interest of a more rigorous training regimen for the birds. With that reprieve granted, conversation abruptly stopped, for there was a crowd gathered to welcome the newest members of the village. Three sweet-faced piglets trotted about the space, watched closely by several young children and a rowdy contingent of the Home Guard, who had outfitted the little pen with its short fence and sturdily built troughs for food and water. She smiled at Mr Battlesby, who stood off by himself at the edge of the pen; he did not respond in kind.

Olive pulled open the gate, thankful she'd had the foresight to wear trousers and boots that morning, and stepped into the pen, careful to set the latch behind her. Her nose twitched, and she flicked a glance to the far corner, where a makeshift barrow was positioned in the shade. She'd enlisted Hen and Jonathon to go around and collect scraps at kitchen doors, and judging by the haul, the whole village was investing in a future bright with bacon.

Stepping carefully through the muck, she caught the piglets up one by one, intent on giving each a thorough looking over, from their wrinkled little snouts to their twirly pink tails. "Well, that's easy enough," she announced when it was done. "The girls both have black spots on their rumps, and this little chap has a marking like a monocle around his right eye." She was pleased to see that they all looked entirely healthy and even rather adorable. One of the girls was a trifle runty, but she had the sweetest liquid eyes and fuzzy nose. Mrs Crandall's two small daughters, trussed up in their coats against the chilly breeze, were quite enamoured with the trio, judging by the fuss they made when it was time to move along. Keeping her gaze trained on the piglets as they rooted about in the muck, Olive said briskly, "They'll need names, of course."

Instantly, the peanut gallery of gawkers began calling out possible names, everything from Benji, Marigold, and Tilly to Trotter, Haggis, and Gammon, the latter suggestions raucously put forth by a portly old fellow wearing the armband of the Home Guard and a flat cap of blue and red tartan. Olive almost expected to hear the sharp tap of an umbrella ferrule—and Miss

Husselbee's strident tones calling a halt to the nonsense—but it didn't come. Instead, there were tears pricking the backs of her eyes, threatening to blur her vision.

"All right, thank you," she said quellingly as the competition became as spirited as an auction, with shouts going up from every direction. "When they're decided, I'll post their names on the pen," she promised.

With nods all around, the men unhitched themselves from the fence and turned to go. Mr Battlesby's hooded gaze seemed full of suspicion and was aimed directly at Aldridge, but as Olive opened her mouth to speak to him, he turned brusquely away.

Aldridge, who was looking less starchily official, with his forearms resting against the top fence rail, turned his gaze to follow the man's ambling retreat. "It might be easier all around if they don't have names," he suggested.

Olive stared at him. "Are we not to talk to them, either, or show them any affection? Is it better that their lives should be miserable simply because they are bound for the dinner table?"

A hand clapped comradely against Aldridge's shoulder, and Mr Duerden advised, "Pick your battles, son. This one"—he flicked his head to indicate Olive and shot her a wink—"is willing to die on every hill."

Olive's lips twisted wryly. "He's no stranger to such battles, Mr Duerden," she said tartly, spearing Aldridge with a look. "You needn't worry about him." She turned back towards the piglets as the men moved off, snickering among themselves. Judging by the general bonhomie of the group, their next stop would be the Fox and Duck.

When their voices had faded away, he spoke. "Swilly, Finn, and Eske."

Olive swivelled to stare once again at Aldridge's long length, which was folded over the fence. "Pardon?"

"Swilly, Finn, and Eske," he repeated. "All three are rivers in County Donegal, Ireland."

"My question was really, What of them?"

The sun had disappeared, swallowed up by scudding clouds that chilled the air and seemed to promise drizzle, if not outright rain, in the hours ahead. In the altered light, every bit of him appeared as if in stark relief—darker, blunter, solid. His eyes, reflecting the sky above, were lit with a fierce intensity and now seemed the colour of shadowed twilight.

"I'm proposing them as names for the pigs."

Olive blinked, letting his suggestions roll over themselves in her head, trying them out even as she wondered if he was having her on. His face gave nothing away, and she wondered what had prompted his thoroughly unexpected outburst. Was it a bit of homesickness? A desperate white flag sent up in hopes of avoiding yet another argument? Or was it an olive branch? There was no way to tell without asking him outright, and even then, his answer might not be truthful. But without a clue, she was determined to settle on the latter.

She glanced behind her, and her gaze arrowed to where the animals in question were currently prodding their rosy pink snouts at the edges of the tipped barrow, evidently tantalised by the nauseating aroma of scraps.

"Finn," she called, feeling absurdly self-conscious. But instantly, one head lifted quizzically—the monocled male, his mouth ringed in some questionable food matter—and she couldn't help but grin. "Well, I suppose that settles that." She carefully navigated the muck in the pen and laid a hand on the warm back of the smaller of the two girls. "You can be Swilly, and she'll be Eske." She grinned at Aldridge, and his lips curved ever so slightly.

He said no more on the subject, which meant one more mystery filed in the TOP SECRET folder, which she imagined held all the answers regarding Jameson Aldridge. It should have irked her. She didn't like deliberate secrecy; she felt it implied an underlying mistrust. But she, too, was going to need to learn to pick her battles.

"Pigs and pigeons," he said musingly as they started for home.

"Don't worry, Captain Aldridge. I can manage them both quite well."

He didn't dare argue. With an exhausted sigh, she tucked her arm into his and leaned unconsciously into his warmth. Her immediate thought was that it was a very sturdy arm, but she refused to think any more about it.

"Tell me more about the mission," she urged.

With a sigh of his own, he informed her that the upcoming mission would actually be a second attempt of Operation Josephine B. The first had been scrapped due to an equipment malfunction and had ended with a crash landing at home that had injured its six-man Polish team. This time, they'd be sending a team from Baker Street's RF Section, which was linked to de Gaulle's Free French. She was quick to remind him that three pigeons would be going along, as well. They'd all be parachuted into France, near Pessac, and tasked with planting explosives and incendiary devices that would disable the transformer station there. As the station controlled a Nazi submarine base, a successful sabotage mission would be a coup for the Allies.

"And your expectations for the pigeons?" she asked quietly.

"Immediate information—success or failure. We might not otherwise get confirmation for weeks or even months."

Olive nodded, suddenly eager to get her hands on a map and plot out the birds' likely route home.

After a moment, he spoke again, this time with a trace of humour in his voice.

"Would it shock you to learn that the explosive devices designed for this mission use a condom?" Not certain whether or not he was teasing, she didn't answer. "The prophylactic is used to waterproof the delay switch, which, for the time being, happens to be an aniseed ball." He slipped his hand into his pocket and produced a little bag of the sweets. Feeling suddenly, marvellously, in on the secret, Olive grinned at him, selected an aniseed ball from the bag, and popped it into her mouth. "A fair bit of irony that the devices are called *limpet* mines," he said, clearly in a punchy mood himself.

But it quickly faded, and his typical reserve had slid back into place by the time they reached the lodge.

After hauling a fifty-pound sack of pigeon corn around the barn to the back of the garden, where a little shed stood forgotten in the shade of a sprawling apple tree, he looked around him in silence. He didn't appear convinced by her assertion that this was the perfect hiding place for the contraband, but then he wasn't aware of her father's aversion to earthly pastimes. Jonathon had been given free reign and full responsibility of their back garden the day he'd arrived, and no one had interfered since.

Content for once to have her advice accepted without debate, she refrained from comment. But when he yanked his jersey over his head, exposing a white cotton undershirt and the outline of corded muscles beneath, she stared unabashedly as her teeth clamped down on her lower lip. Her thoughts were instantly mired in memories of Liam and those rare evenings her flatmate had been away. Some things, she'd discovered, worked better than others at keeping spirits up.

Without warning, he lunged unexpectedly sideways, careening roughly against her and sending her teeth considerably deeper than intended. Clutching his arm, Olive winced in pain as she tried to regain her balance. "What is it? What's the matter?" she demanded, her heart rate beginning to speed as her eyes roved in confusion.

Her gaze fell on a familiar calico cat stepping gingerly along the wall of the shed, heading for the open door. Olive managed to swing it shut before the animal could nip inside, prompting a scornful look and a twitch of its ear. One glance at Aldridge showed a nearly identical reaction as he stared at the unrepentant creature. Olive flicked her gaze between the pair of them, touching the back of her finger to the fresh cut on her lip. It was going to swell, she was sure of it. One more thing to explain without truly explaining.

"You *really* need to get hold of yourself," she scolded, her voice awash with exasperation, even as she stared in admiration at the solid strength of him. "A liaison with this loft requires you to occasionally come into contact with cats. Are you prepared to face your irrational dislike of them and do what's necessary in the face of these harmless creatures?" she demanded in a parody of his earlier gravity.

"It's entirely possible I should have let you warn me off that first day. You may not have your father's notoriety, but as far as I'm concerned, you have plenty of your own." He pulled his gaze away from the cat and promptly focused on her lips. "Did I do that?" Chagrin warring with concern, he stepped closer. "Let me see."

"It's nothing."

"You're bleeding."

"Because I bloody bit it when you shied away from Psyche." In response to his raised eyebrow, she clarified. "The pigeons are all named for characters from children's literature, and the barn animals' names are pulled from mythology. And, evidently, the pigs are to be named for the geography of Ireland."

"Naturally." And then he was pulling her fingers away to stare more intently at her mouth. He dusted his hand against the leg of his trousers, settled his thumb in the centre of her lower lip, and rolled it gently away from her teeth.

"It's nothing," she objected, her words slurring slightly, as a shiver of awareness ran through her.

He ignored her. "There's a tiny gash," he confirmed, releasing his hold as he met her eyes. "And it's already swelling a bit." Waiting a beat, he added, "The good news is, you've got a ready-made explanation."

It took a moment, his steady gaze on hers, eyebrows raised expectantly, but when it hit, she felt the dull thud of blood pumping in her throat, her lip, and her temples. "Right. I should have thought of that straightaway. A little more proof for the pudding. You'll be the talk of the village." No need to tell him he already was—the gossip had little to do with her and everything to do with his striking face and smartly uniformed physique.

"And you? Will you weather the resultant talk?"

"Oh, I'll be on the fast track to fallen womanhood," she said dryly. "But no one will blame me—except possibly my father. You've yet to win him over. He could tell you weren't suitably impressed with his pigeons."

He snorted. "I suppose that lends the whole business a certain amount of credibility, doesn't it? What father doesn't dislike the man courting his daughter, at least initially?" Shrugging good-naturedly, he said, "All right, then? I'm sorry for that."

"It's fine. I shouldn't have been biting my lip."

She checked to see that the shed door was tightly latched and started back through the garden. A glance at the parlour window confirmed that Harriet was there, reclined on her chaise, smoking a cigarette. She raised her hand in a wave. Olive returned the gesture and was turning to warn Aldridge when he slipped his hand into hers. She tensed, forced to remember all over again that it was merely a cover.

"Oh, what a tangled web we weave," Olive quoted, plastering a wide, besotted smile on her face and trying to relax the stiffness in her shoulders. He squeezed her hand, and for a single lovely moment, she didn't feel quite so alone in her deception.

"She'll wonder why you've removed some of your clothing."

"I don't suppose we can just go with the same story . . ."

She cut her eyes around at him. He grinned. "Point taken. I assume you'll come up with something."

The conversation paused while he slipped his jersey back on, but the moment his head was free, he carried on.

"As far as anyone is concerned, your FANY training doesn't start until next week. Use these remaining days of freedom"— the sardonic quirk of his lips at that designator was unexpected, to say the least—"to ensure everything is in order for Sunday." He levelled her with a long look. "I don't plan to see you until then unless there's a change in plan. Put in a call to Brickendon-bury if you have a problem, and I'll come to you."

Back at the car, he handed her a folded uniform and a small canvas bag full of rings, colour-coded for Baker Street. They were intended to help identify her birds if they lost their way, and thereby ensure any messages they carried were forwarded to the appropriate personnel.

"I can't use these," she said abruptly.

"Why not?"

"The rings have to be slipped over a chick's foot while it's still bendable. Only veteran flyers—full-grown birds at least three seasons old—can be used for these missions. The young birds don't yet have the training or the stamina."

"Fine. You can use them going forward, for the younger birds."

"If I slip these rings on our chicks, they'll stay on for the life of the birds. I don't think there's anyone in the world resourceful enough to explain that to my father." She handed the bag back.

He cursed but took it, then rubbed a hand across his jaw.

"Don't worry. The birds will make their own way back, but if they do happen to get lost, their rings are marked with nomen-clature specific to the Bright loft. Eventually, they'll show up here. Rest assured that any messages will be delivered to Brick-endonbury straightaway, more quickly for the loan of the Wel-bike."

He snorted and said offhandedly, "What did you make of the test message that Hook carried back?"

Olive stared at him, giving nothing away. "I'd forgotten all about it. I called you when it arrived. It's still in its canister, as you never came to retrieve it. Shall I get it?"

His eyes met hers, assessing. "You do understand that you're not to read any message without proper authorisation."

"I understood the first time you told me." She'd learned her lesson, and she suspected he knew it.

"Quite. It's rather uncanny how literally nothing goes as planned in my dealings with you, Miss Bright."

"It's the cats, Captain Aldridge," she said snarkily.

He laughed then, one short chuckle, before stepping toward her. "In case your stepmother is still watching," he said before he cupped the back of her neck and planted a warm kiss on her forehead.

Olive could think of nothing to say, and when he turned and walked away from her, she was left to stare after him. Her first impression of Jameson Aldridge had not prepared her for his skilful handling of their forced flirtation, which left her wondering whether he'd had a bit of practice in this sort of cover story. All she knew of him was that he'd lost his sister in the Blitz; everything else was a mystery, and the closer he guarded his secrets, the more she itched to uncover them. He didn't seem to be similarly intrigued where she was concerned. Perhaps he knew everything already. With this possibility hovering in her thoughts, she walked back to the lodge and slipped upstairs.

Wednesday, 27 November 1940
Peregrine Hall, Pipley
Hertfordshire

It was a victory felt through the Commonwealth when a few intrepid young girls stormed a Boy Scout rally in 1908 and informed Lieutenant General Lord Baden-Powell, in no uncertain terms, that girls were quite as capable as boys. It prompted him, quite rightly, to found a partner organisation in their honour.

Despite being well past the age of inclusion, I couldn't help but embrace the spirit of the Guides, as well as their motto: Be Prepared. Both have served me quite well, in Pipley and farther afield. I've gone so far as to devise my own set of challenges in the hopes of bettering myself and my little village.

There have been some challenges I feared I'd never master; the Nurture badge, in particular, was unexpectedly difficult. Having set myself to teach a fumbly-fingered R.D. to knit, I couldn't have predicted that the true test of my efforts would come in instructing the woman how to make a proper cup of tea. But I prevailed; tea was brewed—and enjoyed!—and a pair of socks knit for some unsuspecting soldier. It was a good day, and I must say, I'm prouder of that badge than any other.

I may not officially be a Girl Guide, but preparedness is most certainly my watchword. I'm never without my umbrella, pencil, or paper, and I very often have my binoculars, as well. If the Germans do decide to invade, they will rue the day they tussled with me.

V.A.E. Husselbee

Chapter 13

The conversation on market day resolved itself into two camps: gossip concerning Miss Husselbee's murder and chatter surrounding the contest that had been devised as an impromptu distraction from said murder to raise money for the Red Cross. The ladies of the village had poured forth in their chapeaux, shillings in hand, all hoping to win Best Decorated Spring Hat and be awarded the grand prize: a lemon, sent by someone's cousin all the way from the United States.

As she wended her way through the crowd, a study in comportment as she attempted to balance the lavish arrangement of wildflowers, feathers, and fern fronds affixed to her hat—there might even have been a mushroom or two—Olive's only thought was to reach the judge's table without running into Aldridge.

Eager to avoid all aspects of the contest, Olive had declined to enter. But as she'd stepped into the parlour that morning, the curls of silver smoke already in evidence, it was clear fate had other plans. Harriet had collaborated with Jonathon on a particularly elaborate creation and had been very much looking forward to showing it off. In the throes of yet another bad day, she had admitted she wasn't feeling up to venturing into the village and had solemnly asked Olive to go in her stead—it was a good cause, after all. Olive had, naturally, acquiesced. She would have worn the hat straight up the drive to Brickendonbury if Harriet had asked.

Olive had stayed up late the night before, poring over the cryptic entries in Miss Husselbee's notebook, searching for a hidden clue and coming up short. The entire process had thoroughly frustrated and exhausted her. As a result, she was wandering the stalls on the high street, fuzzy headed and distracted, and was quite relieved to drop Harriet's shillings into the tin and leave the hat, positioned to best advantage, beside a brown felt number that looked as if it had been turned inside out to cradle a taxidermised bird and its trio of eggs. Free of the cumbersome weight, Olive experienced an odd sensation of floating and gazed up at the blue-grey sky, feeling fanciful. Mrs Crabbleton promptly bumped into her, wearing a cloche hat utterly engulfed in puffy white hydrangea blossoms, which made her look like a bobble-headed ninny. Olive smiled encouragingly and murmured, "Tremendous."

Despite the warmer weather, and the more regular appearance of the sun, summer was still a ways off, and as such, the offerings at the various stalls were less than exciting. While imaginations were bursting with stone fruit and berries, tomatoes and corn, and the surplus that would be used to set up jam and chutney, instead they had beets, winter squash, and a few late cabbages, all of which had ceased to inspire any excitement months ago, if they ever had. Rather glumly, she drifted away a bit, not in any mood for gossip.

When she noticed Leo and Margaret tucked into the shadow of the lych-gate, talking earnestly, she couldn't help but agree with Harriet's decision that Margaret would be a perfect Jane Bennet, opposite Leo's Charles Bingley. As she looked on, Leo took hold of Margaret's upper arms and gave her a frustrated shake. Tugging away, her composure cracked, Margaret's fingers clutched the locket that hung around her neck. His brow an angry furrow, Leo suddenly glanced up and raked his frustrated gaze over the lane until it settled inevitably on Olive. Feeling suddenly gauche, Olive raised her hand in a tentative greeting. Ever conscious of the conduct befitting a vicar, he struggled for composure, the frustration fading from his face to be replaced by a polite smile. Without even glancing in her direction, Margaret turned and walked away. While Leo stared grimly after her, Olive was struck by how the couple's lives were mirroring their character roles: they'd moved past the early days of infatuation into loneliness and uncertainty. She could only hope for a happy ending.

As she walked toward Forrester's Garage, she marshalled her thoughts. Margaret was quite obviously hiding something, and while Olive didn't believe her friend was responsible for the Sergeant Major's death, it was entirely possible that Margaret knew something that could lead to finding the killer. Maybe she knew who'd done it and why.

What else could *it be? What sort of secret would need to be kept assiduously hidden away from every living soul?*

Olive stopped walking, stunned into immobility as a thought occurred to her. Could it possibly be that straightforward? Could Margaret's secret be the same sort she was harbouring herself? She frowned, stepping slowly now, keeping her eyes trained on the never-ending line of the yew hedge.

Margaret's behaviour did not hint at a person working clandestine operations for the War Office. For one thing, she was too emotional, vacillating between anger, desperation, guilt, and even fear. While Olive had, admittedly, experienced her share of anger since being approached, all of it had been conveniently directed at Aldridge. Add to that the fact that her friend was making no real attempt to devise an excuse for her odd behaviour—her reason for arguing with the Sergeant Major was flimsy at best. If she was truly involved in some sort of top-secret business, she'd have a cover story. Olive decided she could safely eliminate that possibility, which meant she was stymied all over again.

In truth, it came as no surprise. She'd only scratched the surface of every clue, rather than seek out the curiosities and inconsistencies that surrounded it. Poirot would surely have been disgusted with her, but, really, what could he expect? It wasn't as if she had any experience with this sort of thing—if she was to compare herself to any of Mrs Christie's sleuths, it should be Frankie and Bobby. Having mired herself in a murder investigation, Frankie described the experience as slipping between the covers of a book. Olive understood this utterly. Added to her discombobulation was the disadvantage of being rather alone in the matter. Aldridge wasn't any help, she didn't want to involve Jonathon, and who else was there now that George was gone? No one. It wasn't her responsibility, but her curiosity—not to mention her sense of justice—was well and truly piqued, and the prospect of solving Miss Husselbee's murder was an enticing challenge. She could do this.

Olive closed her eyes, determined to focus.

The scene of a moment ago ran back in her mind like a cinema reel: Leo's freckled knuckles, showing pale against the sleeve of Margaret's violet jumper, the worry and shame evident on both their faces, and Margaret's fist pressed tightly to her collarbone, her locket tucked inside.

The locket. It was clearly dear to Margaret, but she'd never shown it to Olive. It couldn't be from Leo—a treasured keepsake from her beloved fiancé would never have been skipped over in all their gossipy chats. Olive brightened, feeling somewhat vindicated. The locket was undoubtedly quite irrelevant, but it was a curiosity, maybe even a clue.

Resolved to quiz her friend about it at the next opportunity that presented itself, Olive rounded the corner and ran smack into Violet Darling. Both reached out to steady themselves, but when the other woman would have pulled away, Olive tightened her grip.

A legitimate suspect had literally fallen into her hands, and Olive didn't want to let her go. Still, a curious look from Violet prompted her release.

Violet Darling had been absent from the village for nearly ten years. It was difficult to imagine that she'd be prompted to murder someone within twenty-fours of her return. Even if it was Miss Husselbee. Then again, the Sergeant Major *had* threatened to expose her—but with what? It was precisely the sort of answer that had eluded Olive over the course of her short-lived investigation. To say nothing of the fact that Violet Darling intrigued her. The woman was an enigma: simultaneously fragile and self-possessed, villager and stranger, mysterious and relatable all at once. A chance to talk to her, away from ears perpetually pricked for gossip, was too good to pass up.

Her avid gaze swept over Violet Darling in her trim periwinkle jumper and full navy skirt, a magenta patterned scarf covering her red-gold curls. In contrast, Olive's worn boots, shabby tweed jacket, and quickly pinned-up hair, likely mussed by the hat, were surely a bit cringeworthy. But now wasn't the time to quibble. "Miss Violet," she said brightly. "I was hoping to get a chance to talk to you."

"I object to you using that godawful honorific. You've grown up quite a bit since I left. Why don't we pretend we're of an age," Violet suggested blandly.

"Fair enough," Olive agreed, turning so that she was now headed in the direction that Violet was going. "I rather think Miss Rose enjoys that little bit of extra fuss, but the two of you are quite different, aren't you?"

Violet slid her a sloe-eyed glance. "What was your first clue?"

"You were the sister who stole away the man I fancied myself in love with." The words had just popped out, and now they hung like fog in the air between them. "I suspect Miss Rose didn't even like him," Olive finished awkwardly.

After a beat of stunned silence, Violet laughed, a full, throaty sound that seemed to have been stolen from someone else entirely. "I'd forgotten how mouthy you are. In a twelve-year-old, it's too tedious, but in a twentysomething, it's rather fun."

Olive shrugged, relaxing a bit as she let her memory drift back. "I was smitten the first time Emory Hammond roared down Mangrove Lane in his shiny silver coupe, nearly sending me and my bicycle careening onto the verge. That devil-may-care smile of his was dangerously distracting. And my crush only deepened with each subsequent glimpse of it."

She glanced over to see Violet staring into the distance, perhaps remembering the beginning of her own love affair. But then she blinked suddenly, fumbled in the pocket of her skirt, and pulled out a packet of cigarettes and a trim gold lighter. Her fingers shook ever so slightly as she tussled with the breeze for a reliable flame. Once she'd taken a long drag and puffed it away, she answered, her eyes faraway. "He was very charming. But you're right. Rose didn't like him. She thought him a slippery fellow."

Olive thought back to their chat the night of the Daffodil Dance. Violet had steered her away from the name Hammond, but she'd been too distracted to pursue the topic. Now, hearing her use of the past tense, the reality clicked into place.

"What do you mean, he *was*? What happened to him?"

Judging by Violet's raised eyebrows, she'd heard the odd note of accusation shading Olive's words. "He died," she said flatly. "It was rather a shock for me, too."

"Of course. I'm sorry," Olive said, chagrined. "Was it recently?"

"It was years ago." She'd crossed one arm over her midsection and propped the other elbow on top, holding the cigarette poised at the edge of her lips, as she stared out over the fields, lost in her own thoughts. "Shall I tell you a secret?"

A thrill of excitement zipped through Olive's veins at this serendipitous offer. "Only if you want to," she said, fighting to keep her voice nonchalant.

A moment passed, and several strolling steps along the river, and Olive wondered if she'd changed her mind. There was a pebble in her boot, but she didn't want to risk the distraction required to get it out.

"We ran away together, but we never married," Violet said almost carelessly, tapping away the ash from her cigarette.

Olive slowed her steps, startled but carefully considering this new information, trying to figure if it was a clue or simply a point of interest. "That's why you're still a Darling."

Violet's lips curved in a rueful smile. "I was determined to be a famous author even then, and Emory was insistent that we'd have more fun as ourselves than as a tedious married couple. He had a lot of ideas," she said, her eyes glazed with memory. "Not all of them worked out the way he'd planned."

Olive bit her lip, her mind grasping at something just out of reach; then suddenly she understood. "*That's* what Miss Husselbee—"

Eyes the colour of stormy seas snapped back to the present, only to be shuttled off again to focus on a more recent memory. "Yes," she said abruptly, somewhat breathlessly. "Running off with a man is bad enough, but if you don't actually get married . . ." She shook her head, clicking her tongue against her teeth. "Well, then you've set yourself up for a lecture and assorted threats from the village busybody." Her lips quirked with what might have been pain. "Too many years have passed for it to make any difference now—I'm the village pariah as it is—but Verity lived by a different set of standards, the impossible sort." The implication that they'd ultimately led to her murder hung between them in the silence.

"So, you weren't at all concerned that she knew and evidently planned on revealing your secret?"

She turned her head and gazed shrewdly at Olive. "You're try-ing to solve her murder, aren't you?" She threw down her fin-ished cigarette and stepped on it, then viciously ground the little nub into the dust.

Olive's teeth once again worried at her lip. Given the amount of waffling she was doing, she wasn't entirely certain how to an-swer.

Violet went on, "If I sew an *A* on my chest like Hester Prynne, do you suppose I'll be eliminated as a suspect?" She was punchy now, and Olive chalked it up to painful memories prompted by an ambush of sorts.

"Please don't do that," Olive said feelingly. "You'll send the village into such a tizzy, we may never recover." She kicked at a stone, the one in her boot having somehow taken care of itself. "And besides, I don't believe you did it."

Me, I do not eliminate a suspect so easily, Poirot's voice whispered in her ear. Olive roundly shushed it.

This vote of confidence seemed enough for Violet, because she didn't say any more on the topic, and for a little while, they walked in silence, eventually crossing over the bridge to wander back toward the village. The scatter of pebbles underfoot blended pleasantly with the chirp and titter of birds darting amidst the hedgerow, searching for early fruit, and Olive spent the time de-ciding how to frame her next question.

"Do you have any idea where the cake came from?"

"The infamous meat and potato cake? None. I saw it there on the table and instantly decided it was going to be the life of the party." She paused before adding, "Irrefutable evidence that the war has officially reached Pipley."

She was once again staring out over the countryside, and Olive wondered what she could be thinking of them all, and where she was wishing to be instead. "Was anyone manning the table be-fore you arrived?"

"There were plenty of women, tittering like hens, but it didn't appear as if anyone in particular was in charge."

"And no one took any notice of a tent card with the word *Spam* on it?"

She shrugged, the movement efficiently indicating her utter lack of interest in village matters. "Perhaps there was more pressing gossip."

Olive couldn't argue with that logic. And while she had the distinct feeling further questioning would get her nowhere, she nevertheless tried again. "And after Miss Husselbee ate her slice? What happened to the rest of it?"

Violet looked at her, her eyes shifting focus yet again. "I've no idea. I carried the punchbowl into the kitchen when it needed to be refilled and took the opportunity to slip out the back door." Once again, she pulled out the packet of cigarettes, then promptly said a word in a language Olive didn't recognise. It sounded very like a curse. "I've run out." She peered at Olive from beneath lowered lids. "I don't suppose you have any?"

"Sorry, no. I find they make it hard to breathe."

"For me the opposite is true," she confided. She crossed her arms and splayed her fidgety fingers over her skin, dug her nails in gently. "The smoke creates a murky little room where I can escape for a moment from the rest of the world. And breathe."

Staring at her profile, Olive couldn't help but think of a painted china doll that had cracked ever so slightly, the broken slivers falling inward, so that she could never be repaired. With every movement, those tiny pieces jangled inside her, bitter reminders of her life's little tragedies.

"I suppose if I felt like that," Olive said, "I might take up smoking, breathing be damned." She wondered suddenly if that was the reason Harriet took refuge in her little enamelled box.

"You really shouldn't. It's a nasty habit," Violet said. The corner of her mouth edged up in a sly smile, which prompted an answering one from Olive.

"Why did you never come back?" she asked quietly.

"There was no reason to—and plenty of reasons not to. But fate intervened, disguised as a simple-minded tyrant, and here I am, already mired in intrigue." Violet laughed humourlessly.

"In fairness, you'll be playing the much-loved role of Elizabeth Bennet for the foreseeable future."

The road curved, and in the distance, the red brick and the Tudor striped gables of the Fox and Duck stood out against the azure spring sky. Olive wondered if that was where they were heading.

"A fact that has not endeared me to anyone," Violet said, her eyes world-weary. "With the possible exception of your stepmother," she added, staving off Olive's protest. "I honestly don't know what possessed me to agree to do it. Likely I was so shocked to be offered something other than the role of scandalous Lydia or flighty Kitty, I went out of my head." She flicked a sly glance at Olive. "Rose, meanwhile, seems quite content with the role of Mary."

Conversation lapsed, and the fizzy symphony of bumblebees and dragonfly wings sent a relaxing calm over Olive's thoughts. She forgot the hat contest, the locket, the missing diary entries, and Aldridge. The sounds of market day were pleasantly muted, and the war seemed very far away.

Violet stooped to pick up a long, limber branch, stripped by weather or wildlife from one of the trees that towered above them. She was holding it as she would a sabre, swishing it through the air, testing its heft. "I rather expected the tall, dark, and broody officer you brought to the dance to be cast as Fitzwilliam Darcy," she said slyly. "But then, I suppose, you would have wanted to be Lizzy."

"Darcy was difficult," Olive said, refusing to rise to the bait, "particularly seeing as the village is left with men better suited to play Mr Bennet or Mr Collins. Harriet couldn't even convince most of them to do that."

"Yes, well, Dr Ware was resistant at first, but he's evidently come round." Olive had been baffled when Harriet had informed her he'd changed his mind; neither had any idea who'd convinced him. But there was a secret little smile playing about Violet's lips as they reached the crossroads that fronted the pub. Violet stared at the carved sign hanging over the door, her eyes lit with apparent nostalgia. "Coming in for a drink?" she asked, moving backwards, as if drawn by an invisible string.

"No time. I hadn't actually planned to walk this far. I was meant to be checking in at the garage."

"I'm sorry to lead you astray," Violet said. "But I think you knew exactly what you were doing. Fair warning, Olive Bright. I fully intend to ferret out *your* secrets when next we meet. All's fair, you know." And with a little wave, she pulled the painted green door open and slipped into the dim interior. Olive was left staring after her, wondering if her skills at deception were shortly to be put to the test.

She retraced her steps back to the high street, only to discover that the winning hat was a trim black one decorated with flowers made of pink wool bouclé and jet beads. The judges had clearly voted sensible over sensational. After hoisting the fanciful allotment that had been Harriet's entry, she propped it back on her head, having decided that wearing it would likely be easier than carrying it. She let herself imagine that the weight of it was helping to focus her thoughts or, at the very least, squishing them together to make room for new ones. As she slowly walked to Forrester's, she ran her mind back over her recent conversation. Violet had been dismissive and rather flippant over Miss Hussel-bee's intentions to ravage her reputation. Had she been bluffing? She'd been uniquely positioned to make the cake appear and disappear, putting it on display just long enough to tempt the Sergeant Major. Then again, judging by her general ennui, anyone could have done the deed right under her nose. Much as

Olive liked Violet Darling, it seemed she couldn't yet eliminate her as a suspect.

She approached the garage from the rear, checking on her porcine charges as she passed. Jonathon, she knew, would be coming by later to fill their troughs, so she needn't worry about that. Instead, she picked them out by name, her thoughts turning to Aldridge as she admired their quizzical little snouts and spry little bodies. Maybe the business of a pig club wouldn't be too bad; then again, she'd been volunteered for the task because no one else had wanted it.

She walked slowly around to the front, where a truck had been backed to fill the tanks with petrol. Skirting the hose, which lay like a snake over the gravel, she slipped into the darkened garage, intending to inquire about her bicycle. She could hear raised voices behind the closed office door and so went to the table along the back wall to retrieve their spare accumulator. She didn't particularly relish lugging it home, but it would be easier than trying to balance it on the Welbike. She set it on the floor beside her, hitched herself onto a stool, and prepared to wait.

The conversation was muffled, although it was clear from the tone of voices that neither man was pleased. She cringed, somewhat dreading the upcoming conversation. George's father was rather brusque at the best of times, and Poppins's stint as a stowaway had disgruntled him. Now he seemed downright angry. She swung her legs, the garbled words swimming through her subconscious, until two things happened simultaneously.

At the very moment Lady Camilla appeared, walking briskly across the yard, dubiously eyeing the lorry, a single word slipped through the cracks of the office door, as clear as if it had been spoken directly to her: *blackmail*.

Olive schooled her features and smiled at the other woman's approach. Lady Camilla was utterly out of place in the dingy garage, smelling freshly of lavender in a pale yellow dress and navy cardigan. Pearls hung from her ears, set off by sharp cheek-bones and an elegant chignon. On her head was a navy blue straw hat, decorated with neatly looped white ribbons tucked amid sprays of daffodils. She was carrying a basket with a tea towel tucked over its contents.

"What a marvellous hat," Lady Camilla said, her words prompting an immediate hush behind the office door.

"It's Harriet's," Olive said quickly, brushing away a fern frond that was now drooping over her left eye.

"I'm afraid it's looking rather thirsty, dear." She put a tentative hand up to assess the daffodils on her own hat. "I would have loved to have won the prize," she confided. "I've been missing the lemon in my tea for *ages*. Perhaps I could pop in on the winner and plead my case," she said mischievously. She looked around at the jumble of tyres, petrol cans, and mechanics' tools crowded into the space and said, "Picking up?" Olive gestured to the bulky accumulator sitting beside her on the floor, and the older woman smiled knowingly. "Harriet is a stickler for her programmes." She held up the basket. "I've brought along some dinner for George's father."

As if on cue, the door to the office opened, emitting a greasy individual in a flat cap, oil-stained dungarees, and a wrinkled grey jacket: Harry Danes. His gaze flicked to each of their hats in turn; then, with a curt nod, he strode out the bay door and bent to grapple with the petrol hose. Mr Forrester stepped through the doorway next and eyed their fancy millinery as he approached.

"Either of those prizewinners?" he asked bluntly, roughly rubbing his hands on a filthy rag. Olive's nose twitched at the incongruent smell of him: petrol and . . . vanilla? Beside her, Lady Camilla's hands were clenched on the handle of the basket.

"Unfortunately, the lemon has slipped through both our grasps," his wife said. "But I've brought a couple of ham rolls and a ginger beer," she said. Her smile was tight as she handed him the basket. "Don't work too hard, darling."

Feeling caught in the middle, Olive spoke up quickly. "I'm picking up"—she hoisted the beast of a battery—"and wanted to inquire about my bicycle."

Mr Forrester swiped stained fingers through the fringe of hair that had fallen onto his forehead, and focused his deep-set blue eyes disconcertingly on her face. "I've had a lot of interruptions in the past few days," he said, flicking a glance at the truck outside that had started with a rumble and was now spitting up gravel as it pulled out of the yard. "I'll have it finished by Friday."

"Until Friday, then," Olive said shortly, grabbing the handle of the accumulator and nodding a goodbye.

"I need to be off, as well," Lady Camilla said briskly. She turned abruptly and fell into step with Olive, and they walked out into the anaemic sunshine. "Will you be at the play rehearsal tomorrow evening?"

It took a moment for Olive's brain to shift gears. "Yes, I'll be there." Prompted by curiosity if nothing else. There was a fair chance that the murderer would be in attendance, as well.

"Wonderful." Lady Camilla beamed.

Her mind still fumbling with what she'd overheard, Olive looked back. Her eyes sifted through the shadows of the garage before coming to rest on Mr Forrester. Her heart thumped painfully as she realised his gaze had tracked them across the yard.

Turning sharply away, she babbled, "Have you had a letter from George yet?"

"Not yet, dear." Lady Camilla reached for Olive's hand and gave it a warm squeeze. Olive could see the dusting of powder that had settled in the fine lines of her face. "We just need to carry on without him for a time. With luck, this war will be over before he even gets his chance in the air."

"I assume Mr Forrester told you that I made George take one

of the pigeons with him." Seeing her start of surprise, Olive fished the letter from her pocket. "This is the message he sent back with her."

George's mother quickly scanned the page, her hands vibrating with some strong emotion. "But where would they send them?" she asked, her composure cracking slightly as she worried over George's reference to a training relocation.

"I've no idea," Olive said, meeting her eyes. "I've been hoping for another letter, but there's been nothing so far."

"Perhaps I can ask my father." Lady Camilla's mouth had settled into a moue of distaste, and she looked sadly at Olive. "Although I'd really rather not. We've not been on speaking terms since I married George's father." She looked down at the letter in her hands and folded it neatly along the creases; then she breathed deeply, as if girding herself for the task ahead. "But," she said brightly, "he's terribly important in the War Office, and I need to know where George is being sent. Needs must." Her fingers clung to the folded letter for another moment before she handed it back to Olive.

"Will you let me know what he says?" Olive asked hopefully.

"Of course, dear." They'd reached the spot where they'd need to part ways, and Lady Camilla reached for her hand. "There's been a lot of talk about your young man, Olive, and while I can certainly see what's drawn you to him, I would caution you to guard your heart carefully. Regret is a terrible thing."

Abruptly flustered, Olive could only imagine she'd misunderstood. "George and I, we're not—"

"Oh, I know, dear. And perhaps I've already immersed myself too thoroughly in the character of Lady Catherine, nosing about in others' business, but I've always been so proud of you and your aspirations, and I wouldn't want you to be deterred from them."

"Thank you, Lady Camilla," Olive said, somewhat baffled by

the well-meant advice. "I'll keep that in mind." They said good-bye, and she watched the retreating form of George's mother for a moment before turning away.

Her walk home, typically pleasant, was dogged by two ominous words: *blackmail* and *regret*. Not to mention an enormous, unwieldy hat.

Chapter 14

Wednesday, 7th May

The following morning, Olive was once again zipping along the lanes, hunched over the Welbike, as the early morning chill ripped through her jumper and stung her cheeks. Much like the day before, she'd tiptoed out of the house well before dawn, gathered the musketeers, and rolled the motorbike away from the lodge before cringing at its start-up roar. As the sky faded from inky black to midnight blue, she ferried them over the countryside, turning this way and that, in a meandering, circuitous route. Finally, she stopped on an unfamiliar village green and tossed them, one by one, into a dark blueberry sky.

Pigeons weren't inclined to fly in the dark; the lack of visibility constrained their abilities, causing them to get confused. If they couldn't use the sun or identify landmarks to get their bearings, they might fly off in the wrong direction and go hundreds of miles searching for home, never to find their way back. She and her father had never truly worried about training their birds for night flying; the races were all held during daylight hours. But given the secret nature of these missions, the drop times would either be late or very early, and an urgent message would need to be sent home in darkness. So, she was using the days remaining to try to give them a little practice. Beyond that, she could merely hope for the best.

As she watched, they wheeled in circles, going higher and higher, scanning the landscape for a recognisable landmark, before finally heading off in what she hoped was the right direction. Having managed to get a bit turned around herself, she couldn't immediately tell for certain.

"Race you back, boys. And Poppins," she called quietly after them as the little village began to wake. It occurred to her that she was helping it right along with the noise of the throttle, and so she set off. The way back was peppered with wrong turns and backtracks, but Olive didn't mind the extra trouble. She was lost in her thoughts and the shifting, brightening colours above her: lavender, blush, and gold. She whizzed past lorries, waved to farmers and Land Girls out early, and even stopped to ask directions of a couple of the Home Guard who were dismantling a signpost she'd passed not thirty minutes previously. Worries over a German invasion had not dissipated one bit.

She slowed the motorbike to a stop as she neared Pipley, and shut off the engine. After a couple hours of chilly, buzzing speed, she was ready for a bit of calm and quiet and a respite from the wind. She climbed off the Welbike and closed her eyes for a single peaceful moment as she wheeled it along the side of the road. She almost missed the rabbit that bounded in front of her, darted along the verge, and disappeared into the wood beyond. Her eyes followed the graceful flash of movement until it disappeared from view. But just as she was turning back to look where she was going, another movement, deeper among the trees, drew her gaze. Curious, she propped the motorbike against a sturdy trunk, then slipped into the dimness of the wood, feeling suddenly giddy, as if poised for a rare sighting of a wryneck woodpecker.

She was startled to instead see a man, mostly hidden from

view, busy at some task. Instinctively, she ducked back behind a birch tree, not wanting to be caught spying. What, she wondered, was he doing in the woods so early? Checking rabbit traps? Olive winced, remembering the creature that had bounded across her path, and inched forward, craning her neck.

Whoever it was, he was holding a shovel, and a basket sat on the ground beside him. Taken by themselves, those observations were barely even interesting, but when he started digging, the grim sound of it sent a prickle over her skin.

Olive tried to imagine possible scenarios. He could be foraging for mushrooms or digging up wild daffodils; he might have even taken the initiative and embarked on a medicinal plants scheme of his own. Surely there were other useful plants to be collected. Belladonna perhaps, or rose hips. Although it was too early in the year to gather either of those. So, she waited and watched.

After a moment, she was exasperated with her cloak-and-dagger efforts and was poised to set off again when the digging stopped abruptly and he turned. She caught the glint of spectacles and a flash of colour as an egg yolk–yellow handkerchief was swept across his brow before being tucked away again. Recognition came swiftly and, on its heels, relief. It was only Dr Ware. Likely he was collecting some specimen or other for research purposes, and she could put her overactive imagination to rest. Perhaps *this* was his secret. She stepped carefully backwards and turned away, ready to be off again and anxious not to be noticed. But Miss Husselbee's voice hovered at her ear. *I wouldn't trust him if I were you.* Cursing to herself, she swivelled dutifully back.

In between sneaking peeks at his progress, she leaned back against the birch and let her eyes drift closed. After several iterations, they blinked open; the sounds had stopped. Cautiously peering around the tree, she realised Dr Ware had disappeared.

Prompted by the imaginary thump of Miss Husselbee's umbrella, she proceeded to tramp through the woods to the spot where Dr Ware had wielded his shovel. Olive frowned down at the patch of turned earth. The hollows she would have expected—evidence of something having been recently removed—were absent. There was only a mounded square the approximate size of one of her pigeon carriers. Anxious to get on with things, she made a quick decision: *In for a penny, in for a pound.*

She scavenged for a sturdy stick and got to work. As the loamy soil was nudged slowly away, she could begin to see the first clues of what was buried there, and couldn't stop herself from further frenzied digging.

Aldridge never would have stooped to spying on the village chemist, but she'd followed her instincts straight down the rabbit hole. Vindication, however, was not nearly so sweet, as she stared down into the unassuming grave of a tidy row of field mice, each of them covered in horrible raw pink lesions.

She had just let out a shuddering sigh when she heard the light tread of footsteps just behind her.

Her heart setting off at a gallop, Olive spun around, relieved to find Henrietta Gibbons standing there, staring past her, down at the little grave. She was wearing her Girl Guides uniform—blue serge skirt and blue cotton blouse—the sleeves rolled haphazardly to the elbows, the tights drooping a bit about the knees. Her hair, tucked under the brimmed Guides hat, wispily framed her pale face.

"Do you suppose those are the ones I sold him?"

Not wanting to burden the girl with responsibility, Olive answered quickly. "Surely not."

"What's wrong with them?" she asked, stepping closer as she peered down at them. Before Olive could stop her, she'd crouched beside the little grave.

"Don't touch them," Olive said sharply, prompting Hen to stare quizzically up at her. "I don't know what's wrong with them, but whatever it is, Dr Ware appears to want it kept secret."

Hen shot up. "Why don't we go ask him, then." She moved to push past Olive and tramp out of the woods, but Olive caught her arm.

"It might be better, for now, if he doesn't know what we've discovered, if you know what I mean." She looked directly into the round green eyes and slowly lifted an eyebrow, appealing to the girl's love of information. "Let me see what I can find out first. Deal?"

Hen glanced again into the grave, then turned her gaze back to Olive, her lips tight and her eyes sad. She extended her arm, her long, pale fingers hovering in wait of a solemn pact. "Deal," she agreed.

When the girl would have pulled away, Olive tugged her back. "What are you doing out this early?"

"Same as you. War work." This was said as nonchalantly as if the answer had been birdwatching.

"What *do* you mean?" Had Jonathon given away their secret? She could clearly picture Aldridge's raised hand gripping the back of his neck in furious exasperation.

"You're out training pigeons in the hopes that they might eventually be used to carry important messages for our side. I'm out on berry reconnaissance. The first wild strawberries are nearly ripe, and we need to get them tucked away and ready for preservation before the birds get to them."

Olive smiled awkwardly, relief making her legs feel like jelly. The girl must have noticed the pigeon carrier strapped to the motorbike. "Quite right. Carry on, then."

Hen lingered a moment longer, holding Olive in a thoughtful gaze, before spinning on her heel and slinking quietly through the brush back to the road.

Olive scooped the dirt back over the mice and laid a curly fern leaf over the spot. Then she, too, slipped out of the trees and turned the Welbike toward the village. She had business in the church graveyard.

The whispery shadows of that hallowed spot were like a balm to her frazzled mind. Having left the motorbike on the other side of the lych-gate, tucked amid the budding jasmine, she walked through and paused a moment, letting the silence crowd closer. Taking care to avoid the wild crocuses pushing up through the dark earth, she skirted the other gravestones and stepped purposefully toward her mother's, where it sat in the shade of an ancient gnarled yew in the far corner. As usual, it felt as if she was visiting the temple of a Greek oracle, that there was wisdom here if she could just understand how to parse it.

She settled in beside the familiar plot, folding her legs under her. As was her ritual, she ran her finger over the carved epitaph, which had never truly made sense to her child's mind.

SERENA OCTAVIA BRIGHT

1897–1930

A FIGHTING SPIRIT WITH A FRAGILE SOUL

Fragile would surely have applied to her mother's body after the tuberculosis had settled into her lungs; her soul, Olive was quite certain, had been resilient until the very end. But her father had been impervious to questions. Tight-lipped and stoic, he'd been determined to lock the painful memories away and move on. Lewis, too, had manfully soldiered on, leaving her to grieve on her own. As a result, Olive had felt the loss of her mother twice as cruelly, and she still thought of her often. For whatever reason, Serena Bright had recently been on Miss Husselbee's mind, as well.

She brushed away the detritus of spring showers, then wiped her hand on the seat of her trousers. A cluster of crocus blooms crowded near the edge of the grave, but they were already fading with the onset of warmer days. One of the luminescent purple flowers had tumbled off its stem, and Olive cradled it in her hand, running a gentle finger over the silken petals.

Leaning lightly against the chilly headstone, she scanned the graveyard, needing to be certain no one was about before she said the words aloud. Content she was alone, she peered up through the canopy of leaves toward the church steeple and quietly confided, "I've not started yet, but I'm to be a FANY." She smiled. "I might even do some driving, but it won't be on the front lines." A petal came free and fluttered to the ground. "I'm to be stationed at Brickendonbury." Her voice had gone flat with the final admission, and the silence suddenly felt heavy with disappointment.

In the dimness of the graveyard, she felt overshadowed, the shine on her recent success dimmed by the feeling that she could never hope to measure up to the example set by her mother in the last war.

"I had bigger plans," she insisted, her shoulders tightly defensive, "but I gave them up for the pigeons." And other responsibilities, but she wouldn't mention Harriet or the pig club. She gave the base of the flower a quick twist between her finger and thumb, then released it, letting it twirl away from her, to spin in the air, until it finally came to rest on a furry patch of yellowgreen moss. "Our birds are going to be put to work for the war effort, flying secret missions home from occupied Europe."

She paused before revealing the next bit, her stomach clenched with guilt, but she forged on with an up tilt of her chin. "Dad doesn't know, and I can't tell him." Olive sighed, then tried to inject a little happy optimism into her tone. "I intend to make the best of things, even if I am at the mercy of a man with a lacklustre imagination and a penchant for brooding stares. He was already frustrating, but now he outranks me, which means he's going to be entirely insufferable." She snorted, newly resolved to give as good as she got. In that way, at least, she would take after her mother. "His name is Captain Jameson Aldridge, but from now on, I'm going to make it a point to call him Jamie. I'll tell you that part of the story another time."

Spurred by her little spark of defiance, she rose with alacrity and slid her gaze once more over the words she knew by heart. With any luck, she'd have a chance to prove her own fighting spirit, that is, beyond her regular bickerings with Aldridge. Eager, for once, to get away, out of reach of the silence, which now felt disapproving and oddly oppressive, Olive laid her fingers to her lips and pressed them with a kiss before brushing them against her mother's headstone. Then she stepped nimbly across the graveyard and out through the gate. She needed to get on with things.

A hand suddenly gripped her upper arm, spun her around, and hustled her back through the gate. Olive had tensed, ready to jab her elbow into a sensitive spot on the assailant's anatomy, only to realise it was Margaret, her face bare of cosmetics and looking rather helpless.

"What is it?" Olive demanded, feeling cranky to have been caught unaware, particularly so soon after those private moments at her mother's grave. *If she'd overheard . . .*

"I need to talk to you." Margaret spoke in a whisper, and her eyes looked hunted, darting frenetically, as she dragged Olive deeper into the shadows beside the vestry.

Olive's mood shifted instantly, as burgeoning curiosity once again overtook her. "Is this about the secret you've been keeping from everyone?"

Margaret looked near to tears, flushed and dewy-eyed. Rather than answer, she dropped down onto a crumbling stone bench nearly covered with ivy, pulling a handkerchief from her pocket. Not entirely certain the bench could hold the pair of them without collapsing, Olive decided not to risk it and instead leaned against the cool stone wall.

"Not everyone, apparently," Margaret said bitterly.

"You realise it no longer matters that Miss Husselbee had worked it out," Olive said calmly.

"It does if she told someone," Margaret hissed.

"I'm sure she wouldn't have—"

"Really? Then how do you explain this?" her friend said, fury having supplanted the worry. She turned a folded sheet out of her pocket and thrust it at Olive.

As she took it, Olive was acutely aware of the leaves shifting above them. No one else was about, but a shiver crawled over her, like a warning from beyond the grave. Which was silly, because Miss Husselbee hadn't even been buried yet. And because that was entirely far-fetched. Thoroughly exasperated with herself, she scanned the words, blinked, and read them again.

> *Your London secret is no longer your own. I'm willing to safeguard what I've discovered, for a price. You have one week to leave £2 under the loose tile in the corner of the Fox and Duck WC, and it will go no further.*

There was nothing written on the back, and the words on the front looked misshapen and tentative, as if they'd been written by a child.

"This is blackmail," Olive said slowly. Only yesterday she'd overheard that very word in a heated conversation between Mr Forrester and Harry Danes.

She glanced at her friend, whose beseeching look had switched to one of exasperation.

"You're hot on the case, Sherlock."

Ignoring her, Olive said, "Where did you get it?"

"It was pushed through the mail slot, bold as brass. Aunt Eloise was having a chat and a cuppa with Lady Camilla, who'd stopped in to pick up the blankets for the refugees, and when they came through from the kitchen, it was sitting on the rug in the hall. The envelope was marked the same as this, with my name in great leaning capital letters." She stared distastefully at the blackmail note, a wrinkle forming over her nose. "It's not handwriting I recognise, which I suppose is rather the point."

"What about the neighbours?" Olive quizzed. "Did anyone see who delivered it?"

"The doctor's next door, and he was out. The Darlings are on the other side, and while the prodigal sister was likely at home, I doubt we'll get any help from that quarter. She keeps to herself."

Probably working on her next novel, Olive thought, her eyes skimming the note again. *Your London secret.* She peered at her friend. "If it really is only your modelling," she said carefully, "then what does it matter if it comes out? The consequences couldn't possibly be worse than giving in to a blackmailer, particularly if Leo already knows."

Margaret paled, her features pinched. "There is something else," she said, carefully straightening her skirt. "But please don't ask me what it is." Her voice broke, but she took a deep, steadying breath and went on. "I know I came to you for help, and it's killing you not to know, but honestly, why can't it be my secret? Aren't I entitled to a bit of privacy?" Her lower lip jutted, a perfect crescent of pink.

"That depends on what you've done," Olive said quietly, refolding the note and handing it back. When Margaret looked at her crossly, she elaborated. "For instance, if you've killed someone, I'd say there are people who have a right to know—your family, your fiancé, random villagers, fearing your murderous ways will be turned on them."

Margaret surged to her feet, going eye to eye with Olive, and quietly ground out the words, "I did *not* kill that woman."

"It was only an illustrative example," Olive insisted. "And you must admit, it looks rather suspicious."

"Only to you! No one else overheard my argument with Miss Husselbee, and I daresay if the blackmailer thought her death could be pinned on me, he or she would have mentioned that and attempted to extort more money, although two pounds is really quite greedy."

"I would think," Olive said consideringly, "the price would

depend on the secret. And two pounds *is* rather a lot . . ." She let her words trail off and slowly raised a single eyebrow, trying for a balance of curiosity and discretion.

Margaret's hand went unerringly to the locket nestled at her throat. "Oh, give over! You're not going to convince me to tell— even if that *is* the most sensible way forward. And if that means you won't help me, then I'll hunt down the blackmailing devil on my own," she vowed, then turned to stalk off. Thoroughly exasperated, Olive laid a ready hand on her arm and gave a sharp tug.

Clearly, now was not the time to press her about the locket; that would have to wait.

"If I left it to you, you'd leave the two pounds and hang about the pub, dashing into the WC between every occupant—not, I daresay, a very pleasant task. We need some clues, Watson." George's lopsided smile flashed, bittersweet, in her thoughts, but Olive shifted it aside to get on with things. "The pub was actually a stroke of genius. It muddies the water. Anyone in the village could wander into the pub's WC at any time; it will be nearly impossible for you to keep track."

Margaret's shoulders slumped as she considered this. Olive stared at the grey headstones standing sentry over mouldering bones. Miss Husselbee would shortly be relegated to their number.

She frowned. "Did Miss Husselbee tell you how she came to discover your secret?"

Margaret looked uncertain and chose her words carefully. "A friend, she said."

"A friend in London?" Olive prompted. Getting a nod, she went on, "Then, unless you're famous in London—or infamous—Miss Husselbee was likely the only one in the village who knew your secret. I don't believe she would have told anyone . . . at least not on purpose."

Margaret huffed in disbelief.

"It's possible," Olive said slowly, "that she wrote about you."

It would have been perfectly in character for Miss Husselbee to wring out her disapproval with Margaret while doing her duty for Britain. As to the mysterious page left in the typewriter, with its mention of festering evil . . . that couldn't be Margaret, surely. Whatever it was, that particular sin had apparently been discovered recently, which likely meant it hadn't been mentioned in any of the Sergeant Major's previous entries. Olive now suspected those had fallen into the hands of a blackmailer.

"Wrote about me? You don't mean in those diaries she did for Mass Observation?" Margaret's mouth had opened on a little *o* of horror.

Olive pulled her back to the bench, now willing to risk a collapse, and sat facing her. "Was the confrontation by the river the first time Miss Husselbee approached you about your"—she winced—"sordid past?"

"Yes," her friend confirmed grimly. "But not for lack of trying. I've been avoiding her."

"She must have found out about it some time ago, and no doubt promptly wrote a scathing report for Mass Observation. Her April diaries were never submitted, and now they're missing," Olive said carefully. "I suspect someone got hold of those pages and recognised the opportunity for blackmail. Which means you might not be the only victim."

"That is *not* a comforting thought." Margaret tapped the sole of her shoe against a fallen leaf, pressing it into the moist earth.

"Hardly," Olive agreed. "Particularly given that someone is dead."

Margaret's eyes and mouth widened simultaneously. "You don't think . . . ?"

"It makes sense. If the Sergeant Major had confronted someone with a bigger secret than yours, or a bigger temper"—she winked, dispelling Margaret's ire before it blossomed—"he or she might have decided to get rid of her, snatch the evidence intended for Mass Observation, and use the extraneous tittle-tattle to make a little cash on the side."

"The beast! What should we do?"

Margaret was looking at her intently, without a whiff of doubt that Olive would make this go away. Why couldn't Aldridge have just a *modicum* of that trust? She thought of the little notebook, dumped back into her hands with the bossy directive that it be taken to the police. It might be best if she kept it a little while longer, in the interest of helping Margaret. Surely, it held a clue.

"We need to narrow the field of suspects as best we can," Olive said emphatically.

"Well, work fast. I'll pay to keep my secret, and I'll find a way to go on paying if that's what's required." Her fists clenched in her lap. "But eventually, I'll discover the identity of the black-mailer, and then I *will* do murder."

This announcement didn't even faze Olive; she was busy thinking of George, and desperately hoping his father was not capable of the crimes she suddenly suspected him of.

"Yes, I'd like to speak to Captain Jameson Aldridge, please." Olive clutched the receiver as she stood in the dark of the hall, waiting for him to pick up. She'd buzzed home, enjoying the roar of sound that followed her up and down the lanes, and made straight for the telephone, feeling entirely justified. Yesterday Aldridge had been smugly convinced that Margaret was the murderer, but today, Olive thought winningly, she may as well have proof to the contrary. It was entirely likely that Margaret's black-mailer and Miss Husselbee's murderer were one and the same, thereby leaving her friend in the clear. She couldn't fathom how Mr Forrester fit into things. Was he another victim or a criminal? She tapped her foot and worried at a hangnail, as the waiting went on for some time.

"Aldridge here." His voice was gruff and abrupt and startled

Olive so thoroughly that she straightened suddenly, tugging at the line and nearly knocking the telephone off the table. She took a deep breath, schooling her brain to speak cryptically in case anyone was lurking nearby.

"Hello, Jamie," she said, wishing she could trade her coquettish manner for a straightforward "You were wrong."

A beat of silence and then, "Hello, Olive." The unspoken words hummed over the phone lines between them: *This had better be important.*

"Do you remember our argument yesterday?"

"There were several. To which are you referring?" His voice was both wary and impatient, as if he dreaded what she would say but wanted to get it over with.

"The one regarding a friend of mine," she clarified.

"I remember."

"Well, she's lately received a letter."

"The sort that involves secrets and money?" he asked wryly.

"The very same," she said, tipping up her chin. As she straightened a crooked frame on the wall, she wondered if he was reading between the lines and now understood that Margaret couldn't possibly be the murderer.

"In that case, I'd advise *you* to leave it alone, and *her* to go to the police." Olive blustered objections, but he cut right through them like a knife through Victoria sponge. "If her character is as good as you've insinuated, she has nothing to worry about."

Olive stood in silence in the dim hallway; she'd suddenly realised that beneath the burning desire to prove him wrong had lain a kindled hope that he might see his way around to helping her.

"You can always be depended upon," she said through clenched teeth, "for advice." She felt a fool. He'd made it quite clear he wasn't concerned over, or invested in, any village shenanigans, murder included, so long as they didn't touch Station XVII. *Fine. Good.* That meant she no longer needed to trouble herself asking his opinion—and certainly not his permission.

"Can I assume we've managed to come to an understanding?" he asked pleasantly.

"Certainly," she agreed, smiling. Let him assume whatever the hell he wanted. She hung up with a violent clatter, then growled in frustration. After a moment, she took a deep breath, straightened her shoulders, and walked calmly down the hall on her way upstairs.

"Is that you, Olive?" Harriet called, prompting her to peer around the door of the parlour, where her stepmother reclined, trouser-clad legs extended under a lap desk appointed with pen, paper, and a fortifying cup of tea. Her feet, tucked into trim sapphire-blue slippers, looked fragile somehow.

"Did you need something?" Olive said, her smile fighting against her clenched jaw muscles.

"No, dear. I only wanted to make certain you hadn't been ambushed in the hall and weren't fighting for your life."

Olive sighed, leaning back against the door. "I'm sorry. That wasn't particularly well done of me. I rang up Jamie to clarify a few things."

Harriet nodded in understanding. "Not the answers you wanted, then?"

"Quite."

Harriet lifted her teacup and took a sip. "Don't be too hard on him. War is not conducive to budding romance. The pair of you just have to work harder, because life is infinitely brighter when you find that one person who makes your heart stutter."

Olive felt certain she flushed to the roots of her hair. Getting along with Jameson Aldridge—or whatever his name was—was work enough. If they added romance—the legitimate sort—they were liable to kill each other.

Harriet was not expecting a response, so Olive made her escape, fleeing upstairs to her room and tapping the door closed. She slipped her hand beneath the mattress and unearthed Miss Husselbee's notebook. She tossed it on the bed, flopped down beside it, and turned on her stomach to go through it yet again. Aldridge might not be inclined to involve himself in the village's little dramas, but he was an outsider. Her entire life was wrapped up in its goings-on, and lately too many of them were suspicious. Miss Husselbee's machinations had somehow touched her mother, Margaret, Dr Ware, George's father, and who knew how many others. Her only intention was to help undo a bit of the damage; the police could handle the rest, and she could get back to worrying about everything else.

Other than the lovely red tomato that Jonathon had proudly carried in from the garden, dinner was a grim affair. Over modest plates of shepherd's pie, her father had filled them in on the results of the day's inquest, quickly summarising the proceedings that had led to a ruling of death by misadventure. A cake made with Spam and potatoes, it had been determined, was certainly someone's idea of a joke, and the foxglove, which grew wild in many village gardens, had most likely been collected in error, in lieu of the intended edible herb. The guilty party, the judge had allowed, was likely apprehensive about coming forward now that the "cake" had proved to be fatal. Clearly, no one thought it odd that it had been served on a plate belonging to no one, kept in the village hall.

"So that's an end to it," he said, discreetly scraping his plate clean.

Olive grimaced, unable to do more than push the chunks of meat and vegetables around her plate. As she shifted her gaze around the table—from her father's plate, to Harriet's, and around to Jonathon's—she marvelled at their ability to dissociate a meal of tinned meat and potatoes tucked into a gummy pastry crust from a cake, recently confirmed as the cause of death in a police investigation, made of the same basic ingredients.

A murder weapon.

The words resonated in her mind, prompting gooseflesh to

cover her body and a shiver to crawl its length. Wanting only a cup of tea and a biscuit, she leaned back in her chair.

"That can't possibly be an end to it," she insisted. "Someone quite obviously wanted her dead and went to a lot of trouble to target her specifically."

"Olive," Harriet protested. "Accidents do happen."

She swivelled her head to look at her stepmother, her eyes blazing with certitude. "*This* particular accident shouldn't have happened—not here. The entire Pipley WI, not to mention half the village, was instructed on the identification, uses, and risks of the plant, which has grown wild in our gardens and woods for ages. But within a year of the lecture and our efforts for the Oxford Medicinal Plants Scheme, there's been a murder by foxglove."

"It's coincidence, nothing more. As troubling as it is to accept." The low rumble of her father's voice should have been reassuring, but it wasn't.

"If it was truly an accident or coincidence, then where did the cake disappear to? I dared Jamie to try it, and he was willing, but when we came in—when I dragged him to the refreshments table, that is—it was gone. An *entire cake*, missing only one slice, whisked away, no one seeming to know by whom. No one else was given a chance to taste it, or they, too, would be dead." She stopped, and her words echoed back at her, shaking her composure. *Jamie would be dead.* Her hands began to tremble with shock, moral outrage, and . . . something else.

"You're seeing conspiracies where there is only happenstance and tragedy," her father said firmly. His demeanour, however, communicated quite clearly that it was simply easier to accept the inquest ruling and pretend that there wasn't a murderer living among them.

"What if I found evidence that proves otherwise?" She wasn't yet ready to admit that she'd purloined a pocket notebook off a dead woman and subsequently burgled her home and ransacked her desk, but if needs must . . .

Jonathon's head whipped up with interest, but Olive kept her eyes on her father. His own had narrowed curiously as he leaned back in his chair and crossed his arms, exposed to the elbows by rolled shirtsleeves, over his chest. "You? You're already sufficiently out of your element at the manor, with little enough time for all that's expected of you there and here. How on earth do you think you'd manage to root out a murderer?" He held his hands up in front of him, as if to clear the air of such foolishness. "It doesn't matter, because even if such a thing was within your grasp, no one would thank you for challenging the verdict."

"Isn't anyone else concerned with the injustice?" she demanded.

Her father leaned forward and propped his elbows on the table. "Verity Husselbee was a busybody, and she had plenty of enemies—probably too many with means, motive, and opportunity. The authorities might have agreed that a thorough investigation would drain their resources when they're already stretched to their limits with tasks laid on by the government and the military. She's got no family to object, and the killer—if there was one—is likely now done with murder. It could have been decided," he said gravely, "to sweep this under the rug."

Harriet's eyes were shiny with tears, but she didn't argue. Jonathon kept his eyes downcast as he manoeuvred a scatter of spilled salt into the shape of an arrow.

"But that's horrible," Olive protested, feeling sick despite her still-empty stomach.

"There will always be those sacrificed for the greater good, my girl," he said, the lines on his face seeming more pronounced. "And in these dark days, the stakes are much higher."

Olive knew he was thinking of Lewis, who'd gone off to war with the greatest of intentions. An academic at heart, he never could stand to see any creature being bullied or abused, so naturally, the rise of the Nazi regime had enraged him. When it had been discovered he could speak Greek and was quite skilled at tracking and foraging and, most surprising of all, hand-to-hand fighting, they'd sent him up into the Pindus Mountains of Greece, near Parnassus. In his first letter home he'd told them he couldn't believe his luck—the old Gods were with him. She desperately hoped they were. As far as she was concerned, the stakes were enormous, but this was Pipley.

She ground her teeth in frustration. First, Aldridge and now the inquest officials, the coroner, and the jury. Not to mention her father. No one had the time or inclination to dig deeper and discover what had truly happened to Miss Husselbee. It simply wasn't fair. Well, if everyone else was too busy or distracted to see justice done, then it was up to her.

Her optimistic zeal wavered after only a moment. What if something larger was at work here? What of that mysterious diary entry rolled carefully back into the typewriter at Peregrine Hall? What of Dr Ware's dead mice, Margaret's secret, and Violet Darling's mysterious past, to say nothing of Mr Battlesby's troubled mind? Her shoulders dropped as she realised that no one else was likely even aware of the harsh words, veiled threats, and disturbing air of menace that had prompted her to investigate. And she couldn't possibly elaborate right now.

It was difficult to believe that a verdict of death by misadventure had tidily dispatched a shockingly unexpected death straight into the annals of village gossip.

Her thoughts turned faithlessly to Aldridge, even though he'd made his loyalties quite plain on the telephone. A further appeal would surely tear at the gossamer strands that had newly begun to bind them together. She couldn't risk it. Which meant she was quite on her own. Her amateur sleuthing would need to carry on until she uncovered the truth.

If she were to get anywhere, she'd need to be objective rather than sentimental. As much as she'd prefer not to believe that anyone in the village could have harboured murderous intentions towards Miss Husselbee, it was critical that she resign herself to the reality that someone had. She couldn't keep discounting viable suspects simply out of squeamish uncertainty. But the alternative was going to require a full measure of courage.

After a subdued dinner, they all retired to her father's study, but only Olive seemed troubled by a rumbling stomach and a distressed mind. Harriet reclined on the sofa, her too-thin legs having been crossed with effort. She held a hardbound copy of *Pride and Prejudice* in one hand and a glossy black fountain pen in the other. A journal bound in bottle-green leather lay on her lap. Her father was dividing his attention equally between the evening's radio broadcast and the latest edition of the newspaper, with plenty of muffled oaths for each. Jonathon had his back propped against the side of her father's chair and his knees raised in a makeshift desk as he busily scribbled plans for some project or other with Kíli stretched out beside him.

Olive sat curled up on the window seat, leaning against the blackout curtain, which moments ago had been tugged closed against the fading twilight. She was mentally sifting through the developments and discoveries of the past few days, trying to slot them into categories: potential clue or general village shenanigans.

"Olive," her stepmother said, peering at her over the gold wire rims of the spectacles she used only for reading and serious business, "do you need me to find someone else to manage the pig club? It seems as if a great many things are demanding your attention at the moment, and I don't want you run ragged."

As Olive pondered how best to answer and whether the question held an underlying suspicion, there was a loud crackle of pages as her father folded his newspaper onto his lap.

"It's inconceivable to me that it's come to this. The idea that a bunch of blithering idiots would put their personal grudges against me and my birds before the safety and security of this great nation." He shook his head in disbelief as deep lines scored this wide forehead. "But it seems the Pigeon Service has hung us out to dry." The anger abruptly faded, replaced by weary disappointment, and he rubbed one large calloused hand over his chin. "You mustn't worry," he said, almost to himself. "I'll fix this. But until I do," he added, with a glance at Olive, "you might want to focus on your other responsibilities and leave the pigeons to fend for themselves."

Olive couldn't imagine what it had cost her father to make such a suggestion, but she couldn't spare even a moment for misplaced sympathy. She caught Jonathon's eye, both of them conscious of the new difficulty this suggestion would pose. The pigeons had become her main responsibility, and she reported directly to Captain Aldridge. Ostensibly following her father's advice would add a whole new level of cunning to an already duplicitous situation. She blinked at him, her thoughts darting and desperate for purchase on any believable justification to continue on as they were.

"I'm heading up to London tomorrow for some veterinary supplies," her father informed them all casually. "Some things have become impossible to get hold of, and if I can't find them there, I'll have to start improvising. Perhaps I can have a talk with the committee while I'm there." His eyes had taken on a faraway look, and he was nodding slowly to himself.

"No," Olive blurted, the word springing like a tiger into the cosy little room. "I just meant," she said, back-pedalling, "don't put yourself to the trouble. I'll write to them and explain our situation, remind them of our legacy of champions. I'll convince them." She let out the nervous breath clogging her lungs.

Her father had peered around the wings of his chair to get a better look at her. His face was as downtrodden as she'd ever seen it. "Tell them we'll supply our pigeons with no strings attached." He sighed. "It's time we swallow our pride. We're past the point in this war where we can cling to ideals. Better to let our birds do their best in the hands of amateurs. Any lives they can save will be worth the sacrifice."

Olive was struck momentarily dumb, but seeing the pride in the smile Harriet bestowed on her father, she rallied. "You wouldn't, by any chance, want to take one of the birds on the train with you . . . ?" She let the words trail off suggestively. "If the best we can do for now is keep them conditioned, then so be it."

She was relieved to see a mischievous smile edge out the grimness of Rupert Bright's demeanour. "You're incorrigible—a chip off the old block," he said with a wink. "Excellent idea. I'll take Lancelot. He never really had a chance to prove himself before the war."

"Good thinking," she agreed. "We're not faring too badly in the food department, either. Jonathon will shortly be supplying the birds with greens from the garden, and we'll forage where we need to. We'll make do."

"Excellent," he said, then pondered the situation for a moment before rattling his newspaper back into place. Olive leaned back against the window, sighing with relief at having found a bit of success without the need for outright deception.

The radio had begun a slow croon of a song Olive didn't recognise, but Harriet hummed along lightly under her breath. "Violet Darling is sure to make a good job of Lizzy Bennet," she allowed. Her eyebrows tipped coyly up. "But I would have so enjoyed seeing what you could have done with the part," she informed her stepdaughter, "particularly if Captain Aldridge had agreed to play Mr Darcy."

Olive smiled, wondering which of the pair of them would have been more miserable. She stilled as a flicker of an idea sifted through her thoughts. Captain Aldridge may very well balk at donning a cravat as the lead romantic role in the village play, but he might be willing to arrange a second impersonation on their behalf. It was simple, really, and she couldn't believe she hadn't thought of it before. If a liaison officer from the National Pigeon Service—one of the agents at Brickendonbury would do brilliantly—were to show up and convince her father that the Bright loft would be accepted on a trial basis, it would go a long way toward explaining away her work as a pigeoneer for Station XVII. After all, Aldridge's appearance at the loft had nearly duped her. This could work, and she planned on convincing him at the next possible opportunity.

You must allow me to tell you how ardently I require your assistance. . . .

Monday, 3 March 1941
Peregrine Hall, Pipley
Hertfordshire

*H.W. and I got off on the wrong foot from the very begin-
ning. Men don't care to be contradicted, particularly if it's in
regard to a topic in which they fancy themselves something of
an expert. Then again, most men fancy themselves experts on
all manner of topics, which, I have found, can result in conversations fraught with conflict.*

*The man in question and I were discussing the comparative
benefits of pharmaceutical tonics and lozenges versus homemade remedies. Given that he is attempting to sell the
former, it can come as no surprise that he would tout the benefit of that sort. I'm sure I need not say that he was not able
to convince me, but I will admit that he is quite knowledgeable on the topic.*

*Since then, I've kept rather a close eye on him. He flatly re-
fuses to discuss his research, preferring to keep his own coun-
cil. He walks along the river, shaking his head, muttering to
himself, perspiration slick on his brow. He's started collecting
empty canisters and bottles, squirreling them away for some
mysterious use. What can he be hiding? I can only assume it's
something unsavoury, possibly even traitorous. I worry he
might be planning to incapacitate us all in preparation for a
German invasion, and so I will remain ever vigilant.*

V.A.E. Husselbee

Chapter 15

Olive spent the misty grey morning in the dovecote, scraping out the boxes, raking the gravel, and generally making sure everything was in readiness. The first Bright birds would be loaded into carriers for their flight across the Channel in only three days, and Olive was starting to feel fluttery. Lancelot had slipped in at midday, his short flight from London apparently uneventful. Her father, thankfully, would be hours yet, so there was no one to question her focused efforts.

She'd set each of the four birds—Poppins and the musketeers—into a pan of clean water to wash, and now they stood, shimmying about, twitching their wings dry. In the middle of this performance, Jonathon flung open the door to the dovecote, holding a ball of twine and flashing a toothy grin. "We'll booby-trap the cage door," he exclaimed. "All we need is a bell."

Olive propped the rake she'd been using against the wall to give this suggestion her full attention.

They'd already determined that the missions would need to be treated essentially as long-distance races, which meant they'd have to control the comings and goings of all the birds in order to efficiently track those returning home. Whereas before, they'd been clocking in birds for a purse and prestige, now they were awaiting information that could help turn the tide of the war. As before, timing was everything.

The pigeonholes in the cupola would be sealed from the inside, while a single unglazed window at the back of the dovecote would have its shutters lashed opened and a cage attached, allowing returning birds to pass through a levered door into a confined space, thereby making message retrieval quick and efficient.

They were, however, facing a new difficulty: it would be impossible to predict when a pigeon might fly home. A crash landing could prompt a bird's release almost immediately, in hopes of spurring a rescue, but otherwise there could be a delay of hours—perhaps days—depending on the timing chosen for the mission's sabotage. She and Jonathon couldn't be constantly patrolling, staring up at the sky, on watch for returning birds. That, more than anything else, would expose their secret arrangement with Station XVII.

Rupert Bright would certainly notice the conversion of the loft to its race day configuration, but Olive was certain she could convince him that keeping their birds under careful watch would work to their advantage, pending a visit from the NPS. Explaining the need for a bell would be, in Olive's opinion, a different matter altogether.

"He needn't know we've rigged it," Jonathon insisted, reading both her mind and her dubious frown. "We'll tie one end of the twine to the hinged gate on the window cage and run the other through the garden and up the wall to my room."

Olive bit her lip. It could work; Jonathon would be able to hear the bell whenever he was at home—either in his room or the garden—and the jingling would instantly mobilise him.

"Brilliant," she agreed, nodding. "With the dovecote adjacent to the garden, and your room just above, it could work. You might have to tell Dad and Harriet you're practicing for the Christmas handbell choir, but needs must."

"I'm sure Hen can get her hands on a bell for us." Naturally. That girl had her finger in every pie. "Do you think Captain Aldridge will be impressed?"

Olive considered. "Perhaps. It's more likely he hasn't given the matter any consideration at all. He'll expect everything to work like clockwork. And only notice if it doesn't," she said grimly. "But we don't need his affirmation."

He nodded agreeably, and she glanced around her, hands on hips. The place was looking spit-spot, with clean, scalded gravel, fresh straw in the nesting boxes and water in the pan, and plenty of feed, covertly fetched from the shed.

"Are there any green vegetables ready in the garden yet? It would be lovely if we could supplement their diet before the flight," she said.

"Unfortunately, the peas aren't ready yet—I know they'd be your first choice—but there are some tender young cabbages."

"Perfect," she said, then took a deep, contented breath and dipped her hands into her jacket pockets. The tips of her fingers skimmed something rough and rounded, and she drew it out. It was the button she'd found beneath Miss Husselbee's desk. "Jonathon," she said, holding it up, "isn't Hen's brother in the Royal Navy?"

He glanced at it and stilled as his eyes went wide. A moment later, his shoulders slumped guiltily, the twine hanging forgotten against his leg. "She keeps that button in her pocket, and she told me where she'd lost it. It wasn't my idea, I swear."

"*What* wasn't your idea?"

"To lie to you."

Olive's eyes flared in surprise. Miss Husselbee had once barked at him, "What do you think, young man?" and he'd informed the old harridan that he thought she wasn't being very nice. He *wasn't* one to lie, a fact that had worried her slightly when he was made to sign the Official Secrets Act.

"What was the lie?" she asked carefully.

"Remember I told you I found Miss Husselbee's body?"

It was the last thing she would have expected him to say, and for a moment, she was boggled. "If you didn't find her, then who did?"

Now he looked flustered. "I *did* find her," he insisted. "But I wasn't the only one."

Olive let out the breath she'd been holding. "Let me guess. Henrietta Gibbons was with you."

He nodded.

"Why would she run off and leave you to deal with that alone? I thought she was made of sterner stuff."

"We wanted to win the salvage contest," he said helplessly. His ears were pink with embarrassment, and his face was racked with guilt.

"You've lost me."

With an embarrassed sigh, he glanced at the pigeons lurking in the boxes beside him. They appeared as curious as Olive. "Miss Husselbee was going to give us her scrap paper." He scuffed his right foot over the gravel, sending bits of rock skipping across the dovecote floor. "We stopped by the Hall after school on Friday, but Miss Husselbee was out. The contest deadline was Saturday morning, and we were neck and neck with Jimmy Gilroy, so we needed that paper. We planned to go and get it from her after the dance." He'd started fidgeting, his thoughts no doubt shifting back to the memory of that night.

"And . . . ?" Olive prompted gently.

"Hen and I slipped out right after Miss Husselbee, planning to catch up with her, but we never did. And when we got to Peregrine Hall, she wasn't there. We waited a bit, but eventually, we walked back to the lodge and found her beside the dovecote."

At the mercy of her muddled mind, the Sergeant Major had mistakenly gone to Blackcap Lodge and so had been alone in her last, desperate moments.

"Did she truly say my mother's name?" Olive inquired. She

must have looked dubious, because he answered in the defensive.

"I swear," he said stoutly.

"I believe you. I just can't make sense of it. But get back to your story," she said encouragingly.

Grimly, he pressed on. "When we knew she was dead, and there was nothing we could do, Hen insisted we needed to fetch the paper she'd promised us. Otherwise we'd have to deal with the police and might lose our chance at the contest. The prize is five shillings, and we'd planned to split it."

"Hen should never have been wandering alone in the dark," Olive scolded. "Any sort of wastrel could be lurking about— English *or* German." Unfortunately, the poor girl was probably well used to fending for herself; Mrs Gibbons tended to be rather oblivious.

His face flamed. "She said not to worry, that she knew where to aim if she had any trouble."

"Perhaps *she* should be our first line of defence in the event of an invasion," Olive murmured caustically.

"She got the paper, and we got our collection weighed in on time." His face fell. "But Jimmy Gilroy—"

Olive was no longer paying attention. She was thinking back to the day she'd burgled Miss Husselbee's library at Peregrine Hall and found an unfinished diary entry, presumably intended for Mass Observation. There'd been no scrap paper anywhere, only blank paper in the drawer and that single sheet—also seemingly blank—in the typewriter. Because Hen had got there first.

"Where did she find the paper?" she demanded, stepping toward Jonathon, her heartbeat kicking up as she realised what must have happened to those diaries.

"There was a stack of newspapers in the kitchen, but with everyone off at the dance, she went looking for more. She found some in a tray on Miss Husselbee's desk—typed pages with a newspaper on top."

Olive felt the breath go out of her as her eyes shuttered closed.

"I told her it was wrong," Jonathon insisted miserably, "but she said we weren't hurting anyone, that Miss Husselbee had wanted us to have them. But then she lost her button, and we worried that the police—"

Olive gripped Jonathon's upper arms, her hands vibrating with urgency. "Don't worry about the police, and I'll return the button. Only tell me, where did you take the scrap?" She refused to believe that Hen was the blackmailer.

"To Forrester's Garage," he said, his eyes wide with alarm, the muscles of his face slack with shock. "Why do you want to know?"

Her thoughts instantly shifted back to those moments spent waiting in the darkness of the garage while George's father argued with Harry Danes. One of them had clearly used the word *blackmail*. Could they have found the diaries and decided to capitalise on their contents?

If they hadn't, someone else certainly had.

"I can't tell you," she said, hanging the rake on the hook by the door. "But I need to go and see if any of it is still there." Olive bolted out of the dovecote, with Jonathon hot on her heels.

"Can I go with you?" he pleaded. He was obviously feeling guilty and hoping to make amends.

"Come on."

She wheeled the motorbike out of the barn, climbed on, scooted forward on the seat, and nodded to Jonathon to climb on behind her as she started the engine. "Hang on tight!" she yelled before gunning them down the drive and onto the lane. The Welbike bounced over a stone in the road, lifting Jonathon off the seat. He tightened his grip on her waist, as Olive worried that she was already too late.

Miss Husselbee had set the stage for disaster, and Hen had unwittingly raised the curtain. Olive's own deceptions, much too recent, thankfully weren't at risk, at least from this quarter. But with the diaries now in the hands of an unscrupulous individual, anyone harbouring an older secret might have cause for concern.

They buzzed to a stop beside the pigpen, propped the motor-bike against the wall of the garage, and hurried along the back of the building. In the far corner was a modest tumbled heap of a scrap pile, with everything stacked chock-a-block alongside everything else. A pair of tyres leaned against a modest pile of collapsed tin cans, and a short stack of newspapers tied up with string sat atop a rusted tractor seat.

"Looks as if it's all been cleared out already to make room for more," Jonathon said, peering at her nervously.

"Damn." She'd expected this, but still she'd hoped. "We'll ask Mr Forrester when it was picked up."

In truth, she'd prefer to steer clear of the man, but the information might prove useful in determining who could have taken the diaries. As the owner of the garage, he was a prime suspect. Particularly as blackmail was a recent concern of his.

Olive could no longer look at the people she had known her entire life without wondering what they might be capable of—Mssr. Poirot would be proud. Her gaze shifted through the cluster of women, and the few token males, gathered in the village hall for a read-through of Harriet's dramatic interpretation of *Pride and Prejudice*. With Harriet still under the weather, Miss Rose had taken charge of getting everyone organised, then carried on, giving notes and directions in between her limited lines as Mary Bennet. In between making notes for her stepmother, Olive couldn't help but assess all the players as possible murderers and blackmailers.

Dr Ware was fidgety and standoffish, thoroughly in character as Mr Darcy but quite suspicious as far as Olive was concerned. Miss Danes's pettiness, while irritating, seemed to play out rather well in her role as George Wickham, and Lady Camilla was a marvellously regal Lady Catherine. She remained in character throughout, her gaze settling on each member of the cast with cool appraisal, and Olive couldn't help but wonder if she was channelling Miss Marple.

Whereas Poirot was ostentatious, peppering all manner of suspects with questions and spontaneously haring off, hot on the trail of a clue, Mrs Christie's spinster sleuth managed to have all the answers fall almost effortlessly into her lap. There was certainly something to be said for a seemingly innocent bit of busy-bodying, a casual gossip, or a chatty tea. But Olive was entirely too restless to be satisfied with such a method.

"Margaret. Leo," Miss Rose called, clapping sharply to interrupt a cosy but unscripted tête-à-tête between the pair. She glared over the rims of her spectacles. "Jane and Bingley are not engaged yet," she reminded them sternly, prompting a respectful nod from him and a good-humoured sigh from her. Margaret's worry and tension seemed to have fled, for the moment at least.

"Nothing gets by Rose," Violet warned. "Particularly nothing untoward. I suspect she'll be keeping a close eye on the intensity of your gaze when it flashes in my direction," she said, looking pointedly at Dr Ware.

Miss Rose ignored her, but Olive registered the subtle tightening of her jaw.

"I'm going to suggest to Harriet that Gillian and I switch roles," Miss Danes informed them, taking advantage of the interruption. "With her face and figure, she'd make a much more convincing man, I think, and the role of Lydia really requires someone more worldly wise." She smiled at George's sister, whose black look offered no misunderstanding as to her feelings on the matter.

"No, you are not," Miss Rose said, quietly emphatic. "The role of George Wickham is much more difficult for a woman to play, which is precisely why Harriet entrusted it to you. If you cannot manage it, we'll find someone more capable," she added, eyebrow raised in question.

Momentarily startled, Miss Danes rallied quickly. "I do see what you mean and what Harriet intended. It's best if I carry on as I am. Such a pivotal role." She moved away, her eyes alight with importance. Lady Camilla eyed her darkly before bestowing an encouraging smile on her daughter. Olive, for one, was heartily enjoying the rare display of gumption from Miss Rose.

The evening went on in much the same fashion, ad nauseam. After what felt to Olive like an eternity of overacting, distraction, and tactful corrections, it was time for refreshments, which had been graciously provided by Miss Danes, leaving Olive to wonder anew about Miss Husselbee's black-market allegations and what they might have prompted. Dr Ware darted eagerly away, perhaps on some nefarious business of his own, but Violet caught him at the door and slipped her arm companionably through his as Rose stared rigidly after them. Olive settled in comfortably, fully intending to question the "suspects" remaining.

There was a dodgy moment as they all stood around, staring dubiously at the golden sponge, no doubt thinking back to the dance and the poisoned cake that had led to Miss Husselbee's death.

"You needn't worry," Miss Danes chirped, turning to carve herself a piece. "I'll go first." Within seconds, she was chewing and swallowing with gusto as they held their collective breath.

Slinking up beside Olive, Margaret snorted, "A true, manly martyr."

Olive grinned as the cast crowded around the table, clearly satisfied that their safety was ensured. She and Margaret waited their turn, each of them silently scanning faces, wondering who among them might be capable of blackmail, to say nothing of murder. They'd seated themselves at a nearby table, toting a sultana bun and a teacup each, when Miss Danes spoke up again.

"Death by misadventure," she tsked. "If Marcellus had ever had cause to meet Verity Husselbee, he'd surely have predicted it."

"Oh, good Lord," Margaret muttered, rubbing her temple, as she turned her head just enough to keep from being overheard. Olive grinned behind her cup of tea. Miss Danes was an avid follower of the famous astrologer's column in the paper. Thus far, the war had gone on seven months longer than he'd predicted, but she continued to hold him in the highest esteem.

"You probably shouldn't say that, you know," Olive teased. "What would Leo say?"

"If I look appropriately chastened, he's quite forgiving," she said airily. Leaning closer, hiding her words behind her bun, she added, "I'm not in the habit of reading that charlatan's column, but if his advice could be interpreted in such a way as to suggest blackmail, then Miss Danes would follow along like a dutiful mouse behind the Pied Piper."

Olive looked at the woman, her face as round and placid as her Victoria sponge. The idea seemed impossible. "Perhaps we can find out where she was when the letter was delivered." She'd learned nothing useful from Mr Forrester—the salvage had been picked up when it usually was, and he'd not seen anyone lurking about. He'd definitely not been keen on being questioned, which had made her all the more suspicious.

Margaret stood abruptly. "I'll go ask her."

Olive blinked. *Well, that's one way.* She tugged at Margaret's sleeve. "Don't be obvious."

"Leave it to me," Margaret said before moving off.

"Misadventure, indeed," Mrs Spencer said, picking up where Miss Danes had left off. Cast as Mrs Bennet, the woman reminded Olive of a friendly weasel, with her beady eyes and wiry hair, tamped down under a hat adorned with a trio of bluebells. "It was murder, plain and simple."

"Surely it was an accident," Gillian protested, her doe-brown eyes appealing.

"Death by foxglove? When so many of us have been trained in

identifying it? I think not." Mrs Spencer squeezed Gillian's hand sympathetically. "I'm not keen on having a murderer in our midst, either, dear, but we can't bury our heads in the sand. What if one of us is next?"

The question silenced them all, and Miss Danes was the first to speak up. "We should all read Marcellus's next column carefully," she said portentously.

"Oh, shut up, Winifred," Lady Camilla snapped, her hand going instantly to the nape of her neck.

Miss Danes looked suitably shocked, her cheeks flushing red with embarrassment and her lower lip quivering in anger. Margaret, beside her, tucked in her lips, while her eyes danced with amusement. Olive shot her a quelling glare.

"I apologise," Lady Camilla said. "You're entitled to your own opinion, no matter how ignorant and ridiculous it might be." She walked purposely toward the kitchen, tugging one of the marcasite combs from her chignon as she went. Olive couldn't help but wonder if the stress of George's absence was taking its toll. The room was once again stunned into silence as Gillian trailed miserably after her. Those remaining clustered together, expressions agog. Miss Rose, sitting off by herself, appeared to be in a state of indecision, wondering whether to follow the pair.

Olive picked up her tea and the bun she hadn't yet touched, and moved closer. "Everyone is dealing with the situation differently," she said quietly, dropping into a chair beside her.

Miss Rose tipped her head down, tangling her fingers in her lap. "Quite."

There were so many questions buzzing about in Olive's head, she didn't know where to begin. *Should I start with murder or ease into it?* The matter was taken out of her hands.

"I know it's silly," Miss Rose began shakily, "but I can't help but feel that if I hadn't begged off with a headache, if I'd been manning the punchbowl as usual, I could have somehow prevented that awful accident." Her voice broke on the final word.

Olive set down her tea on a nearby chair to snake an arm around Miss Rose's narrow shoulders and give them a bolstering squeeze. "You mustn't think like that. No one could have predicted such a thing could happen." She glanced at the librarian and added quietly, "Except the murderer."

Miss Rose's head swivelled, and she stared outright. "You agree with Mrs Spencer? That it was murder?" There was a hint of disbelief in her voice. "You've been reading quite a lot of Agatha Christie lately," she said. "Perhaps it's making you unduly suspicious."

Olive decided it best not to admit that the books had likely set her thoughts on their current path. But circumstances—not to mention a motley collection of clues—had all but confirmed the possibility. Little had Miss Husselbee known when she'd handed over her library book and irritably quipped, "If you've nothing better to do, Miss Bright, why not solve a murder?" that Olive would take to the idea quite so vigorously. Then again, it was possible the Sergeant Major, who'd often scolded Olive's "rampageous curiosity," had sensed her need for distraction. Olive loved mental puzzles and had eagerly sought them out, feeling that the best ones demanded not only a measure of careful thinking but a dose of intuition, and even a few wild guesses, as well. She and Mssr. Poirot had that in common. The sense of satisfaction she felt as the pieces clicked into place was utterly addictive, and endeavouring to keep up with the little Belgian had kept Olive's mind busy during many long, frustrating months. The situation in which she now found herself was quite different: Agatha Christie's murder mysteries were all neatly confined to the pages of a book, whereas this one touched Pipley, making the solving of it desperately important.

She cleared the emotion from her throat before responding, "If there was no evidence to suggest murder, I'd happily abandon that line of thinking, simply because I don't want to consider that someone I know might be a killer."

"I don't understand."

Olive leaned closer. Lowering her voice, she said, "Miss Husselbee was one of very few people liable to try a cake made out of Spam, and once she'd had a slice, that cake disappeared. No one seems to know where it went, a fact I find too convenient and entirely suspicious." She hadn't actually posed the question, but it was there, nonetheless, hanging between them in the silence, and Olive waited for Rose Darling to answer it.

"I suppose," she allowed tentatively. Usually so composed, Miss Rose looked as if she was about to fall apart. She needed more prompting.

"Do *you* have any idea where it came from?"

She seemed startled. "N-no. None at all. My headache was particularly debilitating, so I stayed home and took one of the pills Dr Ware suggested." She raised a fluttery hand to her temple, as if remembering. "I didn't set foot in the hall that day." She'd coloured slightly at the mention of the chemist, but Olive decided this was not the time to pursue the subject of their burgeoning romance.

Olive reached for her bun and took a large bite. She was suddenly struck with a possibility. After chewing quickly and swallowing, she said, "Do you recall anyone borrowing a book that might prove useful in planning a murder?" Miss Rose stared silently, disbelievingly, so Olive quickly clarified the question. "It could be a book on plants or poisons, or some sort of medical tome. Or what about the minutes of the WI meetings? The details given by the Oxford professor in his talk on the medicinal plants scheme could be particularly useful. Aren't they kept in the library?"

Miss Rose rallied and answered in her usual crisp tone. "Yes, they are, but no one has requested them, and I don't recall any books of the sort you mention going out recently."

"I wonder," Olive thought aloud, "if Hercule Poirot has ever solved a case in which foxglove was found to be the murder weapon."

The librarian's face was implacable, and Olive couldn't tell whether she found the notion ridiculous or inspired. But then her expression changed, and she seemed to come to a decision.

"It's possible," she allowed. "Mrs Christie worked in a dispensary during the Great War and was very knowledgeable of medicines and poisons."

"Do you think you might be able to find out?" The question, tumbling out of her, took Olive by surprise. "I'd love to read through it and see if there are any clues to be had." She glanced around. "And I'd much prefer if we could keep this between ourselves."

"Our very own little mystery," Miss Rose said bemusedly. "You can rely on my discretion."

"Excellent," Olive said, rather pleased with herself. Now she could get on with subtly probing questions about Dr Ware and those mice. "Dr Ware is quite good as Mr Darcy, don't you think?"

"He is," Miss Rose agreed, her words clipped.

"I think you would have done equally well as Elizabeth." Olive then added conspiratorially, "I did suggest it to Harriet. The pair of you are so in tune, I think it would have come across as perfectly authentic."

It was the exact right thing to say. Miss Rose's face brightened, her eyes sparkled, and her bony torso seemed to swell with pride. "Yes," she said breathlessly. "We've discovered we have many of the same interests." She smiled shyly and went on. "A few months ago, we both rode up to London for the same lecture. We went for supper afterwards and became better acquainted. We're both fascinated by the natural sciences, and despite his considerable experience, he encourages my questions and suggestions. He's allowed me to—" She broke off abruptly, as if suddenly realising she shouldn't say any more. And before Olive could press her, she stood and gabbled, "I think I'll just pop into the kitchen to make sure everything is all right."

Olive stared after her, wondering what she'd been about to say and suspecting it might be rather important.

Margaret sidled up the moment she'd gone. "I didn't want to interrupt if you were luring a confession out of her," she said.

Olive rolled her eyes. "I wasn't. Were you able to eliminate Miss Danes as your blackmailer?"

"Not exactly," she admitted. "I told her the cinnamon she'd been requesting had come into the store, and I'd gone round to deliver it at midday." She smirked. "It hadn't," Margaret added as an irrelevant aside. "Well, I could tell right off that she was hiding something. Her eyes went as wide as crab apples, and her cheeks flushed a rather blowsy red." She paused for breath, and Olive nodded at her to go on. "I told her I'd knocked but no one had answered, and seeing as I was rather keen to frazzle her, I said I'd peeked in the windows, and where had she been. She was frazzled, all right. She turned into a right shrew." Margaret shook her head, smiling at the memory.

"Well? What happened then?" demanded Olive.

"She said it was none of my business where she'd been, and I'd best not be looking in her windows, or she'd call Leo and the constable, as well. As if I'd have any interest in looking in that harpy's windows." She shuddered.

"She obviously wasn't at home, which means she could have left the blackmail note. And she certainly could have baked a poison cake, particularly as her garden is dotted with foxglove." Olive paused, her thoughts changing direction. "It's possible she received a letter, as well. You said yourself she was hiding something. Perhaps Miss Husselbee peered in her windows before you did and jotted her findings for Mass Observation?"

"I suppose it's possible," Margaret allowed. "Although I'd really rather she be the villain. Imagine that sanctimonious face behind prison bars . . ." This was precisely why Margaret was not Watson material.

"We'll keep investigating," Olive promised. "We have a bit of time yet before the money's due." It was beginning to look as if everyone in the village had a secret, and she was going to have to wade through them all to find the person who was hiding the biggest one of all.

Chapter 16

"Why do you think Miss Husselbee mentioned your mother?" Jonathon asked, squinting up at her through the tousle of nut-brown hair falling over his forehead as he dug in the dirt. They'd brought the four mission-ready pigeons into the garden to search for snails the night's rain had lured into easy reach.

"I suspect it was merely a coincidence. She had, after all, found herself at the lodge and was likely confused and disoriented. But I do appreciate your discretion." She had been poring over the woman's notebook in her spare minutes and had yet to find a reference to her mother amid the baffling shorthand. Hardly surprising, but even so, it was one mystery she was happy to put to rest.

With regards to all the others, however, she couldn't help but be exasperated that the notebook had turned out to be a particularly frustrating red herring. While it was true she'd managed to piece together a few shocking titbits, she hadn't a clue whose conduct had prompted the unfinished Mass Observation diary entry or whose secret might have been worthy of murder. It was entirely likely they were one and the same.

As she sat considering this on a little garden stool, Badger waddled toward a puddle and dipped his head to drink. Jonathon, content with her explanation, had crouched near a cluster of sticks poking out of the ground near his potato plants. As she watched, he tugged them up, one by one, and crowed with triumph when he reached the third.

"Caught the little bugger," he said, hurrying to show Olive his prize.

She stared at the dirty, wrinkled vegetable he held by the stick stabbed through its centre.

"It's a potato," she said.

"Yes, but inside the potato is a wireworm." So saying, he reached into the tuber's hollow centre and, with finger and thumb, pinched the creature by its tail and held it up for her to see. "If we're not careful, they'll eat through our entire crop of onions, carrots, and potatoes. He's the second one I've caught. The first was Hitler. This is Goebbels." With a flick of his hand, he sent the wriggling yellow-brown worm spinning through the air to land between Poppins and Fritz. They pulled him apart, prompting a cheer from both Olive and Jonathon.

"Miss Husselbee showed me how to rig an old potato to lure them in," he said quietly, turning to rebury the tuber trap.

"She would have heartily approved of your choice of names," Olive said stoutly.

When he was finished checking the rest of his traps and pulling a few scattered weeds, he came to stand beside Olive, who was staring down at the pigeons and the song thrush that had joined them in their snail search. She draped her arm around his shoulders. "They're ready," she said quietly but emphatically. "Although I can't help but be nervous for them."

"They'll come home heroes," Jonathon said confidently. "Carrying messages that will change the course of the war." His eyes were alight now. "And Captain Aldridge will be thoroughly abashed he ever doubted them."

Olive scoffed. "Don't be so sure. I get the feeling he doesn't trust what he doesn't understand." She cut her eyes around at Jonathon. "And he most certainly doesn't understand pigeons. Or cats. Or me, for that matter." She smirked. "You see our dilemma."

"I think you're being too hard on him," he insisted.

"Perhaps we ought to have a little wager, Master Maddocks."

Jonathon nodded agreeably.

"Whoever's right gets half the other's next ration of chocolate. What do you think about that?" she said.

"Deal."

They shook on it, and Olive's hand came away coated with pungent dark soil. It reminded her instantly of those dead little mice and Dr Ware. She had promised Hen she'd talk to him but had found herself preoccupied with other suspects. Olive couldn't help but think him entirely harmless, but perhaps a new strategy was in order. Remembering the ease with which Jonathon had ensnared the wireworm, she decided to set a trap of her own.

Dusting her hands on the seat of her trousers, she said hurriedly, "I need to go into Pipley for a bit—my bicycle should be ready by now."

"I'll go with you. I need to make the rounds, collecting scraps for the pigs."

"It seems you've got the short end of the stick as far as the pigs are concerned," she teased.

"I don't mind. They're rather fond of me."

"Yes, well. Don't lean in, expecting appreciative kisses." Her lips formed a moue of distaste. "They're ferociously indiscriminate in their eating habits," she added with a lift of her brows.

Jonathon merely laughed.

"Let's get the pigeons back to the loft," she said. "The cats might be prowling about, and we can't afford to lose any birds—least of all, these."

* * *

One glimpse of Finn, Eske, and little Swilly was all it took to have her thoughts shifting to Jameson Aldridge. They ignored her with precisely the same infuriating insouciance. Just thinking of it had her climbing onto her newly repaired bicycle and pumping hard at the pedals on her way to the chemist's shop. The bare minimum of words had been exchanged with Mr Forrester, all of them laden with suspicion on both sides, and Olive couldn't help but think sadly of George.

Feeling a queasy sense of déjà vu, Olive propped her bicycle beside the shop window, squared her shoulders, and pushed open the door. The shop smelled reassuringly of eucalyptus, bay rum, and wood polish, but the glass counter was dotted with fingerprints and the display cases were slightly disarranged. When Dr Ware finally appeared from the back room, a reason presented itself. His left forearm was wrapped in a bandage, and his shirtsleeves were rolled up to the elbows, but he was flushed and beaming and looking much more himself.

"You've hurt yourself," she said, her scattered thoughts trying to alight on a good explanation for both the injury and the dead mice.

"It's nothing to worry over. A small scratch is all." His hair was rumpled, and there were two red spots at the bridge of his nose, no doubt left by his glasses, which were missing at the moment.

"Well, it must be difficult to keep up with the shop. I'd be happy to help out." She started to move around the counter.

"No need," he said, moving forward, warding her off. "That's very generous, but I can manage quite well."

"Well, if you're certain. I've just come by, hoping to see the mice."

"The mice?" He looked genuinely puzzled.

"Henrietta Gibbons told me she'd caught the cutest little field mice for you. I wondered if I could see them." Olive widened her eyes, trying for limpid naïveté. "I adore the little creatures and never really get a chance to look at them. Our cats are too diligent." She pouted, then worried she was overdoing and stopped.

Dr Ware didn't move for a long moment, despite looking as if he wanted to bolt. In this little game of cat and mouse, she was most definitely the cat. Aldridge would no doubt approve of the comparison. A sheen of perspiration had appeared on Dr Ware's forehead, and his Adam's apple shifted erratically.

His response, when it came, was self-deprecating. "I don't have them anymore, I'm sorry to say."

Olive said, "Oh?"

He huffed out a short, tired breath. "I came across a kestrel while out walking. His wing had been caught on something, some sort of wire perhaps. It seems the Home Guard are stringing wire up everywhere lately. He was hobbling about rather helplessly. I'd planned to scrounge some food for him." He shrugged. "But Henrietta was in the shop that day, picking up for her mother, and I thought it couldn't hurt to ask her. That girl is indefatigable." He looked away and ran a slow hand over the crown of his head. "I'm afraid I had to kill them first," he said apologetically. "The poor fellow never would have caught them if I'd left them alive. The next day I convinced myself we were getting along quite famously, and got rather too close. The brute scratched the dickens out of me," he finished with a laugh, holding his bandaged arm up as proof.

"Oh," Olive said again, her tone less limpid this time. "I hope you spared no time getting the wound doused with alcohol. You certainly don't want to deal with an infection." At his nod, she went on. "That's a relief, then. For you, anyway, not so much the mice. Where is the bird now? Perhaps I could have a look at his injury. You could have brought him to the surgery straightaway."

"No, no. I'm sure he's quite healed by now. If not, he won't be there in any case . . ."

He was very likely right, but that left Olive with no good opportunity to pursue her clumsy questioning. Still, she had to try.

"That was very noble of you, all things considered. He certainly wasn't very grateful, was he?"

"I should have known better," he admitted.

"Harriet was so appreciative that you agreed to play Mr Darcy, and I've told her you're doing splendidly. I hope it hasn't taken too much time away from your work . . . ?" She let the question trail off, but before he could answer, she pressed on. "I know you don't like to discuss it, but I'm very curious, more so given that I was forced to postpone my own studies." The business of busy-bodying, Olive had discovered, was not for the faint of heart.

Dr Ware rubbed two fingers over the furrows on his forehead. She was clearly making him nervous, but she endeavoured not to feel guilty. Poirot certainly had no qualms in his search for the truth and thought nothing of putting people awkwardly on the spot.

He cleared his throat. "I hope you don't think me rude, but I'm really not in the habit of discussing my work. It's rather difficult to explain, particularly in the early stages."

Propping her elbows on the counter and leaning in conspiratorially, she said, "There's *no one* you've taken into your confidence?" She tidied the combs in the box beside her. "Miss Rose, perhaps?" His eyes flashed nervously, and Olive turned the screws. "I suspect her brain is rather like your own. A sponge for knowledge, a hotbed of curiosity." She smiled coyly.

He stepped backwards and stumbled over something on the floor as a blush crested his cheeks and rose even higher. "No, no. That is to say, she has been quite helpful, but I—we—" He heaved a great steadying breath. "I keep my research quite private until I've drawn my conclusions. Now, I really must get back to work."

At that moment, the shop door opened to admit a young woman wearing a dark-green jersey tucked into belted khaki breeches. Her short, curly hair was precisely the same colour as the freckles that dotted her cheeks. She smiled, and Olive wondered if this might be Jonathon's Land Girl. Eager for the interruption, Dr Ware shifted quickly down the counter.

Knowing she'd been routed, Olive said goodbye and stepped outside. Rather disgruntled with her lack of success, she was pushing her bicycle off when she remembered Margaret's fib to Winifred Danes. With Dr Ware busy in the shop, perhaps she could peep in the windows at the back and find a legitimate explanation for the dead mice—the kestrel, she was quite certain, had been contrived for her benefit. It would be too depressing to go away without even the slightest little clue. She turned at the corner and backtracked up the alley behind the shop, with her head on a swivel. She didn't relish the thought of trying to explain herself.

The back of the chemist's was nondescript, with a dusty stoop and two rather dirty windows. She propped her bicycle, glanced once more up and down the alley, and then peered through the first window, squinting into the relative darkness. Unable to see clearly through the grime, she rubbed her jumper-clad elbow over the glass and tried again.

The north wall was comprised of a long counter fit with a sink. It was crowded with chemical equipment—various flasks and beakers, and other glass apparatuses she couldn't identify. The remainder of the space was outfitted with a heavy worktable and wooden stools and chairs, and every last square inch of it was covered with buckets and pans and other dubious receptacles. She squinted harder, trying to see what they contained.

Thwarted in her efforts, she moved to the other window, leading with her elbow this time. She was closer to the sink now, and peering in, she realised that every available flask and beaker was similarly put to use. The odd thing was, it was all one great jumble, with no discernible labels or organisation. It would appear to Olive's amateur eye that Dr Ware had moved past the experimental stage and was producing . . . what, exactly? The better questions were, Why here? Why in secret? Surely this sort of work was better suited to an official laboratory. Unless he was a fifth columnist, working for the enemy. It was too horrid to contemplate. But Miss Husselbee had suspected, perhaps even confirmed, that someone in the village was involved in something evil. If it had been finished, would that diary entry have linked Dr Ware to treasonous acts?

"Most people go around to the front door," said a voice just behind her. "But you're not like most people, are you, Olive Bright?"

Olive whirled, her heart jumping to the base of her throat. "Where did you come from?" she accused Violet Darling. The other woman was standing, perfectly at ease, in trousers the colour of shortbread and a jammy-toned wrap. Despite the cigarette patiently smouldering in her right hand, she put Olive in mind of a cosy tea.

"There are so many ways I could answer that question," she said smoothly, "but I suspect you mean, How did I happen to be walking down this way at the precise moment you were snooping into the back room of the chemist shop?"

"Clever of you," Olive allowed.

Violet flicked the ash from her cigarette and shook her hair back. "I find that people, with their everyday problems and everyday complaints, can be quite ruinous to the imagination. I much prefer to frequent quiet, deserted—even undesirable—locations when I need a temporary respite from my own mind."

"I see. And do you plan to tattle to Dr Ware?" Olive instantly wondered if she'd misstepped. Unlike George, Violet Darling surely wouldn't appreciate such heavy-handed tactics.

"I do think I'd have rather a lot of fun with that. He's rather dishy." When Olive's expression didn't change, she sighed. "Honestly, I couldn't care less what you're doing," she said seriously, her eyes meeting Olive's. "If you want to climb in through the window and have a look around, I'll even keep watch. Maybe I could hoot like an owl if anyone comes."

"That's not necessary, but I appreciate the thought." Her sense of humour, not so much.

Violet shrugged, but when Olive snatched her bicycle and climbed onto the seat, ready to push off, Violet pulled her up short. "Did you at least find what you were looking for?"

Olive's shoulders slumped in frustration. "I didn't know *what* I was looking for."

Violet's eyes widened in understanding and sparkled with mischief. "You're prowling for clues." Her tone imbued the task with all the dignity of making mud pies. "If you'd planned to peer through our windows, I can save you the trouble." She winked. "Rose is out. Walk right through the door," she said with a magnanimous gesture. "You can have carte blanche."

"No thank you," Olive said primly, eager to be off, with the wind cooling her heated cheeks.

"I'm only teasing, darling. Honestly, I'm thrilled you're searching for suspects. That evens the playing field, as far as I'm concerned."

"Then I suppose this whole thing hasn't been a *complete* failure," Olive said sourly.

"You're a clever girl with a desire to see justice done, but the truth always carries a price. Make certain you're willing to pay it." With these portentous words delivered, Violet Darling turned and drifted off down the alley, the smoke curling behind her.

Monday, 21 April 1941
Peregrine Hall, Pipley
Hertfordshire

If R.D. had been on her own the first time we'd crossed paths, I would have thought her simply a shy and quiet young lady of passable but plain prettiness. Unfortunately for her, V.D. was forever in her company all those years ago. I've never seen two sisters as different as those two—utterly disconcerting. R was content to watch the world go by, whereas V was the sort to imagine that it spun strictly for her. If the former was a titmouse, the latter was a peacock, brazenly seeking attention.

As expected, V's vainglorious ways came to a rather fitting end. The girl who craved attention got it in spades when she eloped with the wastrel stepson of a prominent local family. We've not seen hide nor hair of either of them, but a few months ago, R let slip that her sister had written a string of popular sensational novels under an alternate nom de plume.

When pressed to reveal it, she objected that V would not want the secret divulged. Hardly surprising, given that R is entirely content to moulder away in the quiet confines of a lending library, but ridiculous, nonetheless. Having made a success of herself, V would assuredly want to gloat. I will solve this little mystery with or without R's help.

I should mention that, while I would never condone the sort of scandalous activity portrayed in sensational novels, they are rather deliciously entertaining, and I expect V's will be particularly so.

V.A.E. Husselbee

Chapter 17

Olive had never been the sort of girl to sneak out of the house, keep secrets, or shirk punishments. She was the sort to announce her intention, argue its merits and, if forbidden to proceed, pinpoint a loophole and adjust her plans accordingly. Unfortunately, that strategy was insupportable for the foreseeable future. Which was why she'd gone up to bed early, claiming a headache, changed into dark trousers and jacket, and then crept down the stairs under cover of her father's voluble diatribe on Nazi arrogance. With no one but Jonathon the wiser, she'd absconded to the loft, crated the three musketeers, and proceeded to lug them a quarter mile in the dark. Captain Aldridge was waiting, but not patiently.

He climbed out of the car and skirted the bumper as she yanked the back door open and manoeuvred the crate onto the seat.

"You're late," he said grimly. "We agreed to meet at eight. It is now"—his arm shot out and keeled over, exposing his barely illumined watch face—"eight twenty-three."

Having got the birds settled for the drive, she slammed the door shut and glared up at him in the dark. "Chivalry has clearly

gone the way of the onion in this war," she said waspishly, "both
only available on the rare occasion."

He ignored that but reached around her to pull the passenger
door wide. "No one saw you come out with the pigeons?"

"Only Jonathon."

"And if someone catches you coming in? You've come up with
an excuse?"

"With a sobriquet like Lady Resourceful, I would think you
shouldn't even need to ask." She beamed up at him as he slammed
the door shut.

He slipped in beside her and started the engine. Olive closed
her eyes and breathed deeply, hoping to settle the fierce emotions churning a path through her insides: pride, relief, anxious-
ness, anticipation, fear. . . . The sudden scent of liquorice had
her mind shifting back to the night of the dance—and after. Her
eyes flared open to see his right hand hovering in front of her, the
sweet cradled in his palm. Without a word, she plucked it up,
popped it into her mouth, and focused on its sweet liquorice
taste. Her thoughts drifted, and she found herself wondering distractedly if Aldridge tasted the same. This, in turn, prompted a
choking fit and a sound thump on the back from her unwilling
companion.

The next few moments were spent in a tense, humming silence as he drove as fast as he dared down the narrow, rolling
lanes under the light of a full moon.

"Harriet inquired after you this evening," she said sweetly,
savouring the last little bit of sweet drifting on her tongue.

"Regarding?"

"She overheard my half of our phone conversation a few
days ago."

"Ah," he said. "What did you tell her?"

Olive kept her voice as bland as his. "I told her I thought it
was probably time to forgive you."

"And have you?"

"Do you care?"

"Well, I'm curious."

"If that's the extent of your interest, then it hardly matters, does it?"

"Let's talk about something else, shall we?" he said calmly. "When we get there, you're to stay out of the way. The pigeon gear is already prepped, and the agents have all been briefed. Each has read the instructions on handling the birds, and they know the proper protocol. Your expertise is not required this evening. We're on a schedule, and as you may recall, you were late."

She answered stiffly. "I would appreciate a few moments with the birds before they get put into their canisters." Her hands, cradled in her lap, were fidgety with nerves, but she stilled them, not wanting him to see. "I like to speak to them before a long flight. They expect it," she finished, her voice clipped.

He propped his outstretched arm against the steering wheel and glanced out the side window, clearly wanting to object. "If I allow it, am I forgiven?"

"Yes," Olive agreed instantly, feeling an unexpected lump in her throat. In his mind, there was probably nothing to forgive, but she was thankful he wasn't in the mood to lecture.

The rest of the drive seemed to go by much too quickly, and soon they'd pulled to a stop at the edge of the tarmac at RAF Stradishall airfield. Aldridge came quickly around the hood, but Olive had already hopped out to retrieve the pigeons.

He propped his hand on the top of the door as she lifted the crate. "Would you prefer to speak to them now, while you have a little privacy, or do you want to wait until the last moment?"

"I'll wait," she said, her gaze straying past him to the aeroplane that sat ready close by—a snub-nosed Whitley. Jonathon, a tremendous fan of the *Biggles* stories, featuring pilot and adventurer James Bigglesworth, kept her well informed of Britain's many and varied aircraft.

When Aldridge moved to take the crate from her hands, she shook her head. "Part of the ritual."

They walked briskly toward a cluster of men dressed in dark clothes of the sort she'd seen at Brickendonbury: dungarees, jumpers, heavy jackets, and sturdy boots. A trio of cylindrical red canisters sat behind them, awaiting the birds. Everything else, it seemed, had already been put on board.

Aldridge hailed them quietly. "Bonsoir. I assume everything is in readiness." Each nodded in turn, their gazes turning curiously to Olive. "Gentlemen, this is Olive Bright. She is our pigeoneer and has recently been hired on as a FANY to work with us at Station Seventeen." He gestured to the men in turn. "This is Jacques, Philippe, and Roméo."

Olive shook their hands in turn, shivering in the chill night air. A glance at Aldridge informed her that she could wait no longer. She set the crate down carefully, unlatched it, and reached inside for Aramis. She cupped her hands around him and lightly ran her fingers over his chest and the smooth curve of his head. The preparations were done. She'd examined each of the birds earlier, making certain their eyes were bright and healthy and confirming their remex and rectrix feathers were intact on wings and tails, respectively. They'd been fed and watered and had their feet rubbed with petroleum jelly to ensure an unhindered flight. The pep talk was all that remained.

She took a breath and looked the pigeon in the eye. "All right, Aramis," she said quietly. "Every other flight has prepared you for this one, and I've no doubt you're ready. So much more is at stake now, but I trust your instincts and abilities. Jonathon is counting on you to win that bet. Godspeed." Her throat was tight as she nudged him into his personal canister and clipped it shut.

Fritz and Badger had their turns, and in a moment, it was done. She stood and turned and, without looking at Aldridge, addressed the agents. "One of you will see to it that they're fed and given water?"

"*Oui, mademoiselle*," came the answer. It was the one called

Roméo, his eyes twinkling in the light of the moon. "We will do it. My brother used to raise pigeons, but now they are all gone. With any luck, these will come home to you."

She smiled at him, relieved. He would know what to do. A hand gripped her elbow, tugged her back and away as the men lifted the canisters, put a hand up in salute, and turned toward the aeroplane.

"Bonne chance," Aldridge called quietly after them.

"So those were code names?" Olive asked.

"We don't even know their real names," he said dryly. "Their code names were assigned by RF Section."

Olive shifted her gaze toward the cockpit. Though it felt like a lifetime ago, it had been only a week and a half since George left, and she wondered how soon it would be before he was flying similar missions across the Channel in the dark. She knew he was anxious to get on with it, but for her, sitting at home, waiting and worrying, it didn't bear thinking about.

Barely five minutes later, the plane was taxiing down the runway. Her arm shot out, rigid against the night sky, her index and middle fingers forming the V for victory, as tears of pride and hope shimmered in her eyes.

The ride back to the lodge—or as close to it as they dared—was rather solemn, at least on her part. Her thoughts were consumed with worry over their chances. These birds and agents and all of them toiling on the home front, every soldier, airman, and seaman, and the Resistance in every Allied nation. Could they prevail?

The air felt tense and heavy with anticipation, and Olive thought back to those last days in London, before Liam had gone and she'd trooped dutifully home to Pipley. They'd found they were both quite willing to use the impending war as an excuse to gather their rosebuds. Her bed may as well have been strewn with petals. That seemed a lifetime ago, and roses were so lovely. . . .

Olive didn't turn her head but instead slid her eyes to look at Aldridge. They'd be back soon. What would he do if she crawled onto his lap and laid her lips against his? No expectations, no repercussions, merely a consensual release of pent-up emotion and frustration and worry.

"The first time is always the hardest," Aldridge said beside her, sending an electric shock straight through her bones.

She put a hand up to rub her forehead and fought down exasperated laughter. "How many first times have you had?"

He turned to look at her. "What on earth do you mean?"

She smiled to herself. "You told my father you've been declared medically unfit for active service, but you also insisted that your captain's title was earned. So, at the very least, you've had a first time with Station Seventeen and a first time somewhere else."

"So, I have," he said quietly.

"If this is another topic you'd rather not discuss, we can talk about pigs. Or sheep."

"We could," he allowed, "but we might run off the road and barrel straight into a tree out of sheer bloody boredom." Before she could comment, he went on. "Then again, the alternative isn't exactly riveting."

"If you're boring me, I'll speak right up."

"I've no doubt," he said dryly. It took him a moment, and Olive closed her eyes and let the slow lilt of his voice transport her. "I left Ireland just after the war started to join the British Expeditionary Force. We were sent into Belgium straightaway and charged with pushing back the Germans to the river Dyle. A few of us got separated from our division, and with little training and limited supplies, we decided to shift our strategy to undermining their infrastructure." She could picture him, young and fiercely determined, and her heart hitched.

He went on. "We had a bit of success and then got our hands

on some explosive charges. Two of us were tasked with setting the charges on a bridge the Germans were using to transport supplies." His voice had flattened, and Olive felt a cringe of foreboding low in her stomach. "They went off too early," he said simply. "We must have mistimed the fuse, or else the charges were faulty, and we were only twenty-five metres away. I landed in a ditch and was knocked unconscious. I found the body of my partner, Corporal Colin Andrews, in a nearby tree. He wasn't as lucky."

Olive's eyes flew wide, and she jerked her head to look at him even as she felt the clutch to her insides. He didn't turn.

"I didn't walk away completely unscathed, but I managed well enough through the Battle of Dunkirk, until I was back in England. By then I'd been promoted to captain, but that wasn't particularly useful when the doctors discovered that I'd lost partial hearing in one ear and was prone to some rather ferocious headaches. Not long after the army decided it was best to prop me at a desk, I was approached by Baker Street."

Hearing the bitterness in his voice, Olive realised they were more alike than she would have imagined. They were both frustrated by the hand they'd been dealt in this war; they felt guilty to have it so easy when for so many others, every day was a matter of life and death. Perhaps they should stop taking it out on each other.

He slowed the car to a stop at the precise spot he'd waited less than three hours before. "I'll walk you from here. And for once, wait there and let me open the bloody door."

He climbed out, and she waited, her hands shaking slightly at the thought of all he'd already been through. The moment her door opened, she rallied. "I don't need you to walk me home. I'm quite capable."

"Earlier you were lamenting the demise of chivalry," he reminded her. Grudgingly, she took his hand, and he pulled her to her feet.

A spectral white mist was beginning to curl through the long grass, and a shiver ran over her. "I suppose it's one of those things. You miss it when you don't have it. Otherwise it's rather superfluous."

"Quite." It was too dark to read the expression in his eyes as he stared down at her. But as she moved to retrieve the pigeon crate, he laid his palm against the back door. "If we're being superfluous, we might as well go all out."

She was perfectly content to let him carry the bulky thing. They kept to the verge to quiet their footsteps and clung to the shadows, but they were quite alone. She could almost imagine they were the only two people for miles, and was strangely comforted by the solid bulk of him.

"Truce?" she said lightly, peering up at him.

"I was never your enemy, Olive," he said, his voice sounding heavy and tired. Her name on his lips always took her by surprise.

"Perhaps not, but you haven't been on my side from the very beginning."

"Of course I have. We're *all* on the same side. Except for the traitors. But I'm quite certain you're not one of those."

"Don't be obtuse. You know exactly what I mean. You didn't trust me." She held her breath for a long, painful moment as she waited for three dreaded words to fall from his mouth: *I still don't*.

"I've seen the error of my ways," he said lightly. "Some might say I've had it thrown back in my face."

The tightness in her chest eased, and with her face wreathed in shadow, she smiled. She was over the moon that her risky visit to Brickendonbury had worked to her advantage. "I hope you don't expect me to apologise. It was for your own good, Jamie," she said, slipping her arm through his, relieved to have finally got comfortable with the name she was meant to be calling him.

By the following morning, he was Captain Aldridge all over again.

Monday, 12th May

Despite her late night, Olive was up early, wishing the sun had deigned to show its face, as well. As she scanned the murky morning sky and turned up her collar against the pervasive chilly mist, she walked quickly to the dovecote. As far as she knew, the bell hadn't rung overnight, but nevertheless, she eagerly peered into the mounted cage, hoping to see that one of the birds had returned.

She was disappointed. This prompted a flutter of worry, which she attempted to suppress, knowing it wasn't justified. It hardly mattered; she worried about each of the birds when they were far from home, but this was different. So much was riding on their success, on their ability to make the return journey without a hitch. Knowing that she'd likely be frazzled and distracted all day, she decided it was probably best if she kept to herself. She would take one final look at Miss Husselbee's notebook, with its initials and abbreviations and confusing code words—what could "hips and pips" possibly mean?—and hope for the best.

All day long she kept to the garden and dovecote, testing the alert bell at obsessive intervals. She felt simultaneously hyper-alert and desperate for a nap. Her hands were chapped and filthy, her hair was frizzy, and her nerves were shot. Even her sleuthing had turned up nothing useful, although she suspected her utter lack of focus could be contributing to that particular setback. Her skills at deception, however, seemed particularly honed.

Her father had been by, wondering at the dovecote's altered configuration. She'd convinced him it made perfect sense for all the reasons she'd already thought of. "Good thinking," he'd said brusquely, clapping her on the shoulder even as he whistled for Kíli.

Harriet, on the other hand, had confided that she thought she'd heard footsteps on the stairs late the night before, and Olive had quickly admitted she had had trouble sleeping and had felt a touch feverish. She'd slipped outside to sit on the stoop, relishing the cold moonlit night. She had fallen asleep against the door-jamb and had slipped back into bed a few hours later, her toes like icicles.

"Well, I hope you're feeling better today. You look very pale, and rather shattered. Then again, perhaps I'm coming down with it myself. I keep hearing an odd ringing . . ."

After that conversation, Olive had ceased all testing of the bell.

When she heard a car rolling up the drive later that afternoon, she was hoping rather desperately that it was Aldridge. She had nothing to report, but perhaps, somehow, he'd got his hands on some information. It *was* him. But having hurried over, she pulled up short in confusion as he unfolded his tall frame from the driver's seat and speared her with a look of barely controlled fury.

"We need to talk," he growled.

She hitched her hands onto her hips, her mouth open to snap back, but she promptly thought better of it. Jonathon would be back from school shortly, and her father, who'd been holed up in his surgery for the past hour, was liable to pop out of the barn at any moment. Olive spun on her heel and stalked off, leading him around behind the garden shed, out of view of the parlour.

"Keep your voice down," she said, crossing her arms across her chest, waiting for his latest irritation to roll over her.

"You lied to me." He was standing two feet away from her, legs braced, hands stuffed down in his pockets. His face was a fury.

Olive frowned, considering. Had she? Embellished, maybe, but outright lied? "I don't think so."

He leaned toward her and said silkily, "You claimed your mother was a FANY, driving ambulances during the last war."

"Yes," she agreed, waiting for further explanation.

He stared, but when no further response was forthcoming, he growled, "She bloody well wasn't."

"Of course she was," Olive insisted, her own voice rising in irritation.

His angular face looked harder, sharper—almost unrecognisable from that of the man who'd walked her home only hours ago. A frisson of uncertainty skittered along her spine as he carefully enunciated each word. "It's standard policy to look into the backgrounds of anyone coming to work for Baker Street. We had done our research on your father when we approached you, but hadn't looked into your mother. You were, after all, only supplying pigeons. But when it was decided you would become an official FANY, working inside Brickendonbury, privy to the secrets of Station Seventeen, I checked into her. You'd claimed she was on the front lines, heroically recovering the wounded amid the bombs and devastation." Seeing Olive's emphatic nod, he uttered his last words through gritted teeth. "I checked the FANY registry."

He paused, and Olive's eyebrows rose, willing him to go on.

"There is no record of her ever having been a FANY," he said, his jaw rigid.

She shook her head dismissively. "Of course there is. Somewhere there must be." She shrugged. "Probably a page got misplaced, or part of the records are stored somewhere else."

Scoffing, he turned away from her but quickly whipped around again. "You're persisting with your story?"

"Yes. I'm persisting." Olive was in a temper now. "Because it's the truth. You can take it up with my father if you'd like," she challenged.

"Let's," he said coldly, raising one eyebrow to indicate he was prepared to go right now. She hadn't expected this reaction but now smugly turned, already anticipating seeing him taken down a peg.

After finding the surgery empty, they were marching toward the house as Jonathon wheeled onto the drive. With one look at Olive's face, he quickly scrambled after them.

Excellent. There'll be an audience.

She found her father keeping Harriet company on the sofa in the parlour, and as their little procession trailed into the room, she wasted no time on pleasantries. "Captain Aldridge has just accused me of lying about Mother's war work. He insists that she wasn't an ambulance driver," Olive said calmly, "or even a FANY." Her chest rose with emotion and indignation as Kíli rolled to her feet and trotted over to give the officer a sniff. "He refuses to believe me, and so I've brought him along. Perhaps you can convince him." Her introduction finished, she spun away and stared out the French doors, waiting for the glorious moment in which her father set him straight.

It was too long in coming, though, and she had no choice but to turn back to the room, a frown settling heavily on her brow. Her gaze darted to her father, who was looking decidedly uncomfortable, shifted to notice Harriet's distress, and finally flashed on Jonathon, whose confusion likely mirrored her own. She knew Aldridge was watching her, but she refused to meet his eyes.

Moving closer, she demanded, "Why aren't you speaking up for me—for *her*?"

She darted a frustrated glance at Aldridge, who now appeared oddly discomfited. Her father's face had greyed, and he seemed to have shrunk right in front of her. As he bowed his head, she had the sense that he felt a tremendous shame. His words, when they finally came, were little more than whispers.

"Because he's right, Olive."

The wrinkles of confusion dug deeper. "Wait a moment. What do you mean, he's right?" she demanded. "How could he possibly be right? I've heard all the stories. There's a photograph on my dresser. She's posing with her ambulance," she insisted. "It can't all be a lie . . ."

"You'd better all sit down." Harriet's voice drifted through the silent shock that hung over the room. Jonathon slipped to Olive's side, and together, they sank onto the opposite sofa. Aldridge faded from view. Her father took a breath, propped his hands on his knees, and stood. He proceeded to pace, rubbing a rough hand over this mouth and chin as he considered where to begin. When he finally spoke, Olive was riveted.

"Your mother always had the best intentions. She *wanted* to volunteer as a FANY, wanted to help all those suffering on the front lines and in the trenches. She wanted to fetch them all away in an ambulance, to be stitched right up in hospital." His eyes looked bleak and apologetic, but Olive couldn't focus on that; she still couldn't make sense of any of it.

"When I met her at the end of the war, she was sitting alone in a crowded café in Paris, with a table all to herself. She offered to share it, and we sat there together for hours, each of us sharing our own war stories. I was promptly smitten." He looked over at Harriet with a loving smile. "She was like no girl I'd ever met. She was selfless and brave and fiercely intrepid, a heroine who had saved the lives of countless men."

"Yes," Olive said, nodding, "I already know all this."

Her father heaved a great sigh. "What you don't know—what she didn't *want* you to know—is that those were other girls' stories. They were never hers."

A frighteningly dark hole had opened in the pit of Olive's stomach, and it waited hungrily, as she did, for her father to go on.

"She'd worked as a secretary in Paris at the beginning of the war and had a chance to meet FANYs coming into the city when they had a few days off. They convinced her to sign up, and she tried, insisting she be assigned as a driver." He gazed at her soberly. "But she couldn't pass the test."

"The driving test?" Olive asked, puzzled.

He shook his head. "They took her around to the local hospital and walked her through the wards full of injured men—gaping wounds, missing limbs, hideous, heartbreaking burns. She couldn't stomach any of it. She was sick right there in the ward, and the only jobs they had were for drivers and nurses. The Americans snapped her up as a signal operator—she was efficient and spoke fluent French—and she spent the rest of the war sitting in front of a switchboard. She roomed with other girls—FANYs." He huffed out a breath. "And she collected their stories to rewrite her own."

"But why?" Olive demanded, her mind boggled by her mother's deception.

"She had an image in her head of who she wanted to be, and she made it real in the only way she could." He shrugged apologetically. "For years, even I didn't know the truth, and by then it was so much a part of her. The lies never hurt anyone." Olive was about to object when he said quietly, "Except her."

She looked up sharply. "What do you mean?"

"The more she told them, the more the pressure and guilt began to eat at her. She'd have terrible headaches, and she . . ." He ran a hand over his eyes, as if trying to dash away the memories. "She was dependent on her tablets. She'd convinced me it was only headache powder," he insisted. "Only later did I realise what she was taking, all of it supplied by friends in London." He paused, clearly struggling to go on. "The cocaine was enough to garble her memory and stifle the prickings of her conscience. She was in its ruddy clutches. I should've—" He stopped and hung his head, the shame of it all seeming to pour over him. "But I waited too long, and then the illness took hold, and it was all too late."

Olive stared at her father, her face slack with shock. It had all been a lie. Numbness had spread outward from that dark hole, but she knew, when it receded, the hurt would crowd in on her. Olive very much wanted to be alone when that happened—away from her father and Harriet and, most of all, Aldridge. But she had one very important question that needed to be answered first.

"Has someone been blackmailing you to keep that secret?"

"Blackmail?" her father barked, abruptly pulled from his misery. "No, no, of course not." His head swivelled toward Harriet to confirm, but she shook her head, looking simultaneously startled and concerned. "Your mother has been dead too many years for any of it to matter anymore." When Olive didn't respond, he went on, his voice heavy. "I know I should have told you. My only excuse is that I'd made a promise to your mother. You had your memories. What did it matter if they weren't quite true?" He glanced disapprovingly at Aldridge. "What difference does it make that she wasn't a FANY? We were, all of us, against the Boche." He fell silent, then suddenly remembered her question and demanded, "What's this about blackmail?"

"It's nothing. I just wondered. People react to secrets in many different ways," Olive said stiffly, conscious of Aldridge sitting somewhere out of view, listening to all of this—hearing the truth about her mother as she did herself. "Well," she added crisply, bolting to her feet, "you've solved that puzzle. Score one for Captain Aldridge." Curving her lips into a bitter smile felt like curving a bowstring—and she was deathly worried what might happen if she let go. "He's probably anxious to be on his way, so I'll escort him out."

Walking stiffly, Olive moved to the door, then waited politely for her nemesis to follow. Thankfully, she was still in a state of shock and so was relatively unaffected by the shame at not only having lied—albeit unintentionally—to the CO at Station XVII but also having been caught out in such a way. Later, there would be more to say; questions already burned in her mind, but right now, she needed to be alone, to reconcile herself to the certain consequences of this deception.

She led him out through the kitchen, along the garden, and past the dovecote. It was drizzling in earnest, but she barely noticed. Neither spoke until they were well out of earshot, standing beside the car, and Olive got the jump on him.

Staring past his right shoulder, she was all politeness. "It seems I did lie to you, after all, and for that, I'm sorry. I do hope you realise I didn't intentionally deceive you, but I understand that this will mean our liaison is at an end—or will be once this mission is complete."

He sighed and was quiet for a long moment. "I admit, I was livid. I'd let you badger me into advocating a larger role for you at Station Seventeen . . ."

Olive stared in disbelief. He'd spoken up for her?

"And then you waltz onto the grounds and boast of your mother's exploits in the Great War. Exploits I shortly discovered to be entirely false."

She wanted to object but, for once, stayed silent.

"I considered it a betrayal," he added, tipping his head down. Olive's lower lip quivered in understanding. "But," he went on, "it's quite obvious you were unaware of the truth." His voice had softened, and Olive bit her lip, determined to keep her emotions tucked safely away. "So, I'm inclined to chalk the whole thing up as a misunderstanding. As long as we agree that as of now, it's to be only the whole truth."

It was more than she would have expected, but at the moment, she wasn't at all certain it was what she wanted. Could he ever truly trust her again? Would he judge her by her mother's deception? Had their fragile relationship, built on gradual acceptance and respect, been irreconcilably broken? With each of those questions swirling unanswered in her mind, she didn't know what to say. But her thoughts kept repeating the same refrain: *He believed in you and is offering another chance.* She swallowed past the lump in her throat, met his stormy grey eyes, and nodded solemnly. She would find a way to make this work.

Some of the tension seemed to go out of his shoulders. "It might perhaps be best for everyone concerned if we delay your training a bit longer. I need to explain the situation to the men in charge, and you probably need time to . . . think things through," he said awkwardly. "You needn't worry," he added quickly when she would have objected. "There will be plenty of work when you do get there. And I understand you're getting quite a bit of driving practice in the meantime."

Curving her lips into a bland smile, she didn't answer. Let him imagine she was speechless with gratitude when what she really wanted was to curse a blue streak.

"No pigeons back yet, I take it," he said, leaning in to pose the question, as if someone might be listening in.

She shook her head, and he slid past, on his way again, as if he hadn't just roared in and sent her world spinning topsy-turvy. It didn't matter. He was the very least of her concerns right now.

Without even waiting for him to back the car down the drive, she stalked into the barn. It would seem, she thought sourly, Miss Husselbee's final word had merely been a portent of trouble to come. Olive wondered if she'd known. This thought was interrupted by the postman, cycling up to meet her as she wheeled the Welbike over the gravel, eager to be away.

"One of those sure would make my job easier," he said, nodding at the motorbike as he reached into his bag to pull out the letter he handed over with a flourish.

Olive glanced at it and instantly recognised George's handwriting by the little cowlick he always added to the *O* of her name. Her fingers fumbled as she edged it open, and her eyes quickly scanned the words.

8th May, 11:30 a.m.
RAF Brize Norton

Dear Olive,

    Damn if it doesn't seem as if more has happened in Pipley in the week I've been gone than in the twenty-odd years I lived there. If you're having me on, it's not a bit funny, and I will find a way to get even. Miss Husselbee, dead? I fully expected my children's children to run in fear of the tap of that umbrella. And murder by

*Spam? I'm looking forward to a long write-up of your investiga-
tion, complete with suspects, clues, and the unmasking of the murderer. If anyone can puzzle it out, you can, Sherlock. I suppose it's
not possible that she's rigged the whole thing as an elaborate red
herring, and any moment now she'll spring to life again, criticising
the mishandling of the whole affair? I truly wish it were—what a
damn shame.*

*I imagined you'd be chomping at the bit for a little excitement,
but I should have known you'd find it. I expect you've convinced
(or coerced) the NPS to sign you on, as well. Training here marches
on. We're flying Hurricanes, and they're rather old school, but they
certainly get the job done. We've not heard yet if we're being sent
on—although with the weather as cold and wet as it's been, we're
all daydreaming of warmer climes.*

Please say hello to all, with a kiss for my mother and Gillian.

Your devoted Watson,
George

*P.S. You've garnered quite a reputation among the chaps, what
with being a pigeoneer and an amateur sleuth. Half of them have a
crush on you already.*

Olive's shoulders dropped as she refolded the letter and
slipped it into her pocket with the one Poppins had carried back.
She wanted to laugh and cry all at once. If only it *was* a red herring. . . . It made her think of the time, so many years ago now,
when she and George had trailed into the woods after Lewis one
morning. They'd quickly run across a rabbit with its leg caught in
a trap; it had fidgeted so much that its fur was missing on one
side, and there was dread panic in its eyes. Having deftly freed it,
while cursing roundly, Lewis had pressed the poor thing into
George's arms and sent him running for the surgery. Olive was
meant to stay and help him bury the trap. They'd only just

begun digging when they heard the crackling of twigs and a heavy, slurred voice murdering a familiar pub tune. Their eyes met; they knew that voice, and neither was keen to be caught at sabotage by a drunk who very likely had a gun. In an instant, she was running her fingers quickly and carefully along the jaws of the trap, gathering up the rabbit's blood. This she smeared on her wrists and hands, adding a bit to her face for good measure. "I'll get rid of him," she said, "but hurry." Then she was gone.

It had worked brilliantly. While she'd mustered tears, pretended pain and panic, and begged for help, Lewis had buried the remainder of the traps, all while keeping an ear trained on Olive's bloody little drama. He'd reached the surgery shortly after she had, having stopped to clean his hands in the river. A success all around.

It had been a clever diversion, a bloody red herring. Not at all the same as her mother's calculated deception. What would Lewis say when he heard about their mother? And George?

Suddenly exhausted, she turned the motorbike and wheeled it back into the barn. Moments ago, her only thought had been confrontation, no matter how little sense it made to rail at a grave. But the betrayal had sunk in its teeth, and that compulsion had given way to dispassion. She'd been holding herself up to Serena Bright's standard for as long as she could remember, and it had all been a lie—an illusion. The worst part of it was that she was no better, hiding behind her own deception, while others sacrificed so much. Maybe her mother would be proud of her, after all. The thought was a bitter pill.

She didn't want to think about any of it right now, and she didn't have the wherewithal to ponder the motives of a village full of murder suspects, either. Once she confirmed that none of the three musketeers had yet returned, she was going to find a lonely spot somewhere and settle in to read. Not the Agatha Christie— she was in no mood. She'd fetch the Gothic novel she'd pilfered from Miss Husselbee's desk. So deciding, Olive felt the heaviness in her chest lighten somewhat. And as she came around the corner and noticed a biscuit tin left on the dovecote's doorstep, it lightened even further. Jonathon must have left it, hoping to lift her spirits. Perhaps it was another tomato. . . .

Gripping the lid with her fingernails, she worked it off and promptly sent the lot of it clattering back to the ground. Nestled in a bed of straw, quite dead, lay Guinevere, a chequered female hatched only two months before.

Chapter 18

Tuesday, 13th May

She didn't tell Jonathon or her father; it was possible neither would even notice the bird was missing. Instead, Olive worried alone. She'd long ago become acclimated to the sight of dead animals. There was always a flicker of sadness, but no more. For Guinevere, there was more—there was worry and distress, and even fear. No natural predator had tucked her young body into a Cadbury biscuit tin and left her tidily on the doorstep. It had been intentional and deliberate—a warning—and she could think of only two reasons for it. Either someone had discovered her arrangement with Baker Street and was anxious she put an end to it, or else her amateur investigations into Miss Husselbee's murder were making someone very nervous.

She hadn't decided yet whether to tell Aldridge. This could be the final straw, the nail in the coffin of their little arrangement. Too many complications and coincidences to make it worth the risk. And just like that, her role as pigeoneer and FANY, only recently saved, would be officially over. For now, she'd keep the discovery to herself, stay alert for anything out of the ordinary, and refocus her efforts on finding the killer, not to mention Margaret's blackmailer. Time was running out. Rather a serendipitous coincidence, she thought wryly, that her FANY training had been postponed.

She was hiding in the dovecote, alternately distracting herself with the heavy, ominous prose of A *Lady Avenged* while half-heartedly assessing her birds for a possible future mission, when the rambunctious sounds of Jonathon's arrival carried in through the caged window. Seconds later, he slipped through the door, tugging the Girl Guide in behind him.

His eager eyes met Olive's. She shook her head, silently conveying that none of the pigeons had returned, and he sighed, adding, "I've brought Hen along. She wanted to talk to you."

Olive stared at the pair of them, mussed hair, pink cheeks, heaving chests. "It must be something important."

"It's about Dr Ware," Hen said, peering up into the rafters for a fleeting moment before focusing her steady gaze on Olive. "Did you ever find out why he needed those mice?"

Olive glanced at Jonathon, prompting Hen to admit, "I've sworn him to secrecy."

You, and everyone else, poor chap. Luckily, he seemed none the worse for wear. He had moved away to check on the hens in the nesting boxes and appeared to be offering a treat of some sort from a stash in his pocket.

"I tried," Olive admitted. "I asked him outright, and he made up a story about an injured kestrel." She shook her head at the man's pitiable excuse. "So," she said, lingering over the word, "I did a bit of snooping. No luck, I'm afraid. I'm actually *more* confused by what I found."

"What was it?"

Olive couldn't see that it hurt to tell her. "All manner of jars and buckets, crowding every surface of his back room. It was impossible to tell what they contained." Hen's eyes were roving, likely in tandem with her thoughts. "Don't get any ideas, Hen. There's no Guides badge for burglary. Or interrogation."

"True, but someone somewhere might be offering one," she

said thoughtfully, then instantly changed tack. "I'd almost forgotten what I wanted to tell you."

Olive was beginning to be concerned that she needed to keep a close eye on the girl, but Hen's next words put the thought right out of her head.

"After school, Jonathon and I put Swilly on a lead and were going door-to-door in the village, collecting scraps. When we knocked on Dr Ware's door, he didn't answer, but we could hear him moving around, muttering to himself. So, we persisted, and finally, he opened it, and he—"

"He looked awful," Jonathon interrupted.

Hen continued as if he hadn't spoken. "His left arm was wrapped with a bandage, but the edges looked blotchy and quite swollen. And his face was wan and feverish. I told him I'd earned my first-aid badge ages ago, but he insisted he was quite well." She cleared her throat and said primly, "I respectfully disagreed."

"That's when he sent us packing and slammed the door behind us," chimed in Jonathon.

Olive frowned, frustrated and worried over this information, but utterly baffled as to how to proceed. "Let me think for a moment."

Message dutifully delivered, Hen reached into her own pocket and moved to stand beside Jonathon.

Perhaps there was a simple explanation: there'd been an accident in his little laboratory, and he'd already been to see the doctor. As much as Olive wanted to believe that, she didn't. She also didn't want to believe that he was experimenting with dangerous, or possibly even deadly, compounds for nefarious reasons. *But what else could it be?*

Her eyes roved, touching on each pigeon in turn as her thoughts shuffled through each clue she'd uncovered and all the little questions that lodged, unanswered, in the corners of her mind.

As her gaze settled on Jeremy Fisher, a recent blue-bar hatchling, his mother, Wendy, swooped up beside him with a determined flap of feathers. At almost three months old, he was fully grown, but she was always hovering protectively nearby. Whoever had left the biscuit tin was lucky he—or she—hadn't bothered with Jeremy.

Wendy herded the younger bird toward the pan of water on the floor and began vigorously washing herself, sending a spray of water up onto his wings. Resigned, Jeremy rolled himself in the water, then shook himself dry as Wendy looked on dotingly. He'd likely be escorted to dinner next.

Olive's focus shifted to Billy Bones, a young white-chequered cock, who was currently bowing to Poppins. *Oh, goodness.* With Fritz off on a mission somewhere in France, Billy clearly thought the time was ripe for romance. With an ostentatious flap of his wings that sent a downy white feather wafting down beside him, he circled Poppins, who wilfully ignored him, and bowed again. "You haven't a chance," Olive murmured, shaking her head, quizzically eyeing that feather and willing Billy to look elsewhere.

Images became juxtaposed in her mind, and her thoughts darted with possibility. These behaviours were familiar, recognisable. The sort that prompted strong emotions and impetuous decisions—the very sort that led to blackmail . . . and murder. Sitting there, amid the cooing and flapping and general bonhomie of birds, with Hen and Jonathon entirely oblivious, Olive felt suddenly certain she'd pieced together at least one little mystery, possibly two, and the situations for both were entirely unexpected. Rather troublingly, an explanation for Dr Ware's behaviour continued to elude her.

It was time to take the next step in her search for the truth, which meant confronting everyone she suspected of dodgy behaviour. Basically, she could look forward to a lot of awkward little chats and could expect to be a topic of village gossip for the foreseeable future. Perhaps she'd be the new Sergeant Major. Olive's lips twisted in a wry smile. *So be it.*

She stared down at the paperback she'd taken from Miss Husselbee's desk drawer: *A Lady Avenged*. She'd been enjoying her escape to the fictional Travers Hall, with its wide, sloping lawns and mammoth shade trees, where the spirited young governess had fallen in love with the seductively tortured musician who employed her. It reminded Olive vaguely of her days attending school at Brickendonbury Manor—although she'd certainly never harboured feelings for one of her instructors—and was thus rather comforting. But the prospect of finally getting some answers was much more satisfying.

Less than an hour later, having left Jonathon on watch for returning pigeons, Olive stepped inside the chemist's shop, confirmed there were no other customers, and pushed the door shut behind her, twisting the lock. Dr Ware was working at the counter, and as she turned and stepped slowly toward him with her arms crossed, his face went slack with alarm. He didn't look nearly as pathetic as Hen had made out, but he definitely wasn't himself. His bandaged arm was tucked inside a white chemist coat and so concealed from view, but he was chalky white.

"I realise I have no real right to demand them, Dr Ware, but I'm afraid I need answers."

He wilted slightly, but his voice, when he spoke, was firm. "Now, look here—"

Olive put her hand up to forestall any objections or excuses he might make. She wasn't in the mood to be lectured or condescended to. "There was no kestrel. I saw you burying those mice in the wood." His mouth dropped open, but she went ruthlessly on. "When you left, I dug them up. The poor creatures were covered with lesions, and I want to know why." The thought of Guinevere, lying cold and limp in a biscuit tin, sharpened her

tone. The admission, or else the demand, startled him so sufficiently that he sank onto the stool he kept behind the counter.

She paused while he wiped a shaky hand across his forehead
and gathered a few shallow breaths. But when he still didn't
speak, she pressed on.

"Obviously, the kestrel was not responsible for whatever has
happened to your arm, and I have it on good authority that it's
not healing well. It's swollen and very likely infected—"

"But it *is*," Dr Ware interrupted, his tone emphatic. "By that I
mean it *is* healing. Quite marvellously, in fact." It was as if the
mysterious weight that had settled so heavily on his shoulders
was suddenly, inexplicably lighter. As if he'd only been waiting
to be found out.

Olive refused to be deterred from her course. "I'm glad to hear
it, but I'd like to know how you got the injury in the first place."

Once again, he seemed to retreat into himself, and Olive was
forced to lure him out. "Was it part of your experiment?" she
asked shamelessly. His eyes swivelled to stare at her, and she
added, "I'm referring to the one that's prompted you to fill your
back room with buckets and bottles."

Dr Ware let out a deep, shuddering breath. His right hand
tugged away the glasses sliding down his nose. He set them on
the counter to rub furiously at his temples.

Olive hadn't expected this reaction, and it filled her with
dread and prompted an ill-considered outburst. "Please tell me
you're not a traitor." The moment the words were out of her
mouth, Olive regretted them. She was, after all, locked in with
him, with countless chemical compounds at his disposal. In a
brief moment of hysteria, she imagined herself being poisoned
and fed to a kestrel.

Judging by Dr Ware's change in expression, she'd been staring
at him in uncertain horror. He hurried to reassure her.

"No, no. Certainly not," he insisted quite emphatically. He
sighed again but slipped his glasses back on, hopped off the

stool, and began pacing behind the counter. "I will answer all your questions, and if you're satisfied with my responses, I would ask that you keep the matter to yourself." Seeing Olive's nod, he said quickly, "Perhaps this discussion would be best had over a cup of tea. Why don't you come into the kitchen, and I'll put the kettle on. I've got a bit of chocolate, as well, which might settle your nerves. They seem rather frayed."

A few moments later they were sitting in his tiny little kitchen, on opposite sides of the oilcloth-covered table. She'd finished a square of chocolate and half her cup of tea, and was about to nudge his confession along, when he began.

"Not so long ago, I worked as a research chemist for a pharmaceutical company. I enjoyed my work tremendously, so much so that I let it consume me. When I was working, I forgot to eat or sleep, and little by little, my health began to fail." His fingers tapped at the edge of the table, and he didn't meet her eyes, but he went on. "Intent on making a fresh start, I came to Pipley, hoping that life as a village chemist would be a bit less intense. Within a few months, I felt worlds better, but my mind yearned for the challenging, rewarding work I'd left behind." Olive had stayed silent, watching his face, his fingers; now he stilled and lifted his head to look at her. "I need to tell you about my sister."

He went on. "Molly was the youngest of us. I was the oldest, and there were two sisters in between. She was also my favourite . . . the most inquisitive, the most studious, and the best listener by far. Despite—or, perhaps, because of—these qualities, she never married." He was reminiscing now, and Olive wondered if he was feverish, but she bided her time. "Our family hails from York, so when I left for university, I didn't venture home from Oxford very often, and later there was always research to be done . . ." He stopped and swallowed, his lips pressed together and turned down at the corners, and Olive set down her cup and laced her fingers, waiting.

"She'd got a new kitten, which was terrified of our hulking

Irish wolfhound. The little thing clawed Molly's cheek—just a
little scratch, I was told—but it got infected. The bacteria spread
to her face and her lungs, and there was nothing to be done. She
died of sepsis." There was a lost, faraway look in his eyes now,
and Olive knew she needed to tread carefully.

"I'm very sorry, Dr Ware," she said gravely. "But I don't—"

"Dr Alexander Fleming," he continued, as if she hadn't spoken, "discovered that the penicillium mould inhibits the growth
of infectious staphylococci bacteria in nineteen twenty-eight.
Ten years before Molly died. But his discovery languished, unus-
able without further study, until quite recently." His eyes brightened, and he laid a gentle hand on his bandaged arm. "Several
weeks ago, I took the train to London to have dinner with some
old colleagues from the Oxford School of Pathology. Over a quite
expensive bottle of port, they confessed that they'd been tasked
to re-evaluate Fleming's research, to find the active ingredient in
the mould that would allow it to be put into production and used
by His Majesty's forces."

He was excited now, but Olive was eager to skip ahead. "Did
you volunteer yourself as a test subject?" she asked, glancing at
his arm.

"Yes," he said emphatically and then immediately followed up
that shocking statement. "But the situation is a bit more compli-
cated than that."

She gulped down the rest of her tea, hoping it would calm her
nerves. She still wasn't entirely certain Dr Ware was in his right
mind. In fact, she probably shouldn't have accepted a cup of tea,
but that didn't bear thinking about right now. She needed him to
explain the implications of dead mice and a back room crowded
with buckets. And suddenly it was shatteringly clear. "Oh! You've
been doing your own research."

He nodded approvingly. "I obtained a sample of *Penicillium
notatum* and have since propagated the mould culture in every
available bottle and jar." Now his eyes twinkled as he leaned to-

ward her confidingly. "And I've done it—I've managed to isolate a fluid extract that will successfully cure infection."

It had been a process of trial and error. "The mice," she said grimly.

Dr Ware nodded solemnly. "They were martyrs to the cause, I'm afraid."

"You haven't killed anything else, have you?" She didn't know if she could forgive him Guinevere.

"Certainly not. I wish it hadn't been necessary to sacrifice the mice. As soon as I confirmed that the extract was easing their symptoms, I stopped injecting them to keep as much as possible in reserve."

Olive nodded, much relieved. "I take it your arm was martyred, as well."

"I'm afraid so." He grinned. "I'm happy to say, I'm recovering quite nicely."

"Congratulations, Dr Ware," she said, her tension giving way to a flutter of wonder now that the mystery was solved. "But I don't understand the need for such secrecy."

"It's not yet a viable solution, certainly not for the military. All those bottles and jars you saw will yield only the smallest bit of purified antibiotic. I'm keeping it secret so as not to give rise to an untenable situation. There is plenty more work still to be done."

"Does Miss Rose know?" Olive asked expectantly.

Two patches of colour promptly spotted his cheeks as he stood to clear the tea things. "Some of it," he admitted. "She has a rather scientific mind."

Olive merely smiled.

She washed the tea things, and he escorted her back to the shop. "I'm glad you're on our side, Dr Ware," she said, giving his good arm a squeeze.

Much relieved, she stepped out into the sunshine, fully aware that there were still mysteries to be solved, and not all of them would end quite so satisfactorily. Eventually, she would unmask a killer.

A familiar car was turning out of the gate as she approached Blackcap Lodge. Olive stepped onto the verge on the driver's side, a fizzy urgency bubbling inside her—he could only have come for one reason.

The moment he put down the window, she blurted, "Is one of them home again?"

Aldridge's demeanour was typically stoic, but faced with her obvious exuberance, his lips hitched up in response. "If Jonathon has mastered the ability to tell them apart, it seems Fritz is back." He gave her a wry smile. "And," he continued, forestalling the question he believed to be hovering on Olive's tongue, "he brought a message."

Olive momentarily swept that news aside. "Is he injured?" She was anxious to see for herself, but she also wanted to glean as much information as possible while Aldridge was willing to offer it.

"Not as far as I could tell, but as you know, I'm no expert. Jonathon didn't seem concerned."

Breathing a sigh of relief, Olive returned to his earlier comment. "If the message is in code, I suppose you don't yet know what it says."

"Believe it or not, I can, occasionally, be of some use," he said dryly, his mood shaded with resignation.

"You've decoded it already?" she said, clutching the window sill.

He nodded, his hand leisurely propped on the steering wheel, and she waited, eyes wide, for him to fill her in. He didn't, and the memory of their last confrontation flowed over her.

"You're not going to tell me what it says," she said flatly. It wasn't a question; it was a disgruntled realisation. With an understanding nod, she straightened, released her grip on the car door, and turned to stride off.

His arm shot out the window and caught hold of her.

Something akin to an electric shock whipped through her, but his words left her no time to analyse it. "They aborted," he said grimly. "Something about a tension wire above the perimeter wall and sentries on duty inside the power station. And no bicycles on which to make their escape. Not what you'd call a success."

He hadn't let go of her arm, but now his hand seemed almost comforting. "So that's it? They'll be brought home?"

"We sent them over with addresses for a few of our contacts in Paris. With any luck, they'll find help and reconnoitre before trying again."

"Did the message say anything about the other birds?"

He looked uncomfortable, and Olive tensed. "Tell me," she insisted.

"I'm afraid there was an accident on the night of the drop. One of the men landed on a pigeon container."

She nodded, feeling a welling of emotion in her throat. "I suppose you don't know which one." At the shake of his head, she said calmly, "And the last one?"

"That, I don't know. It would be risky for them to hold on to him. It's illegal to have them in France. But if they think they can manage, they might just do it."

She nodded, trying not to reveal any hint of the emotion swirling through her. But something must have shown in her face, because he offered an encouraging smile.

"Don't worry just yet. Roméo told you himself he has experience with pigeons. Trust him to do his best."

Olive nodded, not meeting his gaze.

"Where have you been this afternoon?" he asked.

Olive bristled. "Jonathon is entirely capable of telephoning you, should the need arise. Obviously."

"The question wasn't intended as a reprimand."

She wilted a bit, feeling rather childish. "Oh. Good, then, because I've had quite enough of those this month already."

When her answer wasn't forthcoming, he teased, "You aren't hiding anything, are you?"

"What? No, of course not." She wasn't keeping secrets; she simply wasn't telling him about her continued investigations, because he hadn't expressed the slightest bit of interest.

"Steer clear of misadventure," he said pointedly, "and say hello to the porkers for me, when you get a chance." He flashed her a wicked smile, and in the early twilight, with his dark hair curling around his ears, he put her in mind of a satyr.

She fled.

Friday, 25 April 1941
Peregrine Hall, Pipley
Hertfordshire

If ever I require a reminder that a single ill-considered decision has the potential to wreak havoc on a person's entire existence, I need only look to L.C. She chanced to pull her car into the local garage one summer day many years ago, and so began a tale of forbidden fruit. She should have been out of his reach, and he beneath her notice. But they cast convention aside, and it wasn't long before it all turned to rot. She was too lovely, too accomplished, too ambitious, and he wasn't man enough to rise to meet her.

In her role as president of the Pipley WI, she's met with Lady Denman, exchanged letters with Mrs Roosevelt, and worked tirelessly to encourage and inspire us all. Her husband has merely stood sullenly in her shadow. I hope she hasn't even a little idea that he has sought illicit comfort from one of our number—an effort that required rather more gumption than he's mustered in all the years I've known him. I would spare her the humiliation and have decided to take both parties to task at the next opportunity.

I will endeavour not to enjoy myself, but I make no promises.

V.A.E. Husselbee

Chapter 19

Smartly turned out in a juniper-green dress with mother-of-pearl buttons, Lady Camilla ushered Olive into her parlour, its windows open to the fragrant late afternoon breeze. Having once again hurried into the village the moment Jonathon had returned home from school to relieve her, Olive was breathing quickly, and the ever-present scent of lavender in the house quickly calmed her nerves. She'd effectively been twiddling her thumbs all morning, distractedly skimming chapters of *A Lady Avenged* and shooting curious glances at Fritz, as she worried over the remaining musketeer, the mission, and the conversation ahead.

A number of puzzling circumstances had slotted together in her mind, presenting a possible solution. *One* possible solution. Olive didn't like being wrong, and she certainly didn't like having witnesses when she was, but in this situation, it couldn't be helped.

"I expect you're curious as to whether I've wheedled any information from my father regarding the flying training schools," Lady Camilla said briskly. She'd gestured for Olive to have a seat on the sofa and settled herself on a cream-coloured armchair.

Olive forestalled mentioning the real reason for her visit in order to hear what George's mother might have discovered. She knitted her fingers and waited.

"They're making arrangements for relocation to various out-of-the-way places—particularly Canada and South Africa—but they're not ready to send them just yet," Lady Camilla said, prompting a relieved sigh from Olive. Knowing George was still in England was a small comfort. With any luck, he'd be finished with his training before logistics were arranged and pilots shipped out. Lady Camilla, it appeared, didn't want to get her hopes up. "If he decides to extend his training, perhaps become an instructor, then he'll have to go." She picked an imaginary bit of lint from the skirt of her dress, then laced her fingers. "But," she said brightly, "it's best to take each day as it comes."

Olive frowned, tamping down the creep of worry for George, determined to get on with things. "I actually stopped in to speak to you about Miss Husselbee."

"Oh," she said blankly. "Not about her death, surely? Because I don't know any more than anyone else."

"I wanted to talk to you about her diary," Olive said firmly.

"The little notebook she carried everywhere?" Lady Camilla said fondly. "I'm not sure any one of us escaped a mention. She was always ferreting away little bits of gossip."

"The one she wrote for Mass Observation."

"Oh, yes. Her very own *Tatler*, so to speak," she teased, her smile a trifle brittle. "I'd quite forgotten about it."

"She mailed the diaries off at the start of each new month, but her death prevented the April instalment from going out." Lady Camilla's lips had curved politely as she waited for Olive to come to the point. "Those latest entries were mistakenly collected by a pair of schoolchildren and were left for salvage in the collection spot behind the garage."

George's mother unclasped her fingers, lifted a hand to the back of her neck, and pressed her fingers into the upsweep of her hair. "Well, I suppose it hardly matters. The poor woman is dead. A few missing entries will hardly come amiss. It's probably a blessing, all things considered."

"It matters," Olive said firmly, "because someone retrieved them from the salvage pile. Miss Husselbee was in the habit of recording the private details of people's lives. The sort that could be used for blackmail."

The older woman's eyes widened in dismay, and she tsked her disapproval. "Surely not."

Olive tried not to remember all the times Lady Camilla had seen her with a sticky face or skinned knees. She thought of Hercule Poirot and Jane Marple, and she mustered every bit of gumption she could manage. "It is, in fact, the reason you took them," she said calmly.

Lady Camilla laughed charmingly. "My dear girl, why on earth would you even suggest such a thing?"

Olive shrugged, running her hand nervously over the sofa cushion. "The simplest explanation is usually the correct one. Your presence near the garage would never arouse suspicion. It would have been a simple matter for you to have noticed the typed pages and tucked them away for safekeeping."

"I could have, yes, but then, so could any number of people, my husband included."

"Except that your husband is being blackmailed," Olive said simply. It was a hunch, but one she was determined to play.

"Olive, this is absurd," Lady Camilla insisted, her aristocratic smile firmly in place, "but I'm going to take the accusation as an excuse for a little glass of sherry." She stood, rounded the chair, and moved to the marble-topped table near the window, on which stood a tray of cordial glasses and a few dwindling bottles of liquor. Olive stared as she poured herself that drink.

Lady Camilla Forrester, president of the Pipley WI, George's mother. Olive had admired this elegantly stylish woman her entire life, and she was suddenly caught up in the paralysing grip of uncertainty. Here she sat, accusing George's mother of parlaying Miss Husselbee's official Mass Observation diaries into blackmail fodder. It seemed preposterous, looking at her now, as she gazed bemusedly out the window. Her carefully powdered cheeks, delicately pursed lips, and the perfectly placed marcasite combs tucked into the icy-blond swirl of her chignon.

"Is there anything else?" Lady Camilla said abruptly, not bothering to turn. "Because as it is, you have only a vague suspicion." She deigned to look at Olive. "And," she added dryly, "I'm afraid, a rather inflated sense of your abilities as an amateur sleuth."

"You were there the day Margaret's blackmail letter was delivered. Before following her aunt Eloise to the kitchen, you left the letter on the mat, making it look as if it had been slipped through the mail slot sometime during your visit."

"Is poor Margaret being blackmailed?" She feigned surprise before giving Olive a hard look. "It's a pretty theory, dear, but you have no proof. You've simply slotted me in as the culprit, and I really don't understand why." There was pity in her voice now, mingled subtly with triumph. Olive now knew with absolute certainty that Lady Camilla was the blackmailer. Any thought to sparing the older woman's feelings was abruptly shunted in favour of vindication.

"I suspect it started when you discovered that your husband was involved with Winifred Danes," Olive said calmly. Lady Camilla gasped and likely would have protested, but Olive went on, refusing to be derailed by an interruption. "You very obviously don't like her. Whenever you're thrown into her company, you give yourself away."

"How very observant of you."

Olive blinked in surprise at the ready admission, not at all prepared to go tit for tat. The role Billy Bones had played in advancing her theory would remain her little secret. Lady Camilla walked back to her chair and sat, gracefully erect. She gazed at

Olive expectantly, clearly waiting for her to elaborate, so Olive obliged. "George has always smelled faintly, comfortingly, of lavender, and until recently, so did Mr Forrester. Now there's something else lingering beneath the scent of rubber and petrol, and I realised it smells rather like burnt sugar."

"And, of course, you've noticed that that very aroma clings sickeningly to Miss Danes. I suppose it's perfectly in character for a tart to smell like sugar."

"Yes, well," Olive said, wincing, "I've also noticed that when she's around, you invariably touch the hair at the base of your neck. Sort of a nervous reaction, I suppose."

"It must look like that, yes. But actually, I'm feeling for my combs." With eyebrows raised, she performed the indicated action now, tugging the pair of combs from her hair, which tumbled down past her shoulders. "They were a gift from my mother before I was married," she admitted, staring lovingly down at the art deco accessories with their flash of charcoal sparkle. "They're my touchstone to a happier time, when I was certain of my place in the world." She smiled sadly and added, "Before I wanted to murder anyone."

Olive's stomach turned over in shock, and she froze, blinking wide-eyed at the woman before her. She had suspected Lady Camilla as the blackmailer but was now forced to re-evaluate her theories. And wonder if she should abort this little visit.

"I'm not speaking of Miss Husselbee, Olive," George's mother said lazily, reading her reaction. "She was quite harmless—and invaluable to the WI." She sipped her sherry, her gaze drifting around the feminine room, before going on. "Only two individuals have ever prompted me to think of murder, to imagine sliding the combs from my hair and stabbing them into their devious throats." The words were said so calmly that Olive had to wonder if she was sitting alone with a madwoman.

Olive's gaze shifted to the doorway as she considered her options.

"But," Lady Camilla went on, undeterred, "murder isn't an option for any civilised human being."

The sentiment drew Olive's eyes back to the older woman, whose pinkie finger was dutifully extended. "Blackmail is generally frowned upon in most circles, as well."

"True," she conceded. "But I need the money if I'm going to leave George's father." Olive hoped her mouth hadn't dropped completely open at this revelation. "I was cut off financially when I married him," Lady Camilla went on, "and while I haven't the fortitude to endure the inevitable gossip along with the betrayal, I won't divorce him. So, I'm planning to go away."

As Olive gazed at Lady Camilla's correct posture and brittle demeanour, she realised how unutterably weary she appeared, as if she was soldiering on by strength of character alone.

She lifted a pale hand to her hair, caught herself, and smiled with genuine amusement. "Force of habit. Don't worry. I was thinking of the pair of them, not you, dear."

"But why blackmail Margaret?" Olive insisted, her nerves on edge.

"Of course she would come to you for help. I admit I'm rather surprised she was willing to reveal her secret. Oh, I see she didn't." Olive's expression, it seemed, had once again given her away. Something to work on. "I've never thought Margaret and Leo suited, and when I came across the diary entry and its tremendous secret, all I could think was to keep them from making the same mistake George's father and I had made all those years ago." Her hands fisted. "Margaret would break off the engagement, and I would supplement my savings. Better for everyone."

Olive stared in disbelief. "And if she couldn't pay? You were going to throw her to the wolves?" As a reference to the dynamics of village gossip, it was only a slight exaggeration.

"I was still undecided on that point."

"Is there anyone else unwittingly helping to finance your escape?"

"Rose Darling," Lady Camilla quickly admitted, "but she has money to spare."

"Miss Rose? What could she possibly be hiding?"

"Other than that she's entirely enamoured of Dr Ware, absolutely nothing. But Miss Husselbee's diary was adamant that *he* is hiding something significant. I figured she'd pay to keep him out of trouble. A secret that will bind them together . . . how perfectly romantic."

Olive frowned. "Does George know any of this?" she demanded, utterly stunned by Lady Camilla's Machiavellian strategies.

"No. I'll write to him, but with any luck, by the time he comes home, I'll be living far away from here, with a job and money of my own." Olive didn't bother to correct this misguided interpretation of her ill-gotten gains. "Oh, I see you meant the blackmail. No, of course not."

"You can't go on blackmailing people," Olive protested, "involving them in your plan for revenge."

Lady Camilla finished her sherry and narrowed her eyes consideringly. "Would you be satisfied if I cease blackmailing everyone, save my husband and Miss Danes?"

"You're blackmailing them separately?" Olive demanded. Thank heavens the woman considered murder uncivilised. . . .

Lady Camilla let a little giggle escape before tapping her fingers against her mouth. "I've written the notes to hint at two separate blackmailers, because, you see, their sins go beyond simple adultery. They're in league with Miss Danes's brother in a black-market petrol scheme." She shrugged, a smug little smile playing about her lips. "What can they do but pay?"

Olive thought for a moment and ultimately decided that Mr Forrester and Miss Danes could, at any time, go to the police to report the blackmail. She suspected they wouldn't, for fear of revealing their own nefarious deeds, and so Lady Camilla could take advantage in order to finance her new life far away from them.

Her head was starting to hurt, and she wanted desperately to escape, but there was one more matter to discuss. "I need you to give me the pages of the diary and promise that you won't use any of the information they contain to blackmail anyone else."

Lady Camilla considered this demand, then stood and walked to the bookcases along the far wall. "I appealed to my father for funds, and he's come up with a tidy sum, after all. Honestly, this whole business is rather tawdry, and I'm relieved to be done with it." She lifted down a chinoiserie vase of jade green, pink, and yellow. She inserted her hand and removed a curled sheaf of pages, slightly smudged with indeterminate grime. She replaced the vase and walked to Olive, arm extended to hand it over. "Will you send them on to Mass Observation or dispose of them?"

"I don't want to read them, so if you can assure me that no one will identify Margaret or Dr Ware, or anyone else, from the information contained in these pages, I'll send them on as part of Miss Husselbee's dubious legacy."

She considered a moment, then said, "I believe I can. The one referring to Margaret is on top, though, in case you want to check with her."

Olive nodded. "I'm sorry, Lady Camilla. I really am. And I'm sorry George isn't here to help you through this."

"I should have known you suspected," she said, her smile already seeming more relaxed. "You always were such a clever girl."

Olive smiled back and stood, relieved not to have to ask about Guinevere. Only someone who'd considered Olive a threat would have had a reason for such cruelty. She walked to the door and paused on the threshold. "It might be a good idea to tuck those combs away in your jewellery box for a while in favour of some others. Just as a precautionary measure." She slipped away without waiting for an answer and walked straight to Pratten's Grocery, hoping to set her friend's mind at ease.

Quite easily persuaded to take a cigarette break, Margaret led Olive around to the alley and stood quietly while Olive explained that the diary pages had been recovered and the blackmail was at an end.

"How did you get them? And from whom?" Margaret demanded. And then, with her voice breaking slightly, she added, "I suppose that means you know." She jammed her cigarette between her lips and inhaled as her hand shook.

"I didn't read them," Olive assured her, "but I think I know."

A stream of silver-grey smoke emerged from between Margaret's lips, and Olive remembered the "little room" where Violet Darling imagined she could breathe. "How?" her friend demanded with false bravado.

"Believe it or not, it was the pigeons," Olive said, pulling her friend carefully down beside her onto a stack of empty crates. "Jeremy Fisher hatched in February, and his mother, Wendy, clearly wishes he'd never left the nest. She's doting and watchful, and ruthlessly protective."

Margaret's eyes had glossed with tears, but as her fingers closed over her locket, she shook her head sharply and said, "I don't understand."

"Watching them, I can't help but think of how closely you've been holding on to your secret, and how desperately you cling to that locket." Margaret released a startled, shuddering breath, but Olive went on. "You're never without it, and you never discuss it. Given the thoroughness of our chats about Leo, I have to assume it's not a present from him. You've reached for it each time I've pressed you for answers, and you clutch it as if it holds the secret you're trying to keep safe, but I've never seen you open it."

Now the tears did fall, and Olive laid a hand on her arm. "You don't owe me an explanation, but you shouldn't keep a secret as important as this one clearly is from the man you plan to marry."

But the dam had burst, and now the secret Margaret had refused to share was pouring forth.

"When I was in London, there were bombings every night," she started, her voice flat. "Sometimes lasting hours, shaking your teeth, rattling your bones, making you wonder if there'd be anything left when it was finally quiet and you staggered back above ground. I was going to the same shelter every night, and it was always the same people. My favourite was a musician—a trumpet player at the Catbird Club. His name was Simon Gale." The name caught in her throat. "We kept each other distracted with silly stories and quick card games. But one night the bombs were close, and we were both frazzled. I went home with him, and I thought I was falling in love."

She swallowed, let out a shaky breath, and fumbled for another cigarette. Olive lit it for her, and she went on. "A week later, he was dead, and shortly after that, I found I was in the pudding club." Olive's heart clutched as she thought of her friend, pregnant and alone, with the city crumbling around her. "I told everyone I'd got married—and maybe I would have." She was staring, sightless, into the middle distance, and Olive took her hand. "I held on to the lie even in the hospital when it was time for the baby to be born. But he died," she sobbed. "I would have loved him. I would have lied for him for the rest of my life. But he died."

Olive wrapped her arm tightly around her friend's shoulders as she sobbed. After a few moments, Margaret was smoking raggedly, dabbing her eyes with the hem of her grocer's apron.

"What was his name?" Olive asked softly.

"I called him Simon, after his father. I wear this locket to remember them both, but I don't have a picture of either of them, and their faces are already fading away." Fighting back another wave of sobs, she inhaled deeply, hiccoughed, and rummaged in her pocket for a handkerchief. "I know I should have told Leo, but I didn't know what to say. I didn't know if he'd forgive me, and I didn't want to lose him, as well. A vicar can't very well marry a fallen woman," she said bleakly.

"Why don't you tell him the truth and let Leo decide what he can do," Olive suggested. "I suspect he'll surprise you."

Margaret nodded resignedly and wiped her nose.

"I've decided to send the final diaries on to Mass Observa-tion—a last hurrah from the Sergeant Major," Olive said with a brittle curve of her lips. "But I think you should decide whether you want yours to be included."

She handed over the relevant page and waited as her friend read over it.

When she'd finished, Margaret said, "When I was in hospital, I told the nurse that my husband had died in the bombing and I'd be coming to live with relatives in Pipley. It seems she was ac-quainted with Miss Husselbee and wrote to her, asking about M.G.—Margaret Gale." She handed the page back to Olive. "Go ahead and include it," she said stoutly. "I'm going to talk to Leo."

"It might be wise to tell him about your kidnapping fantasies, as well," Olive suggested.

Her friend nodded, a mischievous twinkle sparkling through the tears.

Regarding the blackmailer, Olive said only that the culprit was struggling with a difficult situation and had succumbed to an error in judgment. Margaret was quick to forgive.

Olive's thoughts boggled at the hush of secrets already re-vealed, but she was determined to remain vigilant. If poor Guin-evere was any clue, the murderer knew she'd appointed herself resident sleuth, and meant to warn her away. She would need to be on her guard.

Chapter 20

Thursday, 15th May

Flush with success, and overwhelmed by the secrets and emotions that had dominated the past few days, Olive decided to give herself a break from the dovecote and Jeremy Fisher a break from his mother. Harriet, who'd been concerned with Olive's subdued reaction to learning the truth about her mother, was delighted with her plans for a day trip to London.

"Imagine you're on holiday," she said with a flap of her hands. "Solve a murder on the train with Monsieur Poirot, go to the cinema, have a cream tea, if you can manage it. Send off your bird and forget all about him—or her—for a few hours. It's been a difficult, frazzling two weeks. Honestly, I wish I was going with you." With this unabashed declaration, she fell back against the cushion of the chaise longue and reached for the enamelled box.

Olive waited until midday, as a concession to her responsibilities as pigeoneer, but when neither Badger nor Aramis had slipped through the cage, she snatched Jeremy from under Wendy's watchful eye and packed him into the wicker carrier. Tired, for the moment, of mysteries of all sorts, she slipped *A Lady Avenged* into her pocketbook and walked to St Margarets station to catch the train. Ready to be rid of the provoking pages of Miss Hussel-

bee's Mass Observation diary, she'd slipped them into an envelope and, with an index finger laid softly against her lips, passed
them conspiratorially to Mrs Petrie at the post office. The cloak-
and-dagger bit had no doubt thrilled the woman to no end.

Olive spent the entire train journey caught up in her novel,
while Jeremy cooed quietly on the seat beside her, gazing curiously out the window. They were nearly to the station when she
gasped aloud, and a tingle of awareness skipped through her
veins. The words swam in front of her as her thoughts darted urgently. She should have picked up on it earlier, but she'd been
distracted, her attention unfocused. She flipped back through
the pages until she'd reached the beginning. As her eyes ran over
the frontispiece, a suspicion began to take hold. And, along with
it, a worry, a shock, a horror.

But something was fretting at the corners of her mind. She
slipped her hand into the pocket of her jacket and closed her fingers over the folded pages tucked inside. It had brought her a
small measure of comfort to keep George's letters near at hand—
as if he was still within reach—but right now it was suspicion that
drove her need for them. She hurriedly pulled them out. Her
gaze skimmed over the first message, carried home by Poppins,
and her heart began to beat in slow, dull thuds as the words sank
in, forcing her to consider another possibility. It was so astonish-
ing as to be almost unbelievable, and yet not quite.

Trying to remain sensibly unruffled, she calmly read through
the second letter, which had been delivered by post a few days
before. Two words caught and held her attention, and her
thoughts strayed back to the dance and the play rehearsal, to
Lewis and George. Possible coalesced into probable. As the train
rumbled down the track, gradually decelerating, the gossamer
strands of her memories wove themselves into an elaborate web
of deception, betrayal, and murder. The book was the key to
everything.

As usual, George had said precisely the right thing, and Olive suddenly felt certain she knew who had killed Miss Husselbee. She had no proof, but as Poirot had demonstrated, sometimes a little idea was enough to catch a killer. A sense of urgency swept through her, and she realised she'd need to forfeit her little holiday. So much for the cream tea.

Her gaze drifted to Jeremy, waiting patiently to be dispatched back to Pipley, and a thought occurred to her. She could send a message ahead, with directions for Jonathon to contact Aldridge. The man quite obviously had access to resources she didn't, and could confirm information critical to her theory. *If* she could convince him to help.

Olive had intentionally brought a canister along, planning to affix it to Jeremy's leg for the journey home. She'd suspected Jonathon would be thrilled to receive a message, no matter how frivolous.

As she carefully printed her instructions onto a slip of rice paper, she tried to manage her expectations. Aldridge would not relish her involvement—and certainly not his own—and would, quite possibly, refuse her request.

"In that case, we'll simply have to make do without him," she told Jeremy, slipping the paper into the canister and tucking it into her pocket. Either way, she planned to be on the next train home again.

When the train chugged to a halt, Olive hurried onto the platform and then out to the street, which was bustling with activity. Crouching beside the station building, she pulled Jeremy from his carrier, attached the canister to his leg and, with a word of luck, tossed him into the air. A pair of children standing nearby watched the first powerful beats of his wings and then twirled to track his progress up over the ragged rooftops, far beyond the bomb damage, which was all too prevalent. Tugging at their mother's hands, they pointed into the sky as he banked, first left and then right, on his way home. Olive hurried back inside, wishing she wasn't at the mercy of the train schedule.

* * *

A bit later, Olive stood outside, staring down at the pigeon carrier, which she'd propped beside the door, as she took a moment to gather her courage. With George gone and Aldridge entirely indifferent, there really was no one to temper her recklessness, but in fairness, she'd taken precautions, and the business had to be got over with, so here she was. With a deep breath, she pushed open the door and stepped inside. The comforting scent of leather and paper did nothing to calm her frazzled nerves, but with a deep breath, she approached Miss Rose's tidy desk.

The mousy-brown head tipped up, and shrewd blue eyes sharpened with curiosity behind the lenses of her spectacles.

"I think I know who killed Miss Husselbee," Olive said in a raspy whisper. She hadn't expected this sleuthing business to be so difficult, and now it seemed the unmasking of the murderer—Poirot's favourite part—would be particularly so.

Miss Rose blinked, quickly rose to her feet, and came around the desk. "Why don't you come into the kitchen," she said, moving around Olive to set the sign in the window and lock the door. "You look quite pale. I'll make you a cup of tea."

Olive nodded and followed her past the bookcases, to the door that went through to the kitchen. But just as they reached it, someone knocked. They turned to see Violet Darling peering in through the glass, beckoning her sister to let her in. Olive clutched her pocketbook tightly and stood motionless as Miss Rose hissed out an exasperated sigh and brushed past her once again to unlock the door.

"Don't tell me you're off to play hooky, Rose?" Violet teased, running a hand over her hair to tame the flyaways, as she stepped inside.

"Don't be ridiculous," her sister said sharply. "Olive is looking rather peaky, and I've offered to make her a cup of tea. Why don't you come along," she said tolerantly.

Violet looked at her sister curiously, then glanced at Olive.

"Why not?" she said with a shrug, then gestured at the pair of them to lead the way.

As Miss Rose swept briskly by her yet again, Olive's mind raced, wondering how this little chat might now play out.

Miss Rose went straight to fill the kettle, then twitched the flowered curtains at the window over the sink closed against the sunlight glancing off the faucet. Olive stepped up beside her, ready to help with the tea things, but Violet tugged her toward the scrubbed and scarred table, saying sotto voce, "Rose prefers to do everything herself. That way, she can be certain it's done precisely how she wants it."

Olive wavered before dropping into a chair beside Violet, and several moments passed in silent, wary perusal.

"Was that a pigeon carrier outside?" Violet finally said. Seeing Olive's nod, she added, "I always expected you'd grow out of that."

"Yes, well, I find that some things defy expectations," Olive replied calmly.

"Well, I certainly never thought I'd agree to play Elizabeth Bennet in a village production of *Pride and Prejudice*," Violet allowed with a half laugh.

"Yes, well, Harriet is quite good at getting her way," Olive said. She hoped Miss Rose hadn't had her heart set on the role.

"I confess, having the chance to flirt with Dr Ware in the role of Fitzwilliam Darcy was what convinced me," Violet admitted.

With a telling flush pinking her cheeks, Miss Rose set the tea tray carefully on the table, sat, and scooted her chair forward. Olive flicked a glance between the sisters, suddenly feeling more awkward than she had only a moment before. She shifted her gaze to the tray and saw that there was a little plate of short-bread to go with the tea. Violet reached for a piece and held it with long, elegant fingers as she broke it in half and sent a flurry of crumbs onto the tidy tabletop. Miss Rose poured out the tea and handed the cups around, one for each of them.

"Olive believes she has solved the mystery of Miss Hussel-bee's murder," Miss Rose said tightly, lifting her cup to her lips.

At a startled sound from Violet, Olive shifted to look at her. She'd abandoned all pretence of casual disinterest and now sat forward, eyes wide. "Really? Do tell. I'm quite desperate to know who had the nerve to kill the old harridan."

Olive decided the tea was quite safe, as they were all having a cup, and took a tiny comforting sip, burning her tongue in the process. Then, without a word, she unsnapped her pocketbook, pulled out *A Lady Avenged*, and laid it on the table.

"Where did you get that?" Violet demanded, with an agitated glance at her sister.

Miss Rose merely stared into the pale depths of her teacup. Olive sipped again, recalling the little speech she'd rehearsed on the train. She hadn't expected to be making it in the presence of Violet Darling.

"Miss Husselbee loaned it to me," she said—it was the truth, more or less—"and I've just finished reading it." She met Violet's eyes. "I didn't realise until almost the very end that you must have written it, even though it should have been obvious. Lila Charmant is a French variation of Violet Darling."

"Yes, well," the author said, "as I told you, I like to keep my private life separate from my professional one."

"That decision seems to have served you rather well," Olive conceded, her mouth dry. "It's allowed you to keep a terrible secret hidden for years." She put the cup to her lips, relieved the tea had cooled sufficiently for a restorative gulp. "Travers Hall felt so familiar—the square tower and majestic cedar tree, and the lawn running down to the river, with its little island and weeping willow—all of it clearly drawn from Brickendonbury and the River Lea. It wasn't difficult to recognise you and Emory in the outspoken governess and the golden-haired musician who'd hired you to care for his charges. But the ending was unexpected, and rather horrible. We all thought you'd run away to marry him, and while you admitted the pair of you never married, you never said that he was murdered."

"He wasn't—" Violet started nervously, only to be cut off by her sister.

"Do be quiet, Violet," Miss Rose snapped. "You were foolish enough to write out all the details to be published in a veritable confession." She flicked a contemptuous glance at the book on the table. "It's thanks only to my efforts in keeping your pseudonym a secret that the entire village hasn't known for years."

Violet, her face sickly pale, peered at Olive and seemed to realise that denying it any further was fruitless. She said flatly, "Emory and I had been spending quite a lot of time in each other's company, and I fancied myself in love with him. In late summer he invited me for a midday picnic, and I imagined he was going to ask me to marry him." Miss Rose snorted, and the only hint that Violet heard her was an up tilt of her chin and a subtle hardening of the muscles of her jaw. "It seems he'd never intended anything of the sort. He wanted something else entirely and had no qualms about taking it." Her hands were clasped tightly in front of her now, and judging by the blankness in her eyes, her mind had travelled back to that fateful day.

"When he was finished, he turned away, scoffing at my expectations of marriage, and I went red with rage. I searched for something, anything I could use to hurt him. I cut my hands tearing at a wild raspberry cane, but when I would have thrashed him with it, he lunged backwards and fell, hitting his head against a rock. It was all a horrible accident," she said, her voice quivering.

Miss Rose reached for a biscuit and took a dainty bite, seemingly detached from the entire business.

Olive felt vaguely dizzy; her vision was beginning to blur at the edges, and her heart rate had begun to speed.

"When he didn't wake up," Violet continued, "I panicked, covered him with branches, and went to fetch Rose." She glanced gratefully at her sister. "We couldn't see an alternative to simply getting rid of the body, so we waited for darkness, tucked stones in his pockets, bound him up, and pushed him into the river. The elopement was Rose's idea—it would explain his disappearance and get me away. She'd searched his pockets and found his banking information. He may never have intended to marry me, but he financed my life on the Continent for years."

Olive slumped against the arm she'd propped on the table, a feeling of nausea having overtaken her. She tried to focus. Something in Violet's confession was nagging at her, just out of reach. "Miss Husselbee wasn't concerned that you hadn't married Emory. She suspected you'd murdered him. Somehow, she'd managed to unearth *A Lady Avenged*—your confession—and she was going to go to the police. She had to be got rid of." Suddenly, like a puzzle piece snicking into place, the proof was plain. Olive was now certain that her theory was correct.

"You said you didn't believe I killed her," Violet objected in confusion.

"I don't," Olive said, her voice vaguely slurred—she really wasn't feeling at all well. "I believe you loved Emory Hammond, and you were the victim of appalling treatment and a dreadful accident." She remembered the pain lurking in Violet's eyes, and the wistfulness in her voice, whenever she spoke of him, and her stalwart acceptance of Miss Husselbee's intentions. She took a steadying sip of tea. "I suspect you've suffered tremendous regret and a guilty conscience, and you were resigned to having the story finally come out, no matter the consequences."

Violet hung her head and silently sobbed.

Olive shifted her gaze, the movement forcing her to close her eyes against a wave of dizziness. Her head tipped sideways, and she fought to right it. "The elopement was the perfect red herring to throw suspicion off the real murderer." She credited George with setting her thoughts to dissimulation, and right now, she'd give anything to have him there beside her. If nothing else, he could hold her head up.

"What do you mean, the real murderer?" Violet demanded.

"I mean Rose," Olive said flatly.

"Rose?" Violet objected. "I already told you, she only helped me get rid of the body."

Olive closed her eyes, then winked one back open. "In the book, the body dragged to the river was pushed and contorted into all manner of positions. It was almost comical. But you claim to have killed Emory in the afternoon. If that were true, at least four hours"—she held up four fingers and stared bemusedly at them—"would have passed before twilight, time enough for rigor mortis to set in. The body would have been relatively stiff." Olive was particularly proud of herself for having picked up on that little detail—especially in the state she was in. "Emory obviously wasn't, which meant he must have been killed much later."

"I don't understand," Violet said unsteadily.

Olive looked expectantly at Miss Rose.

"Very clever," she said agreeably. "Even Miss Husselbee hadn't puzzled it out, judging by her confrontation with Violet at the dance. Oh, yes, she told me all about that."

"Rose, what does she mean?" Violet demanded urgently.

But Olive cut in impatiently. Her stomach was rolling with nausea, and she was determined to say her piece. "The play provided the final piece of the puzzle. Two sisters." She swivelled her gaze between the pair. "One falls for a cad, and the other swoops in to save her. Well, really it was Darcy, but he did it for—"

"Shut up, Olive."

But Olive barrelled on, undeterred by Rose's objection. "The two of you changed the story—tricky of you—none of those bits are in the book," she said, shaking her head. "And Elizabeth Bennet never would have stooped to murder..." Olive suspected she'd got off track; her thoughts were getting gummed up in her brain.

"It wasn't in the book, because that's not what happened," Violet insisted frantically.

"Violet never knew," Rose corrected, her voice steely, "that I suffocated him with his own jacket when I sent her to gather the stones. He was just starting to come around."

Violet's face was ashen with shock and disbelief. "All these years I've kept away, I thought—"

"He deserved to die, Violet," Rose said ruthlessly, "and I deserved a little peace from all your foolishness. You weren't capable of doing it yourself, so I took care of it."

"Rose, how could you?" Violet's hands were beginning to shake, and her demeanour had shifted to wary uncertainty. Olive didn't blame her: Rose had fooled them all. Rubbing her temples, she peered nervously at her sister. "And Miss Husselbee?"

"Dead," Olive confirmed. Both sisters cut their eyes around to look at her. "Murdered. She did it," she said emphatically, pointing at Rose. "She knew Miss Husselbee had got hold of a copy of *A Lady Avenged*, and she played on her patriotic fervour with a poisoned cake made of tinned meat. Diabolical." Olive's head tipped back and forth like a pendulum.

"She suspected the truth—or a version of it, anyway. She'd hinted as much to me," Miss Rose calmly answered her sister. "There was no other choice. You would have confessed to murder and admitted I was there. At the very least, I would have been an accessory. And if someone had managed to figure out the truth, I would have hanged. Emory Hammond deserved what he got, but Verity Husselbee would never have condoned his murder, and I couldn't let her steal my life away. Not when it's just started—"

Violet pushed back from the table and stared at her sister in horror.

Olive stared into her teacup, her mind fuzzy, and tried to focus. Something was very wrong, but whatever it was remained frustratingly out of reach. Instead, her thoughts floated back to the day of the Daffodil Dance. She could picture Miss Rose slipping quietly into the hall before the dance to leave a cake on the refreshments table. A Spam cake, laced with foxglove, meant for the person who'd dug up a long-buried murder. Then suddenly she was dancing with Captain Aldridge, spinning dizzily. . . . She blinked, coming back to the moment with effort.

Her thoughts slogged through her synapses. She'd confided to Miss Rose that she'd solved the murder, and now here they were, having tea. Olive's eyes slowly travelled among the other cups on the table, and she drew her memory back over the preceding minutes. If memory served, neither sister had actually drunk any tea—she should probably have noticed that earlier. The situation seemed to have got away from her, and it now seemed rather likely she'd been poisoned. The trouble was, she no longer had the wherewithal to do anything about it. She thought briefly about sticking her fingers into the back of her throat, but she couldn't make her arms move the right way. She couldn't even muster an appropriate level of panic.

"Don't worry, Olive," Miss Rose said, reading her thoughts as Olive's gaze continued to drift aimlessly from one cup to another. "It will be over quick as a wink. It's rather ironic, really. Agatha Christie not only gave me the idea for the murder weapon, but she also inspired you to imagine yourself an amateur sleuth. A pity, really."

Violet's gaze flicked from her sister to Olive, comprehension dawning. "Rose, you *didn't*," she said, aghast. She stood and pushed back her chair, staring wide-eyed at the table, no doubt wondering if the shortbread had been poisoned.

"You killed Guinevere," Olive said, unable to muster even a modicum of fury in her current state.

Miss Rose frowned then and, with false pity, said, "I suspect she's rather far gone."

"My pigeon," Olive muttered, enunciating slowly. "You killed her when you thought I was closing in."

"Don't be ridiculous," Miss Rose scoffed. "I assumed you'd been rummaging about in Miss Husselbee's diaries, searching for clues, but I certainly never expected you to turn to blackmail. The things she'd written about Dr Ware weren't true, but I couldn't have you spreading rumours—not when his research is so important." Spots of anger had popped out on her cheeks. "I'd planned to deal with you, but you forced my hand, showing up at the library with a murder accusation."

"What has Dr Ware got to do with any of this?" Violet demanded, only to be once again ignored. She looked worriedly at Olive.

"*Listen,*" Olive said sharply, "*I* didn't stoop to murder *or* blackmail. I only ever tried to find out who did. And I was bloody good at it, if I do say so." She nodded emphatically as her thoughts began to drift. Funnily enough, the whole business had all worked out precisely like a mystery novel. All sorts of things— words and memories and pigeons—had clicked, fitting together like one giant village jigsaw, until all the questions had been satisfactorily answered. Except that none of this was satisfactory. . . .

"I'm going for the doctor," Violet insisted.

"You don't want to do that, Violet," her sister said calmly. "I'll tell everyone you killed Emory Hammond."

Olive's eyes fluttered, and her heartbeat soared until there was a roaring in her head. She slipped from the chair just as she imagined Jameson Aldridge riding to her rescue.

Thursday, 15th May, 2:05 p.m.
Victoria Station

I do believe I've solved the mystery of Miss Husselbee's murder, my boy! The whole thing is really quite astounding, and I will catch you up as soon as possible. I know I've exhausted Captain Aldridge's tolerance, but if he happens to be in a genial mood, I'd like his help in confirming my theory. Please give him a ring and ask him to look into the death of Emory Hammond . . . anything he can find on the man, really. If he refuses, I'll handle the matter on my own. I'm taking the next train home from London, and I plan to go straight to the police after I've had a quick chat with Miss Rose.

Home soon,
Olive

Chapter 21

Olive had propped herself on the gate and was carelessly kicking her feet as she waited for Aldridge to come barrelling down the lane. No doubt Harriet thought she was mooning for the man, but in reality, she wanted information. Aramis had hung on, bless him, defying the odds and carrying home a message that could make all the difference to her loft's continued involvement in the war, and she fully intended to learn what it said.

She'd hardly seen Aldridge since her close call—her father had insisted she be given time to recuperate before settling into her job as a FANY—but he'd maintained the fiction of their relationship, delivering a tidily wrapped parcel of aniseed balls, an armful of hydrangea blooms, which she knew grew in profusion on the manor grounds, and a note from Danny Tierney, promising some lessons in self-defence when she was recovered. After that initial visit, he'd called instead, and she'd stood in the hall, within earshot of Harriet, and dutifully flirted with him down the telephone lines. He'd made a point of asking after the pigs by name and occasionally a pigeon, as well. Slowly but surely, the barriers between them were beginning to come down. Since the deadly conclusion of her amateur investigation, she'd adopted a newfound respect for caution and protocol, and he'd lightened his typically brusque demeanour. Not nearly enough, though. She was still working on that.

The gossip surrounding her attempt to ferret out a murderer was only now starting to die down, three weeks after the incident. Everyone told a different version of that disastrous afternoon, but she trusted Aldridge's. He had, after all, been there, and not just as the hallucination she'd imagined. He'd burst in the door just as she'd lost consciousness, while Jonathon and Hen had gone for the doctor. The effect of the activated charcoal and potassium chloride had been quick and thoroughly unpleasant, and likely just in time. As the digoxin had gradually left her system, she'd begun to feel a bit more herself, well enough, at least, to explain how she'd stumbled upon the truth, before being whisked away to Dr Harrington's surgery. It was only later that she'd learned all that had happened.

While Aldridge and Violet had been busy trying to revive her, Miss Rose had drunk the tea from her own cup and slipped out of the hall. Naturally, Hen had followed and been beside her as she'd succumbed to the poison on the river path. There was nothing to be done but offer comfort in those last moments, in which her final words had, rather curiously, been, "Tell Darcy how ardently I admire and love him." Dr Ware had, understandably, been slow to recover from the shock of it all.

Violet had confessed her role in Emory Hammond's murder, but she hadn't been charged. Olive suspected there'd been no discussion of the man's finances. But Aldridge knew. He'd done as she'd asked, and he'd been thorough. But he'd waited until they were quite alone to deliver a fierce and furious lecture. Her head had still been rather fuzzy, though, so she suspected some words had been imagined. Unless an eavesdropper had prompted him to wax sentimental.

And there he was now, speeding down the lane in his bulky

black Austin, churning up a cloud of dust. She jumped from the
gate, wanting to get ahead of the motorcar, and waited for him
near the barn, snatching Psyche mid-skulk and tucking the cat
under her chin.

Stepping out of the car, he eyed her companion suspiciously.
His hair was neat, and his jaw clean shaven, and it seemed as if
he'd been away for a very long time. So long that she felt a faint
awkwardness overtaking her. Judging by the intense gaze he'd
levelled on her face, Aldridge was feeling much the same as always.

"Would you like to pet her?" she teased.

"It appears you're feeling better," he said dryly, making no
move toward the pair of them.

She slipped her hand into her pocket to retrieve the canister
and handed it over. "Will you decode it now? Please."

"Let's go for a drive," he suggested. "That cat stays."

Smirking at the sternness in his voice, she followed him to the
car, dumping the cat in the shade of the cherry tree. The beast already had her eye on the twittering blackcaps in the hedge.
Aldridge's inexplicable aversion to felines brought to mind Violet's bitter reaction to raspberries, which Olive now sadly understood. His little quirk, however, continued to defy reason.

Psyche, it turned out, had been responsible for Guinevere's
death. Mrs Battlesby had casually confessed her husband's good
intentions while mashing potatoes for supper one evening. He'd
come across the cat, slinking out of the loft, and divested her of
her kill. He'd left the pigeon for Olive, tucked out of reach in a
biscuit tin, as a warning to keep the dovecote shut up properly.
He wasn't quite right in the head anymore, Mrs Battlesby had
admitted sadly, and not up to a chat. Olive suspected even Hercule Poirot wouldn't have managed to solve that little mystery.

Aldridge drove to the spot where he'd waited the night of their
first mission, then parked in the long shadows of the wood. He
pulled a little book from his pocket and unrolled the message

tucked carefully into the canister. Olive peered curiously at the jumble of letters but couldn't make any sense of it, so she sat back to wait.

With her head resting on the seat back and her breathing even, the air holding the barest hint of liquorice, she relaxed and hoped for good news. She had no idea how much time passed.

"They did it," Aldridge said abruptly.

Her head came up off the seat. "What happened?"

He was grinning, and there was a gratified gleam in his eye. "They found one of ours, Joël Letac, in Paris and trekked back to Bordeaux. After discovering that the Germans had become rather lax in their security at the power station, they planned the sabotage for last night. They retrieved the gear they'd buried in the woods, broke in, planted the limpet mines on the transformers, and got out, riding their borrowed bicycles to safety in the light of the explosions. It seems they're going to find their way home through Spain, and the Nazis are going to have a lot of recovery work ahead of them."

Olive smiled, the moment bittersweet. It was a victory for all of them. Except Badger. She would find a way to commemorate his sacrifice, as well as that of all those who might come after him. To say nothing of the birds that would come back. In nightmares, her mind still played over the scenario in which Jeremy never found his way home, Jonathon never got her message, and Aldridge didn't come. Her pigeons—all of them—were heroes, and it would be worth every sacrifice she made if they were allowed to do their bit.

She'd put away the photograph that had sat on her dresser, a daily inspiration for so long, and replaced it with one that captured the woman her mother truly was. Olive had let go of the feelings of anger and betrayal and was instead thankful that finally hearing the truth about her mother had helped her to recognise and appreciate her own small efforts in the grand scheme of things.

Her hours of recovery had given her plenty of time to think back over her stint as self-appointed village sleuth, prompted, as it was, by Miss Husselbee's dying declaration. She could only assume the poor woman had confused two long-ago secrets trapped in her befuddled mind. While she'd recently uncovered what she imagined was Violet Darling's grand deception, she'd evidently known about Serena Bright's for years. Judging by what Olive's father had confessed, and the unfinished journal entry had revealed—with a little guesswork thrown in for good measure—it seemed likely that Miss Husselbee had been utterly conflicted by duty and loyalty in those two particular instances. But only one had got her killed.

Generally speaking, the village remained mostly ignorant of the deceptions perpetrated in their midst. But both George and her brother Lewis would need to face their mothers' secrets when they finally did come home. For now, Mr Forrester's black-market scheme with the Daneses continued, but Olive couldn't help but wonder how long it would last. Dr Ware carried on with his research and his role as Mr Darcy. And then there was Margaret. She'd confided in Leo, and they were to be married at the end of the summer. An engraved stone had been placed at the foot of the yew tree in the corner of the cemetery, marked simply IN MEMORY OF SIMON GALE, 1940.

Olive, who would be starting work at the manor house the following week, was anxious for an escape from village affairs, but there'd not yet been a final decision on the pigeons.

"Are you convinced, then?" she said quietly, desperately hoping Aldridge was willing to give her birds this chance.

He looked at her then, and his silence was nerve-wracking, but Olive weathered it unflinchingly. "Your pigeons have met—and exceeded—every expectation. You, however, have been entirely unpredictable and frustratingly insubordinate," he said sternly. Her stomach lurched in response. "But," he went on, and Olive hoped he had no idea what she was suffering, "you have proven yourself to be impressively competent, and your instincts—with one minor exception—have been nearly infallible." He raised a single eyebrow, and Olive bit her lip uncertainly. "Then there's the fact that I've already invested considerable effort in the cover story of being involved with you . . ."

Relief sent a wave of giddiness skipping through her veins. "Do stop, Jamie. I'm blushing," she said artfully.

After a moment's pause, he said gravely, "I hope you know that there is as much courage in staunchly taking on tasks that others would shirk as there is in running headlong into enemy fire."

"So it would seem," she quipped, thinking of her close call. But she smiled. It had been a hard lesson to learn, but she'd found contentment in her circumstances. She'd find a way to make her mark. She fully expected he'd do the same—he had, after all, decided to take a chance on the Bright loft.

His smile flashed, quick and charming, and Olive caught a fleeting glimpse of mischief in his eyes. "A little less drama would be good, though, going forward."

She didn't even try to hold back the grin that spread over her face. It seemed that Jonathon had officially won their bet, and it occurred to Olive that losing had never given her such a thrill. The war was far from over, and it seemed she'd be working with Jameson Aldridge for the foreseeable future. He had no idea what he was in for.

Historical Note

In 1943 Maria Dickin, founder of the veterinary charity People's Dispensary for Sick Animals, instituted an award to be given in recognition of the heroic feats of animals serving with the British Armed Forces or the Civil Defence Service. A bronze medallion, the Dickin Medal bears the words "For Gallantry. We also serve," encircled by a laurel wreath. Fifty-four medals were given for service during the Second World War, thirty-two of them to pigeons—more than to any other animal by far.

When Neville Chamberlain declared war on Germany in September 1939, it was a call to arms for the whole of Britain. Man and beast, everyone was called to do their bit in the fight for their lives. While a cursory glance at the unassuming pigeon offered little hint as to its intelligence, loyalty, stamina, and endurance, history had told an entirely different story. Memories of pigeons' heroic exploits in the Great War had not been forgotten. Prior to that, the unique qualities of the breed had been instrumental in the establishment of Reuters news service. Pigeons had, in fact, been carrying messages in war and peacetime as far back as Greek and Roman times.

Bred and trained to fly hundreds of miles, at an impressive speed, from an unfamiliar location to its home loft, a racing pigeon could carry critical intelligence in a canister strapped to its leg. It filled the gaps left by wireless communications, saving pilots downed in the Channel and regiments under fire. It braved harsh weather conditions, artillery fire, snipers, and predators, at times impeded by considerable injury. It was, in short, a perfect soldier and much needed in the fight against German military might.

As such, British pigeon fanciers were encouraged to join the National Pigeon Service (NPS) and offer their birds to the war effort. Even the King, who had been introduced, with his father, to the sport of racing pigeons by King Leopold II of Belgium, provided birds from the Royal Lofts at Sandringham. The Air Ministry was then responsible for supplying the various branches and organizations of the British war machine. The army set up mobile pigeon lofts on the front lines in Europe, North Africa, India, and the Middle and Far East; and all Royal Air Force bombers and reconnaissance aircraft had at least one pigeon aboard, tucked carefully into its own watertight container, complete with parachute. In the event of an unscheduled landing, the bird would be released, to return to its home loft with the information necessary to facilitate a rescue mission. The Special Operations Executive (SOE), nicknamed Baker Street for its headquarters, used pigeons, as well, dropping the birds along with secret agents behind enemy lines, where both were equally at risk.

SOE agents went through a rigorous training program before being inserted into occupied Europe. They were assessed for physical and mental suitability and then instructed on every little detail of the job that lay ahead—from the proper way to ask for coffee and how to pick a lock, to the quickest way to bring a factory to a grinding halt. Special training schools were established, one of the first being at Brickendonbury Manor in Hertfordshire. It would become Station XVII, the school for sabotage and the site of explosive trials, thus amply contributing to Churchill's directive to "set Europe ablaze," in missions such as Operation Josephine B.

It's entirely possible that Brickendonbury Manor had a pigeoneer like Olive Bright at its disposal. While her husband stayed busy in London as a member of Parliament, Mary Manningham-Buller spent the war years in an Oxfordshire village, raising pigeons for the SOE. Parachuting into France, Holland, and Belgium, her birds were collected by agents on the ground and sent home with intelligence on German troop movements, operations, and newly developed weaponry, all of which was immediately transmitted by motorbike to the War Office in London.

The Germans were also fully cognizant of the wartime benefit

of pigeons: the state-run German National Pigeon Society supplied birds for use by the military, the Schutzstaffel (SS), and the
Gestapo. They were also keenly aware of the threat presented by
Allied pigeons. Not only did they establish a hawking division in
the German Air Force to intercept birds along the Channel, but
they also made the strategic decision to clear the pigeon lofts in
the countries they occupied. The result was that any unidenti-
fied bird—and the person who harbored it—came instantly
under suspicion, their lives forfeited. To the Nazis, these foreign
pigeons signified treachery and betrayal, whereas to the Resistance, the birds symbolised hope and freedom. They were a connection to the Allies—the last strongholds of democracy—and
provided the means for them to assist in the fight.

It was a pigeon named Gustav that brought back the first news
of Operation Neptune, the code name given to the Normandy
landings, also known as D-Day. In order to preserve the critical
element of surprise, the landings were carried out under radio silence, and hundreds of pigeons were standing by, waiting to carry
messages home amid the threat of enemy fire and German-
trained falcons. Gustav flew 150 miles against a thirty-mile-per-
hour headwind in five hours and sixteen minutes, setting a pace
of nearly sixty miles per hour over the duration. He was awarded
the Dickin Medal for this impressive effort.

Over the course of the war, NPS members provided an esti-
mated 200,000 pigeons for use by the British military. What they
accomplished is little short of amazing.